THE
THORN
GIRL

BOOKS BY LAURA ELLIOT

Fragile Lies
Stolen Child
The Prodigal Sister
The Betrayal
Sleep Sister
Guilty
The Wife Before Me

THE
THORN
GIRL

LAURA ELLIOT

Bookouture

Published by Bookouture in 2019

An imprint of Storyfire Ltd.
Carmelite House
50 Victoria Embankment
London EC4Y 0DZ

www.bookouture.com

ISBN: 978-1-83888-625-7
eBook ISBN: 978-1-83888-077-4

Previously published as *In My Mother's Name* (978-1-83888-078-1)

To Sean, the love of my life. Thank you for the golden years.

PROLOGUE

Marianne

Crack! The snap of a branch splitting underfoot draws her to the window. The new moon is visible beyond the trees. Translucent as a clipped fingernail, it cannot break the darkness of this isolated clearing and she is relying on sound to bring him to her. She has spread the rug over the stone floor and lit the lantern. Fifteen minutes late and he will arrive breathless with apologies, excuses. She will silence him with kisses. Their time together is too precious to waste on unnecessary words.

Weeds have sprouted between the cracks in the walls. Ivy twines around the eaves and the raddled chimneybreast. This is the shell of what was once a family home but there is enough evidence of that vanished life to allow them to imagine the cottage as their secret haven. The trees and hedgerows are too overgrown for cars or night-time walkers to venture down the lane and see a lantern flickering.

Her mother does not know she is missing. She will not check on her until the Thorns have finished their readings and left. Some nights, when they have gathered in the parlour below her bedroom, their voices reach upwards. Unknown prayers and chanting, the off-key singing led by Mrs Thornton. They call her Mother Gloria but she's really Liam Thornton's crazy mother.

Tonight, she hopes that the fervour of their singing will allow her time to return home and feign sleep when her mother comes to say goodnight.

Footsteps draw nearer. More dead wood breaking, leaves crunching. She tenses, filled with a sudden unease. This is a heavy tread, unfamiliar. She hears another sound. The low growl of shared laughter. Is he not alone? She shakes her head, knowing that cannot be true.

Silence falls, a hush that waits to be broken. A shape emerges from the darkness, blurred and indistinguishable, then breaks apart, like fissures on a cracked rock. They form into silhouettes, three unique shapes that move towards her with one unified step.

She moves back from the window but it is too late. The cottage door scrapes against the stone floor. The hinges are loose and the door always needs a hard shove to open. Shadows fill the small room, jig against the walls, loom across the ceiling. Two of the intruders are wearing jeans, the other favours cargo pants. This is just a fleeting impression and is instantly forgotten when she notices the black balaclavas covering their faces. Only their eyes are visible and the tallest of the three has a steady gaze. A butcher sizing up the meat he will chop, the point of penetration. He is the leader. She knows this by his stance, the confident way he moves forward as the others fall into step behind him. The second one is bug-eyed with panic or is it anticipation that causes his gaze to dart from her towards the rug on the floor and back again? The eyes of the third are closed, as if the light from the lantern is too dazzling to endure.

Terrorists. She has seen them on TV, accompanying coffins on their final journey or strutting with guns before the cameras, arrogant with the power that terror and anonymity breeds. Yesterday, there was a roadblock on Main Street. Were the police searching for them? Is this one of their 'safe' houses? Has she invaded their territory? She screams, knowing the futility of making herself heard yet hoping he will hear her. He must be on the way. Unless they stopped him, kneecapped him… or worse.

She is caught easily when she tries to run. A hand is clasped across her mouth. Other hands hold her down as a balaclava is pulled over her head. No slit for her eyes on this one but she does not need sight to understand what is about to happen.

They are not terrorists staking a claim on the cottage. They know her, these hooded men, who are taking possession of her. She can tell by the way they handle her, passing her from one to the other with the ease of those who are certain they will not be caught. They are free to take their time and their laughter, no longer muffled, echoes in the suffocating folds of the balaclava until her mind closes them out and she is unable to struggle any longer. Dead wood snapping, splitting her apart as the black, fathomless night folds around her.

PART ONE

CHAPTER ONE

Adele

Twenty-five years later

A swallow fluttered its wings in an attic and everything changed. Adele Foyle had no idea how the bird found its way into the dim, slanted space but there it was, flapping wildly around her. She bit back a cry and ducked as the swallow skimmed over her head before disappearing between the rafters. She could hear it twittering, a siren of alarm that told her it had not yet found an escape route. When it flew into view again, she decided to direct it towards the open trapdoor and release it through one of the windows. Her efforts to do so only added to the bird's distress. Its frantic swooping came to an end when it crashed into the rafters and fell to the floor with a soft thud.

It must be dead, Adele thought, as she knelt beside it. A quick sudden death. Like the one her grandmother had always wanted. A heart attack, swift as a dagger in the dark, Noreen Foyle used to say. But when it came to the end, Noreen's worst fears were realised when she found her sanity slipping slowly away from her. She had been an organised woman. Documents and letters had been filed alphabetically, along with a list of relevant names to be contacted when she died. She had even outlined the type of funeral she wanted, down to the last hymn and prayer. All her affairs were in order long before illness deprived her of the ability to make even the simplest decision. Adele's last responsibility had been to clear out the attic and now, as she prepared to close the trapdoor, all the contents stored there for decades had been removed to charity shops, the recycle centre or binned.

The swallow was stunned, not yet dead. Adele, easing her fingers carefully under the soft feathers, brushed against the edge of a strap. Unable to see what was attached to it, she carried the bird downstairs and out into the back garden. She laid it under a bush and, returning to the attic, reached into the recess between the floor and ceiling. She tugged at the strap and pulled out a black backpack. Camouflaged against the dark rafters, it had been easy to miss during the clear-out. Dust stirred then settled again in an inaudible puff and cobwebs clung to her fingers when she pulled it out. The smell of mould was strong and the backpack was covered with blue speckles. Gaudy stickers stuck to the front flap were still intact: pop stars, hearts, flowers, butterflies, and one defiant two-fingered salute.

Adele brought the backpack to the kitchen and removed a make-up bag containing foundation, eyeshadow and mascara. Cheap and girlie items from the Body Shop that her grandmother would never have used. She delved further into the backpack and shook out a creased nightdress and pyjamas, seven pairs of briefs, socks and a pair of bedroom slippers. A plastic bag with a tie string contained toiletries, a facecloth wrapped around a bar of soap, deodorant and talcum powder, toothpaste and a roll of dental floss. But it was the hairbrush with strands of dark brown hair caught in the bristles that caused her to cry out. A low moan of grief and recognition for someone she had mourned but never known.

She delved into a side pocket and found a diary with a painting of a dolphin on the front cover. Tears stung her eyes when she recognised the handwritten name inside the cover, written with a turquoise dayglo pen. Without reading the entries, she turned a page, then another. The pages were filled with a teenage slapdash scrawl, the pages smudged in places, as if water had dripped on the paper and stippled it. Tears, perhaps? A strip of photographs fell out. They must have been taken in a photo booth and had served as a bookmark. Five images of a teenage girl and a youth, cheeks together, arms around each other, pulling faces, pouting, scowling, laughing. On the back of the strip were written the words 'Marianne and Shane in Bray, August weekend.'

Marianne... Marianne... During her childhood, Adele had used her mother's name like a mantra at night, allowing the syllables to finally lull her to sleep. In her teens she had listened repeatedly to Leonard Cohen singing 'So Long Marianne', the lyrics remaining in her head long after the song ended.

'Your mother is one of God's special angels.' Noreen had created a make-believe paradise and sold it to her young grand-daughter. Sometimes, particularly after she had enjoyed a few glasses of Baileys at Christmas or on her birthday, Noreen would relate some innocuous anecdote about Marianne's childhood. The day she had been lost on a crowded beach. The dog she had loved, the medals she won for long-distance running. How she had danced her way to the finals of a talent contest and won. These anecdotes, though they were pleasant to hear and Adele was always content to listen to them, had never touched her emotionally. They could have been stories about any young girl growing up in a small Irish village; the real story, Adele suspected as she grew older, ran too deep for her grandmother to share.

When she began to demand more meaningful information about her young mother's death, Noreen would snap, 'No good ever comes from stoking the past. Marianne is in heaven. Let her rest in peace.'

The past had remained a locked box, secured with clamped lips, a blank gaze and silence. Unable to find the information that could conjure her mother into a person she could love, Adele eventually stopped trying to coax information from her grandmother. As soon as she finished secondary school, she had enrolled in a media studies course in London and the bonds holding them together loosened even further.

Before she left for London, Noreen had handed her a Kodak envelope containing photographs of Marianne. Two of the photographs showed her posing self-consciously before the camera on the day she started school and, eight years later, her entry into second level. Her First Communion, Confirmation and all her birthdays had been charted until she reached her fifteenth. These photographs had sustained Adele throughout those lonely, early months in London as she struggled to adjust to the city. They provided positive proof that her mother had been a vital living force, not a sylph who had touched earth briefly to give birth to her before floating onwards to some distant nirvana. And, now, here she was again, carefree, hair mussed up, lipstick smudged, her face glowing.

Was this gangling teenager called Shane her father? Adele drank in the sight of him, searching for resemblances between them. His spiky hair, black – same colour as hers. Blue eyes – negative. Hers were brown, inherited from her mother. Like Adele, he tanned easily, a golden sheen on his skin. Different-shaped foreheads; his was higher, but she could see a similarity about their lips. Voluptuous, Daniel always said, and thinking about her fiancé, Adele wished he was there with her to share this moment of discovery.

Hands shaking and moving faster, she flipped towards the last diary entry. It was undated like the others but it must have been written shortly before her birth. She stared out the window at the unmoving swallow. Such a tiny bird, defenceless. A cat would come soon and that would be the end of that. The law of the jungle. She rubbed her hand against her jeans but the cobwebs clung like gum to her fingers. Her mother's death had signalled the beginning of Adele's life. Her instincts warned her that the information contained between those pages could be haunting and raw to read. *No stoking the past.* Noreen's advice echoed in her mind. There must have been a reason why she had never wanted to discuss her daughter's death. Was the story so laden with sadness that she had believed it was better to maintain a brutal silence rather than satisfy Adele's curiosity? The information she had sought could be buried in these scribbled entries. She snapped the diary closed and shoved it into the backpack, along with the other items.

She had sold Noreen's bungalow and all she had to do now was lock the door behind her. Her flight was booked and Daniel was waiting impatiently for her return. She clasped the backpack to her chest and let it rest against the buffeting force of her heart. Outside in the garden the swallow stirred. Adele watched, unable to decide if the breeze had ruffled the feathers or if the bird was still alive. The wings spread outwards and the swallow paused, an instant of indecision before it ascended into the leaves and was lost from sight. Sinking to her knees, Adele removed the diary and began to read.

CHAPTER TWO

The Marianne Diary

I wish it would rain. Lashing rain like whips! Monsoon rain! Hurricane rain! The kind of rain that'll reflect how I <u>REALLY</u> feel. But it's really sunny and the only smudge in the sky is a jet trail heading off to God knows where. Just like me.

I want to know where we're going. Mum says I'll find out soon enough that. She's made sure to keep us apart since IT happened. Three months now. I never thought a day would pass but it did and another followed and now it's ninety-two days since they came for me!

Sergeant Bale said it was important to get to the truth. The nub of the matter, that's what he called it. How could I be sure it wasn't Shane? Three, I told him. Over and over again. They came to the cottage and threw me to the ground and did IT. But all he did was bring his black, hairy eyebrows together, like he didn't believe me, no matter how many times I told him how it was.

Mam's clattering about downstairs. We haven't even left and our house sounds echoey already, like our memories are disappearing into the emptiness we're leaving behind. Everything's packed, all I'm taking with me, that is. I gave most of my clothes to Castaways. It's where I bought them in the first place. Vintage. Second-hand. I don't do brands. That's because I wanted to be different. Turns out I was. Well done, Marianne. Go to the top of the class for your slut star! My clothes won't fit me soon. Vintage or branded, it won't make any difference. Even when I can wear them again, they'll remind me of IT… so it was best to get rid of them.

Mr Lewis said I have to forget Reedstown. This is my new beginning. He stood in my bedroom, like he already owned our house, and said I'd my whole life in front of me and this bad time would soon be forgotten. Hah? It doesn't matter how often the Thorns pray over me. I'll never forget IT, even when I'm old and crazy and pushing a Zimmer!!! Never… never… nor will I be able to forget the things everyone's been saying about me. Horrible things that aren't true and the older girls sniggering and calling me a slut every time they see me.

I've taken down my posters of the Spice Girls. Girl power. Hah. They have it all and they still haven't a clue what a mess-up life is. I've dumped the stars from the ceiling into the rubbish skip. The paint came away and the ceiling looks like it has acne. Dad put the stars up when I was a kid. They're luminous in the dark. After he died, I pretended he was the one in the centre. The brightest one shining down on me.

He would have moved heaven and earth to find them. He would have pulled off their balaclavas and killed them stone dead for doing that terrible thing to me. But he's the one who's dead and I don't even have his stars left to remember him by.

CHAPTER THREE

Adele turned each page carefully, stopping when it seemed impossible to continue, yet always returning to those scribbled entries, greedily devouring each word. Her eyes were stinging when she finished. She closed the diary and rubbed her hand over its sleek cover. The floor beneath her seemed unsteady when she stood. Unreliable and capable of pitching her forward if she did not hold onto the wall for support. She had always imagined her mother as an inexperienced fifteen-year-old, stumbling into pregnancy by way of an innocent, reckless passion. Noreen, too, had nurtured this belief with evasiveness and lies. But within those stark pages the truth had been laid bare.

Adele knew her voice sounded disconnected when she spoke to Daniel on the phone, as if it was being channelled by someone else. She told him she had been forced to cancel her flight and would stay overnight in Crannock. Some problem with house deeds. She was surprised at how easily she lied to him, but then again what she had discovered was too raw to share on a phone call.

In the immediate aftermath of her grandmother's death, a burden had lifted from Adele. She had been unaware of its heaviness until her shoulders lightened and she realised she was free to begin a normal life with Daniel. This sense of release had been followed quickly by grief. She had lost the woman who had reared her, the only family she had ever known; but now, having read the entries in Marianne's diary, this grief was giving way to anger over Noreen's secretiveness. Her thoughts were chaotic when she lay down to sleep, her cheek resting against her mother's nightdress. Shadowy figures roamed through her dreams. She awoke gasping, convinced she was being suffocated by a membrane so heavy she was unable to breathe through it. In the morning, she showered with her mother's soap, a thin lather on her skin, the faint scent still lingering.

She dressed quickly in shorts and a T-shirt. Another hot day; the warm spell had settled into an uncustomary pattern that showed no sign of changing. She took a mug of coffee outside and sat on the window ledge. In the distance, the brown, jagged outlines of the Ox Mountains wavered in the heat haze. Ox, she had always thought, was a strange, clumsy name for those brooding, granite peaks. Noreen had told her that the name was the result of a mistranslation from the Irish language. If it had been correctly translated into English, the range would be known as the Stormy Mountains. Today, the storm clouds were inside her head and the sun, flitting between bobtail clouds, weaved a filigree of light and shade over the slopes. The bungalow sat alone on a bleak curve of the mountain road. It was her inheritance but Adele had experienced only relief when she sold it. The buyer was an elderly author, intent on writing about the mythological creatures, hags and goddesses associated with the mountains' glacial lakes. From her vantage point, Adele could see the glisten of one such lake, the icy stillness hiding the turbulence of its folklore.

Until she was eight years old, she had believed that Marianne had lived her short life in the shadow of the mountain. This belief was shattered when her friend Rihanna told her that Noreen was a 'Dublin Jackeen.' That was what Rihanna's father called her. He said she had only moved to Crannock when Adele was a newborn baby. Astonished to discover that her mother had not played in the same fields as she did, attended the same roadside school or sat in the same shiny pew at mass on Sundays, Adele had pestered her grandmother for more information. Finally, reluctantly, Noreen admitted that she had moved to this isolated hinterland from Reedstown, a village on the north side of Dublin. She had pointed it out to Adele on a map, a smudge of land close to a river, and snapped at her for continuing to ask questions. She could feel a migraine coming on, she'd said. Noreen's migraines were regular occurrences and had the power to stop all awkward questions.

Adele had planned to visit Reedstown after she left home but London had swept her into its vortex and the longing had faded to an occasional, whimsical notion that had, until now, always passed.

CHAPTER FOUR

The Marianne Diary

Mam never looked back when she drove away from Reedstown. The jet trail had broken up and was disappearing into the blue sky. Miss Grimes in science told us that that blue is created from molecules of air scattering light. I keep thinking about such a scattering. How it breaks everything apart in ways that can never be fixed... never ever!!!

All the morning traffic had gone from Main Street and there were just a few people going into mass. I ducked my head when Mam drove past the Garda station in case Sergeant Bale came out. She was holding onto the wheel so tight that her knuckles were ridged like Toblerone. At the traffic lights, she almost crashed into the back of Keith Lewis's new car. The roof was down and Liam Thornton was in the passenger seat. He's been staying in Keith's house since his mam left him again. The children from the national school were going to confession. A big, long crocodile of them and it looked like they were all staring at me. I should be used to that by now but I'm not.

Mrs Thornton put her bony hands on my forehead after IT happened and said she'd blessed me with the oil of forgiveness. I hate her and I hate the Thorns with their screwed-up faces and mean, ugly lips. They worship a God who doesn't exist. If he does, I don't want to know him. He's the God of fanatics. That's all they are with their made-up name. Mum says I have to stop calling them Thorns, they're the Sodality of Thorns and Atonement. Who cares?

She keeps insisting that Mr Lewis was helping us through this terrible time. How? By buying our house for next to nothing? Big deal. I begged her not to sell. All he wanted is our big long garden. She wouldn't listen. I've shamed her in front of everyone and there's nothing to do except start again in a new place where no one knows us. She says Mr Lewis is right. I will forget. That's what time does. Like it's some kind of magic eraser? She's <u>SO</u> wrong!! It doesn't matter how often she tells me I'll be safe and no one will call me names, I'm scared sick of what lies ahead for me.

CHAPTER FIVE

The clenched sensation in Adele's chest eased a little when she flew into Heathrow Airport and saw Daniel waiting for her in arrivals. His arms reached out to welcome her and guide her through the Underground. Such a cacophony of noise, a Tower of Babel compared to the quiet hinterland she had left. She held his arm tightly as they pushed their way onto the Tube.

They had met two years previously when she was doing research for Voice Dox. The clean air policies of Greendene Petro, the company where Daniel worked as an environmental engineer, had been the subject of a documentary she intended to make. The interview had lasted longer than necessary and his request for her phone number in case he thought of any further information that would be useful for her research had been a thinly veiled excuse to see her again. She gave it to him willingly. Six months later, she moved into his luxurious two-bed apartment in Nine Elms. His rent was subsidised by Greendene, one of the perks of the job, he told her, cracking open the champagne and toasting their future.

Shortly afterwards, she brought him to Crannock to meet Noreen. She had been nervous about introducing him, worried that he would be offended by her grandmother's taciturn personality.

Four months had passed since Adele's last visit home and she had been shocked by the change in Noreen's appearance.

Her clothes, stained with food and liquids, hung loosely over her gaunt frame. Food rotted in the fridge and it was evident from her dramatic weight loss that she had stopped cooking for herself. Her mental state was even more alarming. She was frightened of Daniel, unable to remember who he was or why he was in her house. At times, she forgot Adele's name and called her Marianne. Daniel had returned to London alone and, as Adele suspected, when she persuaded Noreen to visit her doctor, scans revealed that she was suffering from the rapid onset of dementia. A month later, Noreen was admitted to a nursing home and Adele travelled back from London every second weekend to see her.

Noreen's outbursts, when she referred to Adele as a slut and a whore, made these visits difficult. Adele tried with photographs and music to bring her back from the abyss but Noreen became mute, as if, at a subconscious level, she knew she could not be trusted to hold her secrets close, as she had done so determinedly throughout her granddaughter's life. A year after she entered the nursing home, she suffered a catastrophic heart attack and was rushed to hospital. She survived until Adele arrived from London and died in the early hours of the following morning.

'It's *so* good to have you back,' Daniel said when they were seated on the Tube.

'It's good to be back,' she said, aware that he was referring not only to the week she had spent sorting out Noreen's possessions but to the time before then, the Sunday nights when she had returned to him, wan and grief-stricken from witnessing her grandmother's rapid decline.

'You sounded so distracted over the house deeds,' he said. 'Did you manage to sort out the problem?'

'I'll tell you about it later.' Perhaps, in the quietness of their apartment, she could relax and speak coherently about her discovery. She leaned her head on his shoulder and he, smiling, slid his hand along the side of her thigh, a gesture invisible to everyone but themselves. Small familiar gestures that she welcomed as they journeyed towards his apartment, where a beef stew was simmering in the slow cooker and would be ready for serving when they arrived.

They would move to Colorado in September.

Greendene was taking on a new pipeline project and Daniel would be heading up the environmental team. A five-year contract, he had told Adele, all expenses, including their accommodation, covered. She had been torn between her excitement at the idea of moving and her responsibility towards her grandmother. Now Noreen could no longer hold her back, but the thought of moving to unfamiliar surroundings no longer filled her with anticipation.

He lit candles when they entered the apartment, and turned on the music. She thought they would tumble to the bed, as they always did when she returned from Ireland, kicking off shoes, unbuttoning, unzipping, greedy and eager for the touch of each other. But this evening, he concentrated on bringing food to the table, a casserole that was as delicious as he had promised. The reason soon became obvious. Their departure date for moving to Colorado had been moved forward.

'It's all happening much faster than planned,' he said. 'Madison wants me in place by next month. I told her it's very short notice and that I needed to discuss everything with you first. She's waiting on my answer. You know what she's like. Today's information needed yesterday.' His laughter belied his uneasiness, his gaze sizing up her shocked expression.

'What about my job?' she asked. 'I'd planned on having three months to finish the projects I've been working on.'

'Can't someone else take them on? I know it won't be an easy ask but I want you with me. Madison has contacts in the media. She says you'll have no problem finding work. If anyone knows how to pull strings, it's her.'

Adele had met Madison Fox, the project manager with Greendene, when she came to London on a business trip some months previously. She was a brittle redhead with a commanding voice and a personality to match. Adele didn't doubt her string-pulling abilities.

'It's a lot to absorb, Daniel. Too much for me right now.'

'You're tired. I understand. We can talk about it again tomorrow.'

'No, let's talk about it now. What if you go on ahead and I follow you?'

'That's the difficulty,' he said. 'The company want the apartment back. One of Greendene's executives is flying in from the States around the same time as we're expected to leave. He'll be moving in here. The removal firm will take care of everything but we need to organise our stuff for them.' He opened his iPad. 'Take a look at this. Madison sent on these photos of our new home.'

The apartment Madison had chosen for them was an Aladdin's cave. High ceilings, gleaming marble and wooden floors, elegant furnishings, glittering chandeliers and a breathtaking view of city lights; all it needed to make it perfect was Adele's approval.

'We can be married in Colorado.' Daniel put the iPad to one side and took her hands in his. 'We love each other. As long as we have that going for us, the rest will be easy.'

Her thoughts were in turmoil as she listened to his reassurances. His enthusiasm overwhelmed her. In comparison, her discovery felt like a dulled pain radiating from her with no sense of direction. She winced as his grip tightened and the hard bite of diamonds pressed against her fingers. He could not afford to mess up. He told her so gently, pleadingly, firmly.

His phone rang. Madison in Colorado. Unable to listen to the one-way exchange, Adele wheeled her case into the bedroom and began to unpack. The curtains were open and from her vantage point she saw him emerge onto the balcony. She watched him gesticulating. His hand language was always faster when he was stressed.

'What did you tell Madison?' she asked when the call ended.

'That you needed time to get used to the idea.'

'I'd say that went down like a lead balloon.'

'She's going to ring back tomorrow,' he admitted. 'I hate putting pressure on you after all you've been through but there's no reason why we can't manage it – that's assuming you want to go with me.'

'What's that supposed to mean?' She hadn't meant to snap but that was how she sounded, tetchy and brusque.

He drew away from her, his eyes narrowing. 'There's something else going on with you. I knew as soon as I saw you in arrivals. Is it the house deeds?'

'I told you I've sorted that out. You've had time to absorb this news but you're asking me to drop everything at a moment's notice and head off to Colorado with you. Why should you or Madison expect me to give you an answer just like that?' She flung herself back against the pillows. 'You can be so selfish at times. Nagging at me to come back when I was trying to look after my grandmother—'

'I never nagged. But every second weekend—' He stopped, aware of the triggers that could start an argument. 'Come on, Adele, let's not argue over this. We'll sleep on it and discuss it again tomorrow.'

'What's to discuss? You've made up your mind.' She wanted to fight with him. To kick the door and fling things on the floor, smash her fists against the walls. Anything to silence the voice in her head, the earworm – so long Marianne… She pulled away from him and ran from the bedroom.

'Just leave me alone and let me sort out my own mind,' she shouted as she slammed the door behind her.

She sat on the window seat in the living room, the lamp angled so that as much light as possible flowed over the pages of the diary. She had read it a number of times already. On each reading she found something new, even though some of the entries rambled into incoherence as her young mother tried to make sense of her situation. How could Daniel hope to understand her confusion about her past when his face was set to his own future, his mind made up?

CHAPTER SIX

The Marianne Diary

Mam drove for hours before we reached Inisada. It's just a few houses and shops and pubs and then we were out in the country again with nothing but cows and sheep. We came to these huge gates. They were open, like we were expected. I thought it was a hotel when I saw a house with the big steps leading to the front door. But it's not a hotel. It's called the House of Atonement and it's where I have to stay until my baby is born.

A woman in a navy cardigan and skirt was waiting for us at the top of the steps. I only realised she was a Thorn when I got close up and saw the crown of thorns engraved on the medallion around her neck. Then it all made sense. My legs were like jelly so I wasn't able to run. Not that I would have got far. Mam was holding my arm, the way she does when she wants me to stand still and listen to her. I cried then and tried to pull away from her. The woman, she's called Miss Bethany, took my other arm, not hard like the way Mam was holding me, just firm in a stop-your-silly-nonsense way.

The hall smelled of polish and fish. Disgusting. We went into an office. MOTHER GLORIA, SUPERIOR COUNSELLOR was written across the door. I couldn't believe it. Liam

Thornton's crazy mother owns this place and I have to call her Mother Gloria.

She talked to Mam about visiting times and things I could do, and not do, and how I would be treated with kindness and understanding. I didn't believe her. I still don't. Mam has dumped me here whether I like it or not. She was crying when she left me but crocodile tears won't change anything. I'm so frightened. What if I never get out of here? If I never see Shane again? If this is my life from now on? Oh God, is this it? Find me Shane... please find me and take me away from this awful house.

I wish I could have left a trail behind. Breadcrumbs or secret signs that he could follow. I kept thinking he'd throw pebbles at my window or leave a note under our hiding stone. He can't have run away. That's just a lie and it's the same as all the other lies those girls have been spreading about me and him. Does he know I've been sent to prison? That's what Atonement is. There are bars on the windows and spikes on the gates and all the doors are locked so that makes it a prison, no matter what Mother Gloria says about it being a holy sanctuary.

CHAPTER SEVEN

Barefooted and wearing a pair of jogging pants, Daniel came from the bedroom and sat down beside her.

'What are you doing, Adele?' he asked.

'Reading this.' Tears stung her cheeks as she handed the diary to him. 'It belonged to my mother. I found it when I was clearing out the attic.'

Shock, anger, disgust, sadness, his expression revealed each emotion as he turned the pages.

'How long have you known about this?' He laid the diary down when he finished reading it and took her into his arms.

'It was inside a backpack I found under the rafters when I was clearing out the attic. My mother must have brought it with her to the mother and baby home where I was born.'

'Was that why you cancelled your flight?'

'Yes.'

'Why didn't you tell me?'

'I couldn't… I still don't know what to say about it or what to do.' She steadied her voice with an effort. 'How could Noreen have kept this information from me?'

'Maybe she intended telling you but events took over—'

'I'll never know. The bag was so well hidden. Like she couldn't bear to throw it out or to keep it. I believe she planned on going to her grave with her secrets.'

'I'm sorry, Adele. So very sorry you've had to find out—'

'I'm *not* sorry.' She was too confused to know if this was true but it felt right to say it aloud. 'My mother was so young to give birth and I've spent my life haunted by the possibility that I killed her. But they were responsible… those three monsters.' She covered her eyes, afraid that the vague shapes she visualised in her mind would assume features that resembled her own. 'I've been searching the web in the hope that there might be something online about a court case from around that time.'

'From twenty-five years back? That would be a long shot.'

'Not really. So much old information is online now. But there's nothing that links to what I've read in her diary. They got away with it, Daniel. My mother was gang-raped…' She shuddered, her stomach churning at the violence the words conveyed. 'My father is out there somewhere. I want to find him.'

'*Find* him?' The indentation between his eyebrows deepened. 'How would you even begin to embark on such a search?'

'At its source. Reedstown. I want to go there and discover what I can about her.' She spoke faster, forestalling his objections. 'I know it's not the right time to make such a decision but I won't be able to move forward until I know what happened… how it happened. They may believe that they got away with it but all crimes leave traces behind. I'm that trace, Daniel. The result of their depravity. The consequences… whatever you want to call it.'

'A gift,' he said. 'That's what you are to me. A precious gift that I love. Come to Colorado with me. Give yourself time to think this through and decide on the steps you can take to begin your search. I'll give you all the support you need and when you feel that you've enough to go on, we'll hire a private investigator.'

He had been born into security, one of three children, all cherished by their parents and rooted in an extended family tree. She trusted him to do as he promised but how could he even begin to understand the depth of her lost identity? Noreen had left her with a property and an income but with no sense of self. Would he ever appreciate the potency of her anger? Like flames on a parched mountainside, it had no boundaries, no cut-off point. It was focused on the men who had killed her mother, for that was what they had done, as cleanly as if they had plunged a knife into her chest. One of those faceless men was her father. His blood ran through her veins. She carried his DNA. Nurture, nature, what did it matter when she hated the genes she had inherited?

'They murdered my mother,' she said. 'This search is my responsibility. She deserves justice for what they did to her. I have to go there, Daniel, and try to tell her story.'

'How do you intend to do that? Walk up to every man you meet and ask him if he murdered your mother? Gang-raped her?' He was unable to hide his scepticism. 'If what your mother wrote is true—'

'*Daniel…*' The same feeling of detachment she had experienced yesterday when she lied to him about the house deeds returned. As if the words in her mother's diary, now that they had been released, would always drown him out.

'I'm not trying to hurt you but you need to slow down. She was fifteen, Adele. She must have been highly emotional and stressed out. Perhaps Shane was responsible and abandoned her. What you've read could have been a story she concocted.'

'Is that what you think? Why would she make up something as sickening as that?' She paced the room, unable to sit still.

'I don't know the truth,' he replied. 'And neither do you. But, if it did happen as she described and those men are still in Reedstown, do you honestly believe you will be able to identify them after all this time?'

'I don't know,' she admitted. 'But the information I've always wanted is in my hands. I've finally found something tangible that has brought me closer to her. I'm going to the mother and baby home in Inisada and see where I was born. Then I'm heading to Reedstown.'

'How long will all that take?' He forced her to stand still and face him.

'I don't know. Please don't try to pin me down to a specific date. I'll join you there as soon as I have answers.'

'Supposing you never find those answers. How long will it take you to accept that reality?'

How long is a piece of string? she thought, but he would not appreciate such a reply. She had no way of naming the tears that scalded her cheeks. Rage or frustration, fear of what she had lost or what she was about to lose? Her sobs were stifled against his shoulder. She was a rape child, not a lovechild, as she had always believed. Speared into being by an unholy trinity.

*

She saw him off at Heathrow Airport. They held each other in a tight, breathless embrace. More promises, reassurances, vows of love. A swallow in an attic. A butterfly in a jungle. Random events. Heartbreaking decisions.

CHAPTER EIGHT

The Marianne Diary

It's over two months since I came to this prison and Miss Bethany never shuts up.

'Pay attention to your work, Number Fifty-Three,' she shouts. 'You don't know how privileged you are. You could be in a laundry washing dirty underwear instead of being allowed to handle sacred objects.'

The medals are awful, shiny and heavy, and Mother Gloria's ugly face is on all of them, showing off like she's the queen of England. Me and Barbara spit on them and rub our saliva all over them. She's my friend and sleeps in the bed next to me. The factory is in three big steel containers at the back of the big house. It's either too hot or too cold. When it's cold we're allowed to wear fingerless gloves. Such luxury!! We're not allowed to talk to each other when we're packing the medals because that will slow production. But we can listen to music. Just classical and hymns. The violins screech inside my head but the hymns wash over me and help me to stay calm.

We do gift packs of Mother Gloria CDs. She's supposed to be meditating with God on them but Barbara says she's crackers and anyone who listens to her recordings is just as *daft. All the candles are made in her image. I like to think of her melting away and becoming a great, big, greasy blob. We pack the books she's written about her apparitions and the holy messages she receives when she's doing one of her weird dances.*

Barbara says it's slave labour. Her father is also a Thorn and lives in the Donegal commune. One of the chosen. Hah. One of the clones, more like. Such drippy, awful women cleaning the house and cooking our meals. All spit and polish in honour of Mother Gloria. Barbara calls Miss Bethany 'The Enforcer' and Miss Elisha 'The Quack' and Miss Rebekah is 'Poison Paws' because of the awful food she cooks.

The men who look after the grounds are worse. I see them looking at Mother Gloria with their beady eyes when she puts on that white robe and it's like she's poured her body into it. When she goes into one of her stupid trances and talks gibberish, those men are not thinking about their prayers, I can tell you that for nothing.

The first time I heard Mother Gloria speaking was just a few weeks after Dad died. She described how she'd seen Jesus on the top of a mountain and how he told her it was her mission in this life to lead an assembly of Thorns into his light and away from the idolaters of sin and the devil. They had to shun those who would try to corrupt them and use the courage of their beliefs to keep on the path of righteousness. By the end of the assembly everyone in the hall was hugging and singing Thorn hymns and their eyes were really scary, like they were rolling around like marbles in their heads. Tears were streaming down Mam's face when she was 'touched' by Mother Gloria. I shrank back and didn't let her put her skinny hands on my head. I couldn't stand all those women and men acting like she'd come down from heaven on a cloud.

Afterwards, I couldn't get her smile out of my head. Like it was a mask that hid how much she loved seeing everyone in her power. Like them. The ones who came for me in their balaclavas. Their masks as fixed as her smile.

Mam says Mother Gloria helped her understand that Dad died when he tried to double-cross Jesus. Crap. He died because a French tourist came out of a side turning on the wrong side of the road and crashed headfirst into his car. Three people wiped out. The French tourist was called Pascal and the woman in Dad's car was Bernice. Where were they going that night? To her apartment or a restaurant? Did they have time to say goodbye? Did he have time to whisper my name? Or Mam's? Did she know about Bernice? I'm afraid to ask and she never says. Never mentions her name and, after the crash, I saw her tearing up the newspapers with Bernice's picture on the front page.

Hate feels like a tiny scab that begins to itch then it becomes infected and grows into a seeping pus. In the beginning I just hated them, the faceless, nameless three. Then it spread to Sergeant Bale, then Davina Maye and Julie Boland and their clique for the horrible things they said about me. I hated the Thorns with their twisted faith, and Mam, who chose them over me. Dad's now wrapped up in my hate. It's his fault that Mam joined the Thorns and 'found her true identity'. That's when everything changed. She didn't seem to notice me any more and there was always another workshop, another conference where she could learn how to help her true self to emerge from the rot of a Godless society.

CHAPTER NINE

Adele

The signpost to Inisada was almost obscured by overgrown hedging. Easy to miss in a car and Adele had passed it twice before she noticed the rusting finger pointing left. She turned onto a road that was going in only one direction. The car juddered over potholes and she was forced to drive dangerously close to a sloping ditch at the edge of the hedgerow. This was Sleeping Beauty territory, the stunted spikiness, the prickling thorns and bristles reminding her of fairy stories from her childhood. How long since anyone had driven along this road, she wondered? Had they been as confused as she was? As frightened by the questions that had brought them here?

Afraid that the tyres would puncture on a pothole, she considered abandoning the car and continuing on foot. A fallen tree blocked the road and took the decision from her. Its roots, wrenched from their sockets, hung like dreadlocks through the clotted earth and briars twined around the shrivelled trunk. After climbing over it, she reached a set of padlocked gates. She imagined them swinging open and closing behind Marianne. Her terror as Noreen drove away and left her imprisoned behind them.

Beyond the gates, she could see the gaunt outlines of a building. Once, it must have been a magnificent stately home but now, roofless and reduced to blackened exterior walls, it was a shell, razed to the ground by a fire. The sign 'House of Atonement' was faded but still visible on the gatepost. Adele walked around the perimeter wall, searching for a gap that would allow her to enter the grounds. The top of the wall was covered with shards of glass and she was unable to find a break in the solid brickwork. Climbing over the gate was impossible. The curves and loops patterning the bottom section could give her a foothold but the sheer iron bars rising into spikes would defeat her. She returned to the car and removed a hammer and chisel. Determined to enter the grounds, she jammed the chisel into the base of the padlock and hammered at it until the fitting broke free.

She walked across a courtyard towards a blackened archway where a door had stood before it was burned to ash. A gaping space led into the ruin. She imagined the fury of the fire as it roared through this three-storey building, the crash of ceilings and floors thundering downwards. Metal frames of beds and other furnishings lay on the ground, twisted into grotesque sculptures. Flimsy trees rooted in metal crevices, flowers and wild grasses sprouted from the mounds of brick and rubble. What had caused this inferno? An electrical fault, a cigarette flung carelessly aside, an accident in the kitchen, or had the fire been started deliberately?

Adele looked upward towards the blue sky and small, skittering clouds. She should have been prepared for the sensations that swept over her but she had no defences left to hold back her grief. She sank to her knees amidst the debris. No one to hear her in this grim monstrosity. Her cries rebounded from the walls and echoed through spaces she had yet to explore. She found the strength to rise again and fight her way through the wreckage. Which room had been the dormitory where the young mothers slept? Where was Gloria Thornton's office? Where was the clinic, the dining hall and prayer room? It was impossible to map her way through the devastation, apart from the kitchen, where a solid stove was one of the only objects to have withstood the heat and retain its shape.

Outside, in a nearby field, someone was using a tractor. The grass swayed, knee-high and dizzy from the heat. Gaunt and black, the walls brooded under the searing sunshine. She reached another courtyard at the back of the house and found three steel containers. The doors were jammed on the first two containers but she managed to enter the third one, which was furthest from the house. The intense heat had warped the crude wooden floorboards and settled a pall of soot everywhere but the interior was still intact. No wonder it had been icy cold in the winter when the only heating was a few electric bars positioned near the top of the walls. Two windows had been cut into the sides of the container and the sun, shining through the corroding frames, glinted on shards of glass. She noticed scattered flecks of black on a long table and moved closer. Medals, she realised, all speckled with soot. She rubbed away the soot on two of the medals with her sleeve and saw the moulding of a woman's profile, surrounded by a woven arch of thorns. The same woman's face was visible on the second medal, a crown of thorns suspended like a halo above her head. Adele shuddered and dropped the medals. Her skin felt clogged, as if soot was penetrating her pores.

She found more medals under the long trestle table. These ones had been packed in cardboard gift boxes. They were free from soot but tarnished by time. The boxes also contained leaflets that claimed the medals had been blessed personally by Mother Gloria. A faded photograph on the leaflet showed her on her knees gazing rapturously upwards towards a shaft of light. Unable to find anything else of interest, Adele returned to the front of the house. The grass, bleached from the sun, was turning yellow and the heat rolled towards her in waves as she moved in and out of the wall's shadows.

A cocker spaniel bounded through the open gates and headed straight towards her.

'Stay, Molly,' an elderly woman shouted at the dog, who immediately came to a standstill, tongue drooling, her bright eyes staring at Adele. The woman hesitated by the entrance, obviously surprised at finding the gates unlocked.

'I see that barriers aren't any obstacle to you.' She walked briskly towards Adele. Her walking boots looked comfortable and well worn, and the blackthorn stick she used had that same sturdy usefulness. She pointed her stick at the blackened hulk and said, 'It was an inferno the last time I stood inside these gates.'

'What happened to it?' Adele asked. 'Were you involved with the cu— sodality?'

'Perish the thought.' The woman snorted. 'They kept to themselves and didn't welcome outsiders – apart from those, like me, who brought supplies to them. I used to run the local supermarket in Inisada. Of course, that's long gone now. No competing against those big shopping centres. And, sure, isn't that what they call progress, I don't think!' Her gaze was direct and compassionate as she took in Adele's unkempt appearance, her reddened eyes. 'You must be one of the babies. You're of an age and, sure, who else would want to visit this wretched place?'

'Do other people come here?'

'A few come, those who were babies and those who gave birth to them.' The woman's briskness steadied Adele. 'But they never make it beyond the gate. I saw your car turning onto the road, if you can call it that any more. I didn't think you'd make it past the fallen tree. But I can tell you've a determined nature.'

'As you have,' said Adele. 'It's tough climbing over that tree.'

'Far too tough for me, girl. My climbing days are long over. I came by the back field. There's a path through the wood that leads to here. Lilian's my name.' Her hand was rough, calloused with age and exposure, but firm as she held Adele in a warm grip. 'Were you adopted out of here, if you don't mind me asking?'

'No, I don't mind,' Adele replied. 'I was reared by my grandmother. My mother died giving birth to me.'

'Well, that's a tragedy sure enough, and a tough start in life. But I hope you've had a happy one.'

Adele blinked tears away. Surely she was all cried out by now. 'My grandmother did her best.'

'That's all any of us can do.'

In its day, the House of Atonement had been a local attraction, she told Adele. Carloads of curious onlookers used to come to buy religious paraphernalia and catch a glimpse of the visionary. Lilian had been one of the sceptics. She rolled her eyes at the possibility of trances and ecstatic revelations. The house had originally belonged to an Anglo-Irish family whose seed and breed died out when their last surviving member, an only child, a daughter, unmarried, became involved with the Thorns in her old age.

'Putty in their hands, she was,' said Lilian. 'Signed over everything to ensure that she would be among the chosen when she popped her clogs, which she managed to conveniently do six months later.' She stood back and looked upwards towards the blackened ruin. 'Rumours were always swirling around this place. That's what happens when people put up walls.' Gently but firmly, Lilian took her arm and turned her away. 'Small steps, that's the best way to approach the past. You've stood in this godforsaken place for long enough. Come back to my house and we can chat about this over a cup of tea.'

She was in her late seventies, she told Adele, but her step was still sprightly. They walked through a wooded area and entered a farmyard where a woman was lifting groceries from the back of her car. She called out to Lilian and waved a greeting at them before entering the farmhouse.

'That's Tricia O'Donnell,' said Lilian. 'She allows me right of way onto their land. My own house is just up the road.'

Adele became aware of birdsong, a riotous medley. Was she just noticing it now or had it been absent from that blighted landscape? Lilian's 'up the road' turned out to be a quarter of a mile away and her house, an old, two-storey building with yellow exterior walls, was the nearest one to the farm. Inside, the smell of turf and dog mingled pleasantly with the scent from an aromatic oil burner.

'A documentary maker. Now, that's an interesting occupation.' Lilian sounded impressed as she set mugs on the table and cut thick slices of home-made soda bread. 'Are you planning on making a documentary about the Thorns?'

'That's my intention.'

'There was a writer chap down here a few years back looking for information. Devil a bit of harm, I thought, telling him what I knew. But Gloria Thornton's son got to hear about it and threatened to bring me to court for slandering his mother's character. He's a nasty piece of work and he certainly put the wind up me. I'm too old for that kind of pressure. Is what I'm telling you off the record?'

'Of course it is. I *am* anxious to make a documentary but, for now, I'm just interested in finding out what I can about that house and the young women who stayed there. Did you know any of them?'

'Most of them were still only girls and I wasn't allowed next or near them. My only contact was with the Thorns who ran the place, and Gloria, of course, when she visited. She asked me once to bring a baby to the States. She'd heard I was planning to visit my sister in Boston. The adoptive parents would meet me at the airport. All perfectly legit, she assured me. Even showed me the paperwork. When I refused, she threatened to boycott my shop. I didn't give a fig for her threats. I never had kids myself, or a husband for that matter. Never wanted a man, nor a woman either. Just a loner, that's always been me.' She leaned down and stroked the dog's ears. 'A dog, my camera, a strong pair of shoes and a long road, that's all I needed to keep me happy. But if I'd had a baby and someone took her or him from me... there'd be blood spilled.'

'Are you telling me she was trafficking those babies?'

'It wasn't called that in those days, of course. No, then it was considered an act of charity to give a baby a good home. Now, it's all out in the open and we can put the right name on it. Gloria Thornton took those babies from their mothers and sold them.'

'You know that for definite?'

'No, sadly I don't. But Charlotte, she was the owner of that house, said something to me before she died. She was in a fever so it would have been easy to ignore it. I chose not to. She said Gloria Thornton had turned her home into an auction block for babies. She was dead by the time it burned down but she would have struck the match had she been around to do so. It was a miracle that only one person died that night. I've never been able to figure out what brought Gloria back into that inferno after she escaped from it.'

'She was rescuing the girls. I read about it.'

'I read those reports myself. All spin, isn't that what they call it nowadays? Gloria went back into the blaze all right but she never came out alive. Overcome by smoke, apparently. There were some inflammable liquids stored in her office and that's what caused the inferno. That road you drove down was as smooth as a ribbon then but it was still a miracle the firemen were able to get everyone to safety. It was sheer pandemonium. The girls were ferried to hospital to be checked out. Poor wee things, shivering and wailing. Thank God their babies survived. I can see you're upset. You wouldn't have been one of those babies, would you?'

'No, I'd been taken from there by then. It's just appalling to think about it.'

'It *was* appalling, especially the behaviour of the Thorns. They wanted to move the girls to their communes. They had one somewhere in West Kerry, if I remember rightly, and another one up in Donegal. But the emergency teams weren't having any of it. They were ferried to hospital to be checked out and discharged into the care of the state, as far as I recall. I took photos. You probably think that was voyeuristic of me and you'd be right, I guess. I was a keen photographer then, still am, to be honest, and I happened to be close to the scene when the fire first broke out.'

'Do you still have the photographs?'

'I'm sure I do. They're somewhere among the clutter. Give me a minute and I'll see what I can find.'

Adele could hear her rummaging about upstairs. Four generations of clutter stored in crates and boxes, Lilian had said. She was empty-handed when she came downstairs.

'I know they're there somewhere,' she fretted. 'If I could just lay my hands on them. Give me your address and I'll send them to you when I find them.'

What address should she give? Colorado was in the future and an address in Reedstown had yet to be found. They exchanged phone numbers and promised to keep in touch.

Shadows were lengthening when Adele clambered over the fallen tree and returned to her car. She did not look behind as she drove away. Nothing to see except the stark remains of a delusion. An auction block where babies were bartered to the highest bidder.

CHAPTER TEN

The Marianne Diary

Barbara can always make me laugh, no matter how down I am. She's only a year older than me but she knows so much. She says I was gang-raped. I should have been brought to a hospital. Then I wouldn't be expecting a baby because they could have done something to stop me becoming pregnant. That's exactly what Fr Breen told Mam but she wouldn't listen to him. She says he's not a proper priest with his hippy, dippy sermons. A mother knows best, she said after he left our house. That was the day after IT happened. I didn't need to go to a hospital and have doctors poking and prodding me and asking questions that no good girl should have to answer. She said the Thorns would fill my bedroom with the Holy Spirit and heal me. If I sought divine forgiveness then clean thoughts would enter my mind again and wash away the bad.

Miss Bethany heard me and Barbara talking one night when we were supposed to be sleeping. The next day Barbara was put into the tank for two days. It's down in the cellar and she says it's a shit hole. She's been moved to a different dormitory and Miss Bethany says I must make restitution for offending God. That means never complaining or telling lies again. Good girls don't get raped. They wear decent clothes

*and keep their legs crossed. Sorry, Miss Bethany, you're so
fucked-up wrong. Sergeant Bale must belong to the Thorns
because that's exactly the kind of thing he said to me when
he was getting to the nub of the matter. He made me feel
tainted, ugly, filthy, different! Stop! Barbara says we have to
fight, fight, fight to stay sane and defeat them.*

*It's hard to do that. I saw Mr Lewis today. He was getting
into his car and Mother Gloria was at the bottom of the steps
talking to him. She said I needed to have my eyes tested when
I asked her if it was him. I was going to argue with her but
when she gets that look in her eyes it's time to shut up. So
what's real? Me and the others, that's what. Siobhan's cries
over the twins. Jenny's bird that she feeds. Lisa's songs that
she sings to her baby so he'll remember her voice when he's
taken. And Barbara with her crazy plan to escape from here.*

*We measured tummies today. Her baby is due a week
after mine. Charlie, he's her boyfriend, is going to rescue her
long before then. At least she can name her baby's father.
Not like me. Who are they? Which one is my baby's father?
Is he the one with the beer breath? Or the one whose teeth
made my lips bleed? Or the one with the smell of smoke on
his clothes? Three blind mice… see how they run… see how
they run… see how they run…*

CHAPTER ELEVEN

Reedstown was a village on a cusp of change, its fields and meadows torn apart by bulldozers and cranes. The Loyvale Hotel was part of this new expansion and Adele would stay there until she found somewhere suitable to rent. This morning she was searching for the cottage where Marianne and Shane had believed they would be safe. Clues to its location were sparse, scribbled entries that described a lane where deadwood snapped underfoot and dangling branches patterned a cracked window. In one of her vague references to Reedstown, Noreen had mentioned that her house had a view of a river. As the Loy ran behind the village, this suggested that the house had stood on a height but would have been close enough to their hiding place for Marianne to meet Shane and return again before the Thorns finished their weekly gathering.

The land on the outskirts of Reedstown had given way to apartment complexes, their balconies overlooking rows of newly occupied houses. The narrowness of the main street running through the centre of the village suggested it had once serviced a sleepy backwater and was now struggling to contain the stream of cars accessing it from the M50 motorway. The village her mother had known was now a busy satellite town and Adele, searching for a tumbledown refuge with a monstrous history, soon realised the futility of her search.

A week had passed since her arrival and this morning she had discovered a derelict cottage, almost invisible behind a screen of ash and elderberry trees. Yesterday, she had checked an abandoned shack in a field of dandelions. Another cottage sagged by the edge of the main road leading into Reedstown, its roof collapsed. She had photographed each location, clicking, clicking, searching for something, a clue from the grave that would scream *This is where I fell into hell.*

She stumbled on a tuft of grass and regained her balance before stepping through the doorway. Standing in the rubble of pizza cartons and rusting beer cans, she opened her arms in an effort to invoke her dead mother's presence. She longed for a ghostly shudder of recognition; anything that would suggest a link between the past and the present, the living and the dead. But there was nothing to alert her, just stinging nettles at her feet and the earthy smell of rot. And thorns, everywhere she looked. Blackberry briars clawing the legs of her jeans. Hawthorn and blackthorn tangling in the hedgerows, and those banks of gorse, its spindly blossom splashing gold against the distant hillside.

Returning to the village centre, she explored the side streets and narrow lanes for evidence that the Thorns would once have worshipped there. Again, she drew a blank. No wooden signage with faded lettering. No dusty, empty pews or arched ceiling that would have echoed with empty promises. No house of prayer where her mother had hidden under a duvet as she listened to the Thorns chanting and singing to a God who would choose them above all others for entry through the gates of heaven.

A man with cropped brown hair and a trim goatee beard emerged from a small convenience store, a takeaway coffee in hand, and caused her to slow her step. He glanced at her as he passed, startled, perhaps, or flattered by her penetrating stare. She continued along Main Street and stopped before a poster of Christy Lewis in the window of his constituency clinic. His penetrating blue gaze suggested that he had years of experience behind him and the knowledge to use the votes of his constituents wisely. His son had followed him into politics. His poster was also on display, a younger version of his father, better looking than the older man, his white teeth gleaming with sincerity.

Later, Adele's hand shook as she filled her rental car with petrol and noticed a stocky man, his black hair thinning at the temples, watching her from another pump, his three children bobbing with impatience in the backseat. Could he be the one, she thought as he drove away? Or the man in a navy business suit, a briefcase slung from his shoulder, who had followed her into the hotel last night. No, she had decided, as she listened to him checking in at reception; like her, he was a stranger in town. She had no reason to assume her father would still be living in Reedstown. He could have moved to Australia, the States, England, anywhere. He could be buried in a graveyard or resting – ashes to ashes, dust to dust – in a cremation urn. She needed objectivity if she was to discover the truth about her birth; reacting emotionally to every male she encountered in the forty-plus age group would destroy her. Yet they continued to stand out like stencils from the passing crowd.

The people she stopped to ask about the Thorns stared blankly at her. Some lived in the newer houses and found it hard to believe that a cult had once existed in Reedstown. The locals shrugged. The Thorns had kept to themselves before moving on to set up their communes elsewhere, said one woman. Why was she raking all that old stuff up again, a querulous old man on a Zimmer asked when she stopped him on Main Street? Gloria Thornton had been a saint and a martyr. God rest her soul, he said as he shuffled on, muttering about outsiders coming into the village to stir old dust.

A brash shopping centre had been built to service the new housing estates but the shops on Main Street still had their old-fashioned exteriors and signs that suggested business had been done under the same family name for generations. The bold modernism of the office of the local newspaper, the *Reedstown Review*, was the exception. Set apart from the older buildings, its frontage and high-domed roof, both made from glass, reminded Adele of a gigantic goldfish bowl. Did the staff feel the same way, exposed, as they were, to the gaze of the public as they bent over their phones and computers, or rode between the floors on a pod-like elevator? Tomorrow morning, she had an appointment with the owner and editor, Robert Molloy.

CHAPTER TWELVE

The Marianne Diary

My baby keeps growing. Strange how such a tiny heart can keep beating when I wish with all my might for it to stop. I tried so hard to do it. Gin was supposed to work. I stole a bottle from William's off-licence. I didn't care if I was caught. That's probably how I got away with it. Murderer, that's what Mam would have called me if she'd known what I was doing. But she'd gone to the Thorn repentance session after the pregnancy test confirmed her worst fear. I drank loads of the gin and ran a hot bath. I was sick as a dog for two days afterwards. Mam thought it was morning sickness. I hoped it was the baby coming away but it clung on. In the gym I did skipping and press-ups and wall climbing and stomach stretching exercises. Nothing worked.

I begged Mum to bring me to England for an abortion. A girl in fifth year did that. We weren't supposed to know but her best friend told another friend and soon it was all over school. She never came back afterwards. Last we heard she was going to grind school to study for her Leaving.

Mam wouldn't listen to me. She said abortion was a crime against the state but, even worse, it was a sin against God. What God? The one with his hands stretched out, all that streaming light coming from his palms? Or the one the Thorns worship? A big bully who says it's wrong to love and be happy and want to dance on clouds. That's what I felt like with Shane. Like everyone was circling around us but no one could break through our love. If this was our lovechild, I'd cradle it. But it's a rape child. A tumour in my belly and I can't tear it out.

I can't wait for it to be born and on its way to America. That's the best place for babies like ours, Mother Gloria says. There are Thorns over there, loads and loads of them, only that's not what they're called. But they all believe that they are the chosen ones and they want our babies to become chosen too. Barbara says that'll happen over her dead body. She loves her baby and Malachi is going to help her to escape. He's different to the other Thorns. He hugged Siobhan Miley when her twins died and brings us sweets and bars of chocolate back from Inisada.

When Barbara puts her hands on her tummy and gets that look in her eyes, like she's far away from us all, just her and her baby in a bubble, I envy her so much. She has love inside her and that helps her to escape, even if it's only for a little while in her mind. But me, there's no escaping that kick... kick... kick... kick... like my baby knows that's all I'll remember when it's gone.

CHAPTER THIRTEEN

Adele

In the reception area of the *Reedstown Review* office, two large photographs hung side by side. One featured the original newspaper office. Modest in comparison to this glass edifice, it had been a two-storey, red-brick building with the *Reedstown Review* sign above the main entrance. The details, inscribed on a brass plaque underneath, stated that the photograph was taken in 1912. The second photograph showed a group of men and women posing outside the new building on the day it was officially opened. According to the inscription, Christy Lewis, Reedstown's local politician, had cut the ribbon.

'Mr Molloy told me to expect you,' the receptionist said when Adele presented her Voice Dox business card at the front desk. 'Something unexpected came up and he's not free to see you until later. He asked me to look after you. My name is Jessica. Would you like tea or coffee?'

'No, thank you.' Adele smiled and held up the cup of iced coffee she had purchased at Katie's Kasket next door.

'Good choice.' Jessica returned her smile. 'Katie makes the best coffee in Reedstown. Isn't it a scorcher outside? Come with me and I'll show you the archive.'

Adele accompanied her down wooden steps into the basement. No sheen of modernity here. The shelves were stacked with cardboard files that stretched from the floor to the ceiling, where a nicotine-stained veneer suggested the archive had once been a popular smoke-filled enclave. Adele was convinced she could still smell the residue of cigarettes and pipes. The tables and chairs had the battered appearance of much use, and framed posters of famous *Reedstown Review* front pages hung from the walls.

'The paper celebrated its centenary six years ago so we have an enormous archive,' said Jessica. 'Much of it is on microfilm but it's still a work in progress. We haven't yet had an opportunity to put our content online. However, the scanner works so whatever information you need should be easy to find. The phone on that table has a direct line to my desk if you need anything. Don't be shy. See you later.'

Alone in the basement, Adele switched on the scanner and began the painstakingly slow work of tracing the moment of her conception. She had roughly estimated when the assault on her mother occurred. After all, as she'd grimly reminded herself when she had been browsing the web, it was not difficult to count back nine months from the date of her birth. Although she had failed to find anything resembling the assault Marianne had outlined in such painful detail in her diary, surely a local publication would have reported such a heinous rape. Even if the victim had remained anonymous, the Gardai had a duty of care to notify the newspaper and issue a warning that Reedstown was a dangerous place to walk alone at night. There must be a link somewhere that would lead her to another link, then another; a chain reaction that would eventually expose the truth.

The newspaper's reach was local, with an emphasis on the parochial. Weddings, funerals, charity events, prize-giving ceremonies, deb nights, every bunfight chronicled; yet Marianne's name never appeared under any caption or in any column of print. Neither did Noreen. No mention of her in the Irish Countrywomen's

Association or the Irish Housewives Association. She wasn't a member of the Reedstown Musical Society nor, apparently, had she ever served on the parish committee. What had she been doing all those years when her only daughter was growing up?

Adele searched for information on Charles Foyle. Her grandfather had died in a car crash when Marianne was ten years old. A musician who played the clarinet in an orchestra, he must have been well known in what was a small community in those days. His death would definitely have been reported. If not a front-page headline or an inside story, it would be recorded in the obituaries. Her frustration grew as she drew a blank once again. She keyed in the name 'Shane'. Unable to add a surname, she watched as numerous results appeared on the screen. She stopped browsing when she saw a photograph of a boys' football team. She estimated the players must have been about twelve when it was taken, a fact confirmed when she read the headline above it. They were the under-thirteen Reedstown Rovers. One boy was instantly recognisable. Younger than he had been in the photographs taken in the photo booth, he posed in the centre of the front row, his grin wide and triumphant. *Shane Reagan*, she read in the caption underneath the winning team. At last, something tangible to give her direction.

The keyboard snapped briskly under her fingers and another photograph appeared. Gloria Thornton, founder of the Sodality of Thorns and Atonement. A mane of silver hair spilled over her shoulders and the ascetic frailty evident in her long, angular face was offset by her eyes. Adele was unable to decide if they were hazel or green. The circle of yellow surrounding the pupils distorted their true colour and added a compelling chilliness to her gaze. Marks on her hands were clearly visible. Were they the sign of a stigmata, as Gloria claimed, or scars from her cancer treatment? She insisted that her recovery from a terminal diagnosis was due to divine intervention that occurred on a mountain top. New demands had come with this gift of healing and were outlined in the interview Adele read. Her disbelief grew as the journalist described Gloria's experience on Croagh Patrick, which she had climbed to celebrate her recovery. On its summit, she had heard the voice of an apostle telling her to establish a sodality of the chosen, who would venerate the crown of thorns Jesus Christ wore to his crucifixion.

The sodality had formed in the mid-eighties when claims of moving statues had dominated the news and droves of worshippers had gathered in grottos to witness such sightings. Adele's anger grew as she continued reading. Why had the *Reedstown Review* given such biased coverage to this woman? Where was the newspaper's objectivity? Its responsibility to search for evidence to back Gloria's claims that she had witnessed visions of indescribable beauty and heard heavenly voices? People flocked to her, defying or ignoring those who ridiculed her visions and called her a charlatan. The coverage she received had mainly been written during the last year of her life. Previous references to the activities of her sodality had been much more impartial and were mainly confined to brief news reports on conferences and campaigns she had organised.

Gloria Thornton had died heroically. An electrical problem in the mother and baby home she had founded had started a fire, which had been exacerbated by chemicals stored in the premises. She had perished in the flames but not before she had led twelve terrified young mothers, some with babies, to safety. The businesses and shops in Reedstown closed down on the morning of her funeral. The Thorns had overflowed the local church, forcing many of the locals to stand outside in the rain. Adele searched for her grandmother in the photographs of the grey, sombre crowd but was unable to find her. Perhaps she was inside, sitting in the front row, weeping with the others over the loss of their founder.

How could sensible Noreen have been so gullible? On her last night, battling demons, she had struggled violently against the drips and constraints used to hold her still. In those final hours, she had found her voice again, but the few words she spoke were so weak and inaudible it was almost impossible for Adele to understand her. Muttered ravings about thorns and hell that made no sense to her at the time. Hell, if it existed, seemed like such an unlikely proposition for her grandmother. Noreen had attended daily mass and prayed at night for such lengthy periods that, sometimes, Adele would find her sleeping by the edge of her bed, her head resting on the duvet, her bare feet freezing on the floorboards. Noreen would awaken, still drowsy, dread freezing her features as she muttered her dead daughter's name, 'Marianne… Marianne,' over and over again.

CHAPTER FOURTEEN

The Marianne Diary

Mam came today and sat in front of me with her glassy stare. She reminded me of a statue, so waxen, and that saintly smile, like just being with me made her a martyr. She's skinny like a stick now and says it's from the work she does in the Hard Wind commune. That's where I'll live when I leave here. But I have to be cleansed first. Mother Gloria says it's important to remove all impurities from mind and body after the baby is born. That will stop me thinking about IT.

Why do I need to be cleansed? I did nothing wrong… but what do I know any more? Maybe I did 'ask for it', as Miss Bethany keeps telling me. Shane made me feel loved. Did I send out signals, an aura or a scent that they picked up and that made them crazy? Whoever they are. Sometimes I think I know them then I get confused again.

Mam is still going on and on about how IT will be nothing more than a distant memory that'll get easier and easier as time goes by. That's the way it was for her when Dad died. How dare she make that comparison. Dad's death was clean and sudden. No gunge and smells and my rape baby kicking like its struggling to escape from my dangerous clutch.

If only it was Shane's baby. But we never did anything. Just touching each other and wanting so much more but afraid, knowing how Mam would freak if she knew. They did IT. One by one… laughing… sometimes their laughter is the only sound I hear. Their smell is still in my nostrils. I hold my breath, thinking that will force it away, but it doesn't. I blow my nose until it starts to bleed but it makes no difference. I rinsed out my nostrils with salt and water but that just made me sick. The smell is worse than the feel of them. But that's mad because smells can't hurt.

Now I have to cope with the smell of paint on top of everything else. That's really sickening. Malachi used to be painter and decorator before he became a Thorn. He was 'inspired' when he heard Mother Gloria speaking at an assembly but all he's done since he joined is paint walls. He has no time to meditate or find the meaning of life. Barbara is still going on about him helping her to escape. Her plan is crazy. The walls here are too high and dangerous with all that glass on top. The gate has a padlock and bolts. And eyes are everywhere. But she has it all planned.

Malachi has been posting letters from her to her boyfriend, Charlie. I'm the only other person who knows and she's sworn me to secrecy. She'll do it when we're on our 'daily constitutional'. That's when we get to walk around the grounds. We're not allowed outside the gates and Miss Bethany walks with us. It's like being back at primary school when we had to walk in a line to confession. We're going to be mothers, and some are mothers, yet we're treated like children. If we protest, we're told we're privileged and that our parents could have sent us to the Magdalene laundry. Barbara says that's stupid because all those laundries will have to close down. No one has told the Thorns. That doesn't surprise me. They don't have anything to do with Catholics or Protestants and anyone who isn't a Thorn.

CHAPTER FIFTEEN

It was stuffy and hot in the basement. Beads of sweat dampened Adele's fringe and trickled along her spine. Her shoulders were stiff with tension, weighted down with frustration. When the door opened, she jerked back from the screen and dashed her hand across her eyes. The man who had entered smiled and crossed the floor towards her, his hand outstretched. His silver hair, short at the sides and with an untidy quiff brushed back from his forehead, was the first thing she noticed about him. Her initial impression that he was an older man changed as he drew nearer. He was in his early to mid-forties, she guessed, and his most distinctive feature was his eyes, dark-brown and with an arresting, inquisitive stare. He appeared to sum her up in an instant and his welcoming handshake told her he liked what he saw.

'I'm Bob Molloy,' he said. 'Sorry if I startled you. Jessica tells me you've been here since early morning. You must be starving. I've having lunch at my desk.' He held up a paper carrier bag with the words Katie's Kasket printed on the front. 'Why don't you join me?'

'Thank you but I'm not hungry. I'd rather keep going.' She pressed her hand to her stomach to stifle the sudden gurgling but the sound was audible enough to make him chuckle.

'Tummy talk,' he said. 'You can't ignore it. Take a break and come back here with a clear head. Katie makes a fantastic tikka chicken wrap but if that's not to your taste you can try the tuna melt. I want to hear what's so fascinating about our archive. We're not used to breaking headline stories in the *Reedstown Review*, more's the pity.'

Unlike the open-plan workstations and the crowded basement, his office was large and airy with a view of the lower level.

'I appreciate you allowing me to check the archives at such short notice,' Adele said when she was seated in front of him, the wraps spread over his desk, hot coffee steaming in takeaway cups.

Meeting his gaze, his wide-set eyes disturbingly like her own, she was beset again by the pummelling suspicion that had marked her visit to Reedstown so far. Was she making eye contact with a man who could be her father? Aware that her palms were clammy, she resisted the urge to rub them against her knees.

'Your email intrigued me,' he said. 'I'm a fan of documentaries, particularly the ones made by Voice Dox. Are you considering making a documentary about Reedstown?' He smiled, as if this possibility amused him. 'If so, that would be a first.'

'Not about Reedstown, specifically.' She answered him carefully. 'I'm interested in cults and the impact they have on the lives of former members.'

'What on earth have cults to do with Reedstown?' He arched his eyebrows, dark by comparison to his hair and so finely shaped that she suspected the regular use of tweezers.

'The Sodality of Thorns and Atonement was founded here in the mid-eighties,' she said. 'Their founder was a local woman which probably explains why they had such a strong following here. I want to find out everything I can about them.'

'It was never proven that they were a cult,' he said. 'Although you wouldn't be the first person to make that accusation. And they weren't confined to Reedstown. Gloria Thornton was big into expansion.' The wry grimace that twisted his mouth suggested he had known her her.

He shook his head when she asked. 'Not her, personally, but I knew her son when I was in my teens. Gloria was seldom around in those days and I didn't pay much attention to her activities. My grandfather was the editor then. I remember him complaining about the abusive phone calls he received if he wrote anything derogatory about the sodality. He hated giving Gloria the oxygen of publicity.'

'I've been reading about her in the archives. She received very positive coverage during the last year of her life yet very little before then. Why was that, do you know?'

He tapped on his laptop, his fingers racing over the keyboard, his eyes on the screen. 'That would be around the time he retired and my own father took over. New broom and all that goes with it. He knew Gloria. I think they went to the same school or were at university together. Whatever it was, they hung out in their younger days so he was more inclined to trust her, unlike my grandfather, who was a born cynic. But the Thorns have been extinct for a long time now.'

'That doesn't make Gloria any less interesting. She must have been very charismatic… or very conniving.'

'The jury is out on that one, I guess. Maybe you can give us the answer.'

'Did she have many children?'

'Just one son.'

'Your friend?'

'I said I know him but Liam Thornton is not my friend.' He held up his hand to forestall her next question. 'I don't have any contact with him so I can't help you there. But be warned. You'll be wasting your time if you intend contacting him. He never talks to anyone about his mother. He made that decision after Gloria died and has never deviated from it since then.'

'Does he still live in Reedstown?'

'Yes, he's still here. But, like I said, he's unapproachable.' He sounded dismissive as he wiped his fingers on a serviette and closed his laptop.

'Can you tell me anything about Noreen Foyle? I believe she was quite an active member of the Thorns?'

'That name doesn't ring a bell. Where did she live?'

'Somewhere in Reedstown, that's all I know.'

'Then I'm sure you'll find something about her in the archives. We were better than any census form when it came to recording the local population. Not so easy now that the developers have moved us into the twenty-first century. Are you sure you're entering the correct information?'

'I thought so. I'll try again and see what I can find.'

'How long have you been with Voice Dox?'

'Three years. I worked as a journalist for a short while after I finished college but I was drawn more to voice than print. What about you? Was it always the *Reedstown Review*?'

'Actually, between you, me and the wall, I always hoped it would *never* be the *Reedstown Review*.' His tone was emphatic, rueful. 'I worked for the *Webster Journal* when I lived in New York.'

'Really?' Adele was impressed. 'I was a subscriber to that magazine until it folded. The essays were so challenging and interesting.'

'Unfortunately, there weren't enough subscribers like you to keep it afloat. Bit of a change from the *Review*.' He heaved an exaggerated sigh and gathered up the wrappings from his desk.

'Why not return to New York?' she asked.

'It's not that easy. I came home when my father was terminally ill. His impending death gave him a certain advantage and he was always a man to grab an opportunity. He made me promise to take over the family newspaper. Hard to refuse a dying wish.

I'm fourth-generation *Reedstown Review*, all of us born with ink under our fingernails. Excuse me—' His phone rang.

'Hi Rachel.' His voice softened as he turned away from Adele. His wife, she guessed. He wore a broad gold band on his finger. Did he have children? Were they the reason for his silver hair? She had detected a trace of New York in his accent, the drawl on the L's, the muffled R's. He must have lived there for quite a long time. What was it like to move from the intellectual austerity of the *Webster Journal* to the *Reedstown Review*, where the frivolous events of village life demanded front-page headlines? His openness had banished her earlier unease. The urge to confide the truth to him swept over her but ebbed away just as quickly. Time enough for another conversation when she had found something concrete on which to build her story.

'Feel free to spend as much time as you need on your research,' he said when he finished his call. 'It was a pleasure meeting you, Adele.'

'Thank you, Mr Molloy.'

'Call me Bob.' His handshake was firm, warm. 'We're an informal bunch here. I hope you find the information you need.'

CHAPTER SIXTEEN

The Marianne Diary

Oh joy. It worked. I never believed I could scream so loudly but I did and now I've no voice left. It had been raining all morning and the trees were glistening when I knelt down and screamed about the devil trying to steal my soul. I wrestled with Miss Bethany when she tried to lift me up and then she was in the mud with me, her white cap off and her long dress up to around her thighs. She was wearing knickers to her knees and I would have laughed crazy like the others if I hadn't been struggling to hold her down.

Barbara was gone, like a ghost flitting, and her boyfriend waiting for her outside the wall. No one saw her go or noticed Malachi opening the gate. She was gone by the time Miss Bethany dragged me to my feet, her face covered in mud and leaves.

There was hell to pay. Miss Bethany keening like a banshee and Mother Gloria doing the Spanish Inquisition on me because I did a terrible thing. A good family were waiting to adopt Barbara's baby and I've left them heartbroken. Sin has blackened my soul and damned it for eternity. Bullshit. Up yours, Mother fucking Gloria.

I keep thinking about Barbara. Is she still running or is she safe? Everyone is still out of sorts since she escaped. Except me… I know I've done something good and that's all that matters for now. I hope she's in England. That was her plan. I helped her to escape and it was worth being sent to the tank for a week.

I talked to my baby for the first time when I was there. I thought I'd be frightened being all on my own with only a mattress and a bucket but I wasn't a bit scared. God, the real God, made it okay for me. Miss Quack Elisha came every day to check the baby's heart and Miss Rebekah sent down her usual poison paws food, which The Quack insisted I eat because a healthy mother means a healthy baby.

It was so quiet in the tank. Deep enough to drown me but I'd company, pummelling heels and fists, hiccups and moments of stillness when I knew my baby was sucking its thumb. I rocked backwards, forwards, and sang lullabies. When I touched my tummy it was like there was a pulse beating in the palm of my hand.

I don't know how to cope with all these new feelings. They've come like a river raging through a tiny chink and sweeping the hate aside to leave love in its place. Too late… too late… yet I was able to ask my baby's forgiveness for drinking the gin. And forgiveness for deciding never to hold it or name it or love it the way a proper mother should.

In the tank, there was time to bring all the bits of that night together. Lightning was no longer zigzagging through my mind but beaming down on my thoughts. That cigarette packet that Shane found on the floor.

'Chinese,' Shane said. I remember his voice shaking and the blood on his hands as he held the box up to the light for

me to see. He said it was a clue. The writing on the package was weird, all squiggles and squares and symbols like the way Amy Zhou writes her name on her copybooks.

I only saw it again in the Garda station before Garda Gunning threw it into the waste bin. It meant nothing to me then but I can't stop thinking about it now. Sergeant Bale kept roaring about it being just litter that had blown in off the road and how Shane was making it up about the writing being Chinese and he'd better stop saying it or he'd be put in a cell. But Shane wouldn't stop shouting and he was still in the cell when Mam came to take me home. I never saw him again.

Three blind mice... see how they run... see how they run...

CHAPTER SEVENTEEN

Back in the basement, Adele sat down at the computer and keyed in the words 'House of Atonement', but was unable to find any further information on the mother and baby home. No follow-up reports on the young women who had been rescued from the fire. Her mother was dead by then, her young body cremated, her ashes scattered on the mountain, and Adele, under Noreen's care, was living in Crannock.

Suddenly, she found herself staring at a photograph of her grandmother. A younger-looking Noreen, she was dressed in a long, tweed coat that Adele remembered from her childhood. Standing among a group of women and men outside St Dominic's church, she was holding a placard aloft. She was part of a protest, Adele realised, and the protesters on either side of her also carried similar signs. From the blurred lettering, Adele could make out that they were protesting against a priest. Father Breen. Marianne had mentioned him in her diary. Their mouths were open, as if they were chanting in unison. She read the names on the caption under the photograph and frowned. A mistake had been made. Noreen – third from the left in the front row – had been captioned as Rosemary Mooney. Adele checked the other names but could not see any sign of her grandmother's correct name. Struck by a sudden thought, she keyed in the name 'Rosemary Mooney' and watched, bewildered, as more photographs of Noreen were uploaded. They all followed the same pattern. Protests outside the local school and cinema, a larger protest outside Dáil Éireann... and, in each one, her grandmother was captioned as Rosemary Mooney. As she scrolled through these old editions of the *Review* Adele saw that the name also featured on many of the letters' pages. Inevitably, these letters were filled with complaints about some or other aspect of Reedstown society or the behaviour of society in general, which, as far as the Thorns were concerned, had lost its moral compass. An address was listed at the bottom of each one.

River View
10 Summit Road
Reedstown
Co. Dublin.

Her fingers shook as she entered the name Marianne Mooney. At last, her mother's young face appeared. Marianne in break-dancing gear, legs akimbo, at some dance festival. In a First Communion photograph with her classmates, hands joined, a soulful expression. Posing in a skimpy singlet and shorts, a trophy raised in both hands. The same electrifying feeling that had come over her in her grandmother's kitchen returned. The pitching floor, the unstable surroundings, the tingling run of fear over her skin. Noreen Foyle had been a fraud. A fanatic. A stranger she had never known, and with a name Adele was unable to recognise. If she pushed too hard against the structures of the life they had shared, would they collapse into nothingness? Was that already happening, she wondered, as she switched off the scanner and rose stiffly to her feet?

*

She turned right at the traffic lights in the centre of the village and drove upwards towards Summit Road. Her mind was dense with questions and a wild curiosity. Here, the houses were detached and luxurious, their walls partially hidden behind mature trees, except for number ten. Bigger than the rest and with an ornate thatched roof, it stood apart from its neighbours. She parked the car in a side road and walked back to the house where her mother had been born. No longer called River View, it had been renamed Hillcrest, which suited its perched position on the brow of the hill. This was a cottage in name only, a manor showhouse that gloried in the intricacies of its thatch, the curves and angles perfectly executed, the edges as rigid as a scrubbing brush. Three cars, two BMWs and a 4 by 4 jeep, were parked on a courtyard in front of the cottage. Two lawns, riotous with flowers and shrubs, fell away on either side of the courtyard.

Lanes bounded by walls ran along either side of Hillcrest. As a child, Marianne must have played in those lanes, bounced balls off the old brickwork. Later, perhaps, she might have kissed Shane there, the two of them in the shadows, breathless with longing, away from Noreen's judgemental gaze. Entering the lane on her right, Adele could see that a recent extension had been added and the building was even larger than its frontage suggested. She was unable to see over the wall but she figured there must be a large back garden stretching to the end of the lane. As she turned to walk across the rear of the lane she was surprised to discover another building, one storey in height and much smaller than Hillcrest, set into the centre of the wall. The name *The Lodge* was carved on the plaque on the wall and a postbox placed beneath the left-hand window was printed with the name *Christy Lewis*. The Lodge had the same pristine appearance as the bigger house and closed shutters on the leaded windows blocked her view of the interior.

She glanced upwards towards Hillcrest and glimpsed someone at a top-storey window. The figure vanished and Adele, unsure if what she had seen was a shadow or trick of the light, was conscious that she was trespassing on someone's private property. Reluctant to be seen lingering any longer, she hurried towards the opposite lane and walked back along the side of Hillcrest.

A statuesque blond woman in cropped white trousers and a loose linen top was waiting for her at the top of the lane. If her authoritative stance was any indication, she was obviously the owner of the house, a fact she confirmed when she said, 'My name is Davina Lewis. Can I ask what you are doing on my premises?'

CHAPTER EIGHTEEN

The Marianne Diary

Oh, God! God! The pain is back again. I want to crouch down and breathe… breathe. They held me down… no, I'm not going to think about that again. I have to think of Shane. His face, the way he laughs, his kisses and everything else. But he's gone too. Everyone's gone… Mam is supposed to be here to hold my hand. That's what she promised the last time she visited. She was mad at Mother Gloria for putting me in the tank. Malachi said they were fighting like hellcats about it. He's leaving here as soon as my baby is born. He hates Atonement and says Hard Wind is just as bad, even though everyone is supposed to be equal and loving and sharing. Maybe that's why Mam was crying so much that last time. She felt the baby kick when she put her cheek against my tummy and promised she'd be back in time for it to be born… I have to stop thinking about IT… but I can't… can't…

The noise the door made when it dragged against the stone floor. I thought it was Shane coming but they were standing there, the three of them looking at me through the slits in their balaclavas. They grabbed me before I could scream and threw me down on the rug. I don't remember much else, except for the stones digging into my back. There was always someone's hand over my mouth so I couldn't shout for help. Even if I had, no one would have heard. No one ever goes near the cottage. It's been empty for forever and that's why I thought it was our perfect hideaway… Oh God… oh God… The Quack says I've got false labour pains and my baby is not due for another two weeks. I'm to stop worrying and there's plenty of time for Mam to get here. It's so easy for her to say that. She's not the one whose baby is going to be taken away. I used to think I wanted that to happen because I couldn't bear the sight of it. Now I know it's because my heart is breaking and I'm never going to be able to fix it… never ever… they took their turns with me and never spoke only to grunt and curse and call God's name. One of them wanted to leave but the other two kept shouting DO IT DO IT DO IT and the taller one pushed him on top of me and then his jeans were pulled off and I couldn't tell if he was struggling to get away from me or be with me the same way as the others. It was like he was crying and cursing at the same time and he ran away as soon as it was over.

I remember the cars that kept passing when Shane tried to get help. His face was covered with bruises and one eye was so swollen he couldn't see out of it. He'd seen the other two leaving but they dragged him off his bike and knocked him out. I keep wondering how we made it to the road when I was so heavy inside with the weight of them. I remember being on my knees and walking and falling again and still the cars went by and wouldn't stop. I remember lights shining and voices shouting and Shane shouting louder than anyone and Sergeant Bale saying he had to get to the nub of the matter. I remember him carrying me from the Garda station to Mam's car and me screaming because I couldn't stand his hands on me… and now it's time… I know it is… it's time to get to the nub…

PART TWO

CHAPTER NINETEEN

Davina

Davina Lewis was used to strangers admiring Hillcrest. The thatched roof stopped them in their tracks. Out came their phones and cameras, their selfie sticks. Keith had not wanted thatch. Conscious of his eco-aware credentials, he had toyed with the idea of solar glass panels, but she had her way in the end. Water reed or, to give it its scientific name, *Phragmites australis*, had proved to be an effective energy saver, and Keith was now convinced it had been his idea in the first place. Hillcrest was unique among the neighbouring houses on Summit Road and that, for Davina, was what mattered. Not for her, personally – she considered herself modest by inclination. But as a politician's wife, and a parliamentary assistant to Christy, it was important to establish a distinctive presence in Reedstown.

The woman came into view again and stopped when she saw The Lodge. Davina moved closer to the window. She prided herself on her ability to recognise trouble. Like a snake in the long grass, trouble could remain invisible yet nearby, too close for comfort but staying inactive until ready to strike. Strictly speaking, the young woman in the tan leather jacket and hip-hugging jeans, a black backpack slung over one shoulder, was not doing anything that unusual. After taking photographs of the front of Hillcrest, she had disappeared down the lane. Moving back from the window, Davina hurried up the stairs and into her bedroom to get a better view. This stranger was definitely loitering, which meant she was either casing Hillcrest with the intention of robbing it or she was planning to doorstep Christy. Her father-in-law was an expert on soundbites and the media loved his opinions on the latest political scandal.

The chances of successfully breaking and entering either Hillcrest or The Lodge were slim. The security system was state of the art. Christy had made sure of that when it was being installed. He wasn't taking any chances with his secrets. The intruder made no attempt to knock on his door. Burglar or journalist, either way she was trespassing and Davina was determined to find out why she was taking so many photographs. Admittedly, The Lodge was cute with its red front door, the box plants at the entrance, the petunias cascading from the hanging baskets and the purple fall of wisteria softening the old brickwork on the rear wall.

She moved back from the window and was waiting at her front gate when the woman emerged from the lane.

'My name is Davina Lewis.' Davina's authoritative tone stopped her in her tracks. 'Can I ask what you are doing on my premises?'

'I'm sorry.' The intruder shoved her mobile phone into the backpack and approached Davina. 'I didn't mean to trespass but I was fascinated by your house. The thatch is amazing. And the lane... that lovely creeper growing along the back wall... it's beautiful.'

For an instant Davina thought she looked familiar but she was unable to think of where or when they might have met. She would have recognised her if she was from the locality but, perhaps, she lived in one of the new houses that had mushroomed around Reedstown in recent years. New voters, new faces – keeping up with a changing landscape was a constant challenge for the politically astute. The impression of familiarity was fleeting and the laminated business card the woman handed to Davina stated that she was a documentary maker/producer with Voice Dox. The company was based in London. As far as Davina was concerned, a documentary maker was akin to a journalist, and was possessed by that same bloodhound mentality. Not that this Adele Foyle would find anything on Keith. His hands were squeaky clean. Christy's reputation, however, always threatened to cast a long, troubling shadow. The sooner he retired the better. He should have done so after his heart attack but he still believed he was invincible.

'What is your documentary about?' she asked. It was a perfectly logical question, yet she sensed a reluctance on Adele's part to answer it.

'I'm still at the initial stage of my research,' she said. 'An idea can be talked out of existence if it's discussed too often before it's properly formed.' She sounded apologetic but Davina was tuned in to evasiveness and this young woman was not answering her question. Why should Hillcrest and The Lodge attract so much attention from a documentary maker? Determined not to let her escape without revealing her true reasons, Davina invited her into her home for coffee. Hug trouble close and find its chinks: it was a policy that had served her well in the past.

'My husband, Keith, and his father are the two sitting TDs for this constituency,' she said when Adele hesitated. 'I've lived all my life in Reedstown and I work as an advisor to both of them. Between us, we have a wealth of knowledge that could be useful if you're making a documentary about the area.'

Over coffee, strong and black, exactly as Davina liked it, she discovered that the documentary maker had no interest in politics. She claimed that she had never heard of Christy Lewis or his son until she arrived in Reedstown. There was no doubting her admiration for Hillcrest though, and Davina, as susceptible to flattery as the next person, gave her a guided tour. She had every reason to be proud of her home. It had been such a nondescript building when Christy lived here, so dated.

Adele's flattery was slightly unnerving. Her gaze was sharp, her brown eyes flashing here and there, but never settling on anything for long. Was she looking for photographs of children? They should be there, fresh-faced and gap-toothed, blowing out candles, opening Christmas presents, standing with their parents outside holiday homes. They had been part of Davina's life plan and she had intended having two, preferably a boy and a girl, when she was in her mid-thirties and ready for marriage. Until then, her career in politics took first preference.

She had only stopped to take stock of her future when she was diagnosed with uterine fibroids soon after her thirty-third birthday. A hysterectomy was deemed necessary. The shock and heartache that followed the operation could have defined her future, if Davina had allowed it to do so. Instead, she decided to focus once again on her career. She had worked as Christy's secretary, research assistant, speechwriter, and political advisor. The cut and thrust of politics challenged her more than ever and she enjoyed the knowledge that the strings she pulled were invisible to everyone but herself. She had had an on-off relationship over the years with Keith and she was well aware that his interest in children was non-existent. He had joked during his wedding speech that he had chased Davina until she stopped running from exhaustion. She was happy to allow him to believe he was the hunter, and not the hunted. She had moved into Hillcrest and had been the brains behind the victory he achieved when he ran as a first-time candidate in the last election.

Shortly afterwards, Christy had suffered his heart attack. Being weakened had not suited him. His contrariness had convinced Davina that change was needed. After some persuasion he agreed to share a constituency clinic on Main Street with his son and have his old one converted into The Lodge. Davina had had a free hand to plan the entire refurbishment of both dwellings and the new-look Hillcrest featured regularly in interior design and architectural magazines.

'You've done a wonderful job, Davina,' said Adele. 'It's hard to believe this was once a house of prayer.'

'Prayer?' Davina's long eyelashes fluttered. 'I'm afraid you've made a mistake. Hillcrest was never a church.'

'I realise that. I was referring to the Sodality of Thorns and Atonement? They used to gather here for their meetings.'

'My house had nothing to do with that sodality. Where on earth did you come by that strange notion?'

'Oh, I thought this was where they met. I've been doing research in the *Reedstown Review*. Rosemary Mooney was a member of the sodality. She was their secretary or, maybe, their PR person. She gave her address as number ten but the house was called River View then.'

'Ah, now I understand. The Lodge used to be called River View. To be honest, it was something of a shack when Rosemary Mooney lived there. My father-in-law bought it from her.'

'So, was this house always here?' Adele's arm embraced the spacious kitchen and the open-plan living area beyond it.

'It was built for my father-in-law and he lived here until he moved into The Lodge. I guess it's easier to live in smaller spaces when one gets older.'

'I guess.' Adele sounded unconvinced. 'Does that mean the land on which Hillcrest is built also once belonged to Rosemary Mooney?'

'Land?' Davina, surprised by the question, laughed, dismissively. 'It was more like a stretch of wasteland and, yes, Hillcrest was built on it. Why do you ask?

'I'm just curious about Rosemary Mooney's background and her involvement in the sodality.'

'Why on earth would anyone be interested in watching a documentary about those weirdos? We used to call them the Thorns.'

'People are always interested in cults and the impact the leaders have on the lives of their followers. Their founder Gloria Thornton came from Reedstown.' Adele sipped her coffee and a shudder, delicate enough to be imagined, passed through her.

'Honestly, Adele. You're way off track here. To call Gloria Thornton the leader of a cult is to stretch the truth by a mile.'

'How would you define such a leader?'

'That crowd in Guyana who followed what's-his-name…?' Davina clicked her fingers. 'Jim Jones, wasn't it? He led his followers into a mass suicide pact? And Charles Manson with his gang of crazies. You're not trying to compare Gloria Thornton to *those* guys.'

'I'm not making that comparison. Those movements were extreme. But Gloria also had an impact on her followers and that had spin-off consequences. Did you know her?'

'I met her a few times. She was always travelling, helping people in crisis and setting up branches of her solidarity.'

'Are you aware that she ran a mother and baby home?'

Davina shrugged. 'It's so long ago, I can't remember.'

'What about Rosemary's daughter? Marianne. Do you remember her?'

Davina controlled an involuntary grimace. The atmosphere had changed and the kitchen felt clammy, as if the last heat of the day was pressing too hard against the patio doors.

'What has she got to do with your documentary?'

'Marianne was taken from here and kept in that home.'

'*Taken*?' Surely she had misheard.

'Taken against her wishes by the Thorns,' Adele replied. 'I want to include her story in my documentary about this *cult*.' The bitter bite of the word, her expression hardening as she stared back at Davina. 'She must have grown up in The Lodge. I'd like to find out what I can about her.'

Her instincts had been right. Adele Foyle was trouble in the making. The idea of Christy being associated with the Thorns horrified her.

'If it's your intention to feature my father-in-law's home as the headquarters of what you insist on calling a cult, then think again,' Davina said. 'As his parliamentary assistant, it's my responsibility to uphold and protect his reputation.'

'I'm a sensitive documentary maker.' She stared around Davina's gleaming kitchen, where everything had a place and purpose, an order. 'There's no reason why your family's reputation should be jeopardised in any way.'

'I'm afraid I can't help you any further. I know nothing about a mother and baby home, nor can I tell you anything about Marianne Mooney.' This conversation was going nowhere and she had wasted enough time entertaining someone whose motives were definitely suspect. 'I've to attend an important meeting this evening, so if you'll excuse me…'

'Of course.' Adele immediately nodded and stood. 'Forgive me, I've taken up so much of your time.'

'I don't mean to be rude but I must insist that you also leave Hillcrest out of your documentary.' Davina made no effort to sound apologetic. 'My husband and I take our privacy very seriously.'

'I appreciate that.' Adele slung the backpack onto her shoulder. 'Don't worry about Hillcrest. It's probably not that important in the overall story I have to investigate.'

Davina waited by the front door until she had driven away. She caught herself chewing the edge of her nail and linked her fingers together. Adele Foyle had been polite and quietly spoken. She had said all the right things about Hillcrest and her reassurances about being a sensitive documentary maker had a ring of truth. But Davina lived by her instincts and she could almost hear them screaming a warning at her. Trouble had entered her house and left its mark on the pristine interior; it was invisible as yet but she had a niggling fear that it could rise, in time, to thumbprint the future.

The meeting in the Loyvale Hotel had been arranged by a group of Reedstown residents. They referred to themselves as 'Old Reedstowners' and were objecting to what they considered to be the unbridled growth of the village. The meeting was also well attended by those in favour of extending development outwards and onward. Keith and his father had planned to attend but their flight from Beijing had been delayed. Some air controllers' strike, probably the French protesting again, Keith said when he rang from the airport. He sounded frustrated, impatient. The trade mission had been successful. Deals were done, contracts signed. Wasting time at an airport was anathema to him and to Christy, who believed that local politics was the bedrock of success on election day. Davina was expected to shine in their absence.

Dynamic as always in her red jacket and matching shoes, her heels adding to her imposing height, she was so impressive that one of the attendees asked when she was going to run for office. This raised a hoot of alarm from the politicians who had attended the meeting and enthusiastic applause from both sides of the divide.

'You played a blinder in there tonight.' Julie Thornton was waiting for her at the end of the meeting. 'Both sides have gone home convinced they won the argument. Keith couldn't have wooed them any better. As for Christy, he would simply have turned the meeting into his own personal soapbox.'

'Thanks, Julie.' Davina relaxed as they walked towards the foyer. 'They were both furious over missing the meeting, but at least the trade mission was successful.'

'I was surprised Christy went with him. He should be taking things easier.'

'You know Christy. He never misses a bunfight. To be honest, he was just there for his contacts. Keith did all the heavy lifting. Thanks to him, he's been able to offer those small enterprises an invaluable opportunity to establish new accounts in a global marketplace.' She was beginning to sound like one of Keith's constituency speeches, which was not surprising, considering she was the author of them.

The meeting had lasted longer than expected and the armchairs in the foyer were empty, apart from one located close to the exit. Davina's step slowed when she recognised the occupant. Adele Foyle had changed from jeans into a short, pale-green dress. Her black hair, loosened from a ponytail, tumbled over her suntanned shoulders. A cup of coffee on the table beside her, long legs crossed, she was immersed in the book she was reading. Anxious to avoid her, Davina quickened her step and was just level with her when Julie spoke again. Her voice attracted Adele's attention. She looked up from the book and, on seeing Davina, she smiled hesitantly, as if she expected another rebuke.

'We meet again,' she said.

'We do indeed.' Davina's smile felt too stretched to be genuine, but Christy claimed a charismatic smile was an essential element of a politician's arsenal.

'I hope your meeting went well.' Adele's expression softened and the book slipped unnoticed to the floor when she rose to her feet. *Remembering Reedstown*, a local history by a local author. Davina recognised the cover.

Up close, Adele Foyle did not look quite so self-assured. Her eyelids were slightly red-rimmed and a slight puffiness under her eyes suggested she had been crying.

'It was an important discussion but it went on way too long.' Davina had no intention of prolonging the conversation but Julie had bent to pick up the book.

'Thank you,' Adele nodded as Julie handed it back to her and both women glanced at Davina, expecting her to introduce them.

'A pleasure meeting you again, Adele.' Davina's grip on Julie's arm warned her to keep walking.

'Nice-looking girl,' said Julie as they headed towards the exit. 'Who is she?'

'She's a documentary maker.'

'Oh, that's interesting. Why didn't you introduce me?'

'Be thankful I didn't. She wants to make a documentary about Gloria.'

'You can't be serious. Why would anyone want to drag all that stuff up again?' Julie glanced back over her shoulder at Adele, then stopped just in time to avoid crashing into the swing doors.

Davina shrugged. 'Your guess is as good as mine.'

'How did you meet her?'

'She called at Hillcrest. Apparently, she found some information on Rosemary Mooney in the *Review* archives. Remember her?'

'Can't say I do.'

'Marianne Mooney's mother.'

'Oh, my God! That poor kid.'

'Poor kid? Is that how you remember her?'

'Yes, it is actually. All that slut naming and jeering. To be honest, I always feel ashamed when I think about it.'

'Then don't think about it,' Davina advised her. 'We were just kids.'

'We were seventeen. What on earth was going on in our heads? It was like we had all been affected by a contagion.'

'Contagion is a bit dramatic, if you don't mind me saying so.'

'Chinese whispers, then? She was only fifteen. She didn't deserve the reputation she acquired.'

'Come on, Julie. Take off the rose-tinted glasses. Marianne Mooney never acted like a fifteen-year-old and, truth be told, she was a slut. She was probably rebelling against her mother's religious mania. Did you know that the Thorns used to hold their meetings in Christy's place? Remember when it was River View?'

'Vaguely.'

'She's *actually* claiming that Marianne Mooney was kidnapped and enslaved in that mother and baby home your mother-in-law used to run. Like it was some kind of Magdalene laundry. At least that's the spin she wants to put on it.'

'Liam won't like that. He's so protective about his mother's reputation.'

'As he's every right to be.' Davina zapped her car and air-kissed her friend's cheek. 'So good to see you again, Julie. You and Liam must come over for lunch some Sunday, and bring Stephanie, of course.'

'That sounds like a plan. We'll do so as soon as Stephanie comes back from France.' Julie waved and headed towards her own car.

Both knew it wouldn't happen but such promises held the last remnants of their friendship together.

A contagion… a Chinese whisper… Driving back to Hill-crest, Davina tried to banish the memory of Marianne Mooney, fifteen years old and pregnant. Bambi eyes that looked too big for her skinny face. Old-fashioned, second-hand clothes and a reputation that made her the butt of bullies, Davina being one of them. Such a strange, hurtful time. One she preferred not to remember. Marianne Mooney was dead and long gone from their lives. She had no idea why Adele Foyle's presence in Reedstown should threaten her but, like that snake, trouble could sometimes be too slippery to grasp.

CHAPTER TWENTY

Adele

The house Adele rented had flooded during the winter storms when the Loy overflowed. Mould had left the occasional blue fingerprint on the walls and the landlord, who was willing to rent it cheaply to her, had apologised for the faint yet persistent smell of damp permeating the rooms. Otherwise, Brooklime was perfect for her needs. The village was too unsettling. Too many faces to scrutinise, appraise, judge. Who were these men? Did they have a history that was herstory? *Stop it... stop it...* Her mind screamed a warning. Concentrate... concentrate... stop scratching at an open wound, appraising strangers, wondering if they had known her mother, damaged her, destroyed her.

Liam Thornton's home and business addresses were easily accessed, as was his email. Acquiring information was not a problem. Adele had read everything she could find about his company. His business acumen, his risk-taking, the growth of his property portfolio. His ruthless pursuit of journalists through the courts if he believed he had been slandered. She checked out his house. Unlike Hillcrest, it was a secluded dwelling at the end of a curved driveway, its entrance guarded by spiked gates, remotely controlled. One evening, Adele parked her car close to the entrance and waited to see if he would appear. She was uneasily aware that cars and people did not loiter with intent on this road of segregated wealth. If they dared do so, she suspected that a squad car would soon arrive and an officious police officer would demand to know the reason why. She glimpsed him driving past but lacked the nerve to leave her car and approach him when he stopped in front of the gates.

Bella, the receptionist at LXT Properties, was polite but un-bending each time Adele rang. *I'll tell Mr Thornton you were in touch again… I'm afraid you've just missed him… would you like to leave a message… yes, of course I'll pass your name on to him.*

In the window of ReedAlong, a small bookshop on Main Street, she had bought a copy of *Remembering Reedstown* and searched in vain for any mention of the Thorns. Brendan Barry, the author, was affable and chatty when she contacted him one evening. They arranged to meet in the Loyvale Hotel the following day.

He was a small, fidgety man with a habit of tapping his left foot off the floor. Adultery had been his Achilles heel, he admitted, which could explain the foot-tapping. Adele stopped noticing it after a while.

'Liam Thornton threatened to destroy my marriage if I mentioned his mother's name in my book.' Brendan was ruefully honest with her. 'He obtained photographs of… let's just say they were of an intimate nature and could have destroyed my marriage. Seeing yourself in flagrante does nothing for one's self-esteem and certainly helps to keep the tomcat in me at home.'

'Are they still in his possession?' Adele asked.

'They are. Which makes *Remembering Reedstown* the most boring book I will ever write.'

'Did you know Gloria Thornton?'

'I was ten when she died,' he said. 'So, I only knew her by reputation. Weirdly scary was how I imagined her. The jury was out as to whether she was a saint or a swindler. The research I did before I started writing the book led me to believe the latter. I heard rumours about illegal adoptions she ran from that mother and baby home in Inisada. It was way off the beaten track—'

'I've been there.'

'Then you know what I'm talking about. As far as I could gather, the rumours were never investigated. But touch Gloria Thornton and you stir a hornets' nest, especially when it comes to her son. Tread carefully, if you decide to go ahead with your documentary.'

She remembered his warning the next time she rang to speak to Liam. The fact that she was on first-name terms with the formidable Bella had done nothing to change the message.

Two days later, she waited for him to emerge from his office on Fitzwilliam Square. *LXT Properties* was engraved on a copper plate outside a handsome Georgian building with a panelled front door, capped with fan-shaped panes of stained glass.

By late afternoon, her patience was rewarded when the door opened and Liam Thornton stood at the top of the steps with a second man. They spoke together for a moment before the second man shook his hand and walked away.

'Mr Thornton, can I have a word with you, please?' Adele dashed up the steps and reached the door just as he was closing it.

If he was surprised by her sudden appearance, he didn't show it, but the snap in his voice told her he had recognised her.

'You're a persistent young woman, Miss Foyle,' he said. 'One could almost accuse you of being a stalker.'

'If you'll let me explain—'

'I've no intention of allowing you to explain anything,' he said. 'If you're not down those steps within the next ten seconds, I'll call security and have you evicted.'

'Your refusal to speak to me won't stop my documentary.' Determined to make him listen, she rushed the words at him. 'I have testimony from a woman who spent time in your mother's House of Atonement. She claimed she was trafficked there and held against her will. I need your cooperation if her testimony is to be disputed.'

'Testimony?' His eyebrows lifted. 'Now, that's an interesting word. Who dared to make such a slanderous claim?'

'I'm not prepared to divulge sources. But I'm willing to discuss her testimony with you.' She held his gaze. One blink from her and she would lose. He still maintained his deadpan expression but she knew she had unsettled him. Otherwise, she would have been marched down the steps by now.

'This had better be worth my attention, Miss Foyle.' The break in tension was almost palpable as he closed the door behind them, then strode ahead of her towards the elevator.

An elaborate chandelier hung from the ceiling of his office and a black and white photograph of an apartment complex took up almost the entire width of the wall behind his desk. It had been photographed at night, the windows radiating bursts of light and adding a surreal appearance to the tall, stately towers. One of his own developments, she presumed. He waved her into a leather armchair. She sank gently into its cushioned softness, aware that arising with dignity from it would be impossible. His own chair, higher and firmer, sent out an unmistakable signal. Liam Thornton was used to imposing his authority on any given situation.

'Ten minutes, Miss Foyle,' he said. 'That's how long you have to convince me you're not wasting my time.'

His suit sat well on him, bespoke tailored, and he had chosen a muted striped tie to wear with his crisp white shirt. Nothing casual about his attire, which he wore like armour, too flawless to distract attention yet creating the impression of a businessman who left nothing to chance.

'I have two opposing narratives for my documentary,' she said. 'I must investigate which one is true. Was Gloria Thornton a holy woman, who ran a sanctuary for pregnant women and provided them with all the support they needed? Or did she force them to work without wages and then, when their babies were born, did she arrange for those children to be illegally adopted? You can tell me which narrative is true.'

'How dare you…' He paused for an instant, seemingly too astonished by her audacity to continue. 'If that is the angle you are going to spin, you'll find yourself in court faster than the time it takes you to turn around and walk from my office.'

'On what grounds will you silence me?'

'Defamation is a serious crime—'

'The reputations of the dead cannot be defamed, Mr Thornton.'

'But their loved ones who are left behind can challenge an obvious untruth. If you persist in peddling the lie that the House of Atonement was anything other than a legitimate organisation run for the benefit of young women at a difficult time of their lives, I assure you I can provide precise documented evidence to the contrary. What can you bring, apart from some so-called testimony you claim to have discovered?'

'It's genuine—'

'Genuine?' His smile was self-assured, confident that whatever documentation he had would stand up to any legal scrutiny. 'I very much doubt that, Ms Foyle. My mother was an inspirational woman. Whether or not she was touched by the divine is a moot point but this I *do* know. She believed utterly that it was her mission to establish a sodality of like-minded people who were determined to find another way to serve their Lord. If she had a failing, it was to place too much trust in others.'

'Others?'

'People like Rosemary Mooney.' He nodded decisively. 'Davina Lewis told me you were enquiring about her. Am I to assume you're investigating her activities for your documentary?'

Hearing the name again, its unfamiliar resonances, and unable to attach it to her grandmother's face, Adele struggled to compose herself.

'She was the spokesperson for your mother's sodality so, yes, I'm interested in her. But I've no idea what you mean by "her activities".'

'I advise you to go back and research Rosemary Mooney. Then you'll have a documentary worth making.'

'In what respect?' She hoped her tone did not betray her uneasiness. 'I've found no references to her, apart from letters she wrote to the papers. What crime are you claiming she committed?'

'After my mother's death, it was discovered that Rosemary Mooney had been embezzling funds from the sodality. Fortunately, Gloria died before the truth was uncovered, so at least she was spared the ordeal of discovering that someone she trusted implicitly had betrayed her.'

'If that was true, Rosemary Mooney was a *criminal*.' How ridiculous that word sounded. 'Why was she never brought to justice?'

'Simple answer, she disappeared. You like a challenge, Ms Foyle. Go find her and leave my mother to rest in peace.' He was watching her carefully, gauging her reaction, waiting for her response. Not by a quiver or a teardrop would Liam Thornton see the impact his words were having on her.

'The only other information I have on Rosemary Mooney is that she brought her daughter to the House of Atonement and that's where the girl died.'

'Ah, yes, the daughter. A troubled kid.' He looked upwards at the glittering chandelier, his intent expression suggesting he was counting each crystal droplet.

'You knew her?'

'By reputation only.' He drew his nostrils together, as if the air in the office offended him. 'Reedstown was a hotbed of gossip in those days and Marianne Mooney was often the butt of it.'

'How so?'

'Nowadays, teenagers call it slut shaming. In our day, she was simply called "the village bike". A handy ride. I'm sure you know what I mean. Sorry if my language offends you. It was the girls, not the lads, who put her name about.'

'Why did they do that?'

'I've already explained the reasons,' he replied. 'But my mother did not indulge in local gossip. Instead, she took Marianne Mooney under her wing and protected her from the opprobrium of her peers. That girl's death was a tragedy that could have been averted if she had made different decisions. This meeting is over, Ms Foyle. If you uncover one single shred of evidence that proves Gloria Thornton was not driven by her faith and a desire to help those young women in her care, we'll speak again.'

Adele blinked as the sharp lines on the photograph behind his desk blurred. Too angry to care about the tears welling in her eyes, she pulled a handful of medals from her pocket and flung them on his desk. 'Slave labour, Mr Thornton. That's the legacy your mother left behind her.'

'Miss Foyle, I'm not impressed by your dramatics. Don't ever make contact again unless you want an injunction taken out against you for harassing me.'

She noticed faint pock marks on his cheeks, more than likely an old acne problem that only became inflamed when he was angry. He reminded her of a painting where too much gloss had been used to smooth over the rough surface.

Outside, standing at the top of the steps, she swayed, overcome by his casual brutality. Vulnerability: he was attuned to it. Slowly, deliberately, he had fractured her mind, filling it with fissures where, only moments before, there had been certainty. Embezzlement. It was too ludicrous to even consider and yet… and yet… Rosemary Mooney, alias Noreen Foyle, had fled to the seclusion of Crannock to live out her days under the rocky gradients of the Ox Mountains. Querulous yet gentle when Adele needed her loving arms. Silent and obstinate when Adele demanded answers that would explain the loneliness of her childhood. Always dressing in dull shades of brown and beige; shades that had allowed her to move inconspicuously through her chosen landscape.

Moving too fast, she collided with a woman who had just reached the top of the steps. She grabbed the railing to keep her balance but Adele, unable to do so, felt the power leaving her legs. She collapsed to her knees and would have tumbled down the steps if the woman had not reached her in time. She helped Adele to her feet and stared with concern at the tears streaming down her face.

'Are you okay, my dear? You came out of there so fast I didn't have time to move aside.'

'I'm fine.' She had grazed her hands in the effort to stop her fall and must have done the same with her knees if the throbbing pain was any indication.

'You're far from fine.' The woman delved into her handbag and produced a tissue. 'Take this and dry your eyes. You're totally shaken. Can I get you a drink of water?' She gestured towards the door, which had closed with an automatic snap behind Adele.

'No, I'm good. Honestly.'

'You're the documentary maker. I thought you looked familiar. Oh dear, were you trying to interview my husband?'

'Your husband?' Adele stared in confusion at her.

'Liam Thornton.'

Adele nodded and dabbed at her eyes. Tears would not advance her search any further. 'I wanted to speak to him about my documentary but our meeting turned out badly.'

'I'm sorry to hear that but not surprised. I'm Julie Thornton. We met in the Loyvale last week. I was coming from a meeting with Davina Lewis.'

'Ah, yes.' Adele had a vague recollection of another woman being there, but she had been so focused on Davina she had hardly noticed her.

'A strong brandy will put you to rights and there's a bar not a stone's throw from here. Come with me.'

'Thank you, but I don't want to delay you.'

'You're not delaying me. I was planning to surprise my husband and lure him out to lunch, but what he doesn't know he won't miss.'

She escorted Adele into a bar, where the cool, darkened interior offered a welcome relief from the sun. 'I've a clinic this afternoon,' she explained as she ordered a brandy for Adele and coffee for herself. 'Otherwise, I'd be happy to join you.'

'Are you a doctor?'

'A counsellor. My clinic is nearby.' She was small in stature and skinny rather than slim; her face betrayed her age but, seen from behind, she could have been mistaken for a young girl. Even her hair, a sleek, chestnut sheen, the fringe hanging low over her eyes, had the simplicity of a child's haircut. 'Davina told me you're making a documentary about my mother-in-law?'

'She's only part of the overall story I want to investigate.'

'How far advanced is your documentary?'

'Not far. I've been to Inisada to see the House of Atonement.'

'What a dreadful name.' Julie's bottom lip turned down. 'Sounds like something from the Dark Ages.'

'Did you know Gloria?'

'Not really. She was always coming and going in those days so I'm not sure if anyone in Reedstown actually knew her. And that includes her son, by the way. Yet, he's quite devoted to her memory, as you've undoubtedly gathered.'

'Why is he so reluctant to talk to me about her?'

'Not just you, my dear. You're not the first person to approach him with questions about Gloria and that strange sodality she ran. Gloria was beloved by her followers and he suffered because of her fame... reputation... notoriety... whatever you like to call it. She's dead a long time but there are still those who would like to trash her sodality. Can you imagine how you would feel if people were intent on destroying your own mother's reputation?'

The village bike... the slut who put out, trailing gossip behind her. A free-for-all... on her knees... legs splayed... no... no... she could not bear it. Somehow, Liam Thornton had found a fault line through which he could enter and work on her from the inside. Was that how Gloria Thornton had operated on those who were vulnerable enough to follow her? He had defiled her mother's memory and Adele had allowed him to do so without plunging a knife into his heart.

His wife was waiting for her reply.

'I guess... I'm sure I'd find it difficult,' she said.

'As I would, also. I adore my mother so I take her love for granted. But all Liam has are memories and he is fiercely protective of them. He won't allow them to be tainted by exaggeration or lies.' Her hair swung over her cheeks as she glanced down at Adele's empty glass. 'Can I order you another?'

'No… no. But thank you for your kindness. Did you know Marianne Mooney?'

'Slightly. Why?'

'She stayed in that mother and baby home.'

'Really?' Julie sounded surprised. 'I know nothing about that.' She finished her coffee and checked her watch, the skin puckering between her eyebrows. 'I have to go now. I've no wish to interfere in your documentary, Adele. But do tread carefully. You're young and ambitious. I'm not saying that as a criticism. I like your spirit – but Gloria was a woman of great complexity and the story of the Thorns is not an easy one to tell. Too many layers to peel away.'

After she'd left, Adele made her way to the ladies and bathed her hands. Her knees were badly grazed but not cut. She should quit now. She suspected that Daniel was becoming weary of her indecisiveness, her inability to give him a firm date for her departure. She touched her jacket pocket where the diary rested. The feel of it gave her courage. Her separation from him would come to an end soon but the separation from her mother that she had experienced at birth was a wound she never realised needed healing until those pages with their pathetic entries had directed her to Reedstown. She was on a quest and she must not allow herself to falter.

CHAPTER TWENTY-ONE

Rachel

Sergeant Rachel Darcy was seldom taken by surprise. Twenty years in the force had hardened her spine, heart and mind. Listening to accusations and denials, she could usually gauge within the first few minutes of an interview whether or not she was hearing the truth. Not that the truth was ever straightforward. As far as Rachel was concerned, it was a complex canvas, woven with many threads; but, always, there was a single strand that she could grasp and decide if the person being interviewed had a case for the Gardai to pursue. On this occasion, though, she was unable to make such a judgement.

A diary found in an attic. A long-kept secret supposedly revealed. The diary suggested that at least some aspect of this story was true. Tense as a spring about to uncoil, Adele Foyle linked her fingers together, as if she was praying rather than making the most disturbing claims. Allegations, not accusations, Rachel reminded herself any time she became too caught up in the drama of the story. A gang-rape, here in Reedstown, never investigated. A resultant pregnancy that killed the young mother shortly after her daughter was born. And here she was, the daughter, leaning determinedly towards Rachel, brown eyes glistening with unshed tears, demanding that a cold case investigation be opened to establish the truth.

'Gloria Thornton exploited the young women in her care in exactly the same way as the Magdalene laundries did.' Her voice rose, as if she expected Rachel to refute this claim. 'That's *exactly* what it was. My mother was forced to work there for nothing until I was born.'

Rachel had no intention of arguing with her. She was familiar with the history of such places. The litany of lies and cover-ups, the harshness of a regime that promised succour but dehumanised the women who had sought shelter there.

'Will you open an investigation?' Adele asked.

In the three weeks since she came to Reedstown, she had been compiling information. She had uncovered documentation that proved the grandmother she knew as Noreen Foyle had changed her name by deed poll. A copy of the document lay on Rachel's desk. The change was made shortly before Adele was born.

She had been to visit the mother and baby home. Her photographs showed the derelict, burned-out ruin of what would once have been a fine, stately home. There was a rusting sign on the gate, with the words 'House of Atonement' still visible. Photocopies of newspaper clippings were added to the growing pile of documentation. Letters of complaint to the *Reedstown Review*, all signed with the name Rosemary Mooney. Images of her protesting with other like-minded Thorns. The moniker was a lot easier than a mouthful like the Sodality of Thorns and Atonement, Rachel thought, as she moved the clippings to one side. She concentrated on this distressed young woman who was offering to provide her DNA to help establish her father's identity.

'There has to be some information about my mother's assault on record,' she insisted. 'With the advances in forensics, you'll be able to establish what really happened.'

'You've made a very damaging allegation.' Rachel needed to slow the pace of this interview. 'All I can promise for now is that we'll check our records. If your mother was here on that night, as she claimed, then her statement will be on file. How long are you staying in Reedstown?'

'As long as it takes to find out the truth.'

'Be under no illusions, the truth, whatever it is, will take time to establish,' Rachel warned her. 'Let's take one step at a time. I have your details, so I'll be in touch as soon as I finish checking through our records.'

She watched from her office window as Adele left the Garda station and hesitated, as if unsure which way to turn. Crossing the road, she disappeared under the arch leading to the river where she had rented a house.

Her name had been familiar to Rachel even before she came to the Garda station and asked to speak to her. Bob had mentioned her visit to the archives. Always looking out for the deeper layer of a story, he had been intrigued by her decision to document a cult that had been extinct for decades. Could her interest in Gloria Thornton have more to do with unearthing the offshore account he believed she'd established during her glory days? An account that had floated her son's property development company. Rachel was familiar with this rumour, for that was all it remained, despite Bob's strenuous efforts to prove it true. But he was wrong about Adele Foyle. She had no interest in exposing corruption. She was after a bigger truth; one that would reveal her father's identity and bring him, along with his two accomplices, to justice. Every word in her mother's diary, even the incoherent entries that suggested the young teenager was on the verge of despair or else a nervous breakdown, was gospel to her. It was Rachel's objective skills that would establish what was real and what was perceived.

Strictly speaking, calling it a 'cold case' was incorrect. The term was usually applied when a case that had remained unsolved for years was reopened. This happened when vital, new evidence had been received or advances in forensics made it possible to begin a fresh investigation. But Adele Foyle was claiming that there had never been an investigation into the rape on Marianne Mooney. Jack Bale was the sergeant then. He had left behind an unblemished reputation when he retired and his handover of responsibility to Rachel had been seamless.

Over the following days, as she worked through the files, she could see that his record-keeping was impeccable as well. Yes, there had been issues within the Garda station. Occasional staff problems, cases that remained unsolved, but, always, the facts about how these challenges were handled had been logged in such painstaking detail that it would be impossible to question them. A crime of the magnitude described in Marianne's diary would have been logged, statements taken. Shane Reagan, for instance – no mention of his name on any file. Where were the photographs displaying Marianne's injuries, the procedures that had been followed when she *allegedly* stumbled into the Garda station? Searching systematically, Rachel was unable to find anything remotely similar to the distressing diary entries she had read. Her mind shied away from the possibility that such a crime had never been investigated but, if that was true, then Adele Foyle had handed her a timebomb.

The brutish personality described in the diary was a stranger to her, yet Marianne's depiction of Jack Bale confirmed her own instinctive reaction to the former sergeant on the first occasion they met. He hadn't wanted to retire but had been forced to do so when he reached the age of sixty. His handshake on being introduced to Rachel, his grip crushing her fingers for a fraction longer than necessary, had warned her that he hid a darker temperament behind his officious manner. It was this memory that triggered an uneasiness in her. Only one thing to do. These days, he spent most of his time fishing on the river but he was always helpful with information whenever Rachel contacted him with a query. She would have to tread with care around his sensitivities but questions had to be asked and answers given if she was to disprove the extraordinary claims written in the diary.

A pair of rubber boots had been left inside the porch, along with a fishing tackle container and a rod. The front door was open and Jack, when he stomped up the hall, still had his hat on, his forehead shaded by the collapsed brim. As always, that hard handshake, as if it was necessary to establish his dominance. She had arrived at the right time, he said. Three speckled trout, gutted and seasoned with thyme and oregano, were splayed on a chopping board. She must share his catch with him. He silenced her protests and waved her into a chair. The innards of the trout glistened in a chrome dish, their blood drying on the blade of a knife. He squeezed lemon juice over the filleted trout, added crushed garlic and a dash of olive oil, his attention focused on the dish he was preparing. He had put on weight since his retirement, his ample stomach straining against his jumper. The remnants of his grey hair had been dragged into a ponytail, a change from his habitual short back and sides. The effect reminded her, unpleasantly, of a rat's tail. He flipped the fish onto two heated plates and removed a salad from the fridge. His kitchen was spotless, no mess. The innards of the trout were transferred to the back garden to be devoured by a hungry cat.

'So, what brings you to this neck of the woods?' He sat heavily into the chair and slathered butter onto a baguette. 'Not having trouble at the station, I hope?'

'No trouble, Jack.' The trout was delicious, the tang of lemon infused with garlic, the pink flesh falling cleanly from the seared skin. 'I'm hoping you can help me out with some information from way back.'

'How far back?'

'Twenty-five years or thereabouts?'

'As it happened under my watch, I'll remember.'

'It concerns an assault on a young girl. A very serious assault if what I've heard has any credibility.'

He was immediately alert, his forehead wrinkling in shock. 'What exactly did you hear?'

'That she was subjected to a gang-rape.' Such a harsh resonance when Rachel spoke the word aloud, and he paused, his fork suspended in mid-air.

'Who made such an accusation?' He brought the fork to his mouth, seemingly unaware that the morsel of fish had fallen back onto his plate, and winced as the prongs clanged against his teeth.

'I didn't say it was an accusation, Jack. At this point, it's merely an allegation. I'm trying to establish if this claim has any validity.'

He broke the crust on the baguette and chewed slowly before asking, 'The name of the alleged victim?'

'Marianne Mooney. I've checked back over the records but I can't find any reference to her or that such a crime was ever reported and investigated.'

'That's your answer then. It has no validity. But that's not surprising. I knew Marianne Mooney.' He split her name into distinct syllables, nodding as he spoke. 'She was little more than a girl, as you say, but that didn't stop her being as promiscuous as…' He paused, as if searching for a sensitive description, then threw his hands outwards in exasperation. 'Let's just say that young Marianne Mooney wasn't behind the bush when it came to putting herself about, if you get my meaning. She was the scourge of her mother, a deeply religious woman, or so we believed. But that's a story for another day. This allegation? What pit has that sprung from?'

'That's confidential, Jack. And it could be a mischievous claim—'

'*Could* be?' His ruddy complexion deepened.

'This girl, Marianne—' Nothing in her demeanour revealed Rachel's nervousness.

'Was a little trollop who, to no one's surprise, was pregnant by the time she was fifteen,' he brusquely interrupted her. 'The lad in question didn't want to know. He'd planned on going to university and fatherhood would have put a stop to his gallop, especially as the girl was underage. He could have been in serious trouble for – how shall I phrase it delicately – *interfering* with a minor. Such a crime could have landed him inside a prison cell instead of some fancy university lecture hall.' He flexed his fingers, opening and closing them into fists.

'That's what would have happened if Rosemary Mooney had had her way,' he went on. 'She had a reputation to uphold. All set to charge young Shane Reagan with rape. She calmed down quickly enough when she realised what would be involved, especially as Carrie Reagan, the lad's mother, swore the sex was consensual. She claimed her son had been fooled into believing the girl was older than fifteen. But I don't want to speak ill of the dead. The kid was taken in her prime, God rest her soul.'

Unable to stomach his pious platitudes, Rachel stopped all pretence of eating. 'Why was Rosemary Mooney's accusation never recorded?'

'What was there to report? Do you note every crazy, insignificant event that crosses your desk?'

'*Insignificant?*'

'Two kids having unprotected sex. A mother furious because she's prematurely going to become a grandmother. When the dust settles, that's exactly what it was. An insignificant event that I never recorded because no charges were ever made. I checked out the location. Quite a nice little hideaway they'd made for themselves. Lay the blanket on the ground, if you get my meaning.'

'Where was this hideaway?'

'Some ruin out by Blake's Hollow. It's gone now, levelled to the ground a few years back to build the shopping centre. The lad's mother was Australian and she decided to return with the lad to her home country before Rosemary Mooney changed her mind about the rape accusation. However, there is something on record that you can check.'

The cat, having finished the innards, sat on the outside window ledge and fixed Rachel with a green, unblinking gaze.

'You're a smart woman, Rachel. Otherwise, you wouldn't be walking in my shoes. Like me, you know when information has meat on it or what is bare bone. Marianne Mooney signed a statement. Check it out when you go back to the station.'

'Why wasn't I able to find it?'

'Rosemary Mooney begged me to keep a lid on the whole fiasco and not bring any more shame on her daughter. I obliged her and filed it under the name Blake's Hollow. I looked upon it as a form of insurance in case Carrie Reagan ever decided to challenge the evidence. Needless to say, that has never happened.'

He jutted his bottom lip. Oily. Rachel looked away. She had absolutely no reason to believe he was lying. The guards working the station at that time had retired, been promoted or died. She had met with an inspector, who had been a young guard in Reedstown when this crime was supposed to have been committed. She respected the inspector's integrity and had no reason to disbelieve him when he said he would definitely remember if such a traumatic event had ever been reported. But what if he had not been on duty on the night the crime occurred? Could it possibly have been hidden from him? A clean-up operation carried out by Jack Bale for reasons best known to himself? He was watching her closely, his eyes narrowed, as if he sensed her thoughts, her doubts.

'Are you questioning my methods, Sergeant?' he demanded.

'I'm doing my job, Jack, which is to try to establish whether or not a rape occurred.'

'Well, legally speaking, a rape did occur, whether or not the sex was two-way traffic, if you get my meaning. But gang-rape, that's a whole different kettle of fish. I'm asking you again, who made this accusation?'

'Marianne Mooney.'

He studied her for an instant. 'Speaking from the grave, then, was she?'

'In a way. Words live on after death. Marianne kept a diary in which she outlined details of her alleged assault. Three unknown assailants were supposedly involved.'

If she had hoped to startle him, she was mistaken. He cleared his plate, swabbing the last of the baguette in the juices.

'I'm glad you said "supposedly". This diary, has it come into your possession?'

'Let's just say I'm aware of its existence.'

'All kids keep diaries. I'm sure you had one yourself. Did you usually write the truth in it?'

'Yes.'

'Always so honest. No wonder you joined the force.' He laughed and scraped the remains of the trout on Rachel's plate into a bowl. He opened the window and left the bowl on the window ledge where the contents were quickly devoured by the cat. 'I don't suppose you'd like to tell me who's in possession of this diary?'

'You know I can't do that. My reason for coming here was to speak to you unofficially and see if the allegation contained in it had any validity. Were you aware that Marianne Mooney stayed in a mother and baby home run by Gloria Thornton?'

'I heard that, right enough. A well-run place, I believe. Not like those laundries.'

'Yet she died there.'

'A tragedy that could easily have been averted if she hadn't been so reckless about her own safety.'

The certainty in his tone, his bullish stare, as if daring her to challenge him, sickened her. She pressed her hand against her ribcage to control an involuntary heave. She would achieve nothing by continuing this conversation.

'You've been very helpful, Jack.' She stood up and held out her hand to him. 'Thanks for the meal. I hadn't realised you were a cordon bleu.'

'There's much you don't know about me, Rachel.' He smiled broadly as he grasped her hand between his own. 'How's that husband of yours keeping?'

'He's well. Busy as always.'

'You've been the cloud in his silver lining. But I suppose you know that.'

'He's also lined my cloud with silver.'

'Ah, but the difference is that you were delighted to move to Reedstown and take over my station. Bob, on the other hand, had to be dragged kicking and screaming back here from New York. Did he ever tell you why he left Reedstown in such a hurry?'

'He moved abroad to gain experience.'

'A noble reason for leaving, right enough.' He smirked, as if her reply amused him. 'Pass on my regards to him. We go back a long way, me and Bobby Molloy.' He sang her husband's name to the air of 'Me and Bobby McGee'. 'Way, way back,' he added. 'Be sure and tell him that now.'

The cat had made its way to the front of the house and was sitting sphinx-like on the gatepost. Jack Bale had that same waiting stillness about him as he stood in his doorway and waited for Rachel to reverse her car and drive away.

She found the file easily. An admission that Shane Reagan had sex with a minor. She hated the language. It bore no relationship to the love story Rachel had read, yet there was no mistaking the young girl's signature at the bottom of the statement. One sheet of paper that denied everything she had written in her diary.

Bob had made their evening meal and set the table on the patio for two. She helped herself to a portion of lasagne and poured a large glass of wine. Time to detach from her job and be in the moment with her husband as they relaxed in the garden they had created together. She was tempted to tell him about Adele Foyle's visit and reveal her true identity. No, she decided. That was a confidential interview, as was her interview with Jack. Despite being married to a newspaperman, she had to follow procedure. Her stomach heaved when she forced a forkful of lasagne into her mouth and gulped it down with wine. The trout... Thinking about it added to her queasiness. She touched her forehead and was surprised to feel a film of sweat on her hairline. Bob's phone rang. He moved from the patio to take the call and she used the excuse to clear away the dishes. His expression was troubled as she walked past. Problems at the news desk. It was always thus, or else she was the one under pressure, both of them bound by the demands of their careers. How they had ever managed to make time to fall in love was a mystery but there was nothing mysterious about their feelings for each other.

Rachel had not been looking for romance when she was transferred to Reedstown. Earlier ventures along its brambled path had made her wary of its sting but everything changed when, at the age of thirty-nine, she met Bob Molloy. He was also in a stage of transition after his return from New York. Still single, without baggage, attractive, kind and in love with her, he seemed too perfect to be true. If she had been inclined to starry-eyed romanticism, her feet would not have touched the ground in the early months of their relationship. The glow lasted and they were married a year after that first meeting.

Adele Foyle was to be married soon. The ring on her engagement finger had glinted when she picked up her mother's diary from Rachel's desk. A sparkler, too flashy for Rachel, who wore a simple solitaire. She had been wearing it for three years now. Weird that it still felt strange on her finger. Not that she wore it often. She preferred her fingers unadorned when she was on duty.

CHAPTER TWENTY-TWO

Adele

No case to answer. Adele should not have been surprised. To expect the truth to slot smoothly into place was foolish; yet she had hoped the sergeant's enquiries would force open a wedge. One that would allow in enough light for an investigation to begin. Whatever her personal feelings were, Sergeant Darcy hid them behind an impassive expression as she explained that no evidence had been found to support the claims in Marianne's diary.

'Even if there was irrefutable evidence and we knew the identity of the perpetrators, the fact that your mother has been dead for the past twenty-four years puts paid to any chance of this crime being investigated,' she explained. 'Usually, when a victim dies then so does their evidence.'

'Are you telling me my mother made this up?' Adele hunched over the desk, her shoulders bowed. 'She *was* brought to this Garda station on the night she was raped. Did you speak to the priest who wanted to bring her to hospital?'

'Father Breen was transferred from Reedstown in the mid-nineties and left the priesthood shortly afterwards. From what I've been able to find out, he lives abroad but no one seems to know where he's located.'

'What about Sergeant Bale?'

'Yes, we spoke. He was adamant that the crime your mother described never took place. He insists that Shane Reagan was the father…' She stopped, as if she was aware of the impact of her words on Adele. 'Jack believes that Shane is your father,' she continued in a softer tone. 'A reluctant one, I'm afraid.'

'No…*no*.' Adele recoiled away from her. 'My mother wanted so much for Shane to be my father but it wasn't him. Jack Bale is lying. He's trying to cover up for those who were responsible? Marianne wouldn't make up something so terrible…she *wouldn't*.'

'I don't mean to be unkind but you've no idea what your mother would or wouldn't do.' Sergeant Darcy was adamant. 'She was underage and she admits in her diary that your grandmother had forbidden her to see this boy. She was obviously distraught over finding herself pregnant at such a young age.'

'Wrong, Sergeant. She was distraught because she was gang-raped.'

Sergeant Darcy slid a sheet of paper across her desk towards her. 'Technically speaking, Shane Reagan could have been accused of raping a minor, even if the sex was consensual. Marianne signed a statement. This signature matches the writing in her diary.' The sergeant's tone, clipped with authority now, prevented Adele from interrupting her. 'He was committing a crime and your mother could have invented this story to protect him. As you can see, it was witnessed by Jack Bale and another guard.'

Adele stared at the sheet of paper the sergeant had placed before her. The statement was brief yet succinct. It accused Shane Reagan of rape and of threatening to kill Marianne if she reported him to the Gardai. The writing wavered before Adele's eyes, her disbelief giving way to confusion as she read the statement again. The sergeant waited until she was finished, her posture sympathetic yet detached. No doubt she was used to people's beliefs and hopes being shattered by irrefutable evidence.

'Why would she do something like that? It doesn't make sense.' Adele pushed the statement away from her. 'She must have signed it under duress.'

'Adele, please think about what you're suggesting. Do you honestly believe that such a crime would not have been thoroughly investigated? Jack Bale served out his tenure as a sergeant in Reedstown with an impeccable reputation. You can't bandy accusations about on such flimsy evidence. I'm sorry I can't give you the answers you want. I did a thorough investigation and came up with nothing to substantiate your claim.'

'What about Gloria Thornton? She ran—'

'Gloria Thornton is dead and cannot defend herself.'

'As is my mother. Yet no one ever investigated her death.'

'I understand your distress but I've taken this as far as I can.'

The sergeant's voice seemed far away, bursts of static as she explained how Adele's grandmother had been prepared to press charges against Shane and how, directly as a result of Jack Bale's intervention, he was able to leave for Australia with his mother. Marianne went to Inisada and died there so that Adele could live. End of story. No case to answer. She had believed there was an empathy between herself and the sergeant; an openness that had allowed her to place her precious diary into the hands of another. Facts were facts... until they weren't.

CHAPTER TWENTY-THREE

Adele

Anglers regularly came to the Loy, bringing folding chairs and picnic baskets. Adele envied their relaxed postures, their patience. There was always tomorrow if the big one got away. Two days after her meeting with Garda Darcy, she was working on her laptop when she noticed one of the anglers standing outside. Expecting him to pass on, she was surprised when he opened the gate. She recognised him as he drew nearer, having seen his photograph in back issues of the *Reedstown Review*.

Marianne had never described Jack Bale's physical appearance in her diary and Adele always visualised him as a looming, menacing presence. In the flesh he was smaller than in her imaginings, yet still tall, about six feet in height, his heavy shoulders balancing his strong, red neck. A battered hat shaded his face and the lumpen shape of dead fish protruded from the plastic bag he carried. The ring on the doorbell was an imperious summons, which she answered after taking a deep, steadying breath.

He reached two fingers to his forehead in a casual salute. She was relieved when he made no effort to shake her hand. She would prefer to crush glass than make physical contact with him.

'Good evening, young lady,' he said. 'I'm Jack Bale.'

'I know who you are, Mr Bale.'

'Well, that gets rid of the formalities,' he said. 'But call me Jack. May I call you Adele?'

'If you wish.'

'I heard on the grapevine that you're new to the area so I thought I'd drop in on my way home and welcome you to Reedstown. I've had a good day on the river and these beauties will go to waste if I don't give them away.'

He opened the bag to show her the contents. She recoiled from the sight of the speckled flesh, so slick yet lifeless, and still exuding the fresh whiff of their existence. 'Look upon these beauties as a welcome-to-Reedstown gesture,' he said. 'I'll bring them into the kitchen and gut them for you. A cup of tea wouldn't go amiss while I'm doing it.'

She fought back the impulse to close the door on him. Nothing could be gained by such a gesture and she knew with a chilling certainty that he had come to her for a reason. 'Please come in.' She stood aside to allow him to enter.

He walked without hesitation ahead of her to the kitchen, where he slid the trout onto a chopping board.

'How are you enjoying our village, Adele? It must seem very slow after London.'

'Everywhere is slow after London,' she replied. 'Reedstown makes a restful change.'

'I was surprised to hear that Larry managed to rent out this place. Thought it was a lost cause after the flooding. Are you settling in okay?'

'So far so good.'

'Not a bit isolated for a young one like yourself?'

'Not at all,' she replied.

'Well, that makes a change from the young ones I know. They'd get withdrawal symptoms if the city lights were switched off. Now, where's a knife I can use to gut these beauties? Ah, this one should do the trick.' He removed a knife from a wooden block and inspected its blade.

'I believe you're a documentary maker,' he went on. 'That must be a fascinating occupation?'

'I enjoy my work.'

'A kindred spirit, I see. I also loved my work. Loved it so much that I dreaded retiring. I thought I'd be bored but, now, I'm busier than ever.' He slid the point of the knife into the belly of the first fish and began to clean it out. 'I took the liberty of watching some of your work, Adele. You have a keen mind and a curious eye. However, you shave close to the edge of truth in the pursuit of sensationalism, if you don't mind me saying so.' His forehead was furrowed with concentration as he delicately worked on the second trout. 'I don't doubt your integrity but I have huge respect for the good work Gloria Thornton did and the comfort she gave to others.'

He filleted the backbone from the fish and swept the innards into the plastic bag. He washed his hands. Large, capable hands, speckled with sun spots.

'These will stink the kitchen out.' He lifted the bag of innards and swung it towards her. 'I'll dump them into the bin and then have that mug of tea.'

Outside in the garden, he slammed the lid of the wheelie bin closed. 'Come out here and have a look at this,' he shouted. 'You'd need to talk to Larry and get him to sort it out.'

When Adele joined him in the garden, he was pointing at a crack on the side wall. 'It's dangerous,' he said. 'Bad foundations. Tell him I know a builder who'll fix it. He'll not charge him an arm or a leg either. It probably happened when the place flooded last winter.'

'I'll tell him.'

'Be sure and do that.' He continued inspecting the wall, pointing at a block that had loosened and complaining about the land on which the house had been built. 'What idiot on the council gave permission for housing to be built on a flood plain?' he said. 'Larry Kavanagh was asking for trouble when he bought this place. Thought he'd make a quick buck on the rent but he didn't reckon on the Loy. It'll flood again, mark my words.'

Bored by his conversation, Adele turned to walk back to the house.

'Jesus H. Christ! Would you look at this?' He had turned his attention to the shed at the bottom of the garden.

Reluctantly, she inspected a truncated pipe that jutted from the shed wall. It appeared to have been abandoned in the middle of its installation. Jack Bale clacked his teeth and heaved his shoulders at the tawdry workmanship he saw everywhere he looked. A bleep on his mobile distracted him. After checking the message, he followed Adele back to the house. He lifted a lemon from the fruit bowl and squeezed it over the fish, added salt, rubbing the granules between his fingers. His sense of his own authority was absolute. Adele imagined him taking her mother's statement, signing his name at the bottom of it, the flourish of his signature.

He clasped his hands around the mug of tea she handed him and said, 'This documentary you're making, where exactly are you going with it?'

'I'm sorry, Mr Bale.' She was startled by his bluntness. 'But I'm not prepared to discuss my work with you.'

'Jack... Jack, no formalities, *please*. I'm worried about it and I'm not going to pretend otherwise. It's come to my notice that you intend presenting Gloria Thornton as the leader of a *cult*. You, as a wordsmith, and, may I add, a very fine one, should appreciate the importance of words. The *right* words.'

The quickening of her heartbeat was an uncomfortable reminder that Marianne had been terrified of this man.

'I can assure you—'

'Who gave you authority to make this documentary?' His interruption was deliberate, challenging. He had a disconcerting gaze, honed from years of interrogations. Getting to the nub of the matter.

'I don't see what business that is of yours,' she replied.

'I intend to make it my business. Liam Thornton has threatened you with an injunction if you continue to stalk him. You blagged your way into his office with the express intention of defaming a woman who is no longer around to defend herself. You were skulking around Davina Lewis's property and using Bob Molloy's archives under false pretences. You've been accosting elderly members of the community and upsetting them with your suggestions that a cult once existed here. And now you're daring to question my tenure in Reedstown. Don't look so startled. I've deep roots in the village and nothing escapes my attention. I ran a tight ship when I was a sergeant and will prove that to you if you dare to impugn my reputation.'

What had Sergeant Darcy told him? Had she named Adele as the person enquiring about Marianne Mooney or had he just put two and two together and made four? It would not be difficult to figure out that a documentary about Gloria Thornton would include questions about a young expectant mother who had stayed in the House of Atonement.

'I rang Voice Dox and spoke to your boss… or should I say, your ex-boss.' His baleful stare added to the appropriateness of his name, she through. 'I'm sure you can imagine her surprise when she heard from me. She was under the impression you'd moved to Colorado and were no longer an employee of her company. She was shocked to discover that you're making a documentary without her imprimatur and using the name of her company under false pretences.'

'That's a total distortion of what happened. My documentary—'

'On the contrary, your documentary is nothing but a con job.'

The clock on the wall struck six and a cuckoo shot in and out of it. Adele had disliked the clock when she first moved into Brooklime but she had come to terms with its shrill occupant and the notes that marked the hours of her days. Her gaze flickered to the shelf where the diary lay next to her phone. Hoping he had not noticed that involuntary glance, she walked to the wall where a picture hung askew and straightened it. Noticing a key that had fallen from the key rack, she replaced it on its hook. This gave her time to compose her features before she rounded on him.

'I'm an independent documentary maker investigating the practices of a sodality that existed here twenty-five years ago. I have only recently left Voice Dox and have not used their name since then. Regarding my tactics, Davina Lewis invited me into Hillcrest. Bob Molloy gave me permission to examine the archives and anyone who spoke to me did so of their own free will. Liam Thornton refused to speak to me and it's his prerogative to seek an injunction, not yours. I intend continuing with my documentary and will not be intimidated by you or anyone else.'

His large frame dominated the kitchen when he stood and leaned his hands on the table. 'Get that crack on the wall sorted out, Miss Foyle. Accidents can happen so easily when we don't take care of the structures. Good evening to you.'

She watched from the window as he closed the gate behind him. The riverbank was busy, parents walking with children, sleek cyclists shrouded in helmets, joggers with pedometers tracking their steps. The smell of fish clung like a vapour in her nostrils. The air was thick with it but there was something else also, a spicy odour that was barely detectable, and could have been imagined, yet it added to the menacing sense of having had her space invaded. She wrapped the gutted trout in paper, her hands shaking as she flung the parcel into the bin. The Loy flowed smoothly onward.

CHAPTER TWENTY-FOUR

Adele

It was still dark outside when Adele awoke. She had been dreaming, a disturbing nightmare, the images already fading. Instead of the slow relief she would usually feel, she was alert and tense. No birdsong broke the silence yet she sensed that dawn was near. Unable to relax back to sleep, she reached for her phone to check the time. It wasn't in its usual place on the bedside table, nor had it fallen on the floor during the night. She shook the duvet, checked under the pillows. Could she have left it in the kitchen or the living room? Definitely not. She had been in bed when she spoke to Daniel, a terse conversation that filled her with unease as it came back to her.

You're stirring a hornets' nest... opening a can of worms... on a wild goose chase... since when had they resorted to clichés? Nowadays, it seemed as if all their conversations boiled down to such trite comments, his impatience becoming clearer with each call. He was finding the transition to Colorado difficult, more demanding than he had expected. She should have listened to him, allowed him time to express his annoyance with executives who rubbished his reports on how to create a greener environment for drilling oil. He wanted her with him, not digging about in muck. And that was what it felt like. Viscid mud that kept sliding through her fingers. How much longer, he asked. How long is a piece of string? Last night, consumed with her own thoughts, she had cut their conversation short, unable to tolerate his questions.

Their angry exchange troubled her as she continued to search for her phone. Kneeling down, she checked under the bed. She even lifted the edge of the mattress in a vain attempt to find it. Had she walked in her sleep? She had done so in the past when she was stressed. Exams, job interviews, a difficult relationship she had endured for a year before ending it. She left the bedroom and went downstairs. Everything looked exactly the same as it had when she went to bed; until she noticed a delicate sprig of brooklime on the living room floor. The blue flower that had given the house its name had been crushed underfoot and feet other than her own had stepped across the wooden floorboards.

Last week she had picked the flower from the riverbank, dried it and placed it between two pages of Marianne's diary. Had someone turned the pages, unaware that the flower had slipped out? Only those crushed petals now remained as evidence that the diary had been removed from its usual spot and was also missing. Unable to believe the evidence of her eyes, her movements became frantic as she pulled out cushions and dragged the contents from drawers, checking places she knew she would never have left it.

The screen remained blank when she switched on her laptop. Attaching the charger made no difference. The container where she kept her USB sticks was empty. Her file of photocopied newspaper clippings from the archives and printed reports downloaded from the internet had also been removed. Everything she had collected since the day that swallow flew between the rafters of her grandmother's attic was gone. While she slept, someone had systematically erased her online presence. Whoever was responsible for this vandalism had not only destroyed her research but, also, had stolen the only meaningful link she had to her mother's existence. Was that someone Jack Bale? She had not seen him on the river since their meeting in Brooklime two days previously. She shook her head. He would not have taken such a risk. But she suspected he was only a hand away from the deed.

Larry answered his front door after her third knock. 'You and I are the only two people with keys.' He was sleepy and irritable, his eyes bloodshot. 'What's missing?'

'A diary and my phone.'

'A phone I can understand but why in God's name would anyone be bothered stealing a diary? What's in it? The third secret of Fatima?' He tightened the belt on his dressing gown and emitted a short bark of laughter.

She stepped back from the sound. 'They wiped my laptop. Everything's gone.'

'I'm not a techie but I'll guarantee that's a local breakdown. Your broadband will be up and running once the powers that be sort out the problem. Do you know what time it is? Five o'clock in the morning and you're after putting my heart crossways over nothing.'

'I'm sorry for waking you but someone *did* break into Brooklime. They must have had a key. There's no sign of forced entry.'

'Are you saying I did it?' His tone sharpened.

'Of course not.'

'Then believe me when I tell you we're the only two with keys. Go back to bed. Finish your sleep and you'll find everything you're looking for in the morning.'

She returned to Brooklime by the river path. The sky was brightening as the sun edged over the bridge that spanned the Loy. The light on the river deepened to coral as it reflected the streeling clouds. It was going to be another hot day. Adele continued running until she reached the shelter of Brooklime's walls.

She thought about Jack Bale, his affability and aggression working off each other, and how he had kept her outside inspecting flaws that were of no importance. Had someone entered the house while they were outside and made a copy of the key? It sounded ludicrous and yet it made perfect sense. Whoever it was would have had to be armed with the right equipment, probably a clam kit. She had seen how the device worked when she was doing research for a Voice Doc documentary on security. It would have taken only a moment to open the hinged device and press the key into the putty-like substance inside it. She remembered the smell rising above the odour of fish. She had forgotten about it but, thinking back, she realised it had reminded her of a spicily scented aftershave.

Sergeant Darcy listened politely to Adele. She admitted that in all her years of processing complaints, she had never dealt with a victim who claimed her online identity had been stolen. A virus, obviously, rare, destructive and untraceable, she said when Adele told her that her laptop was blank, everything wiped. She was patient and polite as she explained that the Gardai did not have the resources to trace this damaging virus, especially when it had left nothing behind except a ruined hard drive.

'It was not a virus,' Adele flatly contradicted her. 'This was done deliberately to sabotage my documentary.' She described her meeting with Liam Thornton and Jack Bale's visit to Brooklime. Under the sergeant's questioning, she heard her arguments fall apart. No, she had heard nothing during the night. No, she had no evidence to prove Jack Bale had warned her off making her documentary. Yes, he had brought fresh fish from the river to her and, yes, she had invited him in for a cup of tea.

'And now my mother's diary's gone,' she said. 'How do you explain that?'

'Could you have left it behind in the Kasket?' Sergeant Darcy sat back in her chair and folded her arms. 'You do a lot of work there on your laptop.'

'How can you even think that?' Adele's distress left the sergeant in no doubt about her reaction to that suggestion. 'You know that my mother's diary is my most precious possession.'

Perhaps it was this distress that persuaded Sergeant Darcy to take the matter a step further. A young guard arrived at Brooklime to check for fingerprints. Apart from Adele's own prints, there were no marks on the wood or glass to suggest a break-in had occurred. The lost USB sticks were probably hidden in drawers, Garda Roberts said. She was the same age as Adele, tech savvy; yet despite all her knowledge, she had once suffered a catastrophic virus attack that had taken her a week to sort out. She was always losing memory sticks and leaving her mobile in pubs and clubs. Adele's phone was probably lying silent, battery dead, in some unsearched crevice in Brooklime. It would turn up when she calmed down and did a thorough search. Her cheerful conversation was as useless as it was irritating.

Adele located a flyer advertising a computer repair shop that had been dropped through the letter box soon after she moved into Brooklime. BootUrBytes was on Barrow Lane behind the Garda station. It was a dingy building, squashed between a charity outlet and a washeteria.

'Not a chance,' Jonathan Wheeler, the owner, said after giving her laptop a cursory examination. 'Best to dump it and get a new one.'

She asked him how everything on her hard drive could be so corrupted that nothing had survived, even in the Cloud.

'Shit happens.' His indifference verged on rudeness.

Adele sensed something else in the atmosphere of his small, cluttered shop. Amusement, she thought, then dismissed this possibility as ridiculous. Why should the two youths working behind the counter, who called the owner 'Grad', find anything funny in her predicament? Why should the laughter that came from beyond the partition dividing the shop from the repair workspace be aimed at her? Adele left the premises, vowing never to return.

She bought a new phone and laptop elsewhere but the wealth of information she had lost was irreplaceable. As for the diary, her only consolation was the copy she had made soon after she moved into Brooklime. What impulse had driven her to photograph each page and store them on a USB key? She wanted to believe that her mother had prompted her to do so. It was comforting to think that somewhere in that other-world, a young girl with tormented eyes was watching over her. Adele had hidden the USB key in the garden shed with the truncated pipe. Unaware of its existence, Jack Bale had stood so close to its hiding place in the cluttered shed but she was too upset to appreciate the irony.

CHAPTER TWENTY-FIVE

Adele

Bob Molloy's ability to listen was what Adele liked most about him. Unlike Sergeant Darcy, who had been unable to hide her scepticism, he listened intently when she told him her research had been stolen.

'Jack Bale knows my documentary is about more than Gloria Thornton and that bothers him,' she said. 'That's why my laptop was wiped. I can't prove he did it but I'm convinced he's responsible.'

'As a newspaperman I know that nothing is ever as straight-forward as it sounds,' he said. 'I figured you were interested in more than the Thorns and their practices. Obviously, my instincts were right. I've been after the same information ever since I came back from New York but I found it impossible to trace her offshore account.'

'What offshore account?' Adele asked.

'That's not what you're trying to track?'

'No. Liam Thornton said funds were embezzled by Rosemary Mooney—'

'He met you.' Unable to hide his surprise, he sat back in his chair and surveyed her. 'You must have used some strong-arm tactics.'

'Let's just say we had an encounter.'

'I've heard that story about Rosemary.' He flattened his hands against the desk and exhaled sharply. 'She was Gloria's mouthpiece, nothing else.'

'You knew her?'

'To be honest, I hardly knew myself in those days. But from what I remember about her, she was a foot soldier, not a leader. Certainly not capable of embezzling the multitudes and lodging the money offshore.'

'Did you know her daughter?'

He hesitated, his brow furrowing before he replied. 'Yes. Her name was Marianne. She left Reedstown with her mother when she was quite young. What has she got to do with your documentary?'

'She's key to it, actually. You're right about the Thorns. They're a sidebar to the real story I want to tell.'

'Meaning?'

'I've reason to believe a crime was committed against Marianne Mooney and covered up by the Gardai. Jack Bale's behaviour has confirmed my suspicions. He's trying to shut me down.'

'What are you talking about?'

She wanted to touch her pocket and feel the diary. Without it, she felt adrift. It had given her courage to keep searching, asking questions, refusing to accept that there was no case to answer.

'Marianne Mooney was raped. The men who did it, there were three of them, were local.'

'By local you mean Reedstown?' His hands remained motionless on his desk, apart from an involuntary reflex from his index fingers. 'Where did this happen?'

'Blake's Hollow.'

'What evidence have you to back this claim?'

'Enough to know it's true.'

'That's not an answer, Adele.'

'I know that Jack Bale is trying to silence me.'

'That's a mighty presumption to make.'

'I've made it. I believe that's why he was so aggressive towards me. Firstly, he denied it to Sergeant Darcy—'

'You spoke to Sergeant Darcy about this?' His tone was as incredulous as his expression.

Adele nodded. 'She checked the records and said there was no case to answer but I don't believe—'

'Let me stop you right there.' He held up his hand, palm facing her. 'I have to declare a personal interest here. Sergeant Darcy is my wife.'

'Your *wife*?' Heat rushed to her cheeks as she absorbed this information. 'I didn't know that.'

'There's no reason why you should.' He cleared his throat before continuing. 'But you need to understand something important. Rachel is absolutely trustworthy and scrupulous. If she says there is no case to answer, then you must accept that she's telling you the truth.'

'She *believes* she's telling me the truth. I wouldn't push this story if I wasn't convinced that Marianne Mooney was gang-raped and then sent off to that mother and baby home run by Gloria Thornton to hide what happened to her. One of those men was the father of her child.'

'Why did you lie to me about your research?' He pushed back from his desk and walked to the window.

'The Thorns are part of her story. Marianne Mooney died when she was in their care.'

'These supposed assailants…?' He hesitated, his back to her. 'Do you have names for them?'

'Not yet.'

'Was that what you were checking in my archives?'

'The crime was never covered by the *Reedstown Review*,' she admitted. 'No mention of a trial or a report that an anonymous teenager had been subjected to such a heinous attack. Don't you find that strange?'

'I find it strange that you would lie to me.' His attention remained fixed on Main Street. 'And strange that you would suggest my father would bury such a story.'

'If Jack Bale covered it up, your father wouldn't have known anything about it.'

'Are you seriously expecting me to believe the Gardai hid evidence of a serious rape that took place in their jurisdiction?' He turned to face her. 'Come on, Adele, you're a journalist. No names. No Garda records. No mention of it in the archives. How can you honestly base a documentary on such flimsy evidence?'

He didn't believe her. Flimsy evidence, just as his wife had said. A flimsy book of evidence, filled with handwriting that had started to fade. Gone now, that small but powerful bond between them. Pulped or burned, and in its place a soulless memory stick on which she had recorded each precious word her mother had written during those final months of her life.

'My father was a reputable editor.' Unable to control his anger, he moved from the window to the wall behind his desk where a replica of the photograph taken at the official opening of the new building hung. He pointed to his father, a silver-haired man with the same sloping cheekbones and thick eyebrows as his son. 'I will not allow you to undermine his reputation. If he'd received the slightest hint that such a terrible crime had been committed, he would have published every detail. Even if Jack Bale had hushed it up, which I don't for a minute believe he did, James Molloy would have battered down the doors of the Garda station for information. As my wife would have done had she given any credibility to your story.'

'I'm trying to join the dots together and find out exactly what happened.' She pleaded with him to listen to her. 'That's why I'm hoping you'll give me space—'

'Space?'

'I want to put a notice in your newspaper asking the public for information on Marianne Mooney's murder?'

'Her *what*?' Exasperation hardened his mouth.

'She died giving birth to the child of the man who raped her. I'd call that murder.'

'You've strayed very far into conspiracy territory, Adele. Tragic and all as Marianne Mooney's pregnancy was, you haven't offered me a shred of evidence to convince me that she wasn't… wasn't…'

'A slut? Is that what you're trying to say?'

'Those teenage years are barbarous.' His eyes glistened with what looked suspiciously like tears but could also have been the hard sheen of denial. 'Cruel things were said about her.'

'Then help me, Bob. You're the voice of Reedstown. Give me space to tell her story—'

'Enough.' His brusque interruption signalled an end to their conversation. 'I've been patient with you but what you're asking is impossible.' He sat back at his desk and pulled his laptop towards him. 'You'll have to excuse me. I've an appointment in five minutes. If you need further archival information, I suggest you use the National Library.'

Out on Main Street, she forced herself to slow down and allow the breeze to cool her cheeks. Rage had become her new normal. It overrode her distress that she had lost someone she believed would have supported her. The story of the Thorns was not an easy one to tell, Julie Thornton had said. Too many layers to peel away. She was right. Layers of lies, contradictions and denials would bury the truth. Marianne's diary was irreplaceable but her mother's words would soon reverberate through Reedstown and far beyond. It was time to demand restitution.

She entered Katie's Kasket and ordered a sandwich with coffee. Overhead, a fan moved slowly but barely stirred the hot air. She forced herself to eat. Living alone, she seldom cooked anything substantial, depending on takeaways and ready-made meals. She and Daniel had loved cooking, vying with each other to produce elaborate meals and forage for unusual herbs and spices.

He contacted her every day on WhatsApp, sending photographs of himself and his team on-site, checking charts, measuring distances, photographing landscapes. Madison Fox featured in some of them, blending in with the others yet always standing close to him. Adele refused to acknowledge the flare of jealousy she experienced when she recognised her dainty figure in a hi-vis suit and helmet. She trusted Daniel, just as he trusted her to complete her search and join him.

She slept restlessly, awakening at the slightest sound. When morning came, she stood at her bedroom window and stared out at the river. An angler was already on the Loy, knee-deep in the silvery flow, his broad outline partially shrouded by the early mist. Even from that distance, she recognised Jack Bale's bulky frame, his arm flung back, then arching forward.

CHAPTER TWENTY-SIX

Julie

Keith Lewis arrived first at Holywell. As always when meeting him unexpectedly, Julie was forced to gather together all her reserves and greet him calmly, politely. She visualised her mind as a locker room filled with compartments that she could open and close at will. He greeted her with a hug, then followed Liam into his home office. Jack Bale arrived shortly afterwards, all bonhomie and compliments about how Julie still looked like a teenager, which she knew to be untrue, but he made it sound believable. Shortly afterwards, Bob Molloy rang the doorbell.

'Good gracious me.' Julie was careful to hide her surprise when she saw him. 'My husband never told me an old boys' reunion was taking place tonight.'

'How are you, Julie?' His expression was terse as he entered the hall and gazed around him. 'This is like stepping back in time.' He stared upward at the soaring ceiling decorated with angel covings and inspected the Christ statue crowned with thorns that stood on a marble table. He nodded in recognition at the religious paintings on the walls. 'I thought you'd tear the place apart when you moved in.'

'Liam doesn't like change,' she replied. 'To be honest, I don't even notice it any more. How's Rachel?'

'She's good. Busy as ever.'

'Give her my regards.'

'Will do.'

She had met Rachel Darcy at Jack Bale's retirement party. For a while it seemed as if they would become friends but, shortly afterwards, Bob Molloy, newly returned from New York, had put paid to that. Not deliberately, Julie would grant him that, but the enmity he felt toward Liam and Keith was as raw as when he first left Reedstown. The hostility dating back to their teens had seemed unbridgeable… until tonight. Her curiosity aroused, Julie was tempted to listen at the door but, like everything in Holywell, it was solid and heavy.

Her husband shared his mother's taste in opulent Italian design, marble and glass, glossy lacquer screens, curves and swirls, plush leather – and Julie, whose taste ran to minimalism, had converted one of the cavernous rooms into her own space. Holywell was simply a shell with a roof and what she called her 'burrow' was her true home.

In her burrow, she snuggled into an armchair and switched on her laptop. As she expected, Stephanie was online. An hour passed without being noticed as she Skyped with her daughter. She missed Stephanie, who was in France for the summer with her grandmother. Cathy Boland had moved to Provence after her husband died. She could have stayed in Reedstown and settled into a resigned widowhood. Instead she chose to paint and chase butterflies and drink red wine in the shade of poplars.

Stephanie would be home in September, fluent in French, and, until then, the house had an echo that only she could fill with her clattering footsteps, her laughter and chatter. She was the one person who made Holywell into a home and not a mausoleum, which was what she and Stephanie called it behind Liam's back.

The meeting was still under way when Julie entered the kitchen and switched on the kettle. Their voices were raised when she knocked on the office door. Unable to make out what they were saying, she opened the door and asked if anyone would like coffee. Liam's face froze when he noticed her. He was leaning towards Bob as if taunting him, his fist clenched. Jack Bale's arms were outstretched to create a barrier between the two men. He looked as authoritative as he used to do when he was strutting around Reedstown in his uniform. The tableau dissolved as everyone turned towards her.

'Coffee, anyone?' Julie asked again, only more nervously this time.

'Thanks, but no thanks.' Keith smiled and held out his arms, as if drawing the tension towards him. 'We'll be out of here in a few more minutes, Julie.'

The men left shortly afterwards but Liam remained in his home office.

'Is it okay to come in now?' Julie hesitated by the open door. 'I didn't mean to disturb anything.'

'Come in.' He had opened a small drinks cabinet and was pouring brandy into a glass. He filled another glass and handed it to her.

'What was the argument about?' she asked.

'What argument?' He stared blankly back at her.

'When I interrupted you. I thought… it was obvious something was going on with you and Bob Molloy?'

'Don't be so dramatic, Julie. We were simply discussing coverage for the Reedstown Festival. You know how pernickety Molloy gets when he's asked to give out free space in his newspaper. Swear to God, you'd think he was publishing the *Washington Post* instead of a glorified newsletter.'

'That's harsh, Liam. He's done a good job with the paper since he took it over.'

'That's an opinion, Julie, not a fact.'

'Why was Jack Bale here?'

'He's treasurer of the festival and Keith's its chair.'

'I though there were eight members on the committee.'

'What's this, Julie? The third degree? We can sometimes make decisions without dragging everyone to a meeting.'

He finished his brandy and poured another. She held her hand over her glass and remained silent. Whatever had upset him, he had no intention of discussing it with her. Nothing new in that.

A cold fish, that was how she objectively summed up her husband after sixteen years of marriage. She had been slow to realise he was incapable of passion. He went through the motions, made the right moves and sounds, foreplay, after-play. Julie had no reason to fault him in those early years. Or define what was wrong? Perhaps, if she had tried to do so, she would have avoided making the one mistake that had kept her in a loveless marriage. These days, she could think just as objectively about the man who had rushed her into a tumultuous, passionate affair. Tall, handsome and unscrupulous, he had had all the attributes necessary to seduce an unhappily married woman – and to end their affair before she could start making demands.

On the night she discovered she was pregnant she had called into Liam's home office where he was working late and seduced him on his desk. A television screen flickered on the wall, the sound mute, business grafts constantly changing as she scattered his carefully arranged documents to the floor. Bending over, she offered herself to him with an abandonment that shook them both to their core. His roughness and her compliance, that was how he always believed Stephanie was conceived. He apologised to Julie afterwards, gently sliding her thong back up over her thighs, kissing the marks he had left on her arms, the cheeks of her arse, on her neck. She forgave him. Two things she knew. That she would never again trigger such uncontrolled wantonness in him and that she had the strength to ensure her secret. She had upheld her side of the bargain since then, and he, unaware that such a soulless contract had been made in his name, adored the child he believed to be his daughter.

He was lying to her about the meeting. She knew the texture of aggression, its abrasive breath fouling the air. She had walked in on an argument that had nothing to do with the annual Reedstown Festival but had everything to do with Adele Foyle. Her name uttered by her husband with the vehemence he usually reserved for a curse.

PART THREE

CHAPTER TWENTY-SEVEN

Davina

Davina switched on the coffee machine. A strong espresso was needed before she undertook a morning in the constituency clinic, where she would handle the mutterings and grievances of constituents; the needy and the greedy, as Keith called them, always with a hand out or looking for a hand up. Not that he ever gave them that impression. Like his father, he switched into what Davina called his 'charm offensive', which convinced the constituent that his or her problem was the only one that mattered to him.

She perched on the high stool beside the breakfast oasis with her coffee and laptop. This precious fifteen minutes allowed her time to check her emails and Facebook. As usual, it had been a busy night on Reedstown Reminiscences. She had set up the Facebook page during Keith's election campaign. It proved to be a brainwave but soon became a victim of its own success. Trying to administer the page was too time-consuming and Davina had handed that responsibility over to a friend's daughter, Martina Spellman, who was studying computer science at Reedstown Community College. Her co-administrator had obviously been approving posts from around the world. Lots of old photographs and quite a few new link-ups, as one-time friends made contact again. Davina scanned the posts – and stopped when she recognised a new name. Martina had accepted Adele Foyle into the group and approved her first post.

Hi Everyone I'm new to Reedstown Reminiscences and looking forward to belonging to your group. My reason for moving to Reedstown is to make a documentary and I hope to remain here until it's complete. I want to document the life of a teenager called Marianne Mooney. She was fifteen when she left Reedstown and had just turned sixteen when she died. That's twenty-four years ago. Does anyone remember her? Unfortunately, my research material has been compromised so I'm back to the beginning of my search. Can you help me? Send on your photos and your memories of Marianne. She was pregnant when she left Reedstown and her baby was delivered in the House of Atonement, which was run by a local Reedstown resident, the late Gloria Thornton. I've set up a blog to tell Marianne's story. This will consist of diary entries Marianne wrote during the final months of her life. You can add to my research or simply browse through Marianne's reminiscences. Lots to find out – lots to tell. Hit the link below and join me on my blog. http:mariannememoriesreedstown.com

How long had this post been up? Midnight. Martina must have approved it before she went to bed. Why was Adele Foyle focusing on Marianne Mooney and her tragically short life? Life was in the present and too fast-moving to be slowed down by negativities from the past. The popularity of Reedstown Reminiscences was that it allowed nostalgia to bask in the glow of happy memories.

Davina hit the link and opened the blog. It was a simple design, no trimmings. One page for diary entries, a second one for photographs. Viewers were invited to submit their own and caption them. Someone had already responded to the request and added a photo of the grey, charmless bungalow once occupied by Rosemary Mooney, the unkempt front and back gardens neglected so that she didn't have to waste time pulling weeds when she could be pulling lost souls into her fantasy world. Christy had brought order to that wilderness. The rampant dandelions and thistles had been concreted over and the lanes leading to his clinic had become well-trodden over the decades.

The diary entry seemed to be about jet trails and monsoons. What interest had anyone in teenage ramblings? She stopped when she came to a redacted name. *Sergeant XXXX said it was important to get to the truth.* That sounded suspiciously like Jack Bale and later, the Mr XXXXX who told her to look to the future was definitely Davina's father-in-law. Christy was already being dragged into the sorry saga of the Thorns.

A photograph of Marianne Mooney stared back at her from the screen. One of those old-fashioned strips of five, taken with Shane Reagan in a photo booth. She was laughing, which was not the image that came to mind when Davina allowed herself to remember the girl. The sight of them together, arms around each other, pulling faces, lips puckered, acting the fool, added to her uneasiness. The handwriting, though slanted and scrawled, was legible, despite some blotches on the page that suggested tears were shed on the day she left Reedstown.

The sky was peerless and the sun, high and fierce, drilled through the kitchen window. It was only an hour since Davina had showered but she must do so again. A long, cool shower to bring down the prickly heat that was spreading over her body as she continued reading what must have been one of the most outra-

geous accusations ever made. A gang-rape, here in Reedstown.
Three perpetrators, that was what Marianne Mooney claimed.
The nerve of her. Everyone who had known her was aware that
Shane Reagan was the only person responsible for her unfortunate
pregnancy. Trouble, the snake: Davina could hear its rattle. Her
heart thudding, she continued reading. Her teeth clenched when
she came to the last line. *Horrible things that aren't true and the
older girls sniggering and calling me a slut every time they see me.*

Julie had described the bullying of Marianne Mooney as a
virus. As far as Davina was concerned, that was way over the
top, but Julie was all drama, so much nervous energy contained
within her skinny frame. Looking back on it, the bullying of
Marianne Mooney had seemed to happen overnight. Until
then, she had been just an insignificant kid who wore weird
clothes and never seemed bothered by the fact that she was an
outsider. Then the stories started, the nudges and giggles when
she walked past. She was called Queen of the Blowjob and it
was reported as gospel that she had been down on her knees in
Loyvale Park one night, drunk and uncaring as she obliged a
line of eager boys. No one ever checked out the rumours. They
were too salacious to withstand the harsh reality of objectivity.
The fact that her mother was a Thorn added an extra dimension
of pleasure to repeating such stories. Then she was gone and
the rumours went with her, evaporating into a shameful silence
that no one acknowledged when they heard she had died giving
birth to her child.

A movement at the patio door distracted her. She moved
away from the breakfast oasis as Christy slid the door open.
He looked so old this morning, unable to disguise the sag and
slope of age. As for those shapeless jogging pants! If the media
could see him now… Davina closed her eyes at the thought of
journalists linking into Adele Foyle's blog. He was agitated, she

could see that at a glance. She knew immediately that he had also checked Facebook.

He nodded towards the oasis, where she had left her laptop. 'You've read the diary, I presume?'

'I'm furious. Did you see the picture someone put up of The Lodge—?'

His face reddened and a vein pulsed on his temple. 'Davina, my home should be the least of your worries this morning. Why did you allow Adele Foyle to join your group?'

'I didn't. Martina approved her.'

'You agreed to take on full responsibility for administering that page when you set it up, so what the fuck is a kid doing handling it?'

'It's too time-consuming to manage by myself.'

'Then you should have closed it down. Have you any idea how many users have shared her post and are, right at this minute, linking into her blog?'

'Not many. The post went up during the night.'

'That makes no difference. Facebook doesn't sleep. That diary entry…' He exhaled heavily. 'It's total nonsense, of course, every word of it, but social media is a cesspit of misinformation. You, of all people, should know that. My name is up there—'

'All she said is that you bought the house and you were kind to her.'

'Kind to her? Is that how you read it? She said I was in her bedroom—'

'Were you?'

'How the fuck would you expect me to remember something that happened twenty-five years ago? I was probably trying to encourage her to look to the future when her pregnancy was behind her. That kid Reagan raped a minor and did a bunk as soon as he was found out.'

His terse tone increased her apprehension. Was he nervous? Over forty years in politics had honed his nerves to steel and nervousness was not an emotion she had ever attributed to him.

'Where's Keith?' he asked. 'I need to speak to him.'

"He's in Government Buildings.'

'What the hell is he doing there?' He pulled at his ear, his glare suggesting that this upset was entirely Davina's fault.

'Working with a cross-party committee on homelessness. He told you about it.'

'Committees, committees… all he'll get from sitting on them is a fat backside. Druggies and drunks, does he really think he's going to make a difference in their lives? Local issues… that's where you get results.'

He had gone off on a tangent, a favourite hobby horse. She let him rant on about the uselessness of today's breed of young politicians with their cross-party committees and consensus. She knew when he was releasing a pressure valve in his mind and not even hearing his own words. Perspiration shimmered on his forehead and his face had a waxen sheen that alarmed her.

'Has he seen this blog?' he demanded.

'I don't know, Christy. He left early this morning.'

'That bitch needs to be stopped in her tracks. The reputation of Reedstown…' He pulled a handkerchief from his pocket and mopped his brow. His mouth had a slackness that reminded her of his bewilderment when his heart attack struck. His breath was coming too fast. No disguising his alarm now as he held on to the edge of the breakfast oasis to steady himself and pressed his other hand against his chest.

'My tablets. Get them. They're on the bathroom shelf—'

Davina helped him into a chair and ran to The Lodge. His laptop was on the coffee table, open. No need to check what he was reading before he barged into Hillcrest. She found his heart tablets in the bathroom and returned to her kitchen, where she was assailed by the sour smell of vomit. Christy bent forward and retched again before collapsing back into the chair. She winced away from the sound. Her lovely kitchen despoiled. She resisted the urge to fetch hot water and disinfectant.

He was still alert when she phoned for an ambulance.

'Save your breath,' she said when he tried to speak. 'The ambulance is on its way.'

The paramedics transferred him immediately to a stretcher.

'Get in touch with Keith?' He grabbed her hand as he was carried from the house.

'Take it easy,' the paramedic advised him. 'Save your energy for your recovery, and that's beginning right now.'

Before following the ambulance, Davina deleted the Facebook post but its tentacles, she knew, had already spread around the world. She deleted Adele Foyle from the list of friends and rang Martina, whose phone went immediately to message. *Leave a number...* Her voice was giddy and young. How could Davina have been so stupid as to leave a teenager in charge of a landmine?

Three hours later, Keith arrived at the hospital. Anxious and flushed, he embraced Davina. She breathed in the sweat of the city; the snarled-up traffic that had delayed him and, before then, the pressure of the enclosed back room where he had been uncontactable.

'The cardiac specialist is with him now,' she said. 'She'll speak to us as soon as she's finished her examination.'

'What was he doing?' Keith demanded. 'He knows he's not supposed to exert himself.'

'He was upset about something that appeared on social media—'

'He never pays any attention to that rubbish.'

'This time he did. It was related to the Reedstown Facebook page.' She stopped as the ward door opened and Sybil Manning swept towards them, her team following behind.

'Mr Lewis, we meet once more.' She extended her hand to Keith. 'I must admit, I wasn't expecting to see your father again quite so soon.'

'How is he?' Keith bestowed his smile on her. The gift that just keeps on giving, Davina thought, still furious with him for taking so long to reach the hospital.

'Thankfully, I'm almost certain he has not suffered another heart attack,' Sybil reassured him. 'But we'll have to wait until the final results come back from the lab. The stents are still doing their job, as is his pacemaker. But stress has obviously been placed on his heart. On this occasion, I suspect it is emotional rather than physical. My suspicion is that he suffered a panic attack.'

'Panic.' Keith's forehead creased with disbelief. 'My father doesn't understand the concept of panic.'

'I suspect he does,' the specialist replied. 'He's adept at hiding it but that doesn't mean it can't affect him. Of course, I'll need the blood results before I make a final diagnosis. We'll keep him in overnight to stabilise his blood pressure. If the tests are clear, he'll be discharged tomorrow.'

Davina had stopped listening. A panic attack related to Adele Foyle's blog. Fear leading to tension leading to panic that got the better of him and was released in a disgusting pool of vomit. She had no intention of returning to a sullied house and had cleaned it up before leaving Hillcrest.

She made an excuse and hurried towards the bathroom, where she took out her phone and checked the mariannememoriesreedstown blog. A second diary entry had been posted. It mentioned Keith and Liam. Their names, not X's. She remembered that car.

A present from his parents for his eighteenth birthday. Keith had driven it like a rally driver until he hit a wall and that was the end of that. Liam would go ballistic when he saw what Adele had written about the mother and baby home. Already, the sharing of information had begun and the blog was bursting at the seams, virtually speaking, with comments. A snake Davina could handle. But a Hydra, now that was a different matter altogether. No matter how many heads were cut off, more would keep appearing. Christy's blood pressure would go through the roof if he saw the online reaction the post had spawned. She needed to take his phone from him, but it would be easier to cut off his right arm.

He was subdued when they entered the small private ward. The sedation he had taken was working and his eyes were slightly glazed, his voice weak. Keith stood at a distance from his father. He had a healthy constitution and was uneasy around illness, unable to understand how it could fell the strongest and reduce them to a pitiful huddle. And that was how his father looked as he struggled to communicate something – a message… a warning… a threat?

Davina was unable to decipher what was going on between father and son but she was familiar with their unspoken hostility. The united front they presented to the world was impossible to maintain in private. Christy was old-school, back rooms and cigarette smoke, to hell with the ban, foul air was essential for the foul decisions that destroyed the opposition. Cross-party support was anathema to him and his self-belief convinced him that his son's political reputation would never equal his own. Davina, whose job nowadays seemed to consist mainly of keeping the peace between them, often wondered if taming lions would be an easier option.

'I sorted it out for you the last time,' Christy whispered just as they were leaving. His words were slurred, yet held enough bitterness to reach his son. 'Now it's your turn to clean up your own shit.'

Keith turned back and bent low over his father's bed. His hand hovered above Christy's mouth. Davina was convinced he would bring it down on those cruel, withered lips. She grabbed her husband's elbow, forced him to look at her.

'Let him rest,' she said. 'He's too drugged to talk sense.'

'I *am* talking sense.' Christy licked his lips, his dry mouth rasping when he swallowed, and stared directly at Davina. 'You're strong, not like him.' He pointed a finger at his son. 'He doesn't deserve any of it but he's had it handed to him on a plate. You've got the balls to stop him fucking it up.'

Was Christy praising her? If so, what kind of drug had they given him? His finger was still suspended, an accusatory digit that Keith ignored as he turned and walked from the ward. Christy grabbed her arm before she could move and half-rose before collapsing back on the pillows. 'Make him talk to you. You'll know how to handle the storm that's coming.'

Keith had reached Hillcrest before her and was sitting at the kitchen oasis, her laptop open in front of him. She was not fooled by his composure. His youthful good looks had weathered well, thanks to a defined bone structure, a thick head of black hair and a razzle-dazzle smile. No wonder the media treated him as a political poster boy.

'Coffee's ready.' He closed the laptop and gestured towards the coffee machine. 'Would you like a cup?'

'No, thanks. Have you read that blog?'

'I skimmed it. Talk about a blast from the past.'

'It landed your father in hospital.'

'His heart landed—'

'You're wrong. It was Adele Foyle's blog. Why should that pathetic diary scare him so much?'

'It didn't. Stop being so melodramatic.'

'*Melodramatic*? Keith, she claimed she was gang-raped.'

'But we all know that isn't true. You remember her reputation? Look at the comments on Facebook. They tell it as it was.'

'You'll always get that negativity, especially when it's anonymous. But others believe her. Your name is mentioned—'

'Because I was driving my car when she went past. Honestly, Davina, your suspicions—'

'Stop *lying* to me.' Her scream, loaded with years of suppression, was full-throated. 'If something is wrong, we need to fix it. And to do that, I need the truth. Were you one of those boys in Loyvale Park that time she—' Davina stopped, unable to comprehend what she might have to tidy up on her husband's behalf. Marianne Mooney putting it about. Such stories. Davina had listened to them once, shared them, even instigated some of them.

'Can you honestly believe I hung around with that little whore?'

'Why not? Half the village did, if the stories are to be believed.'

'They *are* to be believed. But I wasn't part of her pathetic stable. How dare you even hint that I'd stoop so low?'

'Then what did your father mean? What did he cover up on *your* behalf?' Davina shuddered. 'Can you swear to me you never had anything to do with her?'

'I swear. She was a kid. I was hardly aware of her existence. If you remember rightly, I wasn't exactly short of girlfriends in those days.'

Or since… She almost screamed it aloud but that would give her suspicions some twisted form of validity. Suspicion was not proof. Without proof, there was no reason to confront any unpleasantness in her marriage. She had to believe her husband. Anything else was unthinkable.

CHAPTER TWENTY-EIGHT

Rachel

Voices were being raised at the front desk where Garda Roberts was on duty. Rachel could hear them from her office and the impatient rasp of the second voice was too familiar to be ignored for long. Jack Bale, it appeared, had not been afforded due recognition when he demanded to see Rachel without an appointment.

Rachel defused the situation and escorted him into her office.

'Fucking snowflakes, that's what they're training these days.' His cheeks were puffed with anger, the smell of alcohol strong on his breath.

Rachel made a conscious effort not to lean away from him. 'Sit down, Jack, and tell me why you're here,' she said.

'It's obvious why I'm here,' he snapped. 'The voice from the grave, eh? Lies, all fucking lies. It has to be stopped.'

'What on earth are you talking about?'

'Defamation. Character assassination.'

'Who's being defamed?'

'Are you telling me you haven't seen Adele Foyle's blog?'

'Her blog? No, I haven't seen it. I've other things on my mind than surfing the net. What's the problem with it?'

'The *problem*, as you call it, is a diary that Marianne Mooney filled with lies. Lies that undermine my reputation. I won't allow it to continue. I want you to release the statement that little whore made in my presence. I want it posted online and sent to the media in a press release. And that includes the rag your husband owns.'

His arrogance should not surprise her. She had seen flashes of it on other occasions. But his blatant disregard for her authority was new. That diary – she remembered the entries, the unfolding story of a young girl's troubled pregnancy and the fantasy she created around it. A fantasy that Rachel had almost believed until she read Marianne's statement, signed in the presence of Jack Bale and another guard, now deceased.

'What gives you the idea that you can come in here and make such a request?' she asked.

'It's not a request, Sergeant Darcy, it's a demand.'

'Is it, indeed?' Had alcohol affected his judgement or did he really imagine he had the authority to speak to her like that? His breath wafted towards her. She walked to the window and opened it. The noise of traffic was loud but fresh air was needed to dispel the rank smell of alcohol.

'Did you drive here?' she asked when she returned to her desk.

'Ah ha, nice one, Sergeant.' He slapped his hands off his knees. 'I walked. No need to bring out the breathalyser, so can we get back to the subject in hand?'

'We certainly can,' she snapped. 'I'm amazed that a man with your experience of Garda protocol would make such a demand.'

'It's a *demand* that you would do well to heed.' He relaxed back in the chair, legs splayed, his posture deliberately provocative. 'Your husband has skin in the game, whether you realise it or not. Far be it from me to judge a man on his past but being a junkie affected his judgement when he was a lad, especially when it came to the company he kept.'

Hot saliva filled her mouth. She resisted the urge to return to the window. 'I'm going to politely ask you to leave my office,

Jack. If you don't do so, I'll have you evicted. Please don't force me to take that action.'

He stood and bent over her desk. 'I'm warning you, Sergeant. You need to heed my advice. Discuss the matter with your husband and see what he thinks about this blog the entire village is talking about.'

Unable to remain in his company any longer and overcome by another wave of nausea, she muttered an excuse and hurried from her office to the bathroom. Garda Roberts was combing her hair before the mirror, a cascade of auburn curls that she normally tied in a formidable ponytail. She looked startled at being caught with her hands in her hair, or, perhaps, it was the sight of Rachel rushing past her into the nearest cubicle. Unable to control her heaving stomach, or the sounds she made as she vomited, Rachel leaned her head against her arms and tried to steady her breathing before she emerged. Garda Roberts was still in front of the mirror, her hair tidied, her hat sitting squarely on her head.

'Are you okay, Sergeant?' she asked.

'It's a tummy upset,' Rachel explained. 'It hit me during the night. One of those twenty-four-hour bugs. I'm over the worst of it now.'

Garda Roberts seemed convinced. At twenty-three years of age, she must look upon the possibility of Rachel being pregnant with the same disbelief she would feel if her mother announced such news. Rachel returned to her office, relieved to see the former sergeant striding through the front office and down the steps of the station.

Afraid of building up Bob's hopes and then having to dash them, Rachel had waited until he left for work this morning before taking the pregnancy test. During their first year of marriage, they had hoped it would happen. Trends had changed. Motherhood in the late thirties and early forties, while not exactly the norm, was commonplace enough for Rachel to believe she could become pregnant. No reason why it wasn't possible, the gynaecologist told them after the first year had passed. Keep trying. How enthusiastically they had followed his advice. When nothing happened they had accepted that it was not meant to be. No angst, no rancour, they had each other and that was all they needed to complete their circle. Busy… busy… and now, suddenly, drawn up short and counting backwards, she decided to check the possibility.

Positive. Nothing faint about this pink line. Rachel had been filled with disbelief. While she was thinking about other things, nature was sending out signals she had ignored until now. At forty-three she was going to become a mother. Armed with this new awareness, she was unable to understand how she had missed the signs, the slight nausea she had experienced on a few occasions, the overwhelming tiredness that she had attributed to work, the swelling and tenderness of her breasts and, latterly, her impatience with Bob's moroseness. He was bored writing about lightweight politics that never moved beyond road improvement announcements and broken promises to dredge the Loy.

Tonight, she had planned to cook a celebratory dinner. This longed-for news would lift his spirits, give him a new focus. Imagining his delight, Rachel splashed cold water over her face and rinsed out her mouth. She stared at her reflection. Where was the glow she had experienced earlier? The hormonal aura that reflected her happiness? Washed away by an undertow. The news she wanted to share with her husband must wait. It could not be contaminated by innuendo and the jarring suspicions Jack Bale had left in his wake.

*

Such a summer. The grass in their garden had been charred to stubble and the sun, lingering long into the evenings, drew them out of doors to watch the twilight settle. Bob had barbecued steaks and opened wine. She drank water instead. He made no comment when she told him she needed a clear head for tomorrow, when she had to speak at a conference on road safety.

'Jack Bale called to see me this afternoon,' she said.

'Checking on you again, I presume?'

'Who knows what goes on in his mind? He sent you his regards.'

'Ha.' Bob arched his eyebrows, his one vanity, plucked regularly to prevent them forming a unibrow.

'He claims the two of you go back a long way.'

'We don't go way back anywhere,' he replied. 'I detested him when I was a kid and I like him even less now, if it's possible.'

'Why is that?'

He laughed, a short, mirthless guffaw. 'He was a bully and a toad when he was a sergeant. In deep with the big boys. Now, he's a closed trap. All that information inside his thick head and it's impossible to prise it loose.'

Poor Bob. Dragged back from what he called 'serious journalism' to revive the ailing family newspaper, stymied by the Reedstown old guard with their secrets, their winks and nods, their secret deals and untraceable brown envelopes.

'Do you hate being back here?' she asked.

He smiled at her before replying. 'I deal with it by being happy with you.'

'Is that sustainable?'

'As long as you love me, yes.'

He never talked about his troubled youth, apart from one night on their honeymoon when his defences came down. They drank too much wine over their meal and, back in their bedroom, he admitted that he had been bullied in his teens. It destroyed his confidence but drugs restored it, or so he believed until his parents persuaded him to enter rehab. His decision to begin afresh in New York had been the making of him and he left Reedstown when he was nineteen without a backward glance.

'Bale came to the station to complain about Adele Foyle's blog. Have you seen it?' she asked.

'Who hasn't?' He held the wine bottle towards her, then, when she shook her head, topped up his own glass. 'Adele Foyle certainly knows how to throw a grenade into a crowd. That diary has gone viral on social media.'

The chatter of starlings in the bushes was a shrill scold. Rachel shivered and wrapped her pashmina over her shoulders.

'Did you know Marianne?' she asked.

'I remember her.'

'From what I've heard, she had a reputation of sorts.'

'There were stories…' His voice trailed away as he cut into his steak. She had hardly touched the food he had prepared for her but he did not appear to notice.

'Stories?' she prompted.

'Just stories,' he said. 'I never saw any evidence to back them up.'

"You think they were lies, deliberately planted?'

'Who knows? If so, I wasn't involved in spreading them. Not that I'm giving myself any kudos for doing the decent thing. Far from it. I was too stoned to know what was going on under my nose. Marianne Mooney wasn't even in my range of vision.'

He was lying to her. This was a judgement based on her years of experience in the force; yet, in the next breath, she rejected it. She could not allow herself to be caught in a web spun by Jack

Bale. Skin in the game. Why should that phrase undermine her? *We go back a long way, me and Bobby Molloy… Way, way back…* Jack Bale smirking when he said it and she had been afraid to analyse the implied meaning in his words.

She pressed her hand against her stomach. Was that how it began, this protective urge that she had never experienced until now?

'Do you believe her claim? The three blind mice, that's what she calls them. Or do you think Shane Reagan was responsible for her pregnancy?'

She was watching his reaction, as she'd been trained to do in interrogations. Recognising her behaviour, she wanted to sink her face in her hands and cry. The silence stretched between them, taut as elastic, before it snapped. Even the starlings had stopped their chatter and appeared to be waiting, as she was, for his reply.

'I knew Shane.' He cleared his throat before he spoke. 'I used to see them together. They were mad about each other but his mother left Reedstown in a hurry. She was originally from Australia, so she just headed back home.'

'So, you're convinced Shane was the father.'

'To think otherwise is to give credibility to that diary. Marianne Mooney is dead. It's highly unlikely that the truth will ever be known. Adele Foyle told me she'd been in contact with you. She didn't realise we were married.'

'She must have been surprised when you told her.'

'What did she want?'

'That's confidential information, Bob.'

'Come on, Rachel. This is off the record. I'm not going to splash it over the front page.'

'I know that.'

'Then tell me?'

'She showed me the diary.'

'You've read it?'

'All of it. She reported that it had been stolen but she obviously found it again. It's shocking and heartbreaking but I had to make a decision as to its validity. Jack Bale convinced me that such a crime never took place in Reedstown.'

'Well, if anyone should know, it would be him.' His hand was unsteady as he refilled his glass and the wine, slopping over the edge, ran red across the table.

The fruity aroma wafted towards her. Her heightened awareness of smell was another indication that she was on the brink of something new and wonderful. She had to tell him soon. A week ago, she would have considered it an unthinkable act to keep such wonderful news from him. But not tonight when the atmosphere between them was strained... by what? A frisson she could feel but was unable to control or understand.

Later, while he slept, she traced her fingers across the firm slopes of his chest and forced Jack Bale from her mind. *Way, way back...* A meaningless expression that could never be interpreted as a warning. Skin in the game, equally so. She was overreacting, her hormones running riot, her judgement impaired by her pregnancy. She grimaced, knowing she would vehemently reject this suggestion if it was applied to any other pregnant woman. Still sleepless in the small hours, she wondered why happiness, truly fulfilling happiness, had always evaded her until now. And why, when it was so firmly in her grasp, she could already feel it stealing away from her.

CHAPTER TWENTY-NINE

Adele

The incriminating evidence arrived in a parcel postmarked Colorado. It contained a photograph album, so many pages to turn but only two people were visible in each photograph. They had been taken in Arizona, where Daniel had been attending a conference at Greendene Petro's headquarters. He had mentioned the weekend conference to Adele during a previous phone call and she had promptly forgotten about it. A bad mistake, she realised as she stared at the photographs of him and Madison Fox seated together in a vast conference hall, elbows resting side by side. They were laughing together at some activity on stage, their faces turned towards each other. In another photograph, they projected the corporate gloss of authority as they addressed the audience in a coordinated PowerPoint presentation. Adele had tried to remember the theme of the speech, as if it mattered when her thoughts were racing chaotically towards an inevitable conclusion. Something about fracking and how it could eventually cause earthquakes or have some other seismic impact on the environment. Well, they were right on that one, she thought grimly as she viewed the rest of the album. The bars and restaurants they visited, the nightclub where they ended up afterwards, their faces slashed with laser beams, arms akimbo. Madison's flamboyant red hair was shorter than Adele remembered, its self-assured spikes a conduit to her crackling energy. Adele stared at her walking into a restaurant with Daniel. She was wearing pink, her dress short and figure-hugging, her heels as high as gravity permitted. She reminded Adele of a flamingo, leggy and vicious.

Daniel had his excuses ready when he Skyped, his terse expression clearly visible when Adele displayed the photographs to him. She also held the accompanying letter up for his inspection.

Madison Fox always gets when she wants. Be wary of her. This is just a small example of what is going on behind your back. Be warned.
  With kindest regards from
  A friend Who Cares.

'Someone is bent on making mischief,' he said. 'Six of us went to Phoenix. We were part of a team and we spent all our time together. Those photographs were cropped, Photoshopped, whatever. Madison is a friend, nothing more, nothing less—'

'That's not what it looks like from my side of the screen.'

'That's because your vision is distorted.'

'My vision is twenty-twenty. It's obvious there's something going on between you—'

'And if there is, which there *isn't*, who'd blame me?' he snapped. 'I'm amazed you have the time to feel jealous considering all you ever do is blog that diary and deal with all the crap it throws up. You make promises about joining me and break them without a second thought for my feelings. Your obsession with your mother is the most important thing in your life. I don't even come a poor second any more.'

She had never seen him lose his temper until now. She pulled back from the screen, aware that everything was changing between them. Obsession. The word was cruel yet justified, though Adele would have called it her passion. Maybe that was the problem. Passion was the prerogative of the living and she had transferred all that emotional energy on to a dead girl, leaving him clinging to empty promises of a reunion. Soon... soon... how long is a piece of string?

How little he knew about her life. He should have been the first to know about the theft of the diary and the deliberate wiping of her computer. If she had told him, he would have insisted on her leaving Reedstown. Would she have had the will to withstand the pressure he put on her? Now it was too late and the argument that followed had a preordained pattern, as if the decision to end their engagement had already been made. Their future together ending on a storm of accusations and tears. Daniel's tears, not hers. Adele was beyond tears. She was suspended in some limbo land, waiting for a solution she no longer believed was possible.

After he ended the call, she pinched her arm. Yes, she could still feel pain... but little else. Was it that easy to fall out of love? A tap turning off with a quick flick of the wrist. No drips.

She searched the photographs for a clue that would convince her they had been manipulated as Daniel insisted; truncated arms or background figures that could belong to a jostling crowd – but all she saw was a cameo with two faces, their eyes feasting greedily on each other.

When she phoned the Garda station to check for an update on the break-in, Sergeant Darcy advised her to close down the blog for her own safety. She did not state it quite so bluntly, more like a gentle encouragement to let the dead rest and move on with her new life in Colorado. What new life? Adele clamped her lips on the question. Sergeant Darcy was unlikely to be interested in the fact that her engagement to Daniel was over.

The sergeant was right about her leaving Reedstown. Yesterday, a man had spat at Adele in the supermarket. He came right up to her when she was at the fruit section and aimed the globule at her face. He was her own age, his muscular body primed from the gym, his language gathered from the gutter. She had been accosted on Main Street by two elderly women, who had once belonged to the Thorns. Gently but firmly they had told her she was on the highway to hell. And she was being watched. Eyes on her spine, the back of her neck. A tingling nervousness that convinced her she was a lightning rod where danger was concerned.

CHAPTER THIRTY

Julie

Davina's constant phone calls to complain about the blog were disturbing Julie. Their memories of the past were so different and she, unlike Davina, was scalded with guilt. Each time she read another entry, she imagined the pages blotched by tears as Marianne Mooney scribbled frantically and in secret late into the night.

She had been one of those bullies. Bullying was not an attribute she would previously have used to describe herself but the diary had forced her to confront her younger self. That perplexing, ugly time, conveniently forgotten until now. Davina laughed scornfully when Julie compared their behaviour to a 'virus' but, to Julie, it seemed an apt description.

Forgotten incidents kept surfacing. Marianne Mooney's expression as she endured the remarks and open mockery that followed her along school corridors; the taunts that filled the empty space created around her in the school canteen. Her name becoming a byword for graffiti, splashed on the walls of the school bicycle shed and the walls of her house. How had Julie believed that was funny, fair or justified? One memory in particular became more clearly defined with each appearance. Marianne and Keith Lewis standing outside the snooker hall in the village. She had been wearing a floral-patterned dress with bell sleeves and a flouncy hem that ended just above her ankles. Very retro seventies, which had been her style thing. Her chunky blue clogs gave her extra height, yet she still looked tiny against Keith's tall frame. He bent closer to her and grabbed her hat, slapped it on his own head and laughed out at her from under the floppy brim.

'Bitch slut.' Davina had been convinced they were going to kiss, as had Julie. The girl's lips had been slightly parted, as if she was about to offer her mouth to Keith; but, looking back, what Julie now remembered was Marianne's embarrassment as she strained away from him, her skinny body almost flattened against the wall. Such a configuration had not seemed possible then. Not with handsome, swaggering Keith Lewis, who had held her hat out of reach while she struggled to snatch it from him. Shane Reagan, who saw what was happening as he came towards them, broke into a run. Marianne managed to grab her hat back and go towards him, anxious to prevent any contact between the two boys— no, Julie corrected herself, not boys but men, young, virile and dangerous. Davina had hissed a few more insults as Marianne walked away, insults that would later become the template for the gossip that swirled around her when her pregnancy was revealed.

Liam had also been present, observing the tableau as if he were a voyeur and it was being played out for his pleasure. In those days he had been Keith's shadow, a skinny boy with acne, and mortified by his mother's religious zeal. Who would believe that he would fill out into a compact sturdiness or that his skin would be blemish-free as he grew into a confident, driven businessman? So confident that he had persuaded Julie she would be happy with him for the rest of her life.

Liam was as incensed as Davina over the diaries but had failed in his efforts to serve an injunction against the blog. Documented evidence existed that his mother *did* run a mother and baby home in Inisada and that Marianne Mooney delivered her baby there. No overlooking hard facts. But that had only added to his anger.

Julie had seen evidence of the mother and baby home shortly after she moved into Holywell. It was kept in an abandoned building at the end of the garden. The den had been locked for years but Julie had found the key. She had partied there with Davina when they were teenagers and Gloria was away on tour. Drink and drugs, the risks they took then. How confident they had been that they knew it all. Nothing could touch them yet she had been carried from that den suffering from alcoholic poisoning and hospitalised. The arrogance of youth, she had shivered as she entered the den and knelt to examine the boxes and crates that had been salvaged from the mother and baby home. According to Liam, the big house had been gutted so they must have been stored in an outside building. She had been tempted to leave everything alone and relock the door but curiosity got the better of her. She had opened boxes filled with Gloria's unsold books and meditation CDs. Presentation packs of candles and medals were covered in a film of soot. She found stacks of photographs of her mother-in-law in a trance-like state, her eyes gazing skywards, her hands joined in prayer or raised in benediction. Such a strong face, her eyes slightly protruding, her firm mouth softened as if she was greeting a familiar apparition. Julie was tempted to light a match and finish what the original fire had been unable to do.

A small safe was hidden behind the boxes. She tried various combinations to open it and finally succeeded when she used the date Gloria had died. The first document she removed was the last will and testament of Charlotte Greerson, who had willed her house and land to Gloria. A second document authorised Gloria to establish the House of Atonement. Photographs of newborn babies were filed together. Julie opened letters. One was from adoptive parents in Ohio, another from a couple in Atlanta. The photographs that accompanied these letters showed the trinity of adoptive parents and their babies. She delved deeper and found copies of birth certificates and travel itineraries. Christy Lewis's name seemed to leap from the pages of one letter. He had written to Gloria from Boston, where he was on a trade mission. He had taken the time to call on Baby Malcolm's adoptive parents and was happy to report that everything had gone according to plan. Another letter reassured Gloria that the fuss over that 'other incident' had died down. The girl would be in Inisada shortly.

Julie had staggered when she stood, pins and needles running through her feet. She closed the safe and surrounded it again with boxes. Her skin felt clogged with secrets as she hurried from the building and headed straight to the bathroom to shower. She had left that echoing space and never entered it again. Liam had promised to sort out the material and the building was knocked down. The ground on which it stood was now a flagstoned patio. She had looked upon the memorabilia as relics of her mother-in-law's deluded ego but, now, reading about that mother and baby home, she was tormented by the suspicion that she had let valuable information slip heedlessly through her hands.

She counselled women in her clinic, listened when they spoke about the trauma they experienced when they searched for babies taken from them at birth and persuaded against their will to hand over for adoption. A moat of bureaucracy in their way, the drawbridge closed against their pain, their need for information.

CHAPTER THIRTY-ONE

Rachel

Breathing smoothly, Rachel jogged up Summit Road. She was clocking up kilometres on her pedometer and should reach her target today. She used to run marathons before she was transferred to Reedstown and she was familiar with the rush, the high, all those released endorphins making the aches and the strains worthwhile. She drank from her water bottle and shook the remaining water over her face. Bunches of flowers had been left outside Hillcrest. Rachel had heard that this was happening. People were turning what they believed to be the birthplace of Marianne Mooney into a shrine to her memory. She could only imagine Davina's reaction.

An hour later she was behind her desk reading a registered letter in her in-tray. Marked 'Personal/Important Information' and posted in Reedstown, it had arrived in the morning post. Her heart, when she read it, beat to a rhythm that could not be good for the fragile life she carried.

Dear Sergeant Darcy
*   I write to you as a serving politician who has always afforded the* Garda Síochána *my utmost respect. I have always maintained a professional distance between myself and our*

police force but am now compelled to make contact with you on an urgent matter of concern for you and, also, for me.

I'm deeply disturbed and distressed by the antics of a certain young woman, namely Adele Foyle, who claims she is revealing information about an incident that happened in Reedstown many years ago. I am appalled each time I read another outrageous entry on her blog. She came like a plague into our village and her lies must be silenced.

So far, for reasons best known to yourself, you have refused to publish the statement signed by Marianne Mooney at Reedstown Garda Station on the night of 3 April 1994, despite Jack Bale's request that you do so. Therefore, I'm forced to write this letter to you for two reasons. Firstly, you have the means to control the lies that are being spread by Ms Foyle. Secondly, your failure to name those lies could have dire consequences for the man you love. I fear it is only a matter of time before your husband's name is linked to an imaginary crime. If that happens, it will destroy not only his newspaper but also your reputation as a sergeant.

Guilt by association has a powerful pull and my son's untarnished reputation could also be damaged for no other reason than that he once befriended your husband for a brief and oft-regretted period. Drugs were always an issue with Bob Molloy. I'm aware that young people like experimenting with danger. They enjoy disregarding the rules but usually they come out from the dark side, chastened, wiser and ready to assume their responsibilities as sensible adults. Not your husband, though. He was unable to control his habit. This led to a lapse of judgement and he was seen regularly in the company of Marianne Mooney. The girl was highly promiscuous from the time she was thirteen. She looked older than her years and she certainly behaved that way too. Of *course, she became pregnant and concocted this outrageous story of a gang-rape. Believe me, it never happened. She finally confessed the truth to Jack Bale, who sorted it out in a manner that most benefitted the young people at its centre.*

I don't need to remind you of your responsibilities. For no other reason than to save your husband's reputation, release that statement and end this farce once and for all.

Sincerely yours
Christopher Lewis

The noise in the Garda station faded to a dull rumble as she absorbed the threat. Yesterday, on Main Street, he had greeted her in passing. His complexion was flushed, an unnatural ruddiness that made her wonder if he was suffering from high blood pressure. It was after five thirty in the evening; the post would have been collected by then. Nothing in his demeanour had suggested that he had written a letter designed to tear her husband's reputation to shreds. A letter he believed would force her into making a decision based on the ugly reality of self-survival.

She tore the letter into fragments and stuffed them into her pocket. She would burn it when she returned home. Bob would never know that she must choose between Marianne Mooney's desperate writings and the statement she had made in the threatening presence of Jack Bale.

It was dark when she parked her car a short distance from Hillcrest and walked down the lane to The Lodge. She rang the doorbell twice before he answered, his mouth opening with shock when he recognised her.

'Ah, Sergeant, this is a surprise.' He quickly regained his composure. 'As you're out of uniform, I assume this is a social call?'

'Correct, Mr Lewis. May I come in?'

'Of course. You're more than welcome to my humble abode.'

'As a humble abode, it's impressive,' she said. 'Would this have been the original house where Marianne Mooney lived?'

'It was, indeed.'

'I can see why the land would have been of interest to you.'

'Ah… I see you're familiar with the diary's lies. I can assume you, Sergeant, I bought this property at above its market value and the owner was mightily relieved to sell it to me.' He switched off the television and swept his hand towards an armchair. 'Please be seated. Now that you're off duty, may I call you Rachel?'

'If you wish.'

'And may I also offer you a drink?'

'No thank you. I won't be staying long. I was sorry to hear you were in hospital. I hope you're feeling better now.'

'Much better, thank you. How's Bob?'

'As busy as ever.'

'I'm glad to hear it. Success was never built on idleness.' He settled into the armchair opposite her and folded his hands over his stomach. 'Now that we've got the pleasantries out of the way, we can get to the crux of your visit and discuss my letter.'

'No, that's not why I'm here. But, you're right about this being an informal visit. I want to talk to you about Gloria Thornton.'

'Ah, Gloria. A mysterious and imaginative woman. What can I tell you about her that you don't already know?'

'Adele Foyle's blog refers to the adoption of babies to the States.'

'It refers to many things. Frankly, Rachel, as I've already stated, that diary is an outrageous concoction of lies.'

'Regarding these babies who were taken out of Ireland, I wonder how that was achieved. From my enquiries, the House of

Atonement was a private enterprise, yet there is documentation available that claims these adoptions were legitimate. If I were to begin a Garda inquiry to trace the origins of that documentation, I'm certain it would lead the investigation team to some very interesting conclusions.'

'What exactly are you implying?' he asked.

Did you traffic babies and take your cut from wealthy Americans who adopted them? How many were sold? Did you keep tabs on them after Gloria died or did you conveniently forget they existed? Such questions demanded to be asked but how could she frame what was pure speculation on her part?

'I'm sorry if I'm upsetting you, Mr Lewis,' she said. 'You refer to the diary as lies. I've read its entire contents. So far, Adele Foyle is rigorously editing what she publishes on her blog. But some entries, unpublished so far, refer to visits you made to the House of Atonement. Can you tell me what you were doing there? I'm interested in finding out about your relationship with Gloria Thornton.'

'You are treading on very dangerous ground.' His glacial gaze, the aggressive tilt of his head – she had forgotten how formidable he could look.

'The ground on which I stand is quite solid, Mr Lewis. But, regarding that unfortunate letter you sent to me, I'd like to know why are you demanding I release a statement that was taken from Marianne Mooney under what could certainly be called coercion?'

'What gives you the idea that you can come here and question me like this. It's highly irregular—'

'As was your decision to send that letter to me. You could be accused of interfering with police procedure.'

'Only if you report me. And I doubt you'll do that.' His ruddiness had been replaced by an alarming pallor but his voice was still strong. 'Every wretched word written by that capricious little slut was untrue. Let me pass on some sound advice to you, *Sergeant*. Shut your mouth and keep it closed or you might find you've bitten off more that you can chew.'

'Don't ever threaten me—'

'Threaten you? My dear girl, if I were to threaten you, you'd know all about it. That diary is a fake and the truth will be revealed soon enough. I'd advise you to go home now and forget this conversation ever took place.'

'And I would advise you to leave my husband alone. I won't hesitate to bring the full rigour of the law down on you if you ever write a letter like that to me again.'

He was gripping the arms of his chair and breathing heavily when she left, unable any longer to look at his ravaged face where every secret he had ever hoarded was reflected in his eyes.

CHAPTER THIRTY-TWO

Davina

The midnight hour had passed and Davina was still awake. She sighed and moved to the edge of the bed when Keith flung his arm across her, his sleep undisturbed by fears that the past had a way of fingering the present. Christy had brought him up to believe he was invincible. A belief that had transferred into arrogance and the confidence to believe he had no reason to fear those lies.

This morning she had found three more bouquets of flowers propped up in front of the wall outside Hillcrest, handwritten notes with saccharine messages of sympathy attached to them. The words 'In memory of Marianne. R.I.P.' had been written in red on one note while another was covered with emoji love hearts. Unable to cope with the avalanche of comment, Davina had closed down Reedstown Reminiscences. That hadn't stopped the publicity and Hillcrest, having been incorrectly referenced as the meeting hall used by the Thorns, was attracting sightseers. The crazies and the curious, spying through her windows and trampling over her garden. They posted photographs of her house on Facebook and Instagram only they called it Cult Cottage or Thorns' Thatch or other ridiculous, made-up names.

Marianne Mooney's lies were being shared on other sites. New platforms were evolving all the time, some for the express purpose of debunking the diary, others claiming it was shining a light on a hidden scandal. What was Liam Thornton doing? He was supposed to take control of this situation. His mother's reputation was being trashed and he seemed incapable of putting a stop to it. But social media was unstoppable. She had seen cartoons of three mice with blindfolds on sites that also featured three monkeys, paws over ears, mouth, eyes. The Three Musketeers had been Photoshopped, their faces left blank and some wit had encouraged viewers to fill in the spaces with the features of the guilty three.

She left Keith's side and went to the window. The blinds at the back of The Lodge were closed but the light in the living room was on. Christy must still be up. Like his son, he was a sound sleeper, and he was usually in bed by eleven o'clock. Although he rejected his cardiac specialist's opinion that he had experienced a panic attack, he had been going to bed even earlier since he was discharged from hospital. Davina, who knew him better than anyone, understood his fury over his diagnosis. It undermined his credibility. His heart attack had challenged his belief that he was indestructible but he had accepted it as something over which he had no control. A panic attack, however, smacked of weakness and he had warned her and Keith not to mention it to anyone.

He was visible against the blind, a shadow shape that played with light. As she watched it seemed as if the image shifted and divided into two. It changed again as Christy moved away and was lost from sight. She should check on him, see what was keeping him up so late, but he would probably tell her to mind her own business, as he did yesterday afternoon when she called into The Lodge.

He had been sitting at the table in his living room, a writing pad open in front of him, his hand held protectively over a letter he was writing. Unable to banish the memory of his bitterness in the hospital when he had looked at his son, who was supposed to talk to Davina but never did – and was still refusing to do so – she needed someone to understand her fear.

'Why do you want Keith to clean up his own shit?' she had said.

'What do you mean?' Christy had seemed startled, genuinely so. He was bleary-eyed and flushed, his once-strong features bloated. It was obvious that he had forgotten the words he had breathed at his son.

'That's what you told him in the hospital. Don't you remember? You said there was a storm coming.'

'I've no memory of saying anything of the sort.' His waspish tone lacked conviction. 'If I did, it must have been the drugs talking. God knows they pumped enough into me—'

'You were referring to that blog. It's what you were reading when you suffered your panic attack.'

'I *didn't* suffer—'

'Christy, be honest with me. Is there any truth to those diary entries?'

'Don't be ridiculous—'

'Tell me… *tell* me!' Her cries had pitched her fear into the open. 'Who knows what information Adele Foyle is gathering? Keith won't talk to me. You know what he's like. Was he hanging around with that little slut?'

'That little slut, as you call her, is not your problem.' He had gathered himself away from her, frightened by her loss of control. 'If Adele Foyle continues spreading her poison, I know exactly how to manage the situation.'

'You don't understand social media, Christy. Those entries have gone viral. They're trending on Twitter…' She was filled with a crazed desire to shout: *If those diary entries are true and Marianne Mooney was raped, who do you think those three men would be?*

He stood and held her upper arms, his touch firm, reassuring. 'Go back to your house, Davina. When I need your wisdom, I'll ask for it, but it's not necessary on this occasion.' He had fobbed off her questions, silenced her protests and sent her away. He left soon afterwards, driving too fast down Summit Road, as he always did. His plan, if he had one, would be played close to his chest.

She must relax and stop allowing insidious suspicions to prey on her mind. Back in bed, she drifted off to sleep and awoke again into the same spiralling thought process. Logic and common sense were the losers in the early hours. Unable to stay still and listen to Keith's murmuring snores, she slipped on her dressing gown and made her way along the garden path to The Lodge. She unlocked the back door and called Christy's name. No answer. The television was still on, canned laughter, applause. He must have fallen asleep on his recliner. His laptop was open on the kitchen table and she was not surprised to see that he had been checking the latest blog entry. It was now being called *The Marianne Diary*. Adding a *The* in front of those pathetic entries had given it status, more gravitas.

The atmosphere in the small kitchen was claustrophobic. The plots that were hatched here when it was his constituency clinic, the decisions taken, ambitions expanded, hopes dashed. Davina watching, listening, learning the political ropes until she became the backroom guru. The planner who laid down the foundations for each successful election campaign. It was just a matter of time before Christy retired. When that happened, she would be ready to step into his shoes. The Power Couple, shoulder to shoulder with her husband until she outgrew him. But now this uncertainty, this suspicion, the sense that she was losing control was growing stronger every time she read another

diary entry. Checking the latest one, she held on to the edge of
the table for support.

> *'Chinese,' Shane said. I remember his voice shaking and the*
> *blood on his hands as he held the box up to the light for me*
> *to see. He said it was a clue. The writing on the package was*
> *weird, all squiggles and squares and symbols like the way*
> *Amy Zhou writes her name on her copybooks.*

She ignored the sudden urge to return to bed and pull the duvet
over her head. This time she was not leaving until Christy answered her questions. She moved towards the living room and
opened the door. Another blast of laughter from the television
hit her. Something was wrong. She could feel it on her skin, a
prickling sensation that sharpened her awareness as she looked
towards the recliner. Christy's legs were splayed, as if he had
drifted into a half-slumber while watching television, but she
could see that his stillness was absolute. She shook him, shouted
his name as if the force of her voice would bring him back.

Unable to comprehend that he was dead when he looked
so relaxed, she searched for a pulse, convinced it would still be
beating. His head lolled to one side. His body was warm, flaccid,
his face peaceful enough to convince her that death when it
arrived had caught him unawares.

CHAPTER THIRTY-THREE

Rachel

Rachel sat ramrod straight between her colleagues. Her uniform felt tight, too warm for this crowded church. It had been a long service and throats were being cleared, attention drifting. The nausea had been persistent throughout the ceremony and she was afraid she would have to make an undignified bolt down the aisle before the requiem mass drew to a conclusion. Sweat broke out on the back of her neck and she swallowed hard as she focused all her attention on the coffin where the remains of Christy Lewis lay.

Three days had passed since she stood in his home and officially pronounced him dead in the presence of his son and daughter-in-law. The news had spread quickly through Reedstown and Bob was in the office by sunrise preparing the former politician's obituary. A second heart attack. The doctor believed he could have been sleeping when it struck. No pause between life and death, terror stilled before it could latch its claws onto him.

'Unlike my mother,' Keith had said, his boyish good looks in stark contrast to his red-rimmed eyes. 'Cancer took her before her time but at least she was prepared.'

Dazed with shock and disbelief, Davina had made her witness statement, the shake in her hand as she signed it making her signature almost illegible.

Today, she looked majestic in black. Pale but composed. She must be pleased with the turnout. The crowd included top politicians, who formed a guard of honour as Christy's body was borne shoulder-high into the church. A row of uniformed, high-ranking members of the Garda force were also in attendance.

Keith Lewis approached the altar to deliver the eulogy. His ability to hide a party political broadcast within the speech had to be admired, Rachel thought as he described how his father inspired his son to follow in his footsteps.

'I was still in my teens when I accompanied him on one of his first trade missions to China,' he said. 'I saw at first hand his unstinting commitment to furthering the interests of Irish companies abroad. Recently, I had the pleasure of leading a similar trade mission to China. He came with us and the warmth of the welcome we received from everyone we met was due in no small measure to my father's ability to establish not just business contacts but lifetime friendships. Today, those friends have travelled from many countries to celebrate his life and honour his memory.'

The church filled with incense as Christy's coffin, covered with a single, tasteful spray of white roses, was shouldered by the pall bearers. Keith and Liam Thornton, the tallest of the six, brought up the rear.

Once the coffin had been placed inside the hearse, the solemnity that marked the ceremony ended. Laughter was heard, subdued but audible. Mourners crowded around Keith, shaking hands, offering condolences. Rachel turned to find Julie Thornton beside her.

'How are you, Julie?' she asked.

'All good. Cherish what we have. We never know when it can be taken from us.'

'True. Keith gave quite an impressive eulogy.'

'Very impressive. If you must tell a lie, make it a whopper.' Julie's tone was non-committal. 'That goes for the obituary Bob wrote. He couldn't stand the man but needs must. I was glad to see him getting together again with Liam and Keith. Life's too short to allow any unpleasantness from the past to dictate our behaviour.'

'Sorry, Julie, what do you mean?'

'Didn't he mention the meeting?' Julie sounded surprised. 'He met up with Liam and Keith to discuss publicity for the festival?' She took a step back as Keith joined them and turned towards an elderly woman, who had been trying to attract her attention.

'Thank you so much for coming, Sergeant Darcy.' He clasped her hand between his own and smiled. 'My father would have been honoured by the attendance from the Gardai.'

'We do our duty when called upon.'

'And do so with great dignity. Where's Bob? I want to thank him for that excellent obituary he wrote for the *Review*. I know he crossed swords at times with my father but the relationship between the press and the state is not meant to be an easy one. Despite the negative coverage he occasionally received, Christy had great respect for his integrity.'

Rachel's gorge rose. Did he know about the letter? Was he playing cat and mouse with her, uttering meaningless platitudes when they both knew she had been faced with an impossible choice? The funeral director hovered at a polite distance and nodded at Keith. The cortège was ready to leave for the crematorium.

'Will you join us for lunch afterwards?' Keith asked.

'I'm afraid not. I've a busy afternoon ahead of me.'

The cremation ceremony was short. As it neared its end, a violinist played 'The Lark Ascending' and a selection of photographs spanning Christy's life were flashed onto a screen. Listening to the notes rising and falling, Rachel imagined the swoop of a lark as it played with the breeze, the joyous pitch lifting it upwards into the clear, unpolluted air.

Photographs from the recent Chinese trip that Keith mentioned in his eulogy filled the screen. On that occasion Christy was playing second fiddle to his son, but photographs from his earlier trip showed a younger-looking Christy posing at the Great Wall and outside an elaborate temple. Keith was standing between his parents, a cigarette held nonchalantly between his fingers.

She had killed his father. No need for a gun or a knife. Just a battering of words, especially the unspoken ones they had both been afraid to utter. In saner moments, Rachel knew that the official verdict was the correct one and Christy had suffered a second heart attack. But she was unable to banish the memory of their last bitter exchange and now, as she watched the montage of photographs, her breath felt laboured with suspicion. Chinese lettering, its vertical lines, squares, angles, squiggles... she was making a preposterous connection, yet it refused to go away.

'I need to check something in the *Review* archives,' she said as Bob drove them away from the crematorium.

'No problem.' He glanced across at her. 'If you're busy, I can check it for you?'

'It's complicated. I'll do it myself.'

'Will you have time for a coffee in the Kasket afterwards?'

'Afraid not. I'll be catching up all day.'

'Me too. Some funeral, eh?'

'It certainly was. Julie said you were at a meeting in her house recently. You never mentioned it.'

'Didn't I? That's the problem these days. We never have time to sit down and have a decent conversation.' He grimaced across at her. 'Just as well it was a cremation. Otherwise, a stake would have been necessary to keep that man down.'

Had Adele searched only for evidence on the dates after her mother's presumed assault or had she searched backwards, as Rachel was doing? She exhaled sharply as she read a headline on the front page. *Politician Denies Chinese Junket Accusation.* A member of the opposition had claimed that Christy Lewis used taxpayers' money to fund a family holiday in China with his wife and son. The photographs Rachel had seen in the crematorium had been used to illustrate the news item. She checked the date the newspaper was published. Two weeks before the alleged assault on Marianne Mooney took place. She must keep using the word 'alleged'. Otherwise, she would lose her objectivity. Where was the proof that a cigarette packet found at the scene of a crime was anything other than the delusion of a distraught child? If Adele Foyle came to her with such a tenuous connection, she would reject it out of hand.

She continued scanning old newspapers. Keith was photographed regularly, sometimes alone, sometimes with friends. Three young men at a rock festival, stupid, inebriated grins, beer cans in hand, tents in the background. They were photographed at the Reedstown annual scramble, black leather, boots, helmets under their arms as they posed beside their motorbikes. She read the caption underneath. *Best friends Keith Lewis, Bob Molloy and Liam Thornton preparing for the big challenge.*

Shrinking back from the screen, she recognised Bob's swift confident stride as he entered the basement. His hands on her shoulders, that reassuringly familiar touch when he asked if she had found the information she needed.

She nodded, unable to reply. 'I have to get back to work. Another emergency. We'll talk later.'

'Everything okay?' Jessica called out as Rachel left the office.

'All good.' She forced herself to slow down and smile at the receptionist. How could she sound so calm when she was tormented by doubts? By unbelievable suspicions that seemed to have formed beneath some slimy fungus, its spores multiplying.

The red sky had spent its rage and a twilight haze was settling over the garden but she had no desire to go outside. She cooked while Bob chased television channels, unable to decide if he wanted to watch news, sports or a nature documentary.

'Why did you attend Christy's funeral?' she asked when they sat down to eat. 'You detested him yet you wrote a glowing obituary about him. It seems so hypocritical.'

'Hypocritical?' At last she had his attention.

'From what you've always told me, Christy was a gombeen politician whose only interests were his own. You believe Keith is cut from the same cloth. You loathe both of them so I'm trying to understand why you would write that obituary or attend his funeral.'

'Christy Lewis's obituary was written years ago by my father and filed away until the appropriate time. I just updated it. As for the funeral, if everyone allowed their personal feelings to stand in the way of respecting the dead, there'd be a lot of empty churches. What's brought this on?'

'What happened to make you dislike the Lewis's so much? And Liam, too?'

'That's water under the bridge—'

'You told me you were bullied when you were in your teens. Were Keith and Liam responsible?'

'What does it matter?'

'I want to understand. They were your friends—'

'Just for a while.'

'Obviously, they bullied you.'

'Christ, Rachel, you make me sound like a wimp. So, I took a few wallops, some insults. The usual rite of passage. Can we drop the subject, please?'

'Why did they treat you like that?'

'Oh, that's a classic one, Rachel. Blame the victim, not the bullies.'

She was a skilled interrogator, yet she was unable to find the right words to ask her husband why he felt such intense loathing for the two men who used to be his closest friends. All she could do was blurt out her dreaded suspicion.

'Had it anything to do with Marianne Mooney?'

'*What?*' Unable to disguise his shock, he recoiled from the question.

'She was bullied, also. Those rumours about her—'

'I'd nothing to do with spreading them.'

'I believe you, but…'

'But what?' he asked. 'Where exactly is this conversation going?'

'Were those stories about her started by your friends?'

'How often must I say it… they were *not* my friends.' He was out of the chair and pacing, his food forgotten.

She, too, gave up pretending to eat. 'I saw photographs of the three of you together in the archives today. You seemed like such a close-knit group.'

'Is that what you were checking?' The rush of colour to his cheeks added to her unease.

'No, I came upon them by accident.'

'What *were* you checking?'

'Remember the montage of photographs we saw at the crematorium?'

'Get to the point,' he snapped.

'There was one of Keith with a cigarette—' She stopped and allowed the silence to lengthen.

'So?' His impatience was palpable, yet this was a time-standing-still instant when it was still possible to end this conversation and protect what was precious between them.

'It was taken when he was in China. In Marianne's diary she claims Shane Reagan found a cigarette packet with foreign lettering in that cottage. I checked when Keith was in China. It was two weeks before she claims she was assaulted.'

'Ah.' He slumped back into an armchair. 'A cigarette packet with foreign lettering? *Seriously*, Rachel.' He averted his head, as if he was offended by the sight of her. 'You think my feelings towards them are connected in some way with her… that I'm in the frame… Jesus, Rachel? What are you suggesting?'

'I'm trying to understand what is at the heart of this visceral hatred you feel towards them.'

'Drugs.' This sounded like a statement, not an explanation.

'You were dealing?' she asked.

'That was the charge.'

'So, you have a record?'

'No. The charge was dropped. Big favour from Jack Bale but had it gone to trial my so-called friends were willing to give witness against me. I was an addict, never a dealer. Liam was the supplier, though he was just a frontman. Keith had the contacts. Christy found out what was going on, possibly a tip-off from Bale. He knew it would be just a matter of time before we were caught, so he intervened and I was caught in possession.'

'Why did Bale drop the charge?'

'My father pulled strings. That's how things were done here. Bale claimed it was an act of mercy and I could begin again. But not in Reedstown. People like me pulled society down and he wanted me off his patch. So, I went. Does that satisfy you?

Is it an adequate explanation or would you like to continue this inquisition?'

He had never tried to hide the fact that he was a drug addict, clean for twenty-five years but aware that the habit still had its claws in him. Christy Lewis would have had no hesitation in using him as a pawn to save his son's reputation. Just as he had planned to do to her. Bob's explanation made sense, yet it did not satisfy her. Skin in the game... a throwaway comment by a former sergeant with an attitude. She was giving his words enough credibility to destroy her marriage but Bob's answers, instead of satisfying her, just created more questions. Why was he framed in such a ruthless way by people he trusted and believed were his friends? Why had he been viewed as the weak link? The out-of-control one who could bring others down with him? And if he had broken rank, what secrets would he have told? Her husband did not look like a man who had opened his soul to her. In his eyes, she saw desolation. Had it always been there, this impenetrable sadness, shielded from view by his love for her?

'How can you call this an inquisition?' she asked.

'I'm a newspaperman, Rachel. I read the clues between the lines. I know what you're thinking.'

'No, Bob, you don't. I read the clues in what is not spoken and your past has always been a mystery to me. You deny it matters yet you carry it with you. It weighs on you... here.' She pressed her hand against his chest and felt his heart, the hard, drumming beat reverberating off her palm. And his face, she touched that too, felt his clammy heat, and knew that the truth was as far away as it was when she began this conversation.

'I have a decision to make,' she said. 'Should I continue to allow a dead girl to speak from the grave? Or should I silence her by releasing a statement she made in the presence of Jack

Bale, which denies the claim she made in her diary? What am I to do, Bob?'

He swallowed, his throat muscles contracting. 'That has to be your decision, Rachel,' he replied. 'Knowing you, it will be the right one.'

CHAPTER THIRTY-FOUR

Davina

A week since Christy's death and the air in The Lodge was stale. Davina threw out a bunch of wilted flowers and drew back from the stench of stagnant water. She opened windows and doors, allowed light to flood the rooms. She had already been through his office in the constituency clinic, checking his files and shredding where necessary. Today, her chores were more mundane as she scoured and scrubbed in her efforts to remove all traces of her father-in-law from The Lodge. Now that the property market was stable again, she could sell it and raise funds for her various campaigns. The radio was on, white noise in the background … *Now it's your turn to clean up your own shit…* Had she hastened his death with her questions, harried him into a fatal panic attack? She checked herself. What a ridiculous thing to think. It wasn't that easy to kill a monster.

His death had precipitated a by-election. Her moment had come earlier than anticipated and her nomination would be accepted by the party. Keith had been more than a little surprised by the speed with which she moved, the phone calls to influential contacts who owed her… what? Access to Christy, insights into his thoughts, the right word in his ear, the sleight of hand that was sometimes necessary to change his mind? All that and more. Davina's backroom days were over, or they would be as soon as the election results were counted; but not if they were smudged by her father-in-law's murky shadow.

A phone-in programme had started on the radio. One of the callers was discussing her time in the Magdalene laundries. The same routine, mothers seeking lost babies, lost babies now adults seeking mothers. This was a happy story, a reunion that worked out, but Davina still searched for another channel before entering Christy's bedroom.

He had smoked in bed. Her lips puckered in disgust when she saw the ashtray full of butts. Turning the mattress made no difference to the stale smell of tobacco. The rooms would have to be fumigated before she could put the house on the market. Hearing a soft thud, she looked down and saw a book lying on the floor. It must have been hidden under the mattress. She hoped it wasn't porn. Grimacing, she flung it onto the growing pile of rubbish. The cover opened and the words 'Marianne's Diary', written with a turquoise dayglo pen, seemed to rise from the page and hit her between the eyebrows. Hallucinating. She had definitely lost it. And who would blame her when her day had been spent dumping flowers in the green bin and chasing hideous voyeurs from the front of her house?

She picked it up with her fingertips and moaned softly as she turned the pages. Blotches and scribbles, words crossed out and squashed into what space was left on the line. Adele Foyle's decision to edit the contents before she released the entries on her blog had been a wise one that had kept her out of the libel courts; Liam had been unable to put a stop to the blog – but he would have had no difficulty getting an injunction if a judge had seen this material. The wild accusations and incoherent passages, the names dropped carelessly onto the page. Jack Bale: no redaction of his name, or Christy's. No problem roasting Gloria's reputation. No qualms about defaming the dead. How was she managing to continue blogging when Davina was holding the source material in her hands? And why was it here, hidden under a mattress that could have been overturned if the Gardai had decided there was anything suspicious about Christy's death and searched The Lodge? Davina saw her own name, and Julie's also, underlined many times in connection to the stories that had circulated around Reedstown. Her fury grew as she turned the pages. How had this diary come into her father-in-law's possession? Another grubby Christy Lewis secret. He must have planned to dispose of it but was caught short when his heart faltered and stopped.

Adele Foyle must have made a copy of the diary. Had she suspected it would be stolen when she diligently copied each page? She checked the blog. The latest entry was up.

I talked to my baby for the first time when I was there. I thought I'd be frightened being all on my own with only a mattress and a bucket but I wasn't a bit scared. God, the real God, made it okay for me. Miss Quack Elisha came every day to check the baby's heart and Miss Rebekah sent down her usual poison paws food, which The Quack insisted I eat because a healthy mother means a healthy baby.

It was so quiet in the tank. Deep enough to drown me but I'd company, pummelling heels and fists, hiccups and moments of stillness when I knew my baby was sucking its thumb. I rocked backwards, forwards, and sang lullabies. When I touched my tummy it was like there was a pulse beating in the palm of my hand.

Davina touched her cheek and was shocked to discover it was wet. This drivel was dangerously emotive and there was more to come. The blog needed to be closed down, and fast.

Keith arrived home. A flying stopover, he declared as he
headed for the shower. He had a meeting to attend and would
be home late. She was sitting on the edge of the sofa when he
entered the living room. Clean-shaven, his hair still damp, a
cashmere jumper casually slung over his shoulders, he could
have been going anywhere. As always, she found it impossible
to read him.

'Sit down, Keith,' she said. 'I need to discuss something with you.'

'I'm running late for my meeting. Can't it wait until
tomorrow?'

'*Sit.*'

'I'm not a fucking dog, Davina.' He sank reluctantly onto the
sofa. 'What's going on?'

'I found this under the mattress in The Lodge.' She thrust the
diary towards him. 'I thought it was porn at first. Now, I wish
it had been. At least I know where I am with filth. But this…
what am I supposed to think?'

He took the diary from her and turned the pages, his eyes
skimming over the entries.

'How come I found it there?' she asked.

'I've absolutely no idea. When did my father ever confide in me?'

'Don't lie to me, Keith. It's way too late for that. Did Christy
steal it to protect you? Is this what cleaning up *your* shit means?'

Her emphasis jolted him to his feet. He opened his mouth,
closed it again. Her golden-tongued husband whose vocabulary
swept him into power, elected on the first count, was struggling
to explain how his father had stared at him with such loathing
from his hospital bed. Her hand was rising, swinging towards
him. The smack of skin on skin, a furious joy, and he recoiled,
stepped away from her, his eyes narrowed. He shook his head,
his fingers pressed to his reddening cheek.

'I know nothing about it,' he said. 'There never was any *shit* to clear up and if you want our marriage to survive don't you ever again imply that there was.'

Her fury was being replaced by caution. That little slut probably put out to him. Davina only hoped he had had the good sense to resist her, otherwise her diary would roast him on a spit. And if he had been stupid enough to indulge in a momentary weakness and join the line-up in Loy Park, who else had indulged in Marianne Mooney's dubious favours? Keith always had an entourage. Liam, of course. The faithful shadow with his acne and sniffles. He always seemed to have a cold in those days. A neglected waif with his whacko mother touring the countryside, promoting her books and her visions. Bob Molloy came to mind – but he was in never-never land most of the time. Too spaced out on drugs to do anything except hang around them until he went into rehab… and came back twenty-five years later, clean as a new pin.

Davina did not ask questions when she was with Jack Bale and he did not burden her with unnecessary information. She used to laugh at him and call him 'Christy's sidekick/bagman/sycophant', but not any more. Not since he squeezed her elbow at the funeral and said, 'You and Keith can call on me anytime you need me.' She understood that he was giving his allegiance to the new order.

He was not surprised when she showed him the diary. That was reassuring. No smoke and mirrors to distort facts. She agreed with his view that Adele Foyle had stepped way out of line since she arrived in Reedstown. He swiped his phone and showed her a photograph. Transfixed, she stared at the document, a legal and genuine piece of evidence. She was appalled. Why had that not been used to end the charade being enacted online by the blogger? Davina did not ask how he had acquired it. All that concerned her was its value.

The statement he had photographed had been signed by him and another guard. Garda Gunning, she vaguely remembered him. Dead now, a brain haemorrhage at his desk. The way of his passing was quickly forgotten as she read Marianne Mooney's confession. The scheming, lying slut. To think Davina had cried reading that last wretched entry… a momentary weakness that would never be repeated. The original confession was still under wraps in Reedstown Garda Station, Jack told her, but Rachel Darcy's stubbornness was forcing his hand. How had she allowed that blog to run unchecked for so long when she had this evidence at her fingertips? Why hadn't she leaked it? She wouldn't be the first guard to slide something official and private into the public domain. It would have stopped all the speculation and gossip, the corroding suspicion. Davina had struck gold. The means to end a feeding frenzy of misinformation was in her hands.

*

Statement of Miss Marianne Mooney

Address: River View, Reedstown. Co. Dublin.

Occupation: Secondary School Student

My name is Marianne Mooney and I am a fourth year student at St Dominic's Convent, Reedstown. I am fifteen years of age. On the night of 3 April 1994, Shane Reagan from 6 Riverton Crescent, Reedstown, Co. Dublin had intimate relations with me against my will. I asked him to stop but he penetrated me in the full knowledge that I was a minor.

This rape took place in a derelict cottage at Blake's Hollow. He threatened to kill me and burn down my house with my mother in it if I reported him to the Gardai. I have refused a forensic medical examination, against the advice offered to me by Sergeant Jack Bale.

I have read over this statement and it is correct. I have been invited to make any amendments or changes to it and do not wish to do so.

Signed: Marianne Mooney
Witness: Sergeant Jack Bale
Witness: Garda Maurice Gunning
Date: 3 April 1994

Davina had expected an immediate reaction when she posted the statement on an anonymous blog which she named, 'The Marianne Diary Exposed' and she was not disappointed. Opinions varied but the majority of readers who commented were vitriolic in their condemnation of the diary.

Adele Foyle responded, of course she did, fighting back against the fallout. It was a pathetic attempt that did nothing to stem the negative flow. The names were not redacted on this occasion and Davina knew the gloves were off as soon as she read the announcement Adele wrote as her introduction to the entry.

This entry from The Marianne Diary was written earlier in the diary but I omitted it because of its controversial content. I have decided to release it and counteract the leak of a Garda statement that was signed by Marianne on the night she was brought to Reedstown Garda Station by her then boyfriend, Shane Reagan, to report the crime of rape. I believe this statement was coerced

**from her under a brutal interrogation and that she had
no awareness of what she was signing.**

*Shane is a criminal because of me. That's what Mr Lewis
said when I saw him today. He was coming out of Mother
Gloria's office. He pretended not to know me but only stopped
because I kept shouting his name. Christy... Christy... I
knew he'd hate that. So disrespectful. All I wanted to know
was if he'd seen Shane but he got mad and told me to stop
acting the innocent. I must have known Shane would run
away as soon I blamed him for everything.*

*I called him a liar. I never said Shane was to blame,
no matter how often Sergeant Bale forced me to say it. Mr
Lewis's face got so mad I thought he was going to hit me.
He might have only Mother Gloria came out of her office
and told him to cool it. I was crying so much she took me
into the dorm and explained how I'd told the guards what
really happened. She said I told them Shane violated me. I
told her she was making a BIG mistake. The only thing I
signed was the form Sergeant Bale gave me. He said Shane
would go to jail for hitting Garda Gunning if I didn't write
my name at the bottom of it. That's what I did so Shane
could get out of the cell and go home. He'd stopped shouting
about the cigarette packet by then. But I was afraid he was
unconscious because of the blow he got from Sergeant Bale.*

*Mother Gloria said Shane went to Australia with his
mam. I didn't believe her, not at first, but it made sense.
Carrie's from there and it's where Shane was born. He didn't
move to Ireland until he was two and his parents split up.
He's on the other side of the world, upside down to me, and
I want to see him so bad. But that's never going to happen.*

Not when he's in Australia and I'm here packing poxy medals in boxes.

I did a wrong thing. Now Shane is never going to be allowed to come back to Reedstown or he'll be put in jail. All because I wrote my name at the bottom of that page.

CHAPTER THIRTY-FIVE

Adele

Adele removed her engagement ring and left it on the bedside table. An art deco design set in platinum; Daniel had bought it from a jeweller who specialised in vintage jewellery. Should she send it back to him by post or courier? She massaged cream into her hands, the wringing movements becoming faster, more agitated. The diamonds caught the beam from the bedside lamp and glistened with a cold intensity. She switched off the light and the glister from her ring radiated in the retinas of her eyes as she drifted off to sleep.

The crash awoke her. Glass breaking, footsteps stomping across the hall and up the stairs. She reached under the pillow for her phone but before she could remove it, the bedroom door burst open. Blinded in the glare from a torch, she was unable to see anyone, but as she continued to scrabble for her phone, the man holding the torch shouted, 'Sit up, bitch, and put your fucking hands where I can see them.'

Still invisible, he moved closer, she could tell by the torch sweeping towards the ceiling then flickering across the room. Only then was she able to make out his bulky shape and the pale oval of his face, which seemed to hover before her in two halves, but that impression disappeared when he again directed the torch towards her. He repeated the order as she pulled herself upright and put her hands on the duvet. Other footsteps were approaching. Voices were audible and a bark of laughter was silenced by his gruff command to, 'Shut up.'

A scream swelled in her throat. She fought to contain it. No one else would hear her and it would serve no purpose, apart from antagonising them. When someone switched on the bedroom light, the full horror of this break-in was revealed. Three figures stood in a row inside the door. Dressed identically in anoraks, jeans and gloves, all black, their faces were covered by what she first thought were balaclavas. As her eyes adjusted to the brightness she realised why she had seen the first intruder's face in two halves. Hoods covered their heads and their features were hidden behind Mickey Mouse masks, their eyes covered by black blindfolds. They must be able to see through them because they were moving towards her bed with the confidence of the sighted.

The slimmest of the three made a squeaking noise and the figure beside him giggled. She was female, young, her laughter high-pitched, giddy. They parted when they reached Adele's bed, two on the left side and the man who had been the first to enter the room coming to a standstill on her right. She resisted the urge to huddle out of sight under the duvet in a crazed belief that they would disappear. Three blind mice; their significance was only too obvious. This time she was unable to control her scream.

'Shut your mouth, bitch, or I'll shut it for you.' He clenched his gloved hand into a fist and shoved her back against the pillows. Casually, as if he was familiar with the geography of her bed, he reached behind her with his other hand and removed her phone. Dropping it to the floor, he crushed it with his boot.

Leave me alone… get out of here… don't you dare touch me… how banal those words would sound if she tried to speak but her voice was silenced anyway by the choke of fear. She considered diving towards the end of the bed and making a dash for the open door. That would be equally futile. The thought of being held down on the floor and wrestled into stillness was too terrible to contemplate.

'What part of "fuck off" do you not understand, bitch?' His head jutted forward as he moved closer to her and grabbed her chin.

'I don't know...' Her voice was a whisper, almost inaudible. 'What do you mean?'

'You were warned to shut down that blog but you wouldn't listen.' His accent was wrong. It should be harsh and guttural, like the voices she sometimes heard at night on the riverbank. Instead, he sounded as if he was the product of a posh private school. He continued speaking, quoting words from posts she had received, the vile ones, cruel and, until now, anonymous.

The man who had been squeaking held an iPhone towards Adele and said, 'Say cheese, bitch. Say it nice and slow for the birdie.'

Despite the bulkiness of his anorak, he had the tall lankiness of a youth who had yet to fill out into the solidness of adulthood. The woman was clowning it up, pulling at her mock-whiskers in a parodic gesture, then clawing the air with her black-gloved hands. Thugs for hire, tough and vicious. When the youth with the iPhone leaned closer to Adele, she screamed into his face, her fist moving simultaneously and smacking against the side of his head. He staggered backwards and crashed against the woman. This lash of fury drove Adele forward, her arms flailing. For an instant, it seemed possible that she could escape but this hope was dashed when she was grabbed by the first intruder. He was older than the others, his body supple and muscular as he pinned her face-down to the bed and fended off her struggles with a grunt. The woman, recovering her balance, came to his assistance.

Adele continued to struggle, knowing the uselessness of it but determined to fight until there was nothing left to defend. She stiffened, the energy going from her when she felt the muzzle of a gun against the back of her neck.

'My finger is on the trigger,' the older man whispered in her ear. 'If you don't stop screaming, I'll put this bullet through your fucking mouth.' He twisted her around until she was again facing the iPhone. The youth had regained his balance. Part of his mask had been dislodged when Adele struck him. She caught a glimpse of metal studs in one of his ears and the edge of a tattoo under his chin, but this impression was immediately forgotten as the gunman traced the muzzle from her neck to the hollow of her throat.

'You heard the man.' The youth moved from one foot to the other. 'Say cheese. Let me hear it loud and clear.' Once again, he moved towards Adele, but stayed out of range as he clicked. 'Fuckin' deadly pose,' he said. 'Hold it right there.'

The woman giggled, a hand to her mouth, as the gunman used the gun to probe the opening of Adele's nightdress. So, this was what was meant by helplessness. The feeling that she had been taken over by someone who had the power to exert total control over her mind and body. She had been moved to fury by the descriptions in Marianne's diary but she had never understood the true revulsion and horror her mother must have known that night. Adele could feel it now, her limbs slack with terror as she stared at each identical mask, her senses attuned to every word, every movement. The clicking of the camera phone, the youth's heavy breathing. So much noise but the hammer-beat of her heart was louder still. She imagined it shattered, the bullet exiting her back, her lungs collapsing.

'Cheese.' Drowning in their mockery, she was forced to repeat the word as the gunman pressed the barrel between her breasts and then, slowly and deliberately, moved it downwards, sliding it over her stomach, his intent so obvious that the female intruder, no longer laughing, turned her head away.

'Where is the USB key?' he asked.

'I don't have one—' Adele stopped, her thighs clenched against the cold press of steel, knowing he could probe deeper and more insistently if he chose.

The youth with the iPhone moved into position, clicking, clicking. Adele nodded towards the bedside table. The woman opened the drawer and removed the memory stick.

'This had better be the only copy,' she said.

Too petrified to reply, Adele could only nod.

'Shut down that fucking blog or the next time we come for you we'll rip you apart,' the gunman said. 'But before closing it down, you'll post a final blog and admit that The Marianne Diary was fake. Do you understand?'

The force of the gun against her skin drained the last of her courage. Tears flooded her eyes, flowed down her cheeks as she nodded again.

'Say it,' he demanded. 'I want to hear you say it for the record.'

The youth pressed the record app on his phone and held it towards her mouth. Her muscles were rigid, her jaw locked.

'Say it,' the gunman roared.

Her voice was a croak when she spoke, an unrecognisable sound that betrayed her mother's truth.

'And don't even think of going to the police,' he continued. 'There's nothing they can do for you that we can't undo. Just keep remembering that and you'll be okay.' Obviously unable to resist a final assault, he pushed the barrel between her thighs and prodded deeper, laughing when she closed her eyes against the terrifying pressure he was exerting.

'Leave her alone.' The woman spoke directly to him. 'Let's get out of here.'

Without answering, he slid the weapon into the pocket of his anorak and switched off the light. The darkness pressed against her eyelids. She listened to them leaving, heard the crunch of glass under their feet, the slam of the hall door. When she was sure they were no longer in the house, she opened her eyes and reached for the bedside lamp. She was briefly thankful for the woman's intervention, her sudden anxiety to end the games and depart; but her reason became clear when Adele discovered that her engagement ring was missing from the bedside table. Perhaps tomorrow she would mourn it but for now, its loss seemed inconsequential.

She left her bedroom and walked over the shattered glass, unheeding of a shard that penetrated the sole of her bedroom slipper and drew blood. Every window downstairs had been broken but they had not trashed the house.

Outside, the river was awash with moonlight. Bulrushes speared the night, serried ranks that Jack Bale would snap aside when he next cast his line into the dark-green flow. She had no doubt in her mind that he had organised tonight's attack. Intimidation. It had worked perfectly. Unable to remain any longer in the house, she closed the door behind her.

Her car's tyres had been slashed. She hesitated, her plan to escape in the car thwarted. Larry's house was within walking distance but they could be hiding in the undergrowth, waiting for another opportunity to attack.

The riverbank was hard, the grass dry and withered from lack of rain, yet the ground felt like quicksand as she ran towards his house. Overhanging branches threw grotesque shadows before her and added to her confusion. She fell once, her face smacking off the rutted path. Blood seeped from a gash on her forehead, but she was hardly aware of the wound as she staggered to her feet.

Larry's irritated expression when he opened the door changed to one of concern as he took in the sight of her in her nightdress, her forehead still bleeding. He caught her in his arms just before she collapsed and supported her into the murky gloom of his living room, where the odours of a late-night curry and the beer that washed it down still hung in the air. He bandaged her foot and forehead, calmed her down when she beseeched him not to alert the Gardai. She expected her voice to crack, the wailing to begin. Her composure surprised her but she was confusing it with numbness, as she would later realise.

"This can't go unreported,' he said. 'The police will have to be notified.' He handed her a glass of brandy and stood over her until she finished it. 'What if they come back and burn you out… or shoot up the house. You can't stay there any longer. It's too dangerous.'

She nodded. The brandy steadied her, made it possible to ask him if she could use his phone to ring Daniel. Five o'clock in the morning in Reedstown but in Colorado it was party time. She heard the background choruses of conversation and music when his phone was answered. Bar sounds, always recognisable, as was the husky, female voice in the background when Daniel asked who was calling. Adele made no reply as she ended the call and handed the phone back to Larry.

CHAPTER THIRTY-SIX

Adele

For three days she was unable to leave her room at the Loyvale Hotel. She ordered room service when she was hungry and spent most of her time in bed. Her short, fitful periods of sleep were filled with nightmares. Larry organised new tyres for her car and, having managed to retrieve the memory card from the broken fragments of her smashed phone, arrived with a new one. He reckoned he knew who the vandals were.

'Shitty little river rats,' he called them. 'A toe up the arse would soon sort that lot out.'

He was referring to the teenagers who gathered by the river at night. Pills and weed, needles also. Local youths who knew their terrain and blended into the shadows at the hint of a Garda raid. Adele had often heard them when she was closing her bedroom window before going to bed, their raucous laughter, their raised voices, the slap of their running footsteps. She didn't believe they were to blame. Her gunman, the leader of the trio, had been older, more adept at terror. He had been sent with a message and had every reason to believe it had been successfully delivered. She was seized by dread every time she recalled the crash of glass, the footsteps on the stairs, the rasp of their breath, their inane squeaks and giggles.

She had known the risk she was taking by retaliating with that last entry. Believing that Sergeant Darcy had released her mother's statement without contacting her first, she had been consumed with rage as she tried to cope with the immediate online reaction. The screen on her laptop should have been fogged with bile by the abuse she had received, the name-calling and death threats. She was convinced there was a concerted effort behind the negative reaction; an echo of the verbal campaign orchestrated against her mother all those years ago. The message didn't change, just the medium for its delivery. But Sergeant Darcy had not leaked the statement. Adele had realised this as soon as the intruders burst into the bedroom.

She was not physically hurt, yet the pressure her attacker had used felt like an intolerable ache; his intentions clear as he pressed the gun closer, closer, and in that clenched instant, she had sought desperately for her mother's comfort. She had willed Marianne to tear aside the veil that separated them. If such a connection existed between them then that was the moment it should have been made manifest. But there had been no ghostly voice exhorting her to be brave. Three blind mice... they had smashed the tenuous bond she had formed with her mother and laughed – like those others had – as they did so. *One by one... laughing... sometimes their laughter is the only sound I hear.* She no longer needed the diary to understand the subjugation Marianne had endured. Her ordeal had been subsumed into her own experience, her own encounter with evil.

Her grandmother had been right. Nothing except scorched memories came from stoking the past. Yet, the past was all around her. Messages kept arriving on her laptop. Women who had shared Marianne's experiences in other mother and baby homes. She did not want to read them. Her mother's heartache was more than enough to bear. She had come to Reedstown to discover her father's identity, not to be a voice for women who had been wronged and were demanding justice and information. But that was what they were asking her to do. She sighed as she opened her email account and read the latest messages. How could she post a blog denying the diary's claims? She had written words to that effect, brief, damning and apologetic, she had stated that she accepted responsibility for the fraud that had been carried out through the publication of The Marianne Diary. Every time she felt she was ready to publish the post and deal with the opprobrium that would be heaped upon her, she found herself unable to take that final step.

On the third afternoon, she forced herself to leave the hotel room and go for a walk along the river. She felt weightless, as if she was venturing out after a long illness and was trying to find her balance again. A group of joggers ran past, followed by an elderly woman wheeling her dog in a buggy. The woman came most afternoons, her terrier sitting upright, his eyes darting towards birds he could no longer chase. The wending riverbank should have been a place of peace yet, for Adele, it was filled with unseen spectres. She hurried past Brooklime. A glazier had installed new windows. She needed to remove her possessions but she was not yet ready to return to the house.

An hour later she entered the Kasket, where Katie insisted the coffee and cupcake was her treat. Larry had told her what happened. Like him, she was convinced it was the 'river rats'. She was heartily sick of chasing them from the Kasket, knowing they would eat and run without paying.

Bob Molloy was sitting by the window staring out into Main Street. Was he waiting for his wife to emerge from the Garda station and join him? Despite Larry's encouragement, Adele had steadfastly refused to report her assault. The cold press of steel against her skin kept her silent. Nothing, she believed, would ever dispel that sensation, or the belief that the gunman would not hesitate to pull the trigger the next time.

She had not spoken to Bob Molloy since his refusal to allow her space in his newspaper. He nodded at her, then looked away, unsmiling. She found a table close to the wall. She needed shelter around her, something she could touch for reassurance.

The café door opened and three people, a woman and two men, entered. The woman wore a pair of zigzag patterned leggings and a white top stretched over her ample stomach. The younger of the two men was dressed in mock army fatigues but it was the older man, in tailored shorts and an open-neck shirt, his gaze hidden behind a pair of sunglasses, who held her attention. She recognised him from the computer shop on Barrow Lane. He walked towards a two-seater table next to her. Other larger tables were available but he pulled an extra chair around the one he had chosen. His spicy aftershave, laid on with a heavy hand, wafted towards her. She remembered the odour in her kitchen when Jack Bale had called to warn her off. Slight yet pungent enough to be differentiated from the smell of freshly gutted trout, She would have recognised it that night if terror had not ripped the memory from her.

When the woman looked towards Adele, her gaze hard and direct, she knew they had followed her into the Kasket. The flashback came instantly. She was back in the bedroom again, his gun sliding over her body, her skin glassy with sweat as she stared into the nothingness of their collective gaze. Now, as they crowded around her, she pressed her shoulder against the wall, willed it to slide apart like the door of a vault and hide her.

They ignored her for a while and talked among themselves about a concert they had attended the previous night. The younger two called him 'Grad', their attention focused on everything he said. No wonder they had been laughing at her when she brought her useless laptop into BootUrBytes.

'Have you heard the latest from the Loyvale Hotel?' asked the woman after Katie had taken their order. 'They're dealing with a mice infestation. That's *so* gross. The exterminators have been called in. It's particularly bad in room 32.' She stared boldly at Adele, her high-pitched voice no longer indistinct behind a mask.

The younger man made faint but persistent squeaking sounds, his fingers scrabbling along the surface of the table.

'Word on the street is that it's worse down by the river,' said Grad. 'Rats. Big problem there. Bigger than cats, I've been told. Traps are useless. You'd need a bullet to take the bastards out.'

The same private-school accent; she could remember it clearly now. *If you don't stop screaming, I'll put this bullet through your fucking mouth.*

Adele pushed back her chair and stood. He blocked her way, feinting this way and that as she tried to walk past him.

'You're invading my space.' She would not blink, not this time. 'Let me pass or I'll report you for harassing me.'

'Invading my space,' the youth repeated in an exaggerated whine. 'She thinks she's a fucking space invader.' He had taken her photograph that night and, despite knowing she recognised him, he lifted his mobile and did the same again.

Brazen and unmasked, they were confident that the terror they had inflicted on her would keep them safe.

'Harassing you?' Grad said. 'Perish the thought, Adele. I'm a great admirer of your blog. When can I expect to read your next post?'

'Get out of my way.' His sunglasses reminded her of blindfolds. She saw her reflection pinned like a fly to the mirrored lens.

'No need to be rude,' he said. 'We're worried about your safety. Those long walks you take by the river. One false move and you could end up as fish feed.'

'Leave her alone.' Unnoticed by the group, Bob Molloy had approached the table.

'Whoa, man, don't stress.' Grad held up two fingers in an exaggerated peace gesture and stepped back from her. 'I was just giving the lady some advice.'

'Then let me repeat myself.' The editor's hands balled into fists as he confronted the younger man. 'Leave her alone then fuck off back to whatever stone you crawled out from under.'

He wanted a fight. Up close, Adele could see the change in him since their last encounter. The hardness that had descended on him when she spoke about Marianne Mooney had intensified and his aggressive stance dared Grad to make a wrong move. What then? A gun pulled?

Katie was striding towards them now. She looked capable of ejecting both men by the scruff of their necks but Adele was already leaving, looking neither to right nor left as she hurried towards the exit. She kept walking until she reached the car park at the back of the shopping centre. Once inside, the doors locked, she allowed the trembling to take over. She had to leave Reedstown or she would go mad. Her head exploding. What else could it do with all the rage it contained? And the fear – how was she to battle back when she was imprisoned by it, made mute and helpless? There was nothing but an unfulfilled dream to hold her here. Every record of her mother's experience had been taken from her. But the words Marianne had written in her diary were indelibly etched on her mind. That was the only place where they would be safe.

CHAPTER THIRTY-SEVEN

Rachel

Katie's Kasket was quiet, the brief lull between elevenses and lunch. Rachel found an empty table, ordered herbal tea and a Danish pastry. The Garda station was visible from the window and she kept her sunglasses on, hoping they would provide a barrier between herself and the public. A futile gesture, she realised, when a man entered the café and made his way towards her.

'Good day to you, Sergeant.' He pointed at an empty chair. 'Mind if I join you for a few minutes?'

'By all means.' Rachel pushed her sunglasses into her hair and smiled politely at him. He was a bulky man, low-slung jeans over wide hips, a mop of sandy hair streaked with grey. He looked familiar but she was unable to remember his name.

'Larry Kavanagh.' He offered her a strong, weathered hand. 'We met during the flooding last year.'

'Ah, yes, of course. How are you, Larry? Weren't you one of the volunteers?' Knee-deep in water and manning a pump, he was in waders and an oilskin then.

'Fat lot of good it did me.' His expression crumpled, ruefully. 'My place will probably flood again this winter. Not the one I live in but the one I rent by the river.'

'If I remember rightly, you were worried about your insurance.'

'It worked out okay in the end but I'll not be able to insure again if the same thing happens this winter. But that's not the issue here. I just wanted to check if you'd any success finding out who broke into my property the other night?'

'You had a robbery?' Rachel asked. So much for her quiet interlude.

'I reported it to the young one at the front desk. Told her it was those yobs… little feicers. If they're not robbing shops they're shooting up by the river. I swear to God, Sergeant, Reedstown is turning into a crime zone. Those yobs smashed their way into my property and broke the windows just for the hell of it. My tenant was scared out of her wits when she came banging on my door in the small hours. And that's the second time it's happened to her. Not that the first time was as serious. Stealing an online identity seemed daft when she told me. Now I'd believe anything.'

'Are you talking about Adele Foyle?'

'Yes. That's her, right enough.' Larry nodded vigorously. 'The one with the blog everyone's talking about. What do you make of it, Sergeant?' He paused as Katie arrived at their table with his cappuccino and Rachel's order. 'I'm a blow-in to Reedstown so I wasn't around then. But if it did happen like the kid in the diary describes, then it's a bloody disgrace those wankers weren't brought to justice. That's got me to thinking that there're those in the community who'd like that blog closed down. They've certainly gone about it the right way. My place is a mess but she's terrified to report what happened to her. She was holed up in the Loyvale Hotel for a few days but now she's gone and moved back to Brooklime.'

The Danish pastry, custard and pistachio, her favourite, was delicious but Rachel had lost her appetite after one bite. Her herbal tea cooled at her elbow. The uneasy feeling building inside her whenever she thought about Adele was becoming too familiar. Rachel had phoned her when she discovered that the statement Marianne Mooney had made in the Garda station had gone online. A leak from Garda files. She had her suspicions as to how it had happened but Jack Bale left no fingerprints. There had been no response from Adele's phone, apart from an automated voice stating that her number was uncontactable.

'What was taken during the break-in?' Rachel asked.

'Nothing,' Larry replied. 'That's the strange thing. One of them stamped on her phone and, like I said, they wrecked my front door and windows. Oh, yeah, they slashed the tyres on her car as well. There were three of them, apparently. Apart from the vandalism, they didn't steal anything, though I noticed she's not wearing her engagement ring. She's either broken up with her lad or else it's been taken. All that blogging hasn't done her a bit of good and them little river rats will do anything to line their pockets for those who throw a few euros their way. Is the heat getting to you, Sergeant? You've gone very pale, if you don't mind me saying so.'

'No, I'm okay, Larry.' His concerned expression swam in and out of her gaze. 'Just getting anxious about the time.' She pushed herself upwards, a clumsy movement that caused the table to wobble. 'I've been off duty for a couple of days but I'll check that out and be in touch with an update.'

Outside, the air was heavy and oppressive. If only it would rain and clear away the dust. An Irish summer like this one was rare and the sun's glister had bleached the landscape. Farmers were complaining about lack of fodder for their cattle and gardeners were being warned to avoid the garden hose. Rachel longed for clouds. The lowering dark ones that could suddenly sweep into view and change everything. Perhaps, then, the oppressive feeling that was dragging her down would pass and her energy would be restored. So, too, would her ability to think calmly, rationally, as she had been trained to do.

Why was Adele so reluctant to make a report? Lack of evidence had never stopped her in the past. Was she afraid Rachel wouldn't take her seriously again? Unlike a stolen online identity, slashed tyres were evidence that a crime had been committed. Such an act of vandalism should be investigated.

Back at the station she checked the reports. A guard had called to Brooklime and taken fingerprints. Nothing suspicious was found in the shattered glass or the bedroom. Perhaps Larry was right and the youths who hung around the river at night were responsible for the break-in. They knew the Loy as well as they knew the aisles of shopping centres, and had their alibis in place when they were taken in for questioning. Rachel had no difficulty believing they had vandalised Adele's car and smashed their way into the house, but stealing her online identity would have been way beyond their combined brainpower.

The fogginess suddenly cleared from her mind. Jonathan Wheeler, expelled from university for hacking into his professor's emails and publishing the more salacious ones online, had come to her attention soon after she was transferred to Reedstown. Unlike Larry's so-called 'river rats', the youths who worked sporadically for him at BootUrBytes appeared to be what he claimed they were, early school leavers looking for work experience. They had abbreviated his graduate status into a nickname and referred to him in reverential terms as 'Grad'. If an online identity was to be destroyed, Grad would have the expertise to do it. Why had she not thought about him until now? The reason was simple. She had not taken Adele's complaint seriously. Robbery was physical, objects taken that could be sold on and converted into cash. A virtual robbery could easily be confused with a computer virus, a broken hard drive, a careless action on the part of the user.

The apartment where Grad lived with his partner, Haylee, had been raided by the drug squad last year. A botched attempt that left the team furious and red-faced, convinced that he had received advance warning. The apartment was clean in every sense of the word. Shining surfaces, shampooed carpets, fresh sheets, domesticity radiating from every corner.

To organise a Garda search of the riverbank for a minor break-in when nothing had been stolen would be difficult. She needed to persuade her superior officer that a more serious crime had been committed. The name Grad Wheeler was enough to instigate such a search and the painstaking trawl along the riverbank for evidence began.

The discovery was made by Garda Roberts, close to the turn-off path leading to the village. The piece of black material she found had snagged under a bush. It was bagged, along with other miscellaneous items that had already been collected.

Back at the Garda station, Rachel hid her disappointment when Garda Roberts' find turned out to be a Mickey Mouse mask. It must have been discarded by a child and had probably been lying there since Halloween or some other children's festival. Her initial reaction changed, though, as she studied the mask. It fitted over the head and was similar to the design of a balaclava. The material looked new, unfaded, the nose and grinning mouth still vividly coloured. She fought back nausea as she stared at the area where the wearer's eyes would be. It was covered by a blindfold. Blind mice, running in threes... at whose behest?

Unable to look at the mask any longer, she checked the rest of the items. Only one had significance. A buckle, no visible rust on it and still gleaming. It was too small to belong to a belt or jacket. A boot then, worn by a biker or a walker. It could also belong to Grad Wheeler, who wore biker boots with metal embellishments – studs, chains, buckles. Hidden in the wild grass along the riverbank, it would have remained unnoticed if the sun had not reflected off its surface and turned it into a splinter of light.

Without advance warning of a Garda raid, Grad's apartment was as untidy as Rachel had expected to find it on the previous occasion. Beer cans, pizza wrappings and coffee cups covered the floor. Graphic novels were ranged neatly together on a bookshelf. Grad, it appeared, was a fan of the genre. Copies of *Hello!* magazine, presumably Haylee's choice of reading, were scattered over the sofa. He remained composed throughout the search. His supercilious expression told Rachel that there was nothing in the apartment to incriminate him. Haylee, poker-faced, hid her uneasiness by flicking through the pages of *Hello!*, but when Garda Roberts shouted from upstairs she flinched and abruptly closed the magazine. Rachel hurried up the stairs to join Garda Roberts while another officer moved into position to block the front door.

An engagement ring had been found in the toe of a pair of black opaque tights. Rachel recognised the distinctive art deco design immediately. It was clear from Grad's furious expression that he had been unaware of its existence. Haylee made this point stridently as they were handcuffed and led away. His boots, minus one buckle, were also removed from the bedroom.

It was dark when Rachel finally left the Garda station. Instead of going home, she turned at Boylan's Corner and headed towards the Loy. The silvery flow mirrored the sheen of the moon and the burble of the river was audible as she walked towards Brooklime. She had already phoned Adele and told her she would give the doorbell two short blasts and a prolonged ring when she arrived.

Adele opened the door cautiously. Her expression was terse, her body tense as she scanned the darkness for shadows.

'I've already told you I'm not interested in adding to Larry's report,' she said.

'I'm not here in an official capacity—'

'Your uniform tells me otherwise.'

'I'm finished for the night. I won't take up much of your time but it's important that we talk.'

'Are you going to tell me how that statement was released?' she asked.

'It was leaked,' Rachel replied. 'I assure you, I'd nothing to do with it and I intend finding out how it happened. I've had a busy day, Adele, and it would help if we could have this conversation indoors.'

Adele shrugged and peered once again into the night before closing the door and leading her into the kitchen. She had been working on her laptop. Three mugs half-filled with cold coffee cluttered the kitchen table.

'You challenged that statement with a very strong response.' Rachel observed the rigid set of the young woman's shoulders, her restless movements as she snapped her laptop closed and cleared away the crockery, clacking the mugs together and dumping them into the sink.

'It was a vicious lie,' Adele snapped. 'Why shouldn't I challenge it?'

'Was that the reason for the break-in?'

'I don't want to talk about it.' She rinsed the mugs and smacked them on to the draining board. 'I told Larry I wasn't prepared to make a report so there's no sense arguing with me about my decision.' She sat down at the table and stared defiantly back at Rachel. 'I'm leaving here as soon as possible and I don't want to get caught up in some police investigation that won't lead anywhere.'

Her engagement ring was missing; instead there was a white circle stark against her tanned skin. Conscious of Rachel's scrutiny, she folded her arms across her chest.

'Is this your property?' Rachel opened a small, velvet bag and emptied the engagement ring on to the table.

Adele's eyes widened when she saw it. As if unsure of its validity, she touched the ring with her index finger, then cradled it in her palm.

'Yes, it's mine,' she said. 'Where did you find it?'

'That's irrelevant for the moment. You'll have to come to the station tomorrow to officially declare it missing before you can claim it back.'

'Okay. I can do that.'

'This ring obviously means a lot to you.'

'It does… did.' She slipped the ring onto her finger and studied the intricate design. 'I was thinking of how I should return it to my ex-fiancé when I lost it.'

'You didn't lose it, Adele. We both know it was stolen. I suspect it was an opportunistic robbery and was not the real reason for the break-in.'

'You're wrong, Sergeant. I lost it somewhere along the riverbank. It's always been a bit too wide for my finger.' Jiggling the ring, she tried to demonstrate its looseness.

'Looks like a perfect fit to me,' said Rachel. 'So, please stop playing games, Adele. We searched the riverbank this afternoon and found a mask discarded in the undergrowth. That led directly to the recovery of your ring.'

Rachel spread the mask before her and Adele, her eyebrows lifting, hunched forward to stare at it. Unable to disguise the impact it was having on her she pressed her hand to her mouth to control the sudden chatter of her teeth.

'Two people have been arrested and will go on trial for robbery and malicious damage to property,' said Rachel. 'It's just a matter of time before we arrest the third. Three blind mice. In the light of what you've posted on your blog, this has to mean something to you.'

'I won't be pressing charges against anyone.' Adele sounded as if all the energy had been flattened from her voice.

'If you were intimidated—'

'I never said I was intimidated. You're putting words in my mouth. I told you I lost my ring. The break-in is Larry's concern, not mine. I'm not prepared to report it.'

'I believe they were sent to silence you.' Rachel was familiar with the methods of intimidation. The branding of fear on skin, the cleaving of the tongue to the mouth.

'From where I'm sitting, they appear to have done an excellent job,' she continued. 'Do you know who they are? I don't mean your attackers. They're hired thugs. But the men you believe are responsible for that crime against your mother. Can you name them? If you have information that will help us find the culprits, you must tell me.'

'Does that mean you believe me?' Adele asked.

'Yes.'

'And the diary?'

'That, also.'

When had that happened? The crossing of that delicate line between disbelief and belief? A transition subtle enough to have caught her unawares. Rachel tried not to think of the enormity of her admission, afraid of where it would lead her. She should be at home with Bob, soft music in the background, his arms around her as she broke the news that she had held inside herself for too long. Instead, she was acting far beyond the call of her official duty, searching for what…? These days, she was in a constant state of alert, insidious thoughts gnawing like a toothache.

'The information you received when you were running your blog must have been overwhelming,' she continued. 'Surely you have your suspicions as to their identity.' She was a trained professional, capable of receiving terrifying information without flinching. Now, she was forced to draw on all her resources to maintain her deadpan expression and not burst into tears of relief when Adele shook her head.

'I don't believe I'll ever find out who they are.' She slid her engagement ring across the table to Rachel. 'I'll call into the station tomorrow and collect my ring but I'm not making accusations against anyone. I'm closing down The Marianne Diary but I'm going to do what I can to help others who have nothing except their memories to mark their time in Atonement.'

Rachel gathered up the bag containing the mask, along with Adele's ring, and prepared to leave.

'You may think you've failed but you've told your mother's story,' she said. 'It's out there now, not trapped under the eaves of an attic.' Rachel handed a business card to her. 'Should you change your mind and want to talk about what happened to you, phone this number.'

She hesitated for an instant before touching the younger woman's shoulders. How brittle they felt, drawn forward like wings in flight, resistant to her touch. Her brown eyes watered as Rachel's ring tangled in her hair.

'If you need me, call any time, day or night' she said and left.

The bleep of a text distracted her as she walked away. Another emergency at the news desk. Bob would be late home. Overcome by relief, she stumbled on loose gravel and almost fell. Outwardly, all seemed normal, if politeness was ever the barometer of their marriage. He had not referred to the conversation they had had on the night of Christy's funeral but they both knew it had marked a turning point in their marriage.

CHAPTER THIRTY-EIGHT

Julie

Social media had been buzzing with comments since Marianne Mooney's Garda statement went online. One devastating anonymous post and her diary was toast. Liam's smile when he saw the statement, tight and satisfied, had slanted towards her.

'There's no way Adele Foyle can come back from that disaster.' He had emerged from the shower, rubbing his hair vigorously and combing it into position, side split, short back and sides. Neat, like everything about him.

'Could Marianne have signed that statement under duress?' Julie had asked. 'She could have been too traumatised to know what she was doing, especially if she was dealing with Jack Bale. And Garda Gunning, if I remember rightly, was cut from the same cloth.'

'Duress?' He knotted his tie and inspected the result in the mirror. 'You speak as if you believe her diary. When did this epiphany take place?' He put on his glasses, rimless, almost invisible against his pale complexion. The summer was a heatwave but he was too busy working to turn his face to the sun.

'I'm simply asking a question, Liam. I remember the rumours that were spread about her—'

'Facts, Julie. *Facts.*'

What facts, she had wanted to shout. What facts were you arguing about when I opened the door of your home office and glimpsed your fear?

'We crucified her, Liam. She was just a kid and we turned on her like a pack of animals. For what? That's what I've never understood. Could Jack Bale have started those rumours and, if so, why?'

He had remained standing, his arms folded, watching her. 'Isn't it rather late in the day to develop a conscience?'

'Everyone is entitled to a conscience,' she replied. 'You need to respect mine. I know how I treated her and my shame belongs only to me.'

'Then go for it, Julie. Self-shame all you like. Just don't expect me to share some form of collective guilt with you.'

He had been incandescent with rage when Adele blogged her response to the statement and published that damning entry about Jack Bale and his coercive tactics. She had not been online since then. Until tonight, Julie was convinced she had closed down her blog, but Adele had fired a final salvo at those who considered The Marianne Diary to be fake. She had apologised for the closure of her website. She gave no reason for her decision but, instead, she had posted a copy of an email she had received from a former resident at The House of Atonement.

My dear Adele, I want to thank you for exposing the conditions that existed in the House of Atonement. I knew Marianne Mooney well. Her diary brought me right back to those days. She was a beautiful, lost young girl, stricken down by an appalling crime. She supported me when I was told my beautiful twin girls died. I moved to New Zealand with my boyfriend when I left the House of Atonement and finally, after years of enquiries, we discovered that our daughters did not die from their premature birth, but were adopted by an American family. I have been in touch with my girls and hope to visit them soon. I consider myself lucky in that my own mother spoke the truth before she died, unlike my father, and gave me a chance to find peace of mind again.

There is so much false information out there. So many obstacles to overcome. Your blog has been a catalyst for me. Please keep blogging. It is never too late to expose a grievous wrong. I'm setting up a website called 'Glorious Survivors Together' for the mothers who spent time in the House of Atonement. This will be a safe space to tell our stories and share information that can help us in our search for the babies who were snatched from us.

Thank you for your courage.

Siobhan Miley

Liam was working late again. With Stephanie still away, it was generally after ten or even eleven when he arrived home and Julie was usually in bed, pretending to be asleep. On an impulse, she googled Siobhan Miley and located her website. Siobhan had issued a statement regretting the closure of Adele's blog and insisted that the final diary entry had exposed the fraudulent Garda statement for what it was.

The air in the attic smelled of dust and neglect. Julie had never entered the attic until tonight when she had been driven by a dangerous compulsion to climb the ladder stairs and investigate what lay beyond the closed trapdoor. She shuddered when she switched on the light. Gloria's possessions were everywhere. Rails of dresses, jackets and coats, protected by plastic covers, expensive brands, many with price tags still attached. Shoes and handbags were still in their boxes. What was wrong with Liam? He should have sent her clothes to a charity shop years ago. Perhaps it had been easier for him to let her presence moulder up here than face the fact that his mother had led two lives, the inspirational fantasist and the compulsive shopaholic.

She was unable to see the boxes that had originally been stored in the den. Liam could have destroyed the contents when the building had been demolished. She was about to give up when she pushed aside a rail of evening dresses and recognised the rattan crate and, next to it, the safe. Did the previous combination still work? Holding her breath, she tried the numbers, and exhaled with relief when the lock clicked open.

The contents were the same as she remembered. The attic was stuffy, a sticky heat that beaded her forehead with sweat. She felt weak, dizzy from having too much information and no knowledge of how to handle it. She found a letter at the back of the safe and unfolded it.

Dear Gloria,

My sincerest apologies for not responding sooner to your last letter. Duties of state occupy my time and demand my constant attention, just as your vocation stretches you to the limits of your responsibilities.

I'm relieved to know that the Mooney girl has settled into your care and is in good health. Her pregnancy is a most unfortunate occurrence but it has been handled with tact and sensitivity. Her time with you will provide her with excellent work experience and keep her gainfully occupied until her confinement ends.

I've heard from her unfortunate mother. She is finding peace of mind in Hard Wind and is grateful for the support she has received. I agree with you that the commune, situated, as it is, on the magnificent west coast of Kerry, is the ideal place for her to recover from her ordeal. Thank the Lord that the fuss over the Mooney incident has died down and a resolution been found to the difficulties that arose because of it.

Liam is like a son to me and is welcome to stay with Keith until you return from your mission. We hope to move into Hillcrest as soon as the new house is finished. Just one slight issue. Jack feels his worth is not valued. It's something we need to discuss when I visit again.

I head to Chicago next week and will meet up with the Bradshaws, as you requested. Their pride in their son is unbounded, as is their gratitude. I will meet with their friends, who are overjoyed to know that through you and your blessed sodality, their travails are over and their dearest wishes about to be realised. Your main responsibility is to provide a reliable and trustworthy courier to deliver this joy safely into their arms.

Write back when you have time and bring me up to date on the girl's progress. She need not worry about her baby's future. A happy and privileged home is ready and waiting for her son or, if ordained by God, her daughter. May he continue to bless your holy work and those in your loving care.

Sincerely yours,

Christy

The years had yellowed the pages but nothing could diminish the hypocrisy that oozed from every line. The coded references and oily reverence, the bland indifference to Marianne's fate. Could Julie have understood those words so clearly if she was not already familiar with the entries in the diary?

Working quickly, she examined the rest of the contents in the safe. She missed her daughter. Stephanie had been keen to spend the summer in France with her grandmother and improve her language skills. She loved her grandmother but Julie suspected there was more than love involved. Escape, that was what Stephanie had sought, a brief respite from the unacknowledged but unrelenting tension the thirteen-year-old sensed between her parents.

Hearing Liam's footsteps, she tensed, unable to believe he had returned early from work. When he entered the attic, she had closed the safe and was back at the rails examining his mother's clothes.

'What are you doing?' he asked. There was nothing threatening in his manner or his tone but she had learned to read his body language: the thrust of his chin, his lips thinning, as if the downward force of his anger had compressed his mouth.

'Why on earth didn't you clear out Gloria's wardrobe after she died?' Julie ran her fingers lightly along the plastic covers. 'All those lovely dresses and coats, her shoes, any charity shop would sell them in a flash.'

'You haven't answered my question,' he said. 'Why are you snooping around her possessions? What are you hoping to find? Evidence that she was selling babies? Is that what you believe, eh? Come on, Julie. Spit it out. Tell me what really goes on behind that serene face you present to the world.'

'Don't I have a right to be curious?' she asked. 'I'm surrounded by her furniture, her religious paraphernalia. You refuse to get rid of anything that belonged to her so I figured her clothes would probably be in the attic.'

'Clever girl. Go to the top of the class.'

'Why do you never discuss her with me? You always claim you're protecting her reputation but what if it doesn't need protecting? She neglected you, Liam. You were only eight years old when your father died yet all she was concerned about was building up her sodality and leaving you in the care of others. Have you ever considered the impact her negligence must have had on you?'

She regretted the words as soon as she uttered them. Discussing Gloria had never been easy. The early stage of their marriage had been fraught with arguments about the influence she still exerted over him. Eventually, Gloria became a taboo subject, an unspoken agreement that Julie would accept his need to keep her possessions around him. An abnormal need, she admitted to Davina in the days when they used to share secrets. It became less of an issue when Stephanie was born and the love they felt at this new arrival created a stronger bond between her and Liam.

'Always the counsellor, even when you're on a very slippery slope,' he said. 'This renewed interest in my mother only happened after that blog went up. Why is that?'

'It has nothing to do with Gloria,' she replied. 'I feel ashamed…'

She struggled to hide her agitation when he moved closer to her.

'Mea culpa, mea culpa, I'm familiar with your refrain.' He fisted his chest three times as he spoke. 'You read those outrageous claims and decided she was the villain. Even what that Garda statement was published you questioned its validity.'

'I simply suggested—'

Her breath shortened when he uncurled his fists and closed his hands around her throat. His grip, light but firm, drew her towards him. Aware of her panic – she was unable to hide it – he pushed her back against the rail. The clothes shook, as if galvanised into life and the dust of decades swirled under the attic light.

'Am I one of your suspects?' he demanded. 'Is that why you're here? Searching for the three blind mice.' His laughter had a higher pitch than usual, feverish, she thought, an alien sound that scraped like a nail inside her head. 'Come on, Julie. Out with it. Do you believe I was involved?'

'Of course I don't. For God's sake, Liam, why would you even ask me such a question?' Would he tighten his grip even more if she struggled? 'I appreciated how upset you were at the way Gloria was portrayed in that diary and I fully supported you in your efforts to bring out an injunction against the blog. But I never for a moment associated you with that alleged assault on Marianne Mooney.' She sounded convincing, reassuring, yet she had no idea if her words were having any impact on him. Lies, all lies, her inner voice taunted her. Ask him about the night Jack Bale came here with Keith and Bob. Ask him why he pretended they had met to discuss the annual Reedstown festival. Ask him why the venom in his voice when he spoke about Adele Foyle had chilled your blood.

Slowly, he relaxed his hand and steadied her. 'You're right about this stuff. I'm going to get rid of everything. Let's get out of here.'

Her palms were slick with sweat as she began to climb down the ladder stairs. He followed her, his feet within inches of her face. If he kicked back at her she would be unable to hold on. The thought that he might do so added to her fear. This was the first time he had ever touched her with violence. No, she corrected herself. The first time was that night in his office when she came to him. She believed she had seduced him but it was he who had held her hair in his fist as he bent her over the desk. That same latent savagery coming to the fore then, as it had just now when he grasped her neck in a hold that suggested he could snap it as easily as he could caress it.

A new day would soon begin in New Zealand. Siobhan Miley would open her blog on a wintery morning and fill her kitchen with sunlight. She would stare at her screen, unable to believe that an anonymous source had contacted her during an Irish night with photographed birth certificates. Certificates that contradicted the fact that all this precious information had been destroyed by fire and it was possible after all for those who had been incarcerated in Atonement to discover the path their children had followed when they were wrenched from their mothers.

CHAPTER THIRTY-NINE

Rachel

Two hair follicles that could read the past and rip apart the future. Rachel's hand trembled as she opened the envelope. The sheet of paper that she removed fluttered gently in response. What wild impulse had driven her to carefully untangle strands of Adele's hair from her ring and preserve them? The same suspicion that had had her pluck strands of hair from the brush Bob used in the mornings. Not knowing was worse than knowing, she had convinced herself as she sent the results to a DNA testing service she trusted. Now, reading the report, this belief was as arid as ash.

Apart from the heave of her breath and the low, anguished cry she gave when she folded the letter and replaced it in the envelope, all was quiet in the bedroom. Was it possible for her world to collapse without a sound? Rachel had never asked him why his hair, so shaggy and black when he was a teenager, had turned grey by his nineteenth birthday. She suspected it had happened during the time when he left home and entered rehab. She had seen photographs of him in those early days in New York, his head almost skull-like in its bareness. But the greying began before then. Oh, yes, Rachel thought, it began the moment he laid hands on Marianne Mooney. Would Adele's shining hair silver before its time? A genetic imprint; it was entirely possible.

She was off duty today, alone in the house she had created with him. The bedroom where they had conceived their child was alight with sunshine. His other child, his unclaimed daughter, had inherited the tenacity that had made him such an insightful journalist when he wrote for the *Webster Journal.* It was only a matter of time before she would uncover her story.

Whatever dark place he inhabited twenty-five years previously had been left behind when he moved away from Reedstown. She wanted to find consolation in this belief; but it was cold comfort and could not change what went before.

The water in the shower was cold. Needles of ice pummelling her body. Her skin looked sickly pale, almost translucent, which described exactly how she felt. Airy, as if she could float away and lose herself in some far-distant stratosphere. She collapsed back on the bed and closed her eyes, unable to bear the images that flashed relentlessly before her eyes.

DO IT DO IT DO IT… Wild boys with their fast bikes and reckless parties, their disregard for their own safety, buoyed up by the invincibility of youth and the belief that days of reckoning never came.

She was dressed and waiting for him when he came home. Their marriage had come undone so suddenly, so rapidly, that he seemed like a stranger who had blundered into her life. And yet… and yet… she hungered for what they had before, for what she had imagined was to come. How uncomplicated love had seemed then. What must it be like to build that love on a lie? To push back the dark side of memory every day? Had there been an interim of freedom, the relief of amnesia, between the events of that terrible night and the appearance of Adele Foyle, whose mind was set on discovering her beginnings?

'What is it, Rachel?' His smile faded when he saw her expression. 'Has something happened in work—?'

'Bob, sit down. I need to talk to you.'

'My God, you're shaking. Come here… tell me what's wrong.'

'Adele Foyle is Marianne Mooney's daughter.'

He was silent as he listened to her. His features had sharpened, as if this information had slashed his mouth into a rictus.

'When did you discover this?' he asked.

'I knew from the beginning.'

'You never told me.'

'I saw no reason to do so. She came to me in confidence and told me she was investigating her mother's past. She was determined to find the man who had fathered her.'

'Why are you telling me this now?'

Did he know what was coming? Could he feel it in the air, like a canary in a mine shaft, a rat on a ship, adrift?

'Your DNA proves you are her biological father.'

Her words folded his body in two. She heard him swallow, his breath sharply expelled. 'You tested…' He was silenced by the enormity of what she had done.

'Hair follicles,' she said. 'Yours and hers. This is the result.'

His hand trembled as he took the report from her. As she let it go, she knew she was sundering their marriage. No explanation, no apology or plea would ever be able to fix it.

'You did this behind my back?' He made no effort to read it. 'Without my permission?'

'Yes.'

'How could you…?' As if realising the ineffectiveness of what he was about to say, he stopped and coughed, dryly. 'You loved me yet you believed I was responsible for such a vicious crime?'

Was he aware that he was speaking in the past tense?

'Read the report,' she said. 'Then we can talk.'

She saw the strength go from his neck as he scanned the sheet of paper before laying it carefully down on the coffee table.

'You could have asked me,' he said. 'You could have been upfront with me instead on trampling over my rights and doing this behind my back.'

'On the night of Christy's funeral, I tried. You fobbed me off with a lie about drugs—'

'That wasn't a lie.'

'Yes, it was. Oh, I've no doubt there was a trumped-up charge that was conveniently dropped to put pressure on you to leave, but why? The "why" was what I kept asking myself. Skin in the game, that was what Jack Bale said. He believed it would silence me. Stop me asking questions. Christy Lewis, too. Both of them believed I would release that statement to protect you and undermine Adele's blog. I couldn't do that, Bob… I couldn't bear…'

For the first time since confronting him her composure cracked. Seemingly unable to bear her anguish, he read the report again, more slowly this time, then let it fall to the floor.

'You were the weak link, that's what Christy called you. He was right. Your conscience would have dragged the other two down with you had you remained here. In New York it was possible for you to forget and build a new life.'

'*Forget?*' Was he angry or in agony as he crashed his fists off his knees? 'You believe it's possible to forget something like that?'

If it was anger, it was a puny thing and she must ignore it. His agony, also, could not affect her. Stay in control, she warned herself… but of what? Her marriage was shattering as they spoke. She willed his voice to strengthen, to boom a denial that would batter her into believing him.

'Adele is your daughter,' she repeated. 'You can demand a retest but the result will still be the same. I see you in her. Your cheeks and eyes, the way she holds her head when she laughs, even your

teeth, that same side tooth out of alignment. Once I mapped
her face, you were all I could see. The real you, the man I fell
in love with, began to disappear and I could only imagine that
young girl crushed on the floor. I knew I would go mad unless
I discovered the truth.' She was crying now, recoiling from him
when he tried to hold her.

'I don't remember any of it.' He was barely audible. 'My
mind is a blank about that night. That's what kept me sane all
those years. But the nightmares, it's there, all of it, jumbled and
chaotic but I know what I did… what *we* did to her.' His voice
trailed away, a lost sound, thick with grief. No fear, not yet. He
was still absorbing the shock of his discovery.

'Did you suspect the child in the diary could be yours?'

'I wondered. But I never made the connection with Adele. I
should have guessed. She was so driven… so angry.'

'Tell me what happened,' she said. 'Tell me everything that
you, Keith and Liam did that night.'

He showed no reaction to the other names. They were a perfect
fit. Three blind mice… see how they run… Would hating him
make this any easier, she wondered as he began to speak?

'She reported Keith for bullying. She saw him in action. He
enjoyed throwing his weight around and there was this shy kid,
he was a bit of a geek, into computers and maths. The perfect
target for Keith. He beat him up one day on his way home from
school. When he discovered Marianne had reported him to the
school principal, he made a bet with myself and Liam that he'd…'
He shook his head. 'You don't need to know.'

'That he'd *fuck* her.' She hurled the word at him. 'I know how
these things work.'

'Yes, that's what he planned to do. Then he'd spread the word
that she was a good lay… or wasn't.' His hands hung desolately
between his knees and she was forced to lean forward to hear him.

'Keith hadn't a chance with her. She was a slight little thing but plucky. And she was in love with Shane Reagan.' He shook his head. 'That night… I'm not using drugs as an excuse—'

'Then don't,' she snapped.

'We'd been drinking, too. Partying in Liam's den when his mother was away on one of her tours. I swear to you, we just meant to scare them… well, that's what I believed. We thought they'd be together but Shane was late going to her.'

She imagined them high as kites, all restraint gone as they were swept along on the high of their collective savagery. He began to cry, such a harsh, ugly sound.

'How did you get away with it?' she asked. She could guess the scenario, the call from Jack Bale to Christy Lewis, the youths, now terrified and sobering fast, confessing. 'Your father and Gloria Thornton must have been involved,' she said. 'How convenient it was to have a ready-made mother and baby home to hide her away.'

'You have it all figured out,' he said. 'What more do you want me to add?'

'Everything,' she wailed. 'What was said? What excuses were made to explain what you'd done? Did you make any attempt to tell the truth? Did you suffer shame… disgust… remorse?' Her voice was unrecognisable, her throat strained with grief. 'Or were you so intent on your own self-survival that all you felt was relief that the grown-ups could take care of everything?'

'We were only eighteen—'

'*Don't.*' She rocked forward and held her hands over her ears. 'She was fifteen and you destroyed her.'

'Please hear me out, Rachel.' He waited until she was still again and able to listen. 'I destroyed myself that night. For years after I left here, I was filled with self-hatred. I sought help, counselling, tablets, I even self-harmed. Nothing helped. I knew the only solution was to make recompense to the person I'd harmed but she was dead and there was nothing, not even a grave to mark her presence. I finally found a shrink who helped me find some peace of mind. That's when I started writing for the *Webster Journal*. The only reason I came back here was because my father was dying. He couldn't look at me on his deathbed, nor I at him. Shame, it's corrosive, no matter how hard you try to suppress it. We only spoke once about that night. That was shortly before he died. I saw the same shame in him. But talking about it released something that had been trapped inside me all those years. It opened me up to the possibility of love—'

'I can't bear to hear this.'

'My father died believing I'd return to New York. The *Review* was to be sold and he accepted that I'd crack up again if I remained here. But I'd met you… do you remember our first meeting at—'

'Stop it… *stop* it.'

'I fell in love with you. It was as simple and as sudden as that. So much time had passed and I thought I deserved to be happy. I took that chance, Rachel. Has our marriage any hope of surviving this?'

'No.' She was exhausted, drained emotionally and also physically, aware that her body was undergoing changes that had nothing and everything to do with the turmoil she was suffering. 'I'm leaving you and moving from Reedstown. I'll submit my letter of resignation to the force tomorrow. All I want from you is your signature on our divorce papers when they come through.'

'It can't be as final as that? Rachel, please—'

'Do you honestly expect it to be otherwise?'

"That person… that monstrous person I was that night… that's not me. It never was. Don't run away from me when I need you most. We can deal with this together—'

'How? That child was forced to sign a statement blaming Shane Reagan and she is not around to refute it. Your daughter believes she was murdered. Technically, she's wrong but if you follow her logic, then yes, you have her mother's blood on your hands.'

'If you'll support me, I'll make my own confession…' His lips continued to move, his eyes implored her, but she was beyond hearing him, seeing him.

'As if you have any chance of bringing Liam Thornton and Keith Lewis to justice.' Twilight had fallen outside and his face was in shadow. He must see her in the same blurred silhouette. She had no desire to turn on the light and confront his ravaged features. He must look like death, she thought. Like the young man who moved to New York, a cadaver who had to learn how to live again.

'I have one last question for you,' she said. 'You had a meeting with the others—'

'Jack was warning us to stay united… I didn't want to know. I was sickened—'

'Had you anything to do with the attack on Adele that took place in Brooklime?'

He shook his head, not in denial but puzzled as he tried to grasp what she meant. 'What attack?'

'She's too terrified to tell me what was done to her. But I know that Grad Wheeler and two others carried it out. They were wearing masks. Three blind mice… no mistaking the symbolism there but they were just the hired help. It was organised by others who are determined to silence her.'

'I swear to you I'd nothing to do with it. Nor did I know anything about it. Was she hurt… what did they do to her?'

'How do you define rape, Bob?'

'Please, Rachel…' Unable to continue, he pressed his hands to his eyes.

'The penis is not always the weapon of choice when committing such a crime.' She was speaking too fast, her anger on the verge of hysteria as she described what a chastened Haylee had confessed to her. 'A gun, for instance, that's a mighty weapon when someone is helpless on a bed. I know what happened to Adele that night. Not a first-hand account, unfortunately. She's too frightened to confide in me but I have a reliable report of what took place in Brooklime when those thugs broke in.'

'As God is my judge, I'd nothing to do with this.' He was on his feet, his face averted as he turned from her and headed towards the living-room door.

'Don't walk away from me, Bob.'

'I'll never walk away from you, Rachel. You're the one who has made that decision.'

'Where are you going?' She followed him up the hall.

'Does it matter?' About to open the front door, he turned back to her, his expression unreadable. Only the tears drying on his cheeks indicated that everything they both held dear had been irrevocably snatched from them.

CHAPTER FORTY

Adele

Adele tidied the kitchen and checked that all the doors and windows were locked. This was the most difficult time of the day; with nothing left to distract her, she was unable to stop thinking about Daniel. Not that she was particularly successful at banishing him from her thoughts at any time. Songs, voices, laughter, couples holding hands, strangers with profiles similar to his… she walked through a world that evoked him at every turn. He invaded her dreams, awakening her on the cusp of pleasure, a sensation so intense that she was unable to separate it from pain.

The doorbell sounded and the outside light switched on automatically. She could see a figure through the glass panels on the front door. She froze as the letter box rattled and opened. A voice, male and familiar, called her name.

'Adele, it's Bob Molloy. I need to talk to you.' She had not seen him since the row in Katie's Kasket when he had drawn the attention of her tormentors from her to him. Unable to understand why he would call so late at night she stood aside for him to enter the house.

'What's wrong?' she asked. 'Has something happened to Sergeant Darcy?'

'Rachel is okay,' he said. 'I didn't mean to frighten you.'

'I'm not frightened. Just surprised to see you.' Only one reason could bring him here. He must have information that related to her blog. Perhaps, he intended giving her space in the *Review* to pursue her search. Too late, Bob, she thought as he stood awkwardly in the living room, his eyes fixed on her with such concentration that she looked away, embarrassed by the hunger of his gaze.

'Sit down, Bob.' She gestured towards a chair. 'Can I get you a drink? I've some beer in the fridge.'

'No… no.' He ignored the armchair and remained standing. 'You closed your blog down very suddenly.'

'It was causing a lot of aggravation.'

'Rachel told me you were attacked over it.'

'Did she?'

'Yes. She said you were afraid to make an official complaint. They frightened you, these intruders.'

'Yes, they frightened me.'

'One of them had a gun, she said.'

'Bob, why are you discussing this with me? Are you going to write something about it in the *Review*? If so, I won't allow it—'

'I'm not… don't be upset. Were they the trio who were bothering you in the Kasket?'

'If you're not going to write about it, what does it matter to you?'

'I figured it had to be them.' He nodded distractedly. 'They'll never bother you again. I can assure you of that.'

Increasingly puzzled by his distress, she remained standing and waited for him to continue.

'That night your mother was attacked—'

'Gang-raped.' How did he know her true identity?

'Gang-raped…' His cheeks had furrows she had never noticed until now. 'Adele, I don't know how to confess this to you.'

'Confess?' The anger he had shown in the café that afternoon had been replaced by desolation. That was the only word that came to mind. Desolation in the slope of his shoulders and the aging of his features. Manifest in his gaze as he stared at her.

'You were one of them,' she whispered. As she spoke she was convinced the floor had shifted like a swing bridge, the sudden sway causing her stomach to pitch, her legs to wobble.

What an effort it took to hold his gaze. To search his tormented features for shades of herself. She thought of Shane, who could have been her father, how she would have loved that, and her mother, stolen from her by childbirth complications, and the harsh expression on her grandmother's face when Adele had asked about the parents who conceived her... and when she screamed at him, this brute who could be her father ... screamed at him to get out of her sight... her voice, shrill with the suppressed fury of her young life... her only intention was to inflict pain on him. To reject his apologies, his pleas, his pathetic excuses that came twenty-four years too late for her.

He stretched out as if to touch her, then, when she recoiled, let his hands hang limply in front of him. He reminded her of a marionette whose strings had been cut and he, as if aware of her thoughts, her growing fury, straightened his shoulders and stared pleadingly at her. She recognised him then. He was the one. Finally, her father had a name, a face. Knowing the blood that flowed between them, and hating it, she flung open the hall door. Get out... get out... get out... Her hand reached out into the darkness and directed him from her life, forever.

CHAPTER FORTY-ONE

Rachel

When an hour had passed and he had not returned or made contact with her, Rachel rang him. His phone went immediately to message. Her thoughts turned darker after another hour had passed and she had still not heard from him. Unable to wait any longer, she drove through the village and out along Loyvalley Road towards the river.

She parked in the car park and continued on foot. A mist had settled over the river. Wispy and as ephemeral as a wraith, it flitted between the trees. The whispery rustle of the reeds was muted, as if they were trapped in the vaporous stillness. The riverbank was deserted. No youths hanging about tonight, no bonfires blazing, no secret deals. She beamed her torch over the shrouded river. A swan rose upwards in an ungainly flap of wings and flew low above the water. Ducks and water hens emerged briefly from the haze and swam in zigzags, as if they had lost their way. Uncertain of her footing on the rutted path, Rachel walked cautiously, knowing there were unseen holes ahead that could twist her ankle. Feathery plumes brushed across her hands when she strayed too close to the reeds. Bubbles erupted under her feet and burst into stinking splatters of mud as she searched for a sign that suggested the night had been disturbed by a tortured mind. She stumbled back to the path, aware that each step she took must be tested.

She stopped outside Brooklime. The house was in darkness. When she rang Adele's number, her phone went immediately to message. Her car was outside. She suspected Adele was deliberately avoiding her. She drove from the river and turned up Summit Road. The downstairs lights were still on in Hillcrest. After a short pause, Davina answered the door. She made no attempt to hide her surprise as she invited Rachel inside.

'I need to speak to Keith.' Rachel didn't move any further than the hall and Davina waited, her eyebrows lifting, for her to elaborate.

'It's important that I speak to him immediately.' She knew she sounded formal and curt. Davina, with a shrug, said, 'If it's private, you'd better see him in his study.'

The study was separate from the open-plan design of the rest of the cottage, a small room festooned with old election posters featuring Christy, and more recent ones with Keith's face. The newest ones, not yet on the street, were stacked against the wall. Davina, Rachel had heard, was hoping to win her late father-in-law's seat when the by-election was announced.

'What a pleasant surprise, Rachel.' Keith's disarming blue eyes sized her up as she entered the room. 'How are you?'

'I'm worried, Keith.' She came straight to the point. 'That's why I'm here. Has Bob been in touch with you?'

'Recently, do you mean?'

'Tonight. Has he called or phoned?'

'No. Not since last week when he was looking for a quote from me for a feature he was writing on the new refugee settlement proposal for Reedstown. Why? Is something wrong?'

'We had an argument about Marianne Mooney. You remember her, I'm sure.'

Perched on the edge of his desk, his hands in his pockets, he seemed utterly relaxed. 'To be honest, I'd totally forgotten her existence until that blog went up. Even then, I found it difficult to remember her. She used to live in The Lodge and the publicity from that blog has had a huge impact on our privacy.'

'I'm sure it's been most inconvenient. If Bob contacts you, it's important that you let me know.' She was already moving towards the door.

'Wait.' He stood before her. His demeanour had changed, not outwardly, but his gaze was wary, speculative. 'What gave you the idea that he would come here?'

'Maybe I should have tried Liam's place. Wasn't that where you all met last time?'

'We had a brief meeting about this year's festival—'

'Keith, save the lies for your wife. I know the truth about the night Marianne Mooney was raped.'

He flinched, a barely perceptible blink, and continued to block her way. 'If you were arguing with Bob about that kid, there's absolutely no reason why he should make contact with me. The only time I ever hear from him is when he demands a quote for his newspaper, which he will inevitably distort.'

'There was nothing distorted about what he told me tonight about that young girl.'

'I've absolutely no idea what you're talking about.' He sounded genuinely puzzled – but then, he had had twenty-five years to perfect the art of lying.

She stepped closer to him. 'I'm talking about the night Marianne Mooney was set upon by three animals. Nine months later she was dead. Consequences, Keith, we can't escape them. Her death was a direct result of what happened to her in Blake's Hollow.'

She walked rapidly away from him, convinced she would feel his hand on her neck. But it was Davina who came from behind her and opened the front door.

'Why did you think your husband would come here?' she asked. She had obviously been listening to their conversation and her anger blistered the air between them. 'Keith was never his friend, even when they were teenagers. Whatever friendship you believe existed between them was entirely in Bob's imagination. I presume you're aware your husband had a serious drug problem?'

'There's nothing in Bob's past that we haven't discussed. *Nothing.*'

'Then you must know that Keith is always careful to avoid him,' she snapped. 'That same principle applies tonight. I suggest you check Barrow Lane in the search for your husband. Isn't that where addicts go when they are looking for a fix?' She closed the door on Rachel before she could reply.

Driving back down Summit Road, Rachel was seized by the need to retrace her footsteps. The river… was it possible? Or a tree, a rope, so easy. Her heart thumped as her apprehension grew. Her phone rang. She recognised the number. Garda Roberts was on night duty at the station. She was young and still inexperienced, and all that was evident as she breathlessly asked Rachel to go immediately to Reedstown University Hospital.

CHAPTER FORTY-TWO

Adele

'There's been a shooting at one of those new apartment complexes.' Adele was in bed when Larry rang her with the news. 'A man is seriously injured. I'm sorry for ringing so late but I thought you should know about it. The shooter was Grad Wheeler.'

The gun. She could see it in his hand, the barrel aimed between her eyebrows, sliding over the curve of her breasts, her taut stomach and onward, taunting her with its power. She sank back against the pillows and swallowed, hard. 'When did this happen, Larry?'

'A few hours ago. You've no reason to worry about that weirdo any more.'

'Who did he shoot?' A thought was building, brick upon brick, and leading her in only one direction.

'Bob Molloy, the newspaper guy. Incredible, isn't it? It's clearly a case of being in the wrong place at the wrong time.'

Black dots danced before her eyes. She heard a swooshing sound, as if waves were washing across shale. She bent her head to her knees and waited for the dizziness to pass. When it did, she could hear her voice screaming... *Get out... get out... get out...* were they to be the last words she would ever speak to him?

'How seriously injured is he?' she asked.

'It's not good, I'm afraid,' said Larry. 'The unfortunate man was shot in the chest. Far as I know, there's not much hope of him surviving.'

Adele had no memory of how she ended the call or how she came to the decision to visit the hospital. It seemed predestined, as if it was the only course of action she could take.

Earlier, she had refused to take Sergeant Darcy's phone call. She had huddled on the bed, her arms wrapped around her knees, until the ringing stopped. Had she been searching for her husband when she rang, wondering if he had called to see Adele? If so, she must have known he was one of the three. Had she been shielding him from justice all along, while fooling Adele into believing she cared about discovering the truth? Adele allowed the thought to fade. This was not the time to be burdened by doubts. Her father was critically ill and she needed to see him one last time.

Two squad cars were parked beside the ambulances at the emergency entrance. Adele hurried through the waiting room, where haggard-faced patients slumped in chairs as they waited their turn to be called. At the check-in desk, a tired-looking receptionist stared from her towards a computer screen.

'What is your relationship to the patient? he asked.

Tongue-tied, she stared at him, the word 'daughter' dying on her lips. Impossible to say it, to claim it, to even contemplate it. Far easier to lie than to admit the truth to this bleary-eyed stranger, who shook his head firmly when she said that Bob Molloy was a business colleague.

'Only close family can be admitted,' he said. 'I'm sorry.'

Adele checked her mobile phone and rang the 'missed call' number. It rang for a long time and she was about to give up when the sergeant answered. Her voice sounded different, high and bewildered, drained of energy.

'I heard… I don't know what to say…' Adele paused as she heard the intake of breath at the other end, the sharpening tone.

'Who is speaking?'

'Adele Foyle. I'm at reception. I had to come. But I'm not allowed up. It's only family.'

She waited for the sergeant to tell her to go home. That this was not Adele's concern; nor the time for futile gestures.

'I'll be with you shortly,' Sergeant Darcy said.

The woman who walked towards Adele seemed to have shrunk since the last time they had spoken. Her pale, lustreless eyes barely focused on Adele when she sat down beside her.

'Why are you here?' she asked.

'He came to see me tonight.' *Get out… get out… get out…* 'I told him to leave me alone. I'd no idea… no idea…' Adele made no effort to stem the tears running down her cheeks.

The sergeant rummaged in her pockets for tissues and handed them to her. 'Come with me,' she said and rose stiffly to her feet.

'She's family,' she called out to the receptionist, who looked up from the computer screen and nodded.

The medical team had done their best, Rachel explained, as they glided upwards in the elevator. He was now on life support but the prognosis was stark. The sounds of the hospital were muted, the nurses moving quietly between the wards, hushed voices soothing restless patients. Two young guards stood to attention when they saw the sergeant coming down the corridor. She spoke briefly to them, then placed her hand on the small of Adele's back and opened a door.

The insistent heart bleeps and rhythmic breathing of the ventilator resonated with life in the ward where Bob Molloy lay. The graphs on the screens moved giddily as they choreographed his final hours. Apart from the dressing on his head he could have been in a dreamless slumber, but Adele knew as soon as she saw him that he had gone elsewhere.

It was all so clear now. The primal surge of recognition when she met him for the first time. How easily she had dismissed that instant, believing it was of no more importance than the speculative glances she had exchanged with other men when she first arrived in Reedstown. How shocked he must have been when she mentioned Marianne. His disbelief that the past could rise and grab him so unexpectedly. She pressed her hand to his forehead. His skin was warm, soft.

Stripped of vitality, his features had been honed to their bare essence. Adele released a long, quivering sigh as she saw herself reflected in the slant of his cheekbones, the arch of his dark eyebrows, his mouth... She turned her head to her shoulder, unable any longer to look at him. Whether it was the presence of death gently waiting, or the clutch of his wife's hand holding on to Adele, she found the hate draining from her. It would return, but later, when she had the strength to endure it.

'I have to go now,' she said.

'Thank you for coming, Adele.' When the sergeant released her hand, the graphs on the screens seemed to jig with an even faster intensity. The bleeps stayed inside Adele's head as she hurried towards the elevator. The mist had given way to rain. It fell with a soundless beat against the glass as the automatic doors opened and released her into the dawn. She lifted her face to the sky and was unable to tell if it was the rain or her tears that soaked her face.

Reedstown Review
    The murder of Robert Molloy, editor and owner of the Reedstown Review, *which occurred last night, has stunned the community of Reedstown. The mood in the newspaper*

where he was respected and admired for his work ethic and integrity is one of deep shock and sadness as his co-workers try to come to terms with his untimely death.

Details are sparse so far but we are reliably informed that Robert (known affectionately to us as Bob) lost his life in an altercation that took place in the car park of a recently built apartment complex. He received one shot directly to his chest and was placed on life support at Reedstown University Hospital. A man has been arrested and is currently being questioned at Reedstown Garda Station. His period of detention has been extended to twenty-four hours.

Bob Molloy was married to Sergeant Rachel Darcy, who is on compassionate leave until further notice. She has requested that the Reedstown Review *be used to convey her gratitude to all those who have offered their assistance and condolences at this tragic time. Funeral details will be released at a future date.*

CHAPTER FORTY-THREE

Adele

Adele merged with the crowd, an anonymous mourner in a beige dress, a nondescript sun hat shading her eyes. Her grandmother had perfected the art of blending into her landscape and Adele hoped that she would be equally unobtrusive at her father's funeral. Father... The hopelessness of the word, its utter waste, yet she kept repeating it, as she had on the morning she left the hospital, repeating it as she drove back to Brooklime; an orphan, destined never to know her parents. She dismissed her brief acquaintance with Bob Molloy as meaningless. His amiable manner and friendly smile had disguised a monstrous secret. How was that possible? His crime should have marked him in some way, blotched his face with guilt and shame.

Her decision as to whether or not she should attend his funeral had been hard fought. That struggle still raged within her even as his coffin was lowered into the earth. Rachel was balanced so precariously at the edge of his grave that Adele feared she could collapse into that ghastly open space. Keith Lewis, standing tall above her, encircled her with his arms and drew her back to safety. She stood between him and his wife, her bowed presence emphasised by their solicitous presence. Was Adele the only person to notice her quick shudder when she moved away from them and scattered a handful of clay on the polished wood?

As the burial came to an end and the crowd broke apart, Adele left. She had no interest in attending the funeral reception in the Loyvale Hotel or in speaking to Rachel. The time they had spent together at the hospital seemed unreal, a dream that belonged to neither sleep nor wakefulness. She was unable to recall the urge that had driven her there, yet there must have been a belief that Rachel needed her and that words would not be necessary to explain her decision. But there was nothing dreamlike about her last encounter with him. His shamed, abject expression would always remain with her. She wanted to brush his face with a different patina, remember him laughing as he wiped a dollop of mayonnaise from his bottom lip, his lively expression as she spoke about documentaries she had made for Voice Dox, even his fury as he confronted Grad Wheeler in the Kasket. Could he possibly have realised he was confronting his murderer? Was that the reason he was dead? She imagined him feeding off his own fury by confronting Grad. This time when Grad aimed the gun, he had pulled the trigger. What if she had listened to him when he stood before her in Brooklime? Would it have made a difference? But what words could he have found that would have eased her rage, earned him her forgiveness?

She had phoned Daniel on the day her father was pronounced dead. She had reached the arc of her story and the hurts that had separated them seemed inconsequential, somehow. An automated voice on his phone told her he was uncontactable. When she rang Greendene Petro, another automated female voice with a southern drawl ordered her to press numbers. Eventually, she reached his answering machine and left a message. 'I need to talk to you, Daniel. I found the person I've been searching for. And now I'm broken. Please ring me.'

She had waited for his call all through that night and the following day. When it did not come she had wrapped his engagement ring in bubble wrap and posted it to him without a covering letter.

Sergeant Darcy came to Brooklime four days after the funeral. What could they say to each other? Small talk seemed impossible under such circumstances; they did not even try to discuss the changing weather or the magnificent send-off Bob had received.

'Under the circumstances I think we should abandon the formalities,' the sergeant said. 'Please call me Rachel.'

She had been to the reading of her husband's will. Her astonishment and shock when she discovered she was now the proprietor of the *Reedstown Review* was still evident. She looked as though she had been handed a poisoned chalice and was desperately anxious to pass it on. She intended selling the newspaper – maybe one of the big conglomerates would be interested – but for now it was business as usual with Bob's subeditor in charge. This brief conversation petered out into an awkward silence, until Adele, handing her a cup of herbal tea, said, 'How long had you known I was his daughter?'

'Not long.' Rachel accepted the cup and stared into the steaming liquid. 'I confronted him as soon as I was certain. That was the last time we spoke.'

The heartache of such a conversation. The pent-up emotions let loose between them. Had he struggled to defend the indefensible? Had she struggled to pardon the unpardonable and, finding that that was impossible, had her anguish driven him out into the night?

'You said he came to your house,' Rachel said. 'Did he give you any indication where he was going afterwards?'

'No. I didn't give him a chance to tell me anything. I couldn't believe that he…' Adele paused, unable to continue.

'Was your father?'

'Yes. And that he was one of the three. He was in agony but I sent him away. Did I send him to his death?'

'You must *never* think that, Adele. What happened to Bob had nothing to do with you.' She was adamant, snapped from her own internal concerns by Adele's question. 'The Gardai haven't yet managed to trace his movements after he left you but they will, I'm sure of it. I wish I could be part of the team but as Bob's wife I'm not allowed to participate in the murder investigation.'

Adele understood the reasons why Rachel Darcy needed to be kept at arm's length from the accused. Her expression suggested that if they removed such constraints, she would tear Grad Wheeler apart, limb by limb.

'How did you find out Bob was my father?' she asked.

'DNA. It wasn't difficult.'

'You had suspicions then?'

'I hoped desperately that they were unfounded. I couldn't live with them… they were destroying my marriage. Destroying what should have been the most perfect time between us.' Her fingers were hooked into a knot of grief that seemed impossible to untangle.

'He seemed so nice, yet he…how could he do that to my mother?'

'Don't ask me to answer that, Adele. He tried to explain but I'm not here to make excuses for him.'

'Do you know the identity of the other two?'

'Nothing that can be proved, especially now that he's… gone…' She paused, as if surprised by the impact the word had on her, then slowly released her breath. 'Now that he's gone there's nothing to implicate them.'

'Who are they?' Adele longed for names, shapes to put on them, but they remained a blank sheet that she might never be able to fill.

'I'm not going to tell you,' Rachel replied. 'It's dangerous information. I know what happened on the night Grad Wheeler attacked you. I've had confirmation from his girlfriend who was a witness to his actions. He came at you with a gun and threatened—'

'Stop.' Unable to listen, Adele silenced her with a wave of her hand.

Was it the same gun that killed him... her father... Rachel's husband? Rachel must have also been grappling with that same awareness when she stood up with a muttered apology and asked where she could find the bathroom. When she returned to the kitchen her eyes were red-rimmed. Adele suspected she had been crying soundlessly behind the closed door, but she seemed more composed. Her years of training came to the fore as she brought their meeting to an end.

So much left unspoken regarding those final hours she had shared with her husband. So much still unsolved regarding the chain of events that had led to his death.

'I'm on compassionate leave for now but when I'm back on duty, I promise I'll do everything I can to bring those men to justice,' she said. The determination of her face could not be doubted. Was it feasible that she would unmask them or was she simply whistling in the wind?

The file being prepared for the DPP would state that Bob Molloy's death was due to misadventure. An unfortunate case of mistaken identity. Grad Wheeler would be charged with manslaughter. The Gardai had received information that his name was on a hit list over the non-payment of a drug debt. Grad knew he was a target and he had mistaken Bob for a hit man. Bob would have sounded furious when he emerged from his car, threatening, and dangerous enough for Grad to turn and fire once. A clean strike.

Over the following weeks, Adele watched Rachel running along the river path in the evenings. She had always run before her husband's death and she was intent on continuing the same routine now. Sometimes she stopped off at Brooklime for a cup of herbal tea, camomile being her tea of choice, not that it helped her to relax. She was taut-strung as a bow wire, her compassionate leave still ongoing. Was it difficult, if not impossible, to cope with being one of the questioned rather than the inquisitor?

'To be honest, I don't know.' She shrugged when Adele asked. 'Right now, I don't think I'm capable of feeling anything.'

She quizzed Adele about her future. Did she intend hanging around Reedstown indefinitely? This time it was Adele who shrugged. She could return to London and gather the scattered rags of her old life around her. But the thought of beginning again without Daniel was too painful to consider. A trip to New Zealand was possible. Siobhan Miley had invited her to visit her home. They could work as a team on *Glorious Survivors Together*. Siobhan had received photographs of birth certificates, anonymous admittedly, but invaluable information, and she was still in a state of disbelief as she processed them.

One evening, alone in Brooklime, Adele wondered about the face of evil. Was it possible to tell the difference? Friend or enemy, they all looked alike to her, bland-faced and unremarkable. Would she pick Jack Bale out from a crowd and think him evil? Grad Wheeler? Bob Molloy? No, she would pass them on the street and assume them to be men with untarnished reputations.

The man hesitating outside the gate, seemingly unable to make up his mind whether or not he should enter, was equally unreadable. Adele watched from behind the curtains as he came to a decision and rang the doorbell. Her car was outside and she had opened the upstairs windows to allow the day's heat to escape. He must know she was cowering out of sight. Did that please him, knowing he had the power to terrify her? Or perhaps he was simply an innocent man sent to read her electricity meter or canvass her opinion on the forthcoming by-election. When she didn't answer by the third ring, he closed the gate behind him and walked to the edge of the river. Two swans swam past him with stately indifference and the dog woman came towards him, wheeling her dog in its buggy as usual. She stopped to speak to him and the man bent to have a conversation with the dog. The elderly woman laughed and clapped her hands before pushing her buggy onwards, the terrier straining to look back at the stranger.

Adele was standing at the front door when he crossed back from the river. He stopped when he saw her and pushed open the gate.

'Adele Foyle,' he said. 'I've wanted to speak to you ever since I read your blog but I've been abroad until now.'

'If you've come to complain about it, let me save you the trouble,' she said. 'I've closed it down.'

'I noticed.' He nodded. 'I'm sure you had your reasons for doing so. But I'm not here to complain.' His smile was hesitant, his eyes searching as they roved over her. 'My name is Shane Reagan.'

His handshake was firm enough to convince her that he was flesh and blood and his arms around her, when she told him she was Marianne's daughter, were strong enough to keep her upright.

In the days that followed, it was difficult to resist the urge to touch him to see if he was real and not some imaginary figure who would disappear if she looked the other way. His story was similar to the entries in Marianne's diary but he breathed life into it. Adele listened raptly as he described how he had been delayed leaving home by his mother on the evening he planned to meet Marianne. A jackdaw had nested in the chimney of their house and the living room filled with smoke when Carrie Reagan lit the fire. By the time the smoke was cleared and the nest dislodged, Shane was thirty minutes late. A bird nesting in a chimney. A bird nesting in an attic. The irony was not lost on either of them.

Hurrying and unaware of anything except that his time with Marianne was so short, he had been taken by surprise when two figures suddenly appeared in front of him and pulled him from his bike. Had he arrived as arranged, he would have fought to his death to protect her and she would have fought alongside him. As it was, he was stunned by one of them before he had time to register what was happening. When he recovered, he staggered into the cottage where Marianne, almost senseless, screamed and cowered away from him. She had scratched at his arms when he tried to lift her, too traumatised to recognise him, until his voice broke through her terror. Only then was he able to carry her from the cottage. She was like a rag doll, he told Adele, and almost as lifeless.

He had found the cigarette packet close to her. The cardboard was too hard and dry for it to be part of the litter that blew into the cottage. He had pocketed it, hardly aware of what he was doing until he reached the Garda station. When he pointed out the Chinese writings on it as he was handing it over he was silenced with a blow to the side of his head from Sergeant Bale and removed to a cell.

He never saw her again. The only people who believed he was innocent were his mother and the local curate, Father Breen, who came with her to the Garda station. He remembered the argument that broke out between the priest and Sergeant Bale as to why Marianne had not been brought to hospital. Rosemary had collected her daughter by then and the Garda statement had been signed. He had always believed Marianne had been coerced into signing it and he had wept openly when he read the last diary entry Adele had posted.

Three days, he said, that was all it took to uproot him from Reedstown and return him to Australia. The only silver lining in that dark cloud had been the reuniting of his parents. Carrie had joined the Reedstown Reminiscences Facebook group to keep up with the friends she had made in Reedstown and when she read the announcement about Adele's blog, she had immediately made Shane aware of it.

He was in Afghanistan then, a war photographer and constantly on the move. So many war zones to cover, he told Adele. Reading the diary was like watching a familiar film, he said. One that he had constantly replayed in his mind, only now the actors were in different positions and the spotlight had a harsher shine on those who had betrayed Marianne.

No wife. There had been opportunities but he had never been able to commit to a long-term relationship. Was Marianne the reason? He was non-committal when Adele asked. Twenty-five years was too long to hold a memory but the sight of her huddled figure on the floor still played on his mind. It was not an image to take with him into any marriage, he admitted.

His jaw hardened when he heard how the chilling touch of a gun pressed to Adele's skin had caused her to abandon her search for justice.

'Where is he now?' he raged. 'Tell me where I can find him.'

She could imagine him felling Grad or his accomplices with one blow. He had the wiry toughness of someone familiar with violence and unfazed by its viciousness. But he would be gone soon and she would be alone again.

'Right now he's in jail, awaiting trial for the murder of my father.' Bluntly and without emotion, she outlined the details of her last conversation with Bob Molloy. How she turned her back on him, unable to accept his truth, his shame, and how, in doing so, he had walked blindly to his death. It was important to remain in control. To allow herself to fall apart increased the chances of never being able to fit the pieces together again. The wrong place at the wrong time. It was all so awfully random – but if anyone understood random tragedy, it was Shane Reagan with his war stories and restless memories. The youthful lustre had gone from his eyes, he admitted. His blue gaze had sharpened, and his expression was whittled down to an acceptance that he would never make sense of chaos.

A swallow in an attic, a strand of hair tangled in an engagement ring, a smoking chimney: all insignificant in their own right until fate arranged them like dominoes and allowed them to fall.

CHAPTER FORTY-FOUR

Davina

The annual Reedstown Festival had been Davina's idea and, now in its fifth year, it was proving to be as successful as she had anticipated. A mix of music, literature and debate, it allowed the village to flex its intellectual muscle. This year she had decided to add a one-day conference with a top-notch line-up of speakers to the programme of events. Her only problem was persuading Babs Shannon to be her guest speaker. The author had a suspicious nature and accepted nothing on trust, which was why Davina had been forced to take a precious day off from her by-election campaign to meet her face-to-face.

She ordered a gin and tonic from the trolley and settled back to enjoy her flight to London. She could ill afford the time to cater to Babs Shannon's ego, but needs must if she was to convince the author that speaking at the Women's Unstoppable March Towards Gender Equality Conference was an offer she could not refuse.

In the grounds of a small hotel – where Babs was obviously well known, if the welcome she received from the staff was any indication – they discussed the conference. Was Davina holding it to inspire women to fight for equality or using it purely as a platform to promote her own political ambitions? The author had a direct stare, not cold, exactly, but challenging, as if she was measuring every word Davina uttered. The garden was scented with summer stock and bounded by a weathered stone wall, an oasis in the centre of London, Babs said. She came here when she was having difficulty with her books and always left feeling rested yet decisive.

She politely grilled Davina on her attitude towards the homeless, on climate change and immigration. How would she address these issues if she was elected? Her scrutiny was unsettling and Davina was tempted to walk away. Her other guest speakers had been only too happy to accept her invitation to speak at the conference, so why was this author playing hard to get? Grovelling was not in Davina's nature; but Babs Shannon ticked many boxes. As a mother of four, she would appeal to the maternally minded. Her seven self-help books, always in the bestseller charts, would appeal to the needy as well as to the ambitious, and her commitment to the issues they were discussing would attract the activists. Babs had addressed audiences at numerous international conferences but, despite her Irish roots, had never agreed to participate in an event in her home country. It would be a feather in Davina's cap if she could add her name to the list of speakers.

'I'm flattered you've taken the time to see me and honoured to have been considered as one of your speakers.' The author's polite tone suggested she was about to refuse. 'I'm still uncertain if it's the right platform for me. I avoid mixing my message with politics and, if you'll forgive my observation, I believe you're using the conference as a means of advancing your own political profile.'

'That will be a side effect,' Davina admitted. 'But I'm genuinely interested in balancing the gender gap. That's why I'm anxious to present not only an inspirational line-up of female speakers but also the most formidable.'

'You think I'm formidable?' Babs sounded amused.

'Yes.'

'In what way?'

'You write with such certainty yet with an understanding and level of clarity that suggests you've overcome many obstacles to achieve your success. I'm a huge fan, have been ever since I read your first book.'

Davina lied with sincerity. She was not a reader of self-help books but Julie, who read them avidly, had filled her in on the details. Obviously, the information was spot on; Babs began to open up, especially when Davina enquired about her children.

'All adults now,' she said. 'But you never stop worrying…' She paused. 'Do you have children?'

'No,' Davina said. 'Not all of us are so blessed.'

For the first time since they met, Babs seemed flustered. 'I'm sorry, I didn't mean to be insensitive.'

'No, please, don't be sorry. I've compensated. My work is fulfilling and this conference, well, I suppose you could call it… my baby.'

Always pick the right words. Christy's voice came back to her. She missed his wiliness. Keith was a pale substitute, too conscious of his poster boy image. She turned her attention back to Babs, who was saying, 'You said Reedstown, yes?'

Davina nodded. Bab's expression was thoughtful as she steepled her fingertips and brought them to her chin. 'I've heard of it, I think. Is it on the north side of Dublin?'

'Yes. Nowadays, it's quite unrecognisable from the place I grew up in. But the changes have been good. Marvellous facilities for young families and a fantastic community spirit that helps our newer residents to assimilate. I'm actively involved…' Seeing Babs's eyes shift to a spot above her shoulder and aware of her tendency to sound like a political newsletter, Davina fell silent.

'Lewis?' The author's tone was questioning. 'Have your family always been involved in politics?'

'My late father-in-law was the local representative. Keith, my husband, followed in his footsteps.'

'And whose footsteps are you following?'

'I walk my own path.'

'But under the Lewis name.' The slight twist of her bottom lip suggested she disapproved of women who abandoned their surnames when they married. 'What was your name before then?'

'Maye.'

'Davina Maye sounds very appealing. Why abandon it? Was your husband's name more powerful?'

She asked the question with a smile, which took the sting from her comment, yet Davina had to control an urge to walk away. Babs Shannon, for all her success, was annoying to be around. She couldn't put her finger on it but it felt very much as if Davina was being judged and found wanting.

'I'm tight on time.' She checked her watch. 'I'd hoped I could convince you to speak at my conference but if you're still set against it then we should end this meeting now.'

The author had a long, graceful neck, which she now inclined towards Davina. 'I'm delighted to accept your invitation.'

'That's absolutely wonderful.' Relieved, Davina stretched out her hand. 'It's going to be a fantastic conference. How long since you visited Ireland?'

'Not since the nineties.'

'Oh, my goodness, what a long time. You'll be amazed by the changes.'

'I'll probably also be amazed by how much some things have remained the same,' the author replied as they shook hands on their agreement.

*

On the flight back to Dublin, Davina struggled against an unexpected swell of alarm. She tried to relax, yet the fluttery sensation of having made a wrong decision persisted. The author's capitulation had been so sudden. No, Davina told herself, playing hard to get was probably just her modus operandi. The fee Davina was offering and the number of books she would sell at the conference had probably been at the back of her mind all the time.

Davina needed to control these snake-like slithers of panic that were attacking her at unexpected times. She was troubled by Keith's attitude, his moodiness since Christy died. Despite their rivalry, she knew how much he had depended on his father for advice. He had seemed to be coping at first but the death of Bob Molloy, and Rachel's unexpected arrival at their house that night, had affected his mood even further. His moroseness was not what she needed when Reedstown and the surrounding areas were festooned with Davina's by-election posters. As the other half of a new political duo, she needed him strong and forward-thinking, but Adele Foyle's continuing toxic presence in Reedstown was not helping; nor was the unexpected arrival of Shane Reagan.

'Davina Maye, I do believe,' he had said yesterday when they met by chance on Main Street.

He jerked his thumb towards one of her election posters. 'Though maybe I should call you Mrs Lewis?'

Confused by the Australian intonations in his accent, she had no idea who he was until he smiled and the years rolled back.

'Shane Reagan...' His name out of her mouth before she could prevent it. 'And yes, the name is Lewis.' She had laughed self-consciously. 'I'm an old-fashioned kinda gal. What are you doing back in Reedstown?'

'Waiting to be arrested.' He still had the same direct gaze Davina remembered, a challenging stare that demanded she remember why he had left Reedstown. 'It's time I had my day in court.'

'Sergeant Bale has retired,' she said. 'So, I wouldn't worry too much about the past. I presume you're here because of that diary?' She was awkward in his company. Too many memories unfolding to allow for easy conversation.

He had nodded. 'Amazing what the internet throws up, isn't it? Just as well it wasn't around when Marianne Mooney's character was being assassinated. Word of mouth was bad enough back in the day but nowadays cyberbullying has added a whole new dimension to it.'

'I'm sorry to say this, Shane, but no one believes that diary.'

'I believe it.'

'Of course, you would say that. But the whole truth was there in her statement for all to read.'

'You still *actually* believe I'm guilty of raping a minor?'

'Obviously not. We all understood it was consensual but, legally speaking, once she signed that statement, you'd committed a crime. Tough, I know. You can call the law an ass and complain about the scales of justice being out of kilter, but your guilt was writ large in black and white.'

'Mmm...' He took a step back, his gaze quizzical. 'I see time has not softened your tongue, Davina. Not that I'd any expectations that it would.'

They parted shortly afterwards. After twenty-five years, they had nothing to say to each other. She heard afterwards that he was staying with Adele in Brooklime and would be participating in her documentary. That woman, always lurking like a viper at the back of Davina's mind.

*

In an effort to distract her thoughts, she opened her laptop and checked the bookings for the conference. Martina Spellman was already spreading the word about Babs on social media. The publicity had only just started yet the response was immediate. The power of the internet. Gratified, she jotted down the opening lines of her keynote address; then deleted them. Later, when she had had time to shake off her uneasiness about Babs Shannon, she would begin again.

CHAPTER FORTY-FIVE

Rachel

The phone rang early in the morning. It was still dark outside, too dark for a call to bring anything other than bad news. Rachel was right to be prepared. Detective Sergeant Kevin Magee broke it gently to her. Grad Wheeler was dead. The man who put a bullet through her husband's chest had been found hanging in his cell. Cocky and confident of an early release, according to the prison warden, he had not been judged by his officers to be a suicide risk.

The morning news came on the radio. Rachel stared dully at the opposite wall as she listened to the details. The prison warden was interviewed, his measured words outlining the procedures in place to prevent such tragedies. He asked how the prison authorities were supposed to know if a prisoner was at risk of suicide when he showed no outward signs of distress?

Why such confidence? Such cockiness? His belief that strings would be pulled to release him. Rachel had no doubt in her mind that he had been murdered by the same person who had sent him to Brooklime to terrify Adele, and to an apartment car park to await her husband's arrival. Murdered to silence him.

*

She moved slowly through the following days. Showering, dressing, eating, jogging, sleeplessness, the same routine. The brisk busyness of Reedstown Garda Station snapped her to attention when she entered it on the fourth day following Grad's death. Detective Sergeant Magee gave her a guarded welcome. He listened politely to her suspicions but believed there was no evidence to suggest Grad Wheeler's death was anything other than a straightforward suicide. The reality of life imprisonment had got to him in the small hours and he had decided to opt out. He swept aside Rachel's concerns with sympathetic but steely determination.

She left the station and crossed the road to the Kasket. Davina's confident and arresting smile was visible on posters attached to telegraph poles. The front of Keith's constituency clinic was adorned with his messages of support for her.

A hush fell when Rachel entered the Kasket. Some diners smiled sympathetically, others turned away. People were embarrassed by her grief, unsure how to support a woman whose husband had been murdered and who was now bereft of justice. A hard one to square, Rachel agreed to herself as she found an empty table. Katie brought her the usual pot of herbal tea and a croissant. She sat with her for a moment and squeezed her hand when Rachel told her she was doing fine… fine.

The arrival of Davina Lewis a short while later caused a frisson of excitement among the diners. She shook hands with those nearest her and stopped to admire a baby in a buggy. She was a consummate performer and she, like her husband, would take to politics like a duck to water. Front of house now and happy to kick the door of the back room closed behind her on the way out. She noticed Rachel just as she was about to kiss the baby's head and, straightening, she crossed the café towards her. They had not spoken since Bob's funeral, when she had sat with Keith in the front pew on the opposite side of the aisle to Rachel. They had acted like chief mourners, accepting handshakes and condolences from the congregation. Rachel had somehow found enough energy to be angry then but, now, she simply felt indifferent as Davina gestured towards the chair opposite her and asked permission before sitting down.

'I intended calling on you this week but I've been so busy.' She leaned forward to touch Rachel's clenched hands and smiled sympathetically. 'I was in the constituency clinic when I saw you leaving the Garda station and decided to have a word. How are you bearing up?'

'Getting by, thank you.'

'You must have been shocked to hear about that young man's death.'

'Very shocked.' As descriptions went, it was probably apt, she thought, but she no longer had the words to define her feelings.

'I need to apologise to you for my behaviour on the night Bob went missing,' Davina said.

'I'd rather not talk about it.' She resisted the urge to leave the café. Davina had a reason for being at her table and she must wait for her to reveal it.

'Hear me out, Rachel,' she said. 'It's important that I clear the air between us. 'Tensions were running high all round and I said some very regrettable things to you. Keith and I would have been so much more supportive if we'd realised how deeply Bob had become involved with Grad Wheeler.'

'What are you implying?' Rachel demanded. 'Bob was *not* involved with Grad Wheeler. You know as well as I do that he was simply in the wrong place at the wrong time.'

'Oh dear, I've upset you. I'm so sorry, Rachel. That's the last thing I intended to do. I assumed you'd read the report—'

'What report?'

'It's just an online piece. Purely speculative.' Davina waved a dismissive hand in the air. 'It's too trivial and sensational to make it to the print media. I'd never have mentioned it if I'd realised you hadn't seen it.'

'Thanks for your concern, Davina. Don't let me detain you any longer. You must have a busy day ahead of you.'

'Non-stop busy until election day,' she said. 'I've a meeting at the clinic with four of my volunteers… which reminds me.' She caught Katie's eye and waggled her five fingers in the air. The barista, who appeared to know everyone's preferences, immediately busied herself at the coffee machine.

'Take care of yourself, Rachel, and take time to recover. I believe you'll be on compassionate leave for an indefinite period, which is good. I'm not one for platitudes but time is a great healer. Sometimes, that's all we have to help us recover from appalling tragedies.' Such determination in her stance, that same ruthless force Rachel had witnessed when she called to Hillcrest in search of her husband on that dreadful night.

On the way to the counter where Katie was placing five coffees on a cardboard tray, she stopped again to exchange pleasantries with the diners and hand out leaflets. Rachel waited until she had left the café before she checked her phone. The feature that had gone online detailed the history of Bob Molloy, respected newspaper owner, now dead, with a history of drug addiction, and Grad Wheeler, known drug dealer, now also dead. Rachel didn't need to read beyond the opening paragraph. She knew the muddy path this story would take until all that remained would be the mud, sticking.

By the following morning her dead husband's youthful history had made it to the broadsheets as well as the tabloids. Publicity was cloying its way towards her like an oil slick and the media had moved into position on the pavement outside her house. She gave them a standard reply. All queries must be handled by the Garda press office. The reporters persisted, waiting for her to emerge or attempting to contact her by phone and email.

Inspector Morrison, her superior officer, made no bones about his reason for extending her compassionate leave. Too many loose ends that needed to be tied up, he explained. Better for her to lie low until all the facts surrounding the two deaths had been thoroughly investigated. It was important on many levels to prove that her husband had not been caught up in a drug deal that went tragically wrong. Unfortunately, due to the circumstances surrounding Bob's death, it would be necessary for a Garda team to search her house. Essential to rule out any personal connection between the two dead men, he said.

The team who arrived managed to be both efficient and sympathetic. Bob's computer and her laptop were removed. Garda Roberts gave her an impulsive hug when the search ended, then stepped quickly back, as if fearing a reprimand.

Afterwards, Rachel felt as if her house had become an unfamiliar terrain and she must make her way carefully through the once-familiar rooms. She thought about the times she had carried out such searches in other people's homes, filled with the conviction that she was doing her duty, weeding out wrongs and balancing the scales of righteousness. She had never once considered the effects that such rigorous, impersonal searches would have on the families of the accused. Their sense of being trapped in a cage of someone else's making and unable to escape.

The reporters had called it a night and the space where they gathered outside the gate was clear when Shane Reagan called with Adele to see her. How relaxed they looked together. An easiness that came from being blameless in events that unfolded without their knowledge yet had ordained their futures.

Rachel felt an instant kinship with him when they shook hands. He understood what it was like to stumble into hell. She was not surprised to discover that he was a war photographer. The Marianne Diary had brought him back to Reedstown, determined to prove that Marianne had been coerced or deceived into signing that statement. He knew about Bob. Adele had told him everything that mattered.

'I liked Bob.' He sounded more bewildered than angry. 'We were friends for a while but we drifted apart when he began to hang around with Keith and Liam. He changed. Drugs… but you know all that.' He had kind eyes, sympathetic.

'He claimed it was only in his dreams that he remembered what happened that night,' said Rachel. Talking about Bob was torturous and she had no sense that it would ever be any easier.

'If it's any consolation to you, I believe he was acting out of character that night,' said Shane. 'He had a serious—'

'What happened to Marianne cannot be blamed on drugs or alcohol.' She was not prepared to make excuses. 'He went there with the intention of doing harm. It turned uglier than planned but evil can never be relied upon to stick to the script.'

Adele's eyes glittered. No sense keeping the names from her now. She had already identified them and was slowly, carefully compiling her information. Her father's daughter. Rachel turned away from her direct gaze and opened a small, wooden casket that Shane had laid before her on the table. Inside it, she found an oblong-shaped box wrapped in sheets of tissue paper. Discoloured by age, it held nine withered cigarettes.

'This is the packet I found in Blake's Hollow,' Shane said. 'I hardly knew what I was doing when I picked it up but I do remember thinking it could have fallen from one of their pockets.'

He told her about how he had claimed the packet was a clue as to the identity of one of the perpetrators; how he was silenced and imprisoned by Sergeant Bale and the box tossed into a bin. How, later, after his mother arrived with Father Breen to take him home, he managed to retrieve it. And how, since then, the box had travelled everywhere with him.

'I look upon it as a kind of talisman,' he explained. 'I know it sounds daft but I believe that as long as I keep it with me, I'll find justice for myself and Marianne. There was only one person I knew who smoked those cigarettes. Keith Lewis. Going to China was a big thing in those days and he had brought a few cartons back with him. I was too shocked and confused to make the link then and when I did, my mother closed down the discussion. Carrie was traumatised by what had happened to me. She was afraid that if she tried to open an inquiry, the statement Marianne made would land me in jail. In hindsight, it seems incredible that we let Bale get away with it but when we heard that Marianne had died that, somehow, seemed to put a seal on the past. My parents were together again. Carrie had gone back to college and I was starting my own degree course, so…' He spread his hands outwards. 'All very trivial in the light of what had been done to Marianne but it's the small, normal things that make it possible to move on from a great wrong.' He was close to tears and Adele, who also looked weepy, said, 'It can't be too late to bring them to justice, Rachel.'

Justice. The word sounded as stale as the cigarettes. She thought of Keith Lewis standing by the side of Bob's grave. How he had laid his hands on her when she staggered, an ostentatious gesture visible to all. Liam Thornton had been there also, staring expressionlessly into the yawning space that would soon be occupied by her husband's coffin. And Davina, so magnificently confident that her husband was untouchable. Was that the same ruthlessness with which she and others had destroyed Marianne's reputation? Was the media focus a continuation of that same campaign? She took the cigarette packet from Shane and rewrapped it. An inquiry into that fateful night would never be opened. But that did not mean she was powerless. Shane Reagan had invested in this crumpled relic. His talisman. Her weapon of choice. She replaced it in its casket and snapped the hinged lid closed.

Jack Bale was surprised to see her. More than surprised, Rachel thought as he faced her in his doorway. She wondered if he would leave her standing outside but, after a slight hesitation, he led her into his kitchen. No trout laid out on this occasion, but the same cat lazed on the outside window ledge.

'A sad, sad time,' he said. 'How are you coping?'

'As well as can be expected, thank you.'

'You're still on compassionate leave, I gather.'

'For the time being, yes.'

'That detective can't be happy with the publicity that's been building in the media.' His gaze gave nothing away. 'Magee thought he had the case wrapped up with sealing wax until the reporters decided there was another angle to it. Are they giving you a hard time, Rachel?'

'Nothing I can't handle, Jack.'

'Takes its toll, though. I see the impact it's having on you. Not sleeping well, I'd hazard to guess.'

'I've a lot on my mind.'

'Well, as you're not a woman given to courtesy calls, I imagine you've come here for a reason.'

'You're quite right, Jack,' she said. 'I'm here to discuss my husband's murder. Grad Wheeler did not shoot him over some botched drug deal, as you're only too well aware. Those lies being reported in the media have originated from only one source. You need to stop them right now.'

'Goodness me, that sounds remarkably like an accusation.' He thrust his chest forward and sat a little straighter.

'You stitched Bob up once and you're intent on doing it again. So, yes, it is an accusation.'

'I understand how grief affects the mind, Sergeant Darcy. That's the only reason I'm willing to overlook such an outrageous comment. I always had the height of respect for your husband—'

'I'm well aware of what you did for Bob. Respect had nothing to do with it.'

'What exactly do you mean?'

'I know who was responsible for the gang-rape of Marianne Mooney.'

'Gang-rape? What a curious term to use.'

'Nonetheless, it's the right one. I have enough evidence to prove you covered up that crime with the connivance of Gloria Thornton, Christy Lewis and my late father-in-law. How much did they pay you to exonerate their sons? Handsomely, I suspect. It must have been so much easier to stitch up Shane Reagan. You forced him to leave the country or else he would stand trial on a trumped up charge that you were prepared to bring against him.'

'How dare you.' His chin jerked, as if the impact of her accusation had landed a punch on him. 'Could I respectfully suggest that you confine yourself to mourning your dead husband instead of attempting to besmirch his reputation? You've no grounds for making such a fantastical accusation and I must warn—'

'Bob is way beyond my care now, Jack. He was haunted by what he did to Marianne—'

'High jinks that got a bit out of control? Come on, Rachel, you're a sensible woman. Forget this nonsense and start building your life again.'

'Like Shane built his life again? Did you know he's back in town? He wants his day in court and is more than happy to produce evidence that he took from the scene of the crime. Papers never refuse ink and, as I now own the *Reedstown Review*, it will take very little effort to redress the balance in Marianne's favour. Call off your media hounds, Jack, or I will destroy you and bring those other two down with you.'

'Don't mess with me, Rachel.' His fury hit her like a heat wave. 'I've a low tolerance level and it doesn't do to test it. That's when I tend to ask questions and demand answers. Like why you never admitted you were the last person to see Christy Lewis on the night he died?'

Before she could respond, he removed his phone from his pocket and swiped the screen.

'Ah, there he is,' he said. 'My dear old friend rang to have a final chat with me.'

Christy Lewis's voice filled his kitchen. The politician's breathless last act. He must have rung Jack shortly after she left The Lodge. After she had harassed him, he claimed. She had threatened him, refused to undertake her professional responsibilities and left him fighting to breathe. A full-blown panic attack and Jack had recorded every word. He must have a cesspit full of such recordings, she thought, kept there until the right occasion presented itself to him.

By the time the recording came to an end, her teeth were clenched together, her jaw rigid.

'Voices from the grave, eh?' he said as he replaced the phone in his pocket. 'They're all around us. Out to bring us down, but only if we let them.'

'Why didn't you call an ambulance for him?'

'No need. I talked him down as I always did when he was upset. Thoroughbreds, those politicians. Always needing reassuring that their past isn't about to catch up with them. However, I miscalculated the impact you had had on him and, sadly, he was gone by the time his daughter-in-law discovered him.'

She was relieved to be able to walk with a steady step to the front door. He made no effort to follow her. He would quash the rumours he had instigated about her husband and the media would fall away from a non-story about a drug deal that went wrong. But he had her cornered, as was his wont when he was challenged. She would continue dancing to his tune unless she found his weak point and drove the knife in deep.

CHAPTER FORTY-SIX

Davina

Poor Rachel. Grief was a savage and it had ravaged her. Davina could have passed her on the street and not recognised her. Hard to imagine she had ever worn a uniform and walked with an authoritative step. She needed to be transferred from Reedstown. That was if she was ever allowed back into the force. The publicity had been appalling but the truth should out. Once an addict, always an addict, as Jack had pointed out the last time they met. The former sergeant had a treasure trove of information gathered over his years of service. He used his information selectively and only leaked it to an eager source within the media when the occasion demanded it. Now, for reasons best known to himself, he had closed down the flow of information and the media had moved on to other stories. No one seemed any closer to finding out what had happened to either of the dead men. Davina would never figure out all that went on in Jack's devious head but she had learned enough to understand why Christy had always kept him close, as she and Keith must now do. But having him on her side did nothing to alleviate her panic.

Like the morning she turned on the television and saw the grey walls of the prison where Grad Wheeler had ended his life. She had known him. Not very well, admittedly, but she had sought his advice when she was setting up her Reedstown Reminiscences page. He had repaired her laptop whenever it gave her trouble, but then she heard a rumour that BootUrBytes was a front for drugs. After that, she never went near the place again but her acquaintance with Grad, however slight, had given her an eerie feeling when she heard about his death. It seemed more personal, somehow.

Christy used to preach about the dangers of guilt by association and the fact that she had had contact with Grad worried her. She had once seen him leaving Jack's house, sauntering from it as if the two of them were the best of friends. Working for Christy had taught her to hold her nose when the occasion demanded and, more importantly, hold her tongue when necessary.

She was finding this increasingly difficult to do. When she was canvassing door to door, she was constantly being asked whether she believed the Garda statement or The Marianne Diary? She had burned the diary, watched the pages brown to ash, yet the debate rumbled on between the two online communities: those who believed Marianne Mooney's story was real and those who insisted it was a fake.

Today, being Saturday, Main Street was busy with weekend shoppers and Davina was busily canvassing them when a woman asked if she would instigate an enquiry into the rape of Marianne Mooney should she be elected.

'It's never too late to right a wrong.' Her voice was shrill and sanctimonious. 'Justice for Marianne… justice for Marianne.'

For a horrifying instant Davina thought others would take up the chant, but Keith moved into position, distracting the woman with his easy charm. He gave her a leaflet detailing the Women's Unstoppable March Towards Gender Equality Conference and offered her free entry to hear Babs Shannon's speech. As a distraction, it worked. Turned out she was a fan and had read all the author's books.

Babs Shannon's decision to speak at the conference was still the major selling point. Her reputation overshadowed the other speakers and Davina's team was doing an excellent job with publicity. Twitter, Instagram, Facebook and other social media sites were the perfect platform, Martina assured her. There would be no cock-ups like the unfortunate Reedstown Reminiscences page; yet still Davina was unable to control those sudden rushes of alarm.

After they returned home from canvassing, Keith poured a large measure of whiskey. He was pale and tense, his anger barely under control. He had never outgrown his teenage tantrums, those sudden eruptions when he would pick on someone over what he perceived as an insult, however slight.

'What are we going to do about Marianne Mooney?' Davina asked when he had finished his drink and poured another.

'What the hell kind of question is that—?' he began.

'The kind you need to address. I feel as if I'm making my way through a fog and will only be able to see the way forward when I know the truth.'

'Oh, for Christ's sake!' His exasperation was a veneer that did little to ease her panic.

'You can't continue lying to me, Keith. Whether you like it or not, we're in this together. Shane Reagan told me he came back to Reedstown to tell his side of the story. Would you be damaged if he had his day in court?'

'I've no idea what you're getting at—'

'Please *don't* insult my intelligence.' The velocity of her scream startled them both. 'Tell me what happened that night.'

He steadied the glass before the whiskey spilled, and took another sip. 'I've no intention of being implicated in some online fantasy that has been utterly rubbished,' he said. 'And you'd be wise to watch the company you keep. Shane Reagan is a—'

'Don't say it.' In one swift movement, she smashed the glass to the ground. She had been waiting for this to happen, had known the stress she carried within herself must finally seek release. Her beautiful house had become a shrine to a long-dead slut. Even though bouquets were no longer being tossed at her doorstep in the same numbers, people still came to stand and stare.

Shocked by her violence, he watched the whiskey seep into the magnificent Turkish rug that was such a focal point in their living room.

'You'd be wise to remember that you were nominated to run for the Party on the strength of the Lewis name and my reputation,' he said. 'Sing from my hymn sheet if you want to win this election.'

His mulish expression; she was familiar with it. Deny... deny... deny... His father was dead but the life lessons he had instilled in his son lived on. Davina must go to the only source she trusted.

Jack Bale was waiting when she arrived at their usual meeting place. Little Loy was a tributary of the main river and the road running along its bank was no longer in use; a cul-de-sac, too overgrown and potholed for cars to venture very far. This was the safest place to meet a man who had made too many enemies over the course of his career.

Davina talked to him about the snake in the grass. The one with the bite of a cobra but capable of lying still until the instant it struck. As always, Jack was deliberate and considered as he revealed to her the details of the 'Mooney incident'. Davina welcomed the term. An 'incident' was controllable. Every day 'incidents' were reported on the daily news and there was always an infrastructure in place to deal with each one. Shane Reagan would never have his day in court, Jack assured her. Nor had Rachel Darcy the power to begin an investigation. She was like a bitch with a bone, intent on besmirching her dead husband's reputation instead of protecting his memory, but he had her under control.

He confirmed what Davina already believed. Keith was there with that slut in Blake's Hollow – with the other two, all there at her behest – beguiling them, Jack was convinced, tempting them, opening herself to their advances. Davina would not think about it, not now or ever, yet it had been necessary to gain that information. Knowledge was, as Jack said, the pathway to power.

Keith was still drinking when she returned to Hillcrest.

'I've been with Jack,' she said. 'He told me the truth about the Mooney *incident*.'

He dug his knuckles into his eyes, too ashamed to look at her. His handsome face was bloated, all bluster and prevarication gone. He begged her forgiveness. Asked her to understand the pressure of being under suspicion for something that happened so long ago he could barely remember it. He had wanted to leave the shack before things got out of control. He had begged the others to stop but he became caught up in the madness and now it could destroy them all… Davina pressed her hand to his mouth and silenced him. Knowing too much, she now realised, could be as dangerous as knowing too little.

She helped him to his feet and guided him up the stairs to bed. She would protect her weak-willed, lily-livered husband for one reason only. She was on the verge of winning her first seat in Dáil Éireann and she would not allow his past to put her future in jeopardy. Something fundamental had shifted in their relationship. His father's guiding hand had gone and he needed Davina's steadying influence more than ever. But there was little pleasure in the knowledge, just the sharp sting of satisfaction.

CHAPTER FORTY-SEVEN

Julie

Her phone was on silent but the persistent vibration against her hip caused Julie to ease it from her jacket pocket. Her client's eyes were closed as he contemplated a new question that had arisen during his session. She sneaked a quick glance at the screen. Liam would never ring her during clinic hours. The fact that he was doing so now, alarmed her.

Can't take call now. Is all okay with Steph? She sent the text and waited anxiously for his response. She imagined her daughter in a car crash, attacked, kidnapped. So many terrifying possibilities… Liam, knowing her fears, simply texted back, *She's okay but you and I need to talk. Cancel your clinic and come home immediately.*

Despite the curtness of his reply, her panic eased. If Stephanie was in trouble, he would be distraught, not irritated by something Julie had done. What that could be was a mystery as they hardly saw each other these days. She had no intention of closing her clinic early but, as luck would have it, her last appointment cancelled and she arrived at Holywell an hour later. The fact that he had taken time off work puzzled her but the reason was clear as soon as she entered the living room and he turned his pale face towards her. The marble-topped table was strewn with letters, documents, certificates, photographs, and Julie's fingerprints were all over them. Invisible prints – but he knew what she had done and there was going to be a reckoning. Why had she entered the attic? She must have known it was not a safe place to venture. Nothing about Gloria had been safe.

He lifted one of the birth certificates and examined it. His manner was not threatening, yet his anger ran like a current through her. Fight or flight? It was always thus and Julie just wanted an end to it… somehow.

"*Glorious Survivors Together*,' he said. 'You've been quite an active little busybody. It was bad enough that you dared to snoop into my mother's private affairs. But to publish them online is unforgivable.'

'I didn't publish—'

'Julie… *Julie*… don't waste your time lying to me. There's only one other person, apart from myself, with access to this information, and that's you.'

She nodded. No sense denying it. 'Why would you want to keep those certificates hidden when there are women desperate for information that rightfully belongs to them?' she asked.

'Rightfully? Don't make me laugh. My mother looked after them when their own families turned their backs on them. She found homes for their babies and they were grateful to her for the care—'

'Liam, are you listening to yourself? You sound like a parody. Have you read the stories they've shared?'

'You mean the manufactured whining? That blog is as fake as the one Adele Foyle ran and she's the brains behind this new scam. You've no idea of the trouble you've caused by copying those certificates.'

'Why should there be any trouble? Everyone is entitled to a birth certificate unless…' She paused. She had opened a can of worms and, in doing so, she had exposed the real reason why he was so protective of his mother's memory. The facts laid out there on the table.

'Unless what?' He challenged her to say it.

'Unless those certificates were gained illegally so that those babies could be adopted abroad. In other words, trafficked.'

'Are you daring to call my mother a trafficker?'

She should stop now. Step back before it was too late. But the urge that drove people over the edge of a cliff, into waters that were too deep, pushed her onward.

'She was your protector, Liam. Just as Christy Lewis and James Molloy protected their own sons when you all went to Blake's Hollow that night. If a father was named on Adele's birth certificate, who would he be?'

The question was out there in all its ugliness and it was too late to claw it back. His smile when he struck her was mirthless and detached. She went down easily, her breath whistling.

When he was finished, his anger as spent as a storm that had passed and left devastation in its wake, he stemmed the bleeding, iced her bruises. Her body was cold, chilled to the marrow, and it hurt her to breathe. Her lips bled each time she tried to speak and she was unable to silence him as he confessed to her, whispering his sins like a fevered child seeking forgiveness.

The swelling and bruising would heal, as would her lips and her ribs. Nothing could heal her marriage. It was over. She had known the risk she was taking when she contacted Siobhan Miley. It seemed a small price to pay for the wrongs done by Gloria. She had weighed up the odds of being discovered and had no regrets that they had been stacked against her. Quits now, the two of them. She was no longer bound to Liam by guilt, and love, if it had ever existed in their marriage, had not served either of them well. The only two people he had ever loved was his mother, whose crazed delusions he had endured, and Stephanie, the child he believed he had fathered. Unlike the authentic birth certificates she had photographed, the one her daughter held told a lie. And that was how it would remain. A delusion she would never shatter.

Keith Lewis's blue eyes, deep enough to drown a body, as they once drowned Julie, no longer enthralled her. She had believed him to be her crucifixion, her addiction. Now, he was neither. She used to wonder if he had forgotten their short-lived affair or if, like herself, he had acquired the skills to carry the memory of it on his shoulders without stooping under its weight. Now, she no longer cared.

CHAPTER FORTY-EIGHT

Adele

The rain began to fall soon after they left Dublin and had softened to a drizzle when they reached Mayo. How dull the landscape looked compared to her last visit, Adele thought, as she drove through the drenched countryside. The trees were losing their summer lustre but the heather still cast a purple bloom over the mountain slopes that framed Inisada. They reached the House of Atonement in the late afternoon. The sun emerged from watery clouds to shine briefly over the burned-our ruin and the magnificence of the rainbow that spanned the blackened walls did nothing to soften their starkness. Shane was visibly upset as he walked from the house to the container, where wires hung from electrical fittings and medals lay like specks of mica on the grimy floor.

After they had seen all that needed seeing, they left the foreboding atmosphere behind and called on Lilian. Adele had been in touch to tell her to expect them and the tea was ready when they arrived. So, also, were the photographs that she had failed to find on Adele's previous visit.

Calm in the midst of mayhem, Lilian had been a good photographer. The people milling around the courtyard must have been unaware of her presence, if the images Adele examined were any indication. Nothing studied about those poses. Shock and terror reflected on the faces of the barefooted, pregnant young women. The Thorns, mostly women in their fifties and older; the men, also, equally traumatised by the blaze as it flung plumes of smoke skywards. Shane viewed each image Lilian laid out on the table with the experienced eye of a professional.

It was easy to trace the progress of the fire. Lilian had taken the earlier photographs when it had been contained to one wing of the house. Those were the clearest images. The later photographs, taken after the fire crew arrived and ordered everyone away from the house, cast an orange glow against the sky and the people watching were mere silhouettes in the background of an inferno.

Shane seemed riveted by an earlier photograph, which he carried to the window for a closer examination.

'What is this?' His shocked exclamation brought Adele to his side. 'I know it can't be her but she looks so like… she's the image of Marianne.' The name he whispered floated towards her and held her still for an instant before she gently corrected him.

'That's not her, Shane. Those poor girls all look so alike.' And they did, like birds tossed from a nest, their white, full-length nightdresses billowing, their hair scraped back from their frightened faces. The girl he had mistaken for her mother carried a swaddled baby in her arms. She appeared to have hunched away from Lilian's camera, as if she feared what its lens would capture. Her protective stance tugged at Adele's heart. Had the baby been wrenched from her arms as soon as the flames were quenched and order restored?

'She's Marianne.' Shane sounded too insistent to be ignored. 'I'd recognise her anywhere.'

'My mother was dead before that fire broke out.' Adele wanted him to stop fantasising. Otherwise, the pressure inside her head would explode. 'Her body had been cremated by then and I was in Crannock with my grandmother. The date is on my birth certificate. I'm sorry, Shane. This fire started seven days later.'

She prised the photograph from him and showed it to Lilian. 'Did you know this girl?' she asked.

'Thirteen of them were staying in Atonement at that time but I was never on personal terms with any of them,' Lilian replied. She slipped on a pair of glasses and peered more closely at the image. 'I barely knew the Thorns and those who had to speak to me did so only when it was necessary. They made sure to keep the girls out of sight whenever those they considered to be 'outsiders' were around.'

Adele had a niggling feeling that something she had read in the *Reedstown Review* contradicted Lilian's memory. 'Thirteen?' she said. 'Did you say that was the number of girls rescued?'

'That's right.'

'I read in a newspaper report that twelve were rescued.'

'That's wrong. Thirteen was the number I counted that night.'

A dazzling flash, that was what it seemed like, attached itself to Shane's bewildering claim. Adele was afraid to look at him because then she would see hope when surely what he claimed was beyond all probability... and yet... and yet... He continued examining the other photographs, searching for another sighting of the girl. One that would confirm his hunch. Adele refused to think of it as anything other than that – a hunch buoyed by his yearnings – but that single blurry image was the only one he could find.

Lilian made tea. What else was she to do when momentous thoughts were being entertained? She cut bread and cheese and opened a jar of home-made chutney. The dog snuffled about under the table and, finding nothing to his satisfaction, barked to go outside.

'Malachi Norris,' said Lilian when the tea was ready to pour. 'He could be the man to ask. He was with the Thorns for a while and stayed on in Inisada after the fire. Not that he ever became part of the community. Far from it. He's a loner. Comes and goes, does a bit of house painting when he's short of cash. I always use him when I need odd jobs done.'

'Where does he live?' Shane asked. Like Adele, he was struggling to eat so as not to offend Lilian's hospitality.

'He has a place out by the waterfall,' she replied. 'It's more like a shack, really, but he keeps it dry and warm, and the isolation suits him well enough.'

'Does he have a telephone number?'

'Perish the thought.' Lilian gave an exaggerated shudder. 'People call on him when they want work done, or he comes to them. He has an instinct that always tells him when he's needed. I'll go with you. He knows me well enough to trust me… but he gets a bleak look about him if I even refer to his time with the Thorns. Rumour had it that his paints accelerated the fire but I don't know the truth of it and Malachi never uses two words when one will do.'

'Marianne mentioned him in her diary,' said Adele. 'He helped her friend to escape.'

'I heard one of them got away all right.' Lilian paused, struck by a sudden thought. 'Winnie O'Donnell, now there's a woman who might be able to help. We walked through her land the last time you were here. Remember?'

Knee-high grass and a woman waving at them as she left her car, it seemed so long ago since Adele had walked towards the farmyard with Lilian, unaware that her life was about to be changed, irrevocably.

A waterfall flowed from a cleft high up on a rocky bluff, gloriously free as it lunged towards the waiting river. Malachi's shack was practically invisible behind a screen of trees. After knocking three times on the wooden door and not receiving an answer, Lilian checked the side wall.

'That's where he leaves his bike.' She pointed at the empty space. 'He could be anywhere. Leave him a note and I'll give it to him when he's back. Let's check with Winnie O'Donnell. She had a fine flock of hens in those days and she used to supply eggs to the Thorns. There was talk in Inisada at the time that she helped one of the girls to escape. Not that she ever admitted to it. She's over a hundred now but still sharp as a tack. She might be able to put a name on this wee girl who has you all in such a state.'

Winnie O'Donnell seemed moulded into her rocking chair. Impossible to imagine her ever rising from it, yet her bright eyes never stopped moving. She surveyed Adele, her head tilted, a smile crinkling her parchment skin.

'Lilian tells me you're the one put The Marianne Diary online.' Her voice quavered but was still distinct. 'Well done, girl. Time that place was shown up for what it was.'

'Do you think you can help us?' Adele asked.

'I might and I might not. My memory's not what it was. It's a shame what age takes from us.'

'It took nothing from you except your weight,' Tricia joked and pointed at a framed photograph on the wall of Winnie in her seventies, a stout, sturdy woman with a formidable expression. 'Cup of tea, anyone? I don't have to ask you.' She surveyed her grandmother fondly. 'Your insides are pure tannin.'

'We've all got to die from something.' Winnie was philosophical. 'Better tea than dementia, that's what I say.'

The atmosphere in this country kitchen with its wood-stained ceiling beams was relaxed and Adele fought to contain her impatience as the chit-chat continued. Finally, the old woman put on her glasses and examined the photograph Shane handed to her.

'Magnifying glass,' she said to Tricia, who found one for her in a drawer.

'So hard to tell,' she sighed apologetically. 'I've a clear recall of the other one who escaped. Big as a mountain she was with that baby still kicking, and prepared to run over nails to get away from yon place.'

'Was Barbara her name?' Adele asked.

'That was it, sure enough.'

'Lilian said you were good to her when she ran away.'

'I hid the pair of them in the barn,' she said. 'Her and the boyfriend, tucked under hay, they were, when the Thorns came looking. I lied to their faces and they were afraid to push me too far. They didn't want the Gardai checking out what they were doing in Atonement. I got rid of them sharpish and the pair of lovebirds escaped the following day. Hidden in a trailer of hay, and it got them to the station in Castlebar. Last I heard they were on the train to Dublin. She sends me a Christmas card every year and I send one back to her.'

'So, you have Barbara's address?'

'It's in my notebook.'

'Would you mind giving it to me? I'd love to contact her about my mother.'

Winnie nodded and picked up the magnifying glass to look again at the photograph. 'This little one was a different kettle of fish altogether when she came here.'

'She came here?' Shane knelt by her side and helped her to focus the magnifying glass on the girl.

'If memory serves me right, she's the other one who bolted. She was a scared wee thing. Such sad tears. That's what I remember most. The tears and the shivers. She smelled of smoke, God love her. Singed, like she'd been up close and personal to that inferno, and almost impossible to get a word out of her. She'd left her baby behind and she was heartsore at that. But something else was wrong. She was too petrified to tell me what it was. She hid behind the sofa when a man came looking for her. A beast of a man, he was, but I was well able for him. Told him... well, never mind what I told him, it's not for young ears. I wouldn't let him in. I played ignorant of seeing anything that night except the house going up in smoke. It used to be a grand house until that daft Charlotte got religious and signed it away. After he left, the girl asked me to ring a priest. I was glad enough to do that for her and he came the next day.'

'A priest?' Shane's voice cracked, as if this information had struck a chord with him.

'That's what she called him, though he was dressed like a regular lad when he arrived to take her away. That's the last I saw of her.' Winnie closed her eyes, her mouth slowly opening as she nodded off.

'She nods off like that all the time,' Tricia said. 'She's told me the same story a dozen times. That's all the remembers from that night. More tea, anyone?'

'No thanks,' said Adele. 'We've taken up enough of your time. Thank Winnie for us and remind her to send Barbara's address to me.'

'I'll see that she does.' Tricia walked with them to the gate and waved them off. The cool air was a relief after the kitchen. Fields of barley rippled in the sunshine but even here, in this peaceful dip of the valley, they could see the blackened gable wall of the House of Atonement.

It was late when they returned to Brooklime. Lilian had given the photographs to Adele and she was anxious to scan them into her laptop. She paced the living room as Shane worked at enlarging, enhancing and sharpening the images. Was he aware of the fever he had unleashed within her? Such headiness was perilous. It raised her to great heights and would make the fall all the harder.

'My God! Look at this.' Shane sat back from the screen and beckoned her over.

Mesmerised, Adele bit into her knuckles as she stared at the enlarged photograph. She realised that the young girl was going towards the camera and not away from it as she had thought at first. Going towards an older woman, who had extended her arms to take the baby from her.

'That's my grandmother.' Her index finger trembled as she pressed it against the screen. Noreen should have been in Crannock caring for a week-old baby yet there she was, gaunt and almost spectral, standing at the edge of the conflagration. She stared at Noreen's rapt gaze; the same gaze that had claimed ownership of Adele so often.

Shane peered intently at the clustered group and zoomed in on another figure. 'That's Jack Bale.' His expression mirrored Adele's confusion. 'What on earth was he doing there?'

Looming behind her waif-like mother, his face just visible over her shoulder, was the former sergeant. He was out of uniform, yet it was impossible to mistake his broad forehead and menacing stare.

'He must be the man Winnie mentioned,' she said. 'Can you see my mother in the other photographs?'

'That's the only one. But it proves Marianne was alive that night and afterwards when Father Breen took her away.'

'You think he was the priest who collected her?'

'Who else could she turn to for help? He's the only person who believed me that night at the Garda station. Marianne would have known she could rely on him.'

'What does it mean, Shane? Did she die afterwards or could she still be…' Adele faltered, unable to utter that wondrous word. She had never known an instant in her twenty-four years when she had believed her mother was alive, except in dreams. The radiance of those dreams, the instant of blissful belief as she awakened. Then, reality, another day dawning, but it was that same bliss she felt now as she stared at the slight figure in the photograph.

'She was alive that night?' Shane seemed equally dazed by this realisation.

Noreen was visible in other photographs. It was obvious from her stance that she was distraught and frightened. She must have been constantly moving around the courtyard, if the different backgrounds were any indication. Shane zoomed in on another photograph that showed the back view of Jack Bale standing at the foot of the steps leading upwards to the house. What connection had he to the House of Atonement? And what was Noreen doing there? It was impossible to know the story that was being played out in the midst of the pandemonium but such questions were irrelevant compared to the bigger one. Could it be… was it possible that Marianne had witnessed the carnage that had ended the life of Gloria Thornton and brought the sodality to its knees?

And afterwards, what then? Had she died on a different date or was she out there somewhere, unaware that her daughter had spent her life yearning to know her?

'Why did my grandmother change the date on my birth certificate? Or tell me my mother was dead if she's not…' Adele bit down hard enough on her lip to draw blood. She had pleaded with her mother so many times to send her a signal. Nothing dramatic, just something that could not be brushed off as a coincidence. Like a butterfly landing on her hand when she was meditating or the scent of a rose in a sterile room. Never once had she experienced anything that suggested such an ethereal link was possible. Could this failure to communicate with her daughter be a sign that she was alive? Like a dangerous star about to fall to earth, this possibility quivered before Adele. She needed to calm down. Marianne must have died at a later date. Otherwise, why had she not torn the world apart as she searched for the baby she had finally been able to love?

PART FOUR

CHAPTER FORTY-NINE

Marianne

Sometimes, when she dwelled too long on the past, she took out her death certificate and examined it. 'Marianne Mooney. Age 16. Cause of death—thromboembolism.' It was such a stark diagnosis, yet that same word always rushed a song through her mind and cast her back into time and tears.

> *Thumbelina, Thumbelina tiny little thing*
> *Thumbelina dance, Thumbelina sing*
> *Thumbelina what's the difference if you're very small?*
> *When your heart is full of love you're nine feet tall.*

She was unable to imagine her baby being tall. Or having eyes of a definite hue. Adele had been dark-haired, a slick of black hair when she was born, smooth as a skullcap against her tiny head. Her Thumbelina, framed forever in a cocoon, her milky gaze, still impenetrable.

Her marriage certificate was the only certificate Marianne possessed that was not fake. George Maclure was seventy years old when they married and still strong enough to appreciate what Parkinson's would take from him. She would have cared for him regardless of certificates but he wanted to make the way ahead as clear-cut as possible for her. His death seemed such an abstract concept then. He was still active and his hand trembled only slightly when he signed the register that made them man and wife.

His deterioration had become more noticeable over the past six months. Sometimes he forgot her name and how she came to be in his care; but nothing, no illness of the mind or limbs, could dim the love he felt for her, or her love for him. Not romantic, nor passionate, but love had other dimensions and theirs had grown from a raw beginning into one that sat easily with both of them. He was in her care now. Time with its corrosive edge was leaving him as helpless as the baby she had abandoned on the night Gloria Thornton died.

In the mornings, when George was showered and dressed, she wheeled him to the veranda where he could watch the birds: the tui with its exotic plumage, the speckled thrush that reminded her of home, as did the chaffinch, and other birds that were once strangers to her until he taught her to recognise them. He had accepted his illness with a quiet dignity that had surprised her in the beginning. He had been a rumbustious personality, and had terrified her when she first came to live with him.

'You'll be here for just a short while,' Rory had assured her when he brought her to Cape Maclure. 'Trust me.'

She had trusted him and, even when she lost the belief that she would ever find her daughter, she still maintained that trust in him. She often wondered how he had managed to acquire her death certificate. He was a priest then, ordained to follow the path of righteousness. The real path, not the one that Gloria Thornton magicked from her craziness. A narcissist. The term had become familiar to Marianne in recent years. When she applied it to Gloria, she decided it was a perfect fit. Visions and grandiose notions, her ability to sway a crowd with her deluded beliefs, her sense of entitlement that convinced her she had the right to take babies from the arms of their mothers and sell them to the highest bidder. Not that Marianne had had the insight or the language to apply that term to Gloria in those days. Gloria was just a monster then. One who had imprisoned her, and others like her, for the sole purpose of stealing their babies.

Ireland had changed. Rory told her so on his last visit. Survivors, that was what they were called, the women who had endured the Magdalene laundries. She thought of Miss Bethany, who had held the laundries as a threat above the heads of those who laboured in Atonement, insisting that packaging Gloria's tatty merchandise was so much more important than washing dirty clothes.

The person she was in those days seemed like a wraith now. She had never before been outside Ireland and when she left for the first time, she did so by stealth. A fake passport. She had never asked Rory how he came by all that fake documentation. He had always moved in strange circles, a prison chaplain before he was sent to Reedstown to become her saviour. It was inevitable that he would eventually leave the priesthood. He claimed that the path to righteousness had too many banana skins for him to manoeuvre and he was better suited using his hands, rather than his words, to aid the stricken.

She did not dwell often on that time. The black dog growled a warning when she did. That was what George called the dark moods that swept her far away from him and onwards to the edge of the cliff. Some mornings, when it lay across her bed, she found it impossible to shift its weight. Then, she longed for an authentic death certificate. One that meant what it said. A deep, peaceful sleep with nothing to penetrate the oblivion.

She had learned techniques to overcome those urges: meditation, yoga, journaling. She had kept a diary when she was in Atonement, but it would have burned with all her other possessions on that terrible night. What did it matter, those ramblings of a child? Nothing mattered except holding Adele close, so close, as she ran through the smoke to hand her over to her mother with a whispered prayer. The previous time her mother had visited Atonement, she had lain her cheek against Marianne's stomach and felt the throb of the baby's heels. She would love her granddaughter and care for her until Marianne could return to claim her.

Inevitably, looking back like this too often caused the black dog to snap at her heels, so it was better to look outwards as the tour boats nosed their way into the fiord. When she glimpsed flashes of light, she knew that photos were being taken of their house – what could be seen of it beyond the trees – and that the tour guides were telling those tourists that it was the home of the reclusive artist, George Maclure, whose great-grandfather once ran the now-defunct Maclure Cannery. Nothing left of the cannery now except rusting steel, the bleached skeletons of fishing boats, and this vast relic of a house that had been built originally for a family of eight. These days, it was occupied only by ghosts, Marianne often thought. One a pale shade of his former self, and herself all hollowed out.

In the evenings she read to her husband. He favoured Westerns; he was a Zane Grey fan: *Forlorn River, The Desert of Wheat, Tales of Lonely Trails*. Recently, he had started asking her to read from her diary; the one she began when she first came to him. At first, she had resisted his request and claimed she was unable to find it. She had no desire to look back to that troubled time, but she soon realised that he was trying to hold on to the circumstances that had drawn them together before that memory was taken from him. Knowing this, she read to him in a steady voice that belied the emotions raging inside her. When would she be able to stop yearning for all she had lost when her mother lifted Adele from her arms and she ran away from the horror of Sergeant Bale's pitiless accusation? Nothing, neither time nor distance, could change the fact that she was a penitent, unrepentant of the crime she had committed yet unable to forgive herself for abandoning her daughter.

CHAPTER FIFTY

Twenty-four years previously

I thought the Tank was the loneliest place in the world to be but here is worse. Mr Maclure tells me I'm safe. When he says I'll get used to living with him, I know he hasn't a clue. How am I supposed to get used to living on the edge of the world? That's what it feels like. All those cliffs and rocks and the waves bashing off them and roaring in my ears.

I stand on the cliff every day and watch for the boat. I know it's on its way. It has to be. Sergeant Bale is the long arm of the law. He always gets to the nub of the matter and he meant it that night when he said I'd spend the rest of my life in jail. He'll come with Garda Gunning and they'll have truncheons and handcuffs and big fists. Maybe they'll throw me into the same cell that Shane was in.

I'm able to picture Shane's face again. I couldn't for ages but now when I see him in my mind, he's got blood all over his mouth and nose so it's not really him I'm seeing, just the blood. I've only been able to do that since Amaia gave me a present of this diary. I told her about the one that got burned in the fire and she said sometimes the only way to make sense of the world is to journal. That's what she does when she's not cleaning and cooking for Mr Maclure or looking after her children. She has five, two boys, three girls, and a husband with tattoos on his face. He's scary but she says he's really only a pussycat

and the tattoos have all sorts of meanings about family and the past.
I don't have a tattoo, or a moko, as Amaia calls it, but I feel as if
everything about me is branded in red on my skin and I'll never be
able to remove it.

I left a moko on Shane. The marks on his arms must have been
a gift from heaven for Sergeant Bale.

Scratches made by my nails, clawing at him, unable to see his face
and believing they had returned. The statement I signed, I thought
that by doing so he would be released but it sent him away to the
other side of the world. We were done for as soon as Sergeant Bale
recognised the cigarette packet. Chinese cigarettes, I smelled the smoke
on Keith that time when he snatched my hat and pressed me against
the wall of the snooker hall. Such a strange smell, smoky and fruity
all mixed up, and it was there again on his stinky breath that night.

The Chinese letters on the box meant nothing to me then but later,
in Atonement, I understood. No wonder Sergeant Bale stopped all
enquiries and ran us out of Reedstown. It was easy to guess who the
other one was. But the third one... I never wanted to believe it was
Bob and I didn't until Adele was born and I saw the cast of him on
her tiny face. It didn't matter then. Later, if I'd been able to keep
her, I could have dealt with all those confused feelings but then, all
that mattered was planning to escape, as Barbara had done.

The cliff when I stand on Cape Maclure is high. Such a long drop
to the rocks below. Today I took one step closer to the edge. Just one
step. It made me sway and the ticklish feeling in the pit of my stomach
was the strongest yet. Mr Maclure says the boat won't come. Only tour
boats enter Maclure Sound and the Gardai have no powers of arrest
in New Zealand. He sounds impatient when he talks to me. Like he
hates me being in his studio or his house and can't figure out how a
teenage killer ended up living with him. I can't figure it out either.
One minute I'm nursing my baby in Atonement, then I'm standing
on a cliff and moving one step closer to the edge every day. I know

lots happened between those two moments. It's just hard to figure it all out. When I try to do so, I end up choking, like the smoke is still in my lungs, and then Amaia gets cross with me because I forgot to take my inhaler again.

The sun was shining like gold on the ocean the first morning I was here. I knew it was night-time in Ireland and I kept thinking of Adele lying in the dark crying for me, like I was crying for her. That's the first time the choking started. Mr Maclure had to ring for the flying doctor, who gave me the inhaler. That's two months ago and the doctor has flown to the cape to see me twice since then. There're lots of seaplanes here. They use them like we use bikes in Ireland. And there's boats too. That's why I can't stop waiting for Sergeant Bale with his big red hands holding on to my arms the way he did that night when he said he was going to put me in jail for life and was throwing away the key because I murdered Gloria Thornton.

CHAPTER FIFTY-ONE

Marianne

This morning George was snoozing on the veranda when she entered his studio. Since his illness had taken his power away, the bristles on his paintbrush were stiff and dry, his palette washed clean. Once a storehouse for the cannery, it was a vast, barn-like building, filled with paintings he had abandoned partway through, or those he had finished and then rejected for reasons she had never understood. His paintings roared. That was the impression they had created in her mind the first time she saw them. Roaring waves and storm-tossed forests, the tumbling fall of rock and ice. The paintings that moved her most were the ones of stunted trees hurtling downwards from the cliffs, their fragile roots torn loose from rocky crevices. Her roots on Cape Maclure were just as shallow but they had enough strength to keep her in a prison with an open door.

George had taught her to paint during those early years but her paintings were too grim to attract buyers. Who wanted to see broken glass on top of walls, bars on a window, an empty cot, flames raging? She seemed to be incapable of painting anything else and after a while she stopped trying. George said she had talent. It was the only time she remembered him being angry with her. Talent was a gift from the heavens and squandering it an unforgivable sin, he stated. Not that he believed in sin, or what he called 'religious balderdash,' which Marianne found strange at first, considering his favourite nephew was a priest.

George was tall then, and strong-limbed, a gruff, loud-voiced and bewildered guardian, saddled with a traumatised young mother. Cape Maclure was his retreat from the world. He had travelled its four corners, tasted fame, love, notoriety, wealth, and all were found wanting. On the cape, named after his great-grandfather, he'd planned to spend his days peacefully painting the landscape of his youth. Instead, he found himself nursing her back from the edges of insanity and despair.

A treasure trove, George told her when his voice was still strong. His paintings, all hers on his death. What would her life on Cape Maclure be like when he died? Would she cling to the solitude of the peninsula or step onto the ferry, as he wanted her to do? She could set up a gallery in Kaikoura. Unseen George Maclure paintings – she would be on to a winner with such a collection, he believed. She found it difficult to believe anyone outside Cape Maclure had ever heard of him but Van, his agent, claimed otherwise.

Trekkers came and went along the cliffs that dominated the peninsula. Sometimes, they stopped at the house and asked for their water bottles to be refilled, but, otherwise, the solitude she shared with her husband was seldom disturbed, apart from the flying doctor, who checked on George every week. Van called occasionally to announce the sale of another George Maclure painting, and Amaia always came to see them when she returned to visit her husband's grave. After she had left to live with her married daughter in Kaikoura, Marianne had taken over the household chores and what was meant to be a temporary arrangement had not changed since.

When he first became ill and they went to Christchurch for a diagnosis, Marianne had been dazed by the noise, the harried faces hurrying towards the wards, the brisk steps of medical staff, the claustrophobic order of confined spaces. Could she ever adapt to new surroundings? Ever shake off the feeling of being watched, judged, convicted? She had had no idea that the fear was still coiled as tightly as ever inside her. The belief that a hand would reach out from the crowd and clasp her in irons. It had been possible to contain her imagination on Cape Maclure, where the small community who lived on the peninsula had long ceased to wonder about the reclusive artist and his much younger wife.

Living on the cape had changed her beyond recognition, she believed. Rory disagreed and said that she still had 'that look'. When she pressed him as to what he meant, he said 'untouched innocence and vulnerability'. It was a strange thing to say to a grown woman who had celebrated her fortieth birthday and was four years a wife. But she understood what he meant. She was an unfinished piece of work, her heart hacked to pieces before it had a chance to fly. Her mind, also, its stunted growth still trapping her in Atonement packing medals in poxy boxes, as Barbara once wrote. She hadn't thought about the poem for years yet the words were still there, learned faithfully and remembered as she recited them loudly in her husband's abandoned studio.

All day we pack in poxy boxes
Mother Gloria's paradoxes.
Blessed with spite, with greed and bile
Medals to bewitch, beguile
Those chosen ones who think their hates
Will bring them through the golden gates.

Such joy to know each crazy Thorn,
Who look upon us with such scorn,
Will kiss the face that's stamped in tin
The face they think is free from sin,
And never know that we've all spat
A glob upon their sacred tat.

Barbara had dismissed her poem as a bit of nonsense. Doggerel, she had called it. She was going to be a *real* writer when she escaped from Atonement, and reveal the truth about the Thorns. Marianne had read all her books. Rory sent them to her as soon as they were released. They were wise and witty, helpful to women who planned on smashing the glass ceiling or to those whose ambitions were simply to seek fulfilment in their own way. She wrote about freedom from fear, how to be confident, content, satisfied and, if her readers had the wisdom to recognise it, how to embrace happiness. But she never wrote about Atonement. Somewhere along the way, she must have decided not to give currency to her past. She had four children. The eldest was called Aaron. Her first book had been dedicated to him.

To my precious Aaron. Who came to me in flight and on
the wings of courage.

Her readers must have wondered what she meant. Not Marianne. Or Malachi, if he still lived and was moved to read her books. Barbara was the one who got away. But the others –what had happened to them? Rory said that those who were there on the night of the fire were taken to hospital to be assessed and then discharged into the care of the State. The illegal adoption of the babies from Atonement had been stopped but Gloria's past activities had been hushed up, he said. The whole damn operation kept under wraps and she was just short of being sanctified for her heroic rescue of the expectant mothers in her care. The Thorns, those who had worked in Atonement, were either dead or had blended back into society, reverting to their own names instead of the Biblical ones they had chosen when they joined Gloria's sodality.

Marianne had longed to shout her truth across the continents. Sometimes she thought she would choke on it, lodged as it was so deeply in her throat when she thought about the young mothers she had known. Mothers, like herself, who had been prodded and poked and bullied into giving their babies away. Elizabeth Green with the red curls. Marianne was unable to forget the sight of her cried-out eyes when they took Conor from her. Miss Bethany used to call him 'that sickly child' but Elizabeth had made him strong with her breast milk. Marianne used to laugh at his cheeks going in and out like tiny bellows, and Elizabeth, all swoony with love, staring down at him. Miss Bethany sent her to Lilian's Foodstore for groceries one afternoon. An hour was the time it took her to walk to Inisada and back. Conor was gone by then. They heard her screams, saw her tears, and then she, too, was gone. Her parents collected her, all stiff-backed and proud, and not listening to a word she said about getting Conor back.

And Siobhan Miley, what about her? Did her twin daughters really die in hospital? Marianne, accompanied by Barbara and Malachi, had gone with her to see a tiny grave, recently dug. Someone had placed a wooden cross with their names, Sarah and Stella, on it. Siobhan had knelt on the mud and traced her fingers across the carved letters of their names. Were her babies in that grave? Or was that another lie? Siobhan would never know.

According to Rory, all their documentation had been lost in the fire. All their precious information turned to ash.

Names were important. Barbara had had a name book, hidden from Miss Bethany, who prowled the dormitory like an anteater sniffing out acts of disobedience. Adele, they discovered, meant nobility. It was the perfect name for her daughter. One that would blot out the horrors of her beginnings. Did her mother hear her through the roar of the fire when she cried out. 'My baby's name is Adele… I'll be back to care for her soon… soon.'

CHAPTER FIFTY-TWO

Twenty-four years previously

My body was toxic with hate when I entered the tank yet something strangely wonderful happened while I was there. I discovered that love could conquer hate. Like a butterfly shedding a chrysalis that was no longer needed, I abandoned hate. My baby stopped being an object I was forced to carry and became real. A little person fully formed in her own right. This love turned everything upside down. I was so stupid to think Mother Gloria would allow me to keep her. I'd put my name to so many forms since Mam left me in Atonement that I must have signed her away to some rich Americans months before she was born.

Mam was supposed to be with me for the birth but Adele came early and easily. No stitches or complications. I kept asking for her. She would fight off the greedy hands reaching out to take her from me. I believed that if I screamed loudly enough someone in that hellhole would heed me. Again, that was just me being stupid. Malachi was the only one who spoke to me, telling me that Adele was a beautiful baby, who looked exactly like me.

The Thorns wouldn't listen to me until the third day, when I was still refusing to eat. That's when Mother Gloria decided that I could have Adele for one day. She made me promise that I'd behave like a 'sensible girl' when I had to give her back. Miss Bethany brought

Adele from the nursery to me and locked us into a room on the ground floor. I was free to sing to Adele, to make silly noises when she smiled. I knew she was smiling even when Miss Bethany insisted that I'd 'gone mad' from the birth and Adele was far too young for such a thing.

I hadn't been allowed to breastfeed her and Miss Bethany came in every few hours with her bottle. Adele was a fitful feeder until I brought her to my breast. I was tense, waiting for the door to be unlocked, but she fed from me as easily as she had been born. My slippery little fish. My lost baby.

The roars of a house in agony, the cries and racing footsteps: it's hard to believe I didn't hear them. The door was strong, the walls thick, and I was unaware of anything except my tiny daughter. I smelled the smoke in the same instant that the lights went out. I'd no idea what was happening until I stood on the bed and looked out of the window. All those flames leaping from the north wing and the courtyard filling up with Thorns and penitents. That's what they called us, penitents who had to atone for our sins, but out in that courtyard, there was nothing to distinguish anyone. They were all just frightened people. I put Adele high up on the wardrobe shelf and banged on the window with the legs of a chair until the glass shattered. My hand began to bleed but air was coming through the bars. I don't know how it happened that my voice reached Malachi. He came to my rescue. I can still hear him at the door, kicking and kicking at it until the lock broke. The smoke had reached us by then. I still couldn't see it but I could feel it stinging my eyes and catching in my throat. I was terrified it would choke Adele as we made our way along the corridor into the main hall. Malachi had a torch and that helped us to see where we were going. Then, suddenly, Mother Gloria was there. I thought she was a ghost at first, the way her long, white robe was floating around her, but she was real and she wanted my baby.

She reached for Adele. 'Give her to me,' she shouted and her eyes were like big, empty holes swallowing me up. But she wasn't looking at me, only at Adele. I was just her mule, her penitent, and she wanted the cargo I was carrying. I pushed her away with my free arm. I never knew I had such strength. Mother strength, that's what it was. It knocked her off balance. I never looked back when she fell. I didn't care if she was hurt. I could hear the flames roaring. They had reached the south wing and the whole house sounded as if it was cracking and breaking up around me. I thought she would follow but she never came out.

Malachi went back in again to find her and when he came out again I thought the person behind him must be Mother Gloria. I was wrong.

Sergeant Bale's bulging eyes and hammering questions belonged to IT. What was he doing in Atonement? I'd no time to run before he grabbed me and forced me to stand in front of him. He told me how I'd killed Mother Gloria. She'd banged her head on the iron fender in the main hall when I pushed her. I'd run off and left her bleeding, dying, and now she was dead. For such a crime I'd spend the rest of my life in jail. My baby would be reared by strangers. She would never know my name or that her mother was a murderer.

That was when I saw Mam in the crowd. She'd arrived at last. I broke free from him and my heart was a magnet drawing me towards her. I was crying and trying to explain that I wanted to keep Adele. I don't remember if she smiled or even if she spoke. All I remember are her arms. How steady they were when she lifted Adele from me and kissed her face. Everything was mad, the burning house and the fire brigade arriving with sirens screaming and the crew pushing everyone out of the courtyard and Sergeant Bale grabbing me again like I was a dangerous criminal trying to escape, which I was, well, not dangerous, just mad with fear. Malachi hit him. I don't know what he used but it knocked Sergeant Bale out. He dragged me down with him when he fell but Malachi pulled me up and told me to run. Mam was crying and holding Adele so tight I was afraid she'd strangle her.

The sergeant was trying to get back up on his feet when Malachi hit him again. The fire engine headlights were flashing off the trees as I ran through the gates. I had bare feet, still in my nightdress, but I never felt the stones, the thistles or the briars.

They gave me shelter at the farm. Dear Winnie. Fr Breen came when she rang him and took me away. I hid in his house for two days and then he brought me to the airport. He has promised hand on heart to find Adele. He will check every highway and byway where Mam could be hiding. She's been accused of robbery but Fr Breen says it's a stitch-up and I'm to stop fretting. When he finds them, he will take them both here to live with me.

I've stopped looking for the boat with the sergeant. It was a silly notion. The only boat I want to see is the ferry bringing Fr Breen, Mam and Adele to me. Sometimes I lose hope. Mr Maclure says it's a dangerous thing to despair. Despair leaves room for dangerous thoughts to creep in… like yesterday.

Would I have jumped into the ocean if he had not been there? He never made a sound as he followed me from his house to the cliff. How did he know that the battering waves were calling to me? I could hear them so clearly. Murderer… murderer. They were telling me that losing my baby was not enough punishment for the crime of murder. Mr Maclure said the sea sings siren songs and I'm never to listen to it again. Ever.

PART FIVE

CHAPTER FIFTY-THREE

Adele

Jack Bale was unable to hide his surprise when he opened his front door and saw them standing outside.

'I heard you were back in town.' He ignored Adele and spoke directly to Shane. 'I'm amazed you have the nerve to show your face around here.'

'After all this time, I would have expected a warmer welcome, Jack. Aren't you going to invite us in?'

'Why the fuck should I do that?'

'We have information that should be of interest to you.'

'We can discuss it on your doorstep, if you'd prefer?' said Adele.

He appeared to notice her for the first time, yet she knew her presence was an itch to him, had been from the first time they met. He hesitated, his colour rising, then shrugged. He closed the front door behind them but moved no further than the hall.

'So, enlighten me.' He thrust his face towards her. 'And make it fast.'

'I want to know why you were in the House of Atonement on the night it burned down?' Adele handed the photograph to him. He would find it impossible to deny the evidence, his strong features recognisable since Shane had clarified the image.

LAURA ELLIOT

'The House of *what*...?' His Adam's apple bobbed violently. 'I haven't an earthly clue what you're taking about.'

'You can't deny that you were there on the night it burned down,' said Shane. 'Your link to Gloria Thornton will be one of the main questions Adele intends to explore in her documentary.'

'I was visiting her.' He coughed to clear his throat and dabbed at his mouth with a handkerchief. 'Gloria was a friend. A good neighbour when she wasn't on the road doing God's work. Do you have any further questions?'

'We certainly do.' Shane pressed his finger on the image of Marianne. 'I'm sure you recognise her.'

He took a pair of glasses from his shirt pocket and held them up to the light, as if searching for smears. Playing for time before he examined the photograph. 'No, I haven't a clue who she is.'

'She's the girl you destroyed.' Shane's hands were clenched as he strained towards him. 'Marianne was supposed to have died before that night, yet there she is. What happened to her?'

'How am I supposed to know?' He met Adele's gaze and looked quickly away. 'You're supposed to be the one who's doing the research.'

'My research was destroyed by thugs,' she said. 'But I don't need to research her name. It was Marianne Mooney. She was my mother.'

His stunned expression was fleeting enough to have been imagined but he was unable to prevent the colour draining from his cheeks.

'I always knew you were a deceitful bitch,' he snapped. 'You've caused nothing but trouble since you came here with your fake identity and lies. How's your thieving grandmother? Still alive, is she? Ready for interrogation?'

'My grandmother is dead. You can't touch her now. And you still haven't told us how you came to be in this photograph?'

'I was in Inisada to advise Gloria Thornton, who contacted me when she discovered that the person whom she trusted most was a thief.' His confidence was returning, his voice hardening. He tapped the photograph, his mockery aimed directly at Adele. 'Rosemary Mooney was clever enough to disappear without trace and take you with her. As for your mother...' He hesitated and frowned as he surveyed Adele from beneath his lizard eyelids. 'She was running from an even bigger crime. But I don't want to speak ill of the dead.'

'Dead?' Shane reached her hand and squeezed it. 'This photograph suggests otherwise.'

'The kid's dead. If you thought she died before the fire, you obviously have the wrong information. Wait here and I'll prove it to you.'

He turned abruptly from them and climbed the stairs. They listened to his heavy tread on the landing, a door slamming. Adele felt her optimism ebbing away, her butterfly hope fading.

'Liam Thornton made the same accusation about my grandmother,' she whispered to Shane as the purposeful sounds from upstairs continued. 'He said she embezzled the sodality's funds—'

Shane's warning pressure on her hand silenced her. Jack Bale was returning.

'Read it.' He handed a document to Adele. 'This one has the correct date.'

Staring at the thick, black writing, Adele realised it was a death certificate with her mother's name on it. Her death was recorded three days after the fire. She was unable to look at Shane as she handed the certificate to him.

'Your mother has been dead a long time and that man standing beside you put her in her coffin,' Jack Bale declared. '*Consent* may be the in-word at the moment but no matter what she wrote in her diary, Shane Reagan was responsible for having carnal knowledge of a minor.'

'You lying, evil swine.' The narrow hall in which they stood seemed too fragile to contain Shane's anger. 'How come you're in possession of Marianne's death certificate?'

'What business is that of yours?'

'I'm making it my business. Answer my question. Who gave it to you?'

'The priest,' he replied. 'The one who left. What was it they were called in the day? A spoiled priest or something like that? Anyway, the religious life all got too much for him so he skedaddled off and left his dog collar behind.'

'Father Breen?' Hope faded from Shane's face and Adele, watching his expression change, whimpered then fell silent. Time enough to mourn her dream when she was alone.

'That's the name right enough,' said Jack. 'I took a copy of it from him when he showed it to me. Nothing like having evidence to counteract lies. Now fuck off out of my house.' He glared at Adele. 'I'm sorry you never knew your mother but it saved you a lot of heartache in the long run. My advice to you is to forget about that documentary and take the next flight out of here. You too, Mr Reagan. The girl is dead. Let her rest in peace.'

Shane would not allow her to drive back to Brooklime. She was too emotional, he said as he sat behind the steering wheel, the tendons on his neck stretched like wires about to snap.

Two days after their encounter with Jack Bale, Shane left on his next assignment. South Sudan, this time. He had no idea how long he would be away. He would continue his efforts to make contact with the former priest. Adele dropped him off at the airport and drove away before he saw her tears. She had lost one father to a bullet. Had she found the perfect father figure just to lose him to another war zone?

Rory Breen. It had been easy enough for Adele to discover his first name. After leaving the priesthood he had worked abroad on famine relief. The agency where he had volunteered was unable to provide her with any up-to-date information, apart from the fact that his last posting was in Darfur during the early noughties. Adele wondered if he was dead. He had worked in dangerous places, disease-ridden and war-torn communities.

She should leave Reedstown now. She was tired chasing rainbows that shimmered then faded, and when she had almost forgotten their sheen, another one appeared to taunt her by demanding that she should check out one last line of enquiry. This time it was the letter from Winnie O'Donnell with Barbara's address.

Dear Barbara,

Winnie O'Donnell was kind enough to give me your address. I hope you don't mind me writing to you. Marianne Mooney was my mother. I believe you knew her when you were staying at the House of Atonement. I found her diary and she mentioned you many times, always with great fondness.

I'm a documentary maker and am hoping to make a documentary about her time there. Would it be possible to meet and talk to you about her? I can fly to London any time that suits you.

I hope I am not stirring unhappy memories by contacting you and would be grateful for any help you can give me.

Best wishes,

Adele Foyle.

*

My dear Adele,

I'm so glad you contacted me. I loved Marianne. She was such a fey and gentle child, and courageous, also. Thanks to her bravery I was able to escape that awful place and live a fulfilled, happy life.

But a grievous wrong was done to her and her death was a tragedy. I've never stopped mourning her. I could fill pages with my memories of her but, instead, I will await your arrival. Please come and see me as soon as possible. We have much to discuss.

Sincerely,
Barbara

CHAPTER FIFTY-FOUR

Adele

It was Daniel who finally lifted her from the belief that she had hit a wall and could go no further in her search for Rory Breen. He rang shortly after Adele's return from London. Her time with Barbara and her family had been as wonderful as she had anticipated but nothing prepared her for her reaction when Daniel contacted her. How could she have forgotten the joy she had always felt whenever she heard his voice on the phone?

'Shane Reagan gave me your new phone number,' he said before she could speak. 'Promise you won't hang up until we've had a chance to talk.'

'I promise,' she replied. 'But why on earth did Shane contact you?'

She knew the answer, of course. Fatherly interference. He had joked about it before he left. Love was as important as blood when it came to bonding and he was everything she had imagined a father would be. And that, it seemed, included putting his nose into her business and trying to sort out her confused and broken heart.

'Those photographs that were sent to you,' he said. 'Why didn't you tell me?'

'I was afraid you'd lie… deny everything.'

'There was *nothing* to deny. You should have trusted me. They were crowd shots taken at that conference. Madison Fox sent them. She edited out the other people. Shane could see that when you showed them to him. You could too, if you'd cared to look.'

'I did look.' But, of course, that was untrue. Jealousy had blinded her to any other explanation, even Shane's insistence that they had been photoshopped.

'He told me about the attack. How could you not let me know, Adele? I would have come to you immediately.'

'I tried to ring you after it happened.'

'A private number. I saw it on my screen. I thought it was one of those scams. He said you also rang me at work on another occasion.'

'Daniel, it doesn't matter—'

'It *does* matter. I checked back. Your call was logged but your message had been deleted. Only one person could do that.'

'Madison?'

'I confronted her.' He sounded grim, purposeful. 'It wasn't pleasant. The upshot is that she's left Greendene. However, that's not why I rang. Shane said you'd received information that led you to believe your mother could be alive. I'm so sorry to hear you finally received confirmation that she died shortly after you were born.'

Unable to speak, she could only nod.

'Are you still there, Adele?'

'I'm here.'

'I've found out something that might help your search for that ex-priest. Greendene has a wide reach and I've tapped into their global contacts. I discovered a Rory Breen who helped in a clean-up operation when Greendene had an oil spill in 2007. Sounds like it could be him. I've nothing more up-to-date but I'll send you a link with his details, if you'll give me your new email address.'

'Thank you, Daniel.' It seemed such a stiff response but it was either that or falling into a wave of emotion that was too turbulent for her to handle. He sounded just as formal when he thanked her for the return of his engagement ring.

'"There was no need to send it back,' he said. 'It was my gift to you.'

'Daniel…' She faltered, afraid to continue yet knowing she must. 'I'm sorry I caused you so much pain.'

'You were going through a hell of a time—'

'But I allowed myself to lose sight of *us*.'

'I should have been more understanding.'

'You were understanding. I never stopped loving you or wishing I was with you. But I was possessed…' She was unable to continue but it didn't matter because his own voice was sweeping towards her, telling her how much he missed her, yearned for her, loved her to distraction. And the wave she had feared was no longer threatening as it swelled and swept them back to a familiar shore.

Rory Breen's C.V. revealed the history of a man who had taken many turns in his life. He was part of a specialist response team who travelled to locations affected by a natural catastrophe or threatened by an oil spill. His last known address was in New York. Adele rang the number and was informed by an automated voice that it was no longer in use. Despite his best efforts, Daniel was unable to find any further information on him.

They were constantly in touch, unable to stop talking, planning their future together, that hurtful separation reminding them how easy it was to let happiness slip carelessly through their fingers.

CHAPTER FIFTY-FIVE

Rachel

The pavement outside Rachel's house was free of journalists yet she ran each morning as if they were still tracking her. She took the route along the river and crossed the narrow, potholed bridge that spanned the Little Loy. The water level was returning to normal, the riverbed no longer visible. She ran like a machine, using pain and endurance as propulsion, but the exercise energised her and convinced her she should return to duty. The feeling evaporated as soon as she returned home. Her energy dipped then and the loneliness that took over was equal only to her despair.

At the end of her compassionate leave she had sought permission to have it extended again. She was unable to bear the thought of investigating other crimes when the mystery surrounding Bob's murder remained unsolved. The shadow of suspicion that had hung over the circumstances of his death had been removed and the conclusion that he had been unfortunate enough to be in the wrong place at the wrong time was once again judged to be the only reason for such a senseless killing. The cliché Rachel had used so often in her line of work now carried a bitter resonance every time she heard it repeated.

One afternoon, when she returned from a run, Adele was sitting on her garden wall.

'I've been waiting for you for over an hour,' she said. 'Why do you never answer your phone these days?'

Rachel shrugged. 'I didn't know you were trying to contact me.'

'Well, I was.' She jumped down from the wall and followed her into the kitchen. 'When are you going back to work?'

'I'm still on compassionate leave.'

'Rachel, you can't outrun your grief. You need to engage your brain as well as your body.'

'I'm not ready yet.'

'Yes, you are. And I've something to show you that will change your mind.'

'Can it wait until I shower?' She was conscious of her flushed face, her hair plastered to her forehead.

'Not until you've seen this.' Adele was glowing, her body aquiver, as if touched by some internal spark, her brown eyes luminous.

She handed a photograph to Rachel and ran her finger lightly over the glossy image of a girl. One girl in the midst of a crowd, all of them trapped in what seemed to be an inferno.

'Who is she, Adele?' she asked.

'Marianne.'

'Marianne?'

'She's my mother, Rachel. And that's me in her arms.'

Rachel sank into the nearest chair and examined the photograph. What was she to make of this? A child, for that was all Marianne Mooney was, a child carrying her baby, flames leaping from the windows of the house behind her.

'I thought she was dead before that fire broke out but I was wrong,' said Adele. 'She died soon afterwards… or so I've been led to believe. Now, I'm not so sure. I'm afraid to hope again but there's something inside me that tells me I must trust my instincts. Look again, Rachel. Do you recognise anyone else?'

It took her a moment to notice Jack Bale, looking younger and even more menacing than he did now. Her astonishment grew as Adele described the encounter that she and Shane had had with him.

'You should have come to me with this information, like you did the last time,' she said.

'You have so much going on.' Adele hesitated. 'We didn't want to burden you with anything else.'

They hadn't trusted her, knowing she was worn down by grief and conflicting loyalties. They must have been disappointed when she told them the cigarette box was too little, too late, to be used as evidence. Justice struck down by time's ruthless gavel. But something had changed and she suspected it was contained in a letter Adele was taking from the pocket of her jacket.

'It arrived this morning.' She opened an envelope postmarked Inisada and handed the letter to her. 'Read it and tell me what you think.'

She waited expectantly as Rachel turned each page, the story unfolding like a ripple of silk that was constantly changing its shape, its shimmering hues.

Dear Adele,

It is a long time since I wrote a letter to anyone. I hope you can read my writing. Lilian told me you called when I was out. I'm sorry I missed you. She said you had questions to ask about your mother. I was upset after she left. Thinking about the Sodality of Thorns and Atonement messes with my head and forces me to remember what a gullible fool I once was.

I joined them after my wife died. We'd been unhappy together and all I could think about were those wasted years, hers and mine. She went to her grave with nothing but regrets. I'd a second chance and I wanted my life to have meaning. I heard Gloria Thornton talking at one of her rallies and I believed that's what would happen in the Hard Wind commune.

I was wrong. Petty squabbles, jealousies and bullying, they were all there beneath the surface but hidden when Gloria visited. She came regularly to tell us to work harder in the fields, harder at fundraising, harder at establishing new markets for the stuff she sold.

Friendships were frowned on but I was drawn to your grandmother. Like me, she had lost her spouse. His death had changed her and, also, like me, she had been fooled by Gloria's charisma.

She was very anxious about her daughter. Gloria didn't like parents visiting Atonement. The expectant mothers were in her care and she claimed those visits upset them for ages afterwards. Your grandmother also suspected that Gloria was siphoning off the sodality's donations and she was trying to put some order on the accounts.

Atonement needed painting and I was sent to do it because I'd been a painter and decorator before I joined the sodality. I was shocked when I saw those young women working long hours in those awful containers. The way they were treated by the Thorns disgusted me. I never had children and this was my chance to be a dad to them. Not that I knew much about fathering but kind words and gestures don't need training.

Me and Marianne helped one of them to escape. Your mother was put into solitude as punishment. That finished me off. I decided to leave as soon as her baby was born. I'd have helped her to escape but the place was guarded like Fort Knox after Barbara got away.

I watched everyone who came to see Gloria. One was a politician. I discovered he was the one who made sure she *had the right documents to send those babies to the States. Oh, they were a right double act, and all the time more people were joining her sodality. We're a needy lot when we're troubled or when we're too lazy to look behind the surface of easy salvation.*

Your grandmother planned on being at your birth. But you were born early and you came quick. Your mother wailed so loud when they tried to take you from her. I swear to God the sound lifted my scalp. To stop her crying, it was agreed she could keep you for a day. But the door of the room was locked and Gloria was the only one with the key.

Another man arrived on that same day. Gloria got a shock when he turned up and she was a difficult woman to startle. They were in her office arguing loud enough for me to hear. I'd been painting in there earlier and was taking a cigarette break outside. He had a loud, hard voice. I could hear him though the open window. I used to carry a small recorder with me to record birdsong but that day I turned it on them. He wanted money but she knew enough to keep him tame, or so I thought. The house burned down that night.

They blamed me for the fire and maybe they were right. I'd knocked a bottle of white spirit over the sheets I used to catch the drips. I'd bundled them up and left them in Gloria's office, intending to bring them to the laundry room later. That's what caused the combustion but the source of the fire was later traced to Gloria's computer. A faulty battery, we were told, but I've never known the truth of that.

The whole house was blazing and everyone was outside by the time the emergency services arrived. All except Marianne. I couldn't find her anywhere. Gloria had forgotten about her in the mayhem and your mother was still locked in that room. It was on the ground floor of the south wing and thanks be to

God the fire hadn't reached her. But she was starting to cough from the smoke and I was fair sure you'd be dead. But you gave a little meow, just like a kitten, half-strangled but alive.

We felt our way along the corridor. There was light from the flames, they were still far enough away not to be an immediate danger. We were just entering the hall when we saw Gloria. She was like a wild thing trying to take you from your mother's arms. Marianne pushed her away so hard she staggered back and that gave us a chance to escape.

I kept expecting Gloria to follow. When she didn't, I ran back in to see what was keeping her. She was on her feet again and the man she'd been with earlier was coming out of another room. The stairs were beginning to blaze and I yelled at them to hurry up. I went back out and was convinced they were coming behind me. But he was the only one who escaped.

He grabbed your mother and accused her of killing Gloria. She'd hit her head when she fell and was already dead when the stairs came down, he said. Your mother kept saying no… no… no… It was obvious she was terrified of him. He was holding her arms and shouting at her about jail. I picked up a stone and smashed him over the head with it. It stunned him and then I saw your mother handing you over to Rosemary. Your grandmother must have arrived when the house was blazing. She took you into her arms and that's the last I saw of any of you.

I heard that your mother died shortly afterwards. That didn't surprise me considering how weak she was and demented with terror. However, I've learned not to take anything at face value so that's something else I've never known the truth of. I wish I could tell you that she's still alive and where you could find her. The only thing I'm sure of is that she did not kill Gloria Thornton. Gloria died either by accident or at the hands of that man.

I watched the sodality fall apart afterwards. Gloria had been their lynchpin. Without her they were just troubled people searching for a new leader. I was done with all that.

I've lived my life simply since then. I meditate to the sounds of the waterfall. More often, I'm distracted by thoughts such as the ones I've just written down but the waterfall brings me solace. I hope you find yours in the knowledge that your mother loved you dearly.

Malachi Norris

Rachel folded the letter and slipped it back into the envelope. Where was the truth in it? So much of it was speculative, and yet she was on tenterhooks when she asked Adele if she had the recorder.

Adele handed a small device to her. Small enough to hold in one's hand and be unnoticed. The atmosphere in the house was changing, igniting. Rachel longed to resist it, to stay becalmed in her own numbness, but she was peering at something through the dissipating fug. As yet it had no shape. Just disjointed limbs seeking a body and she must struggle to hold it together.

'The voices are difficult to hear,' Adele admitted. 'But you'll pick up the gist of their conversation. It's time you returned to work, Sergeant Darcy.'

Before she left, she opened her arms in a spontaneous gesture and Rachel, without hesitating, walked into them. She was aware of Adele stiffening, drawing back, her eyes questioning.

'Did he know?' she whispered, and when Rachel shook her head, she sighed then pressed her hand gently against the growing swell of Rachel's stomach.

*

The tape had been cleaned by forensics and the voices were finally audible. Gloria Thornton spoke softly yet distinctly as she discussed the trafficking of babies. Admittedly, that was not the term she used. Her mission was to find good homes for unfortunate children born with the stain of sin on their brows. Rachel was sickened by her pious utterances. Jack Bale kept interrupting her. No mistaking his forceful tone, his self-assurance as he stated that babies were a lucrative business, especially on the other side of the Atlantic. He was not being paid enough for the risks he was taking, especially as he would be the first to take a fall should the powers that be start asking questions.

'Not near enough, *Mother* Gloria.' His mockery was as pronounced as ever. 'I'm giving you the opportunity to make up the deficit. The Mooney baby, for instance. A girl, I've heard. I wonder if she resembles her mother... or her father?'

'Don't threaten me, Jack.' Gloria spoke calmly. The hypnotic timbre of her voice as she warned him against the sin of greed soon silenced his demands. She was not going to increase his payments and if he insisted on making threats, she had gathered enough evidence to destroy him. Forged documents, kickbacks from property developers, drunk-driving charges quashed, false evidence given in court... his career was an open book to Gloria Thornton and well documented.

'You're overstepping yourself, Jack,' she said. 'I can bring you down as quickly—'

At that point the tape abruptly ended but the story, as far as Rachel was concerned, was only beginning.

Later that evening he opened his front door to her. 'Back so soon,' he said. 'I'm beginning to look forward to these unexpected visits. You'd better come in in case my neighbours start gossiping. A man is never too old to gain a reputation.'

In his spotless kitchen Rachel tried to ignore the uneasy lurch in her stomach. The room was still infused by a fishy smell that nothing, she believed, would eradicate.

'I'm returning to work shortly,' she said.

'Law and order returns to Reedstown.' He smiled and pulled out a chair. 'Sit yourself down there and tell me what's on your mind this time.'

'I'll stand, thanks. I simply wanted to let you know that I'll be opening an investigation into the trafficking of babies from the House of Atonement.'

'The trafficking of what?' He stood before her, legs apart, his hands resting on his hips. 'What the fuck are you talking about?'

'Is there anything you'd like to share with me before the investigation officially begins?'

'Rachel, you've worried me for a long time. Have you seen a counsellor? I'm amazed your superior hasn't had you in for an assessment—'

'You ran a racket with Gloria Thornton and Christy Lewis. Illegal adoptions mean illegal documentation, illegal shortcuts, illegal anything that helped those babies to be brought from Ireland to the States. Your boast that you always ran a tight ship has stood you in good stead until now. But there's always the danger of a stumble, especially when you get too greedy, as you did on the night that hellhole caught fire. Take a moment and listen to this. Like you said before, voices from the grave…'

She switched on the recorder and waited impassively as the voices, clearer now, sealed his fate.

'Where did you get that?' Too stunned to hide his panic, he wiped his forehead yet the sweat still glistened on his brow as he switched off the recorder.

'Come now, Jack, do you honestly expect me to reveal my source?'

'I'm warning you—'

'This evidence is a timebomb waiting to explode,' she said. 'As your two partners are dead, you're the only one left to take the fall. I intend making sure it's a very deep drop. But if you're cooperative, that will make things easier all round.'

'What exactly do you mean by "cooperative"?' he asked eventually.

'Destroy the recording you made with Christy Lewis.'

'And if I do?'

'I destroy this one.'

'Quid pro quo? How do I know you don't have another?'

'I can say the same for you.'

'They used to call this the Cold War.'

'Balance of power, Jack. Isn't that what it's all about?' She would meet him bluff for bluff, and see who blinked first.

CHAPTER FIFTY-SIX

Rachel

The Loy was running high this evening. A week of intermittent rain had broken the hot spell and the earth was greening again as Rachel bent, stretched, flexed. Two hours passed. She was conscious only of her breathing and the steady slap of her running shoes. She crossed the humpbacked bridge over the Little Loy, aware the light was dimming fast and that it was unsafe to run alone along this uneven track.

She slowed down to a walk, conscious that she was the only person on this rough terrain. Branches heavy with leaves obscured the way forward at times and she was forced onto the grass by the edge of the river. The path was just a pale ribbon before her as the twilight deepened. She quickened her pace when she heard a rustle within the thicket, too loud to have been made by an animal. Someone moved from the trees and stood before her. Hooded and crouched, the stance of the figure suggested only one thing. Danger.

'You killed him.' The voice was female, a furious shriek that Rachel recognised, despite the hoodie shading the figure's face. The last time they had spoken, Haylee Ford was loudly demanding a lawyer to refute the accusation that she had stolen an engagement ring. This time she held a knife and when she lunged at

Rachel, narrowly missing her arm, her accusation shattered the tranquillity of the night.

Dazed and disoriented, Rachel swivelled instinctively as Haylee slashed at her again. She managed to remain standing, aware that the woman in front of her was dangerously unbalanced. Kick-boxing had been her favourite sport when she was younger, and it was this combat training that protected her when Haylee lunged again. One well-aimed kick was all that was needed to stun her. Collapsing to her knees, Haylee still held onto the knife until another defensive blow sent her sprawling. The blade of the knife caught the glint of the moon as it fell from her hand. Rachel kicked it into the river and pulled her to her feet.

The fight had gone from Haylee and she was snuffling loudly into her hood. 'You killed Jonathan…' Her voice broke on his name. 'He's dead because of you. You paid those thugs to string him up in his cell.' She was so frightened without the protection of the knife that her knees buckled and she would have collapsed again if Rachel had not held her upright.

Maddened by the belief that Rachel was responsible for the death of her partner, she let loose a tirade of abuse that only one person could have orchestrated.

'Listen to me, Haylee, whatever happened to Gra— Jonathan had nothing to do with me,' she said. 'Someone is feeding you false information. I know who he is, and so do you. He sent you out here to attack me.'

'You're a fuckin' liar…murderer.'

'Do you honestly believe he's going to let you walk away from your crime?' Rachel's warning eventually forced her into silence. 'Jonathan is dead because of him,' she continued. 'So is my husband. You have to talk to me, Haylee. Otherwise, he'll make sure you go the same way.'

'Jonathan never meant to shoot your husband. He thought…'
She began to sob uncontrollably.

'He thought what?' Unable to bear the sound, Rachel resisted
the temptation to grab her by the shoulders and shake her until
her teeth rattled. She continued talking, aware from Haylee's
stance, steadier now but still wary, that she was listening.

'Whatever he told Jonathan that night frightened him enough
to take a gun and commit murder. He signed his own death
warrant by doing so. You need to tell me who is responsible for
the fact that we've both lost the men we loved. Is he the same
person who convinced Jonathan he'd get an early release if he
stayed silent?'

'What does it matter now?' When Haylee lifted her arm, it was
only to wipe her nose with her sleeve. 'They're both dead, aren't
they?' Her voice was thick with an anguish Rachel understood.
'He fed me this shit about you being the bitch what organised
Jonathan's death. Maybe he's right. What the fuck do I know
any more?'

His name dangled just out of reach and when Haylee finally
uttered it, Rachel made her repeat it, but more loudly this time.

'He'll kill me if he knows I've told you.' No longer crying,
she spoke with a sharper awareness. 'I need money to get away
from him. Jonathan's parents won't let me near his apartment.
His money's frozen in the bank and there's no way I can take it
from the ATM.'

'I can help you with money but, first, you have to tell me
what happened. Did my husband go from Jack Bale's house on
to your apartment?'

'That pig cop phoned Jonathan to tell him Kev Spencer was
coming for his money. Gave him the reg of the car so when your
husband got out—' She stopped, obviously aware of the impact
her words were having on Rachel.

'Go on.' She saw it all unfolding in slow motion. Kev Spencer, dangerous in the deadly sense of being a hit man, highly rated for his accuracy. Grad must have been convinced his night of reckoning would be upon him if he did not fire the first shot. She imagined Bob, distraught and furious after confronting Jack Bale. Perhaps he had threatened to reveal all – Rachel could only hope that was true – then driving onwards to confront Grad, who had dared to terrorise his daughter.

Blood pounded in her forehead. The moon seemed just as engorged, its serried peaks and valleys mapping pale-blue capillaries across its face. This time it was Haylee who offered her a steadying hand and coaxed her away from the water's edge. Was she aware, as Rachel was, of the strangeness of their encounter? At any other time, they would have passed each other on the street without a glance, yet now there they were, bonded in loss. Haylee's nervousness was evident as she glanced over her shoulder. There was no one else in sight, no furtive footsteps approaching, no threatening shadows, yet she was trembling until they left the river behind them.

'He promised Jonathan he'd get him released on bail if he kept his mouth shut.' Now that she had opened up to Rachel, she seemed unable to stop. 'We'd everything arranged to escape but then I get a call from his mother to tell me he'd gone and killed himself. She wouldn't listen when I said that was ridiculous. Even if he was going down for life, Jonathan loved himself too much to take a rope to his neck.'

She entered Rachel's house warily. She was defiant and suspicious but, for now, hunger took over as she snatched at the leftover lasagne Rachel heated. To cook for two was still an ingrained habit and there was plenty to spare.

'No way.' Her reply was emphatic when Rachel asked her to talk to Detective Sergeant Magee.

'The Gardai can organise protection for you.' She tried to assuage her suspicions but she could see the fear pooling Haylee's eyes. 'Jack Bale needs to be brought down and you have the information to make it happen—'

'Do you seriously think they'd listen to me?' Her hand shook as she scooped lasagne from the dish to her plate. 'They'd have me behind bars as soon as I opened my mouth.'

'I'll be with you every step of—'

'What part of "no" do you not understand? You said you'd give me money, not some lecture about ratting to the pigs. I want what you promised or I'll… I'll…'

'You'll what, Haylee. Attack me again? Keep trying to outrun Jack Bale?'

'Shut up and give me that money.'

'Please listen to me—'

Haylee was on her feet, this time moving too fast for Rachel to avoid what was coming. The headbutt, vicious and accurate, forced her backwards to the floor. She was too dazed to react when Haylee lifted her foot and aimed it at her stomach. She was kneeling, her hands clasped protectively over this fragile life she carried, when she heard the front door slam.

She saw the blood when she was finally able to make her way to the bathroom. Not much, a smear, but how garish it looked against the white cotton. No… no… no… She kept talking to her baby as she made her way to the front door. Her car was missing. Haylee must have taken the keys from the hook in the hall. She groped for her phone. Only one person would truly appreciate her terror.

'Stay with me… stay with me,' she pleaded as she waited for Adele to arrive.

*

At the hospital, she shuddered as the sonographer applied gel over her stomach. How flat it looked, so deflated, as if this delicate life was already departing. Adele held tightly to her hand as the probe moved, sending out ultrasound waves that would deliver a terrible message. Rachel turned her face away as the calm voice of the stenographer encouraged her to look at the screen.

'Oh my God, Rachel, look,' Adele whispered. 'Look... oh, look!'

Holding tightly to each other, they saw an image, as delicate as the flap of butterfly wings but which was, the sonographer assured them, the steady beat of her baby's heart.

CHAPTER FIFTY-SEVEN

Adele

Once again, it was Daniel who provided Adele with the necessary information on how to contact Rory Breen. This time the telephone number had an Italian prefix. Braced against disappointment as she rang the number, she was tempted to hang up. This phone call would either lift her into the clouds or plunge her back to earth, all hope gone. She had visited Italy once with Daniel. A romantic weekend in Florence. She had been amazed by the accessibility of the historical sights, all only a fingertip away from the immediacy of the present. She felt that same shock of recognition when the phone was answered and a voice said, 'Rory Breen here.' He had the rolling lilt of a Cork accent, his voice gravelly with age. 'Who is this, please?'

She struggled to speak, her mouth suddenly dry, her well-prepared words deserting her.

'Hello… hello. Can I help you?' He must be used to people ringing to report disasters but his tone suggested he was not immune to their distress.

'My name is Adele Foyle,' she said. 'You don't know me but I'm hoping you can help me with some information.'

'If I can, I will certainly oblige.'

'I'm looking for information on Marianne Mooney.' She reached for the wall to steady herself. 'I've reason to believe you knew her.'

Now he was the one to remain silent. She heard the catch of his breath and when he spoke again, he sounded cautious, strained. 'I'm sorry, I didn't catch your name.'

'Adele Foyle. If you know anything about Marianne Mooney—'

'Can I ask in what context?'

'I want to know if she's alive.'

'May I ask why you would expect me to provide you with that information?'

'I need to know…' She hesitated, terrified that the bubble containing such a miraculous possibility was about to burst with a splatter of hopelessness. 'Is she still alive…?'

'Miss Foyle, I've no idea who you are. Or what motive you have for ringing me. This number is private and only used in emergencies. I ask you again, how did you get it?'

'*Please* tell me—'

'I'm not prepared to continue this conversation on the phone. Give me your address and I'll contact you in my own time.'

Afterwards, she sank to the floor and gathered her knees into her chest. She rocked backwards and forwards, as she used to do when she was a child and the world seemed too big to handle. It had always soothed her but tonight she found no relief in the rhythmical movements. She Skyped Daniel, who talked her up the stairs and into bed.

'Just be patient,' he said. 'If Shane said he's one of the good guys then believe him. Good guys don't change. He'll be in touch, I'm sure of it.'

Rory Breen arrived at Brooklime the following day, a rugged-looking man with steely features. She knew who he was as soon as she answered the door. He reminded her of Shane but older and leaner, a weathered face, his sparse, grey hair shaved close to his scalp. What was it about men who ran towards danger that gave them such a focused gaze, she wondered as she invited him in?

'You're Marianne's daughter.' He nodded decisively, as if the sight of her had answered his question. 'I had to be sure. A phone call like that coming out of the blue, well, it could be anyone.'

'You mean someone connected to Jack Bale?'

'Ah, you're acquainted with him then?'

'Very much so. But I didn't intend to scare you when I rang. You're the only lead I have. Please, can you tell me if she is alive?'

All the waiting and wondering, the hope and despair, all compressed into her chest as she waited for his reply.

'Yes, Adele,' he said. 'She is alive.' A simple answer that was powerful enough to split the atom.

'Oh… *oh…*' She was unaware that she was crying until she clasped her hands to her face. 'When can I see her—?'

'Adele, please listen to me. Marianne had reasons for going into hiding. Reasons you will find difficult to understand.'

'I do understand them.'

'How could you?'

'Read this.' She handed Malachi's letter to him. His expression remained inscrutable as he read it. Easy to do when he spent his time controlling chaos.

He passed the letter back to her. His hands were broad and capable. They had lifted her mother from danger and carried her into exile.

'How long have you been searching for her?' he asked.

'Not long. I never thought… my grandmother told me she was dead. I never believed otherwise until Shane came.'

'Shane Reagan?'

'He recognised her from a photograph…' So much to tell each other. It would take all night and the next day. Maybe there would never be enough hours to learn what her life could have been like had fate not intervened.

'My father was Bob Molloy,' she said. 'He was one of the three. The other two were Keith Lewis—'

'And Liam Thornton,' Rory said. 'Those two were inseparable. But Bob… I'd never have imagined…' Unable to hide his shock, he sighed heavily and shook his head, his reaction so similar to Shane's that she drew some comfort from it.

'Where does my mother live?' She thirsted for information, for details that would add substance to the pictures in her mind.

He described an inlet on the South Island of New Zealand. Cape Maclure, it sounded wild and inhospitable, yet he claimed it was a place Marianne had come to love.

'So far away?' Adele said.

'As far as she could get from here,' he admitted. 'It was meant to be only for a short while. She trusted me to find you and your grandmother. God knows I searched high and low down for the sight of you but you had vanished like a fairy child.'

'Into the mist and mountains,' she said. 'My grandmother was always hiding in plain sight.'

Unable to sit still, she walked to the window and stared out at the anglers. Jack Bale was not among them. He was never far from her thoughts. Her mother had written that hate was a seeping wound and that night in the hospital with Rachel, watching the tiny heart beating, Adele had been overwhelmed by a murderous urge to crush him under her heel. Rachel had advised her to be patient. She said it quietly, as if she was watching an internal play and she was the only one who knew how it was going to end.

Adele listened raptly as Rory spoke about his uncle, an artist who had once captured his landscape on canvas but was now slowly dying. Marianne's husband, Adele's stepfather, so much to absorb, so much more to learn.

'How soon can I see my mother?' she asked.

'I need to talk to her, reassure her that you are genuine. She scares easily. Old scars that she never had a chance to heal. She'll be frightened…' Rory joined her at the window and put his arm around her shoulder.

'Make it soon?' she whispered. 'She has nothing to fear.'

He was smiling the following morning when he joined her for breakfast. 'You and I have a long journey ahead of us,' he said. 'You'd better start packing.'

Happiness also seeped, bleeding into her veins and shaking her heart to its core.

CHAPTER FIFTY-EIGHT

Adele

Adele was unable to tell if it was nervousness or the swell of the waves that made her ill as the ferry churned through Maclure Sound. Leaning over the side of the boat, eyes streaming, her hair streeling, she willed the journey to end. Rory, smiling as he gazed at the distant inlet rising out of the sea, ordered her to breathe… breathe…

Now that it was about to happen, she was unable to recapture the rush of exhilaration that had swept her across the world and into this ferry that was pitching her towards her mother. Mother… Mammy… Mama… Mum… Mam… She tried them all and each one sounded unfamiliar on her tongue.

One step at a time, Rory had said. He was right. She straightened and allowed the wind to buffet her. Like the back of a sloping beast, the headland was beginning to shape itself. How brown it looked, how bleak the cliffs, and yet she could see the shapes of trees, and birds whirling into the wind.

So much had happened so fast. It was too easy. After all the obstacles that had been put in her way, something had to go wrong. Why, Rory had asked. Don't you think there was enough wrongness in twenty-four years of separation? As the ferry rounded the side of the headland, sheer columns of rock rose upwards like deadly arms inviting the ferry closer. Adele was relieved when the skipper rounded the bend and the softer lines of Maclure were visible. The ferry nosed its way into the harbour. Passengers gathered their belongings and the drivers returned to their cars. A cluster of people stood on the harbour. It was impossible to make them out from this distance. Was Marianne among them or had she, like Adele, been filled with the same nervousness, unable to face the daughter she believed she had lost forever?

Adele stepped onto the gangplank and recognised her instantly. She would have picked her out in a multitude. Her slim frame and long, brown hair, the face that had stared at Adele from a strip of photographs. She had been laughing then, secure in Shane's arms, whereas now, as she stared towards the disembarking passengers, she reminded Adele of the frightened child she had recognised in Lilian's photograph. She stood perfectly still as Adele walked towards her. She was used to waiting, so many years imagining such a moment. What must she think of her daughter, sickly pale and wind-blown, red-rimmed eyes, leaning like an invalid on Rory's arm as she tried to find her land legs? Marianne's arms were outstretched and the distance Adele had to walk before she could be enfolded in her embrace seemed never-ending. It took only a few more steps before they were together, and it was everything Adele had imagined this moment to be. An explosion of happiness, an overwhelming joy. Afterwards, there would be time to talk far into the night but in that instant, as they clung to each other, it was the knowingness of touch that tore at Adele's senses. Surely it would be impossible to remember the last time she was held this way by her mother – she was three days old – and yet it was there, stored but never forgotten in the angel-space of baby memories; the feeling that she was cocooned, cherished, safe. The evening sky flamed above them, tongues of fire searing the clouds as Marianne took her hand and brought her daughter home.

CHAPTER FIFTY-NINE

Davina

The Unstoppable March was fully booked. No problems there, all boxes ticked. The heatwave was becoming a distant memory but the weather forecast promised occasional blasts of sunshine between the showers. Davina greeted the guest speakers when they arrived and threw open the doors of the green room for refreshments. She checked that all was okay with the camera crews, photographers and journalists in the press room and returned to the foyer to watch the attendees streaming into the Loyvale Hotel conference room. The buzz of conversation and the heighted sense of anticipation was music to her ears. Keith mingled with the audience. As always, women gravitated towards him. Babs Shannon had sounded a little coy on the phone when she asked if he would like to introduce her. Even the staunchest of feminists, it seemed, were not immune to her husband's charms.

Yet, Babs continued to worry her. What bothered Davina most was her inability to put her finger on the reason for those sudden darts of panic. They struck at unexpected times. The blurb, for instance, that Babs had written for insertion into the conference brochure had been vague enough to alarm Davina. Was the self-help author and ardent feminist suggesting that one of the obstacles to overcome in the fight for equality was the damage done to women by women? Davina had relaxed slightly after an anxious phone call to Babs, who insisted that her speech would take the audience by storm.

She flew into Dublin Airport on Friday evening and refused Davina's offer to send a courier to pick her up at the airport. She was spending the night with friends, which struck Davina as curious, since Babs had claimed during their London meeting to have had very little contact with anyone in Ireland since she left. On Saturday morning she arrived at the Loyvale as planned and spent the period before her speech signing her books.

In the conference room, the female politician spoke wittily and wisely about the status of women in government. The female economist was witty and factual. The female stand-up comedian was edgy and witty while the female historian believed there was nothing remotely witty about the subjugation of women through-out the centuries. A lively diverse mix of speakers, Davina began to relax as applause broke out at the end of each presentation, especially when she heard her chosen guests thank her warmly for inviting them to participate in this unstoppable march.

Babs did not join them for lunch. Davina was aware of her absence from the table, even as she entertained, sparkled and engaged the group in conversation.

After lunch, the atmosphere was warm and welcoming when Keith introduced the star speaker. The political poster boy, doing what he did best. Anger soured Davina's mouth but she was adept at hiding her feelings. She sat in the front row beside Julie, who was still wearing her dark glasses. Another dart of alarm, a pitter patter heart beat to remind Davina that marriages with secrets were built on quicksand.

Babs Shannon had style. Her pale-blue dress swished pro-vocatively around her knees as she walked towards the podium. She had good ankles and her high heels, clicking assertively, gave her extra inches. A close-up of her face was visible on the video screens on either side of the stage. Her embracing smile gathered the audience to her but Davina, watching keenly, noticed a touch of nervousness when she stood behind the podium and surveyed the crowded auditorium. Not that anyone else would notice it beneath her self-assured sheen but Davina was locked into a growing belief that she had made a dreadful mistake by inviting Babs Shannon to speak. She still had not read the author's books. Too much canvassing to do, not to mention stiffening her husband's spine every time he tried to talk about that night. That terrible night that seemed incapable of being pushed back into the dark since it saw the light of confession.

Keith's introduction was polished enough to suggest he had memorised every word the author had ever written. An expectant silence settled over the audience as the applause died away and he turned to leave the stage.

'Stay,' Babs said. 'We need some gender balance here. Don't you agree, Sisters?'

The audience laughed obligingly and clapped. Keith bowed towards Babs and remained in position on the opposite podium.

'I've spent weeks working on my speech,' she began. 'It's filled with the most up-to-date research and statistics. But the bottom line is what matters and all you want to know from me is… are we on an unstoppable match towards equality? I can answer you with one word. Yes. We will get there in the end. But the path is bloody and, as this is a long march, I decided to tear up my speech and share with you my own story. My own long march. You won't have read about it in any of my books. Nor have I spoken about it in the media or at conferences like this one today.'

Davina pressed her fingers to her chest. This was not in the script and Keith, unable to move from his podium, seemed unsure whether he should be alarmed or enthralled. She looked around her. The audience were alert, leaning forward in their seats, reluctant to miss a word from the stage.

'Sisters, you may wonder what gave rise to my desire to revisit a time in my life I believed I'd left behind forever,' Babs continued. 'I decided early on in my career that dwelling on periods of great unhappiness would hinder my way forward. It would consume my energy, slow my footsteps. I kept my own counsel about my past when I was questioned by journalists. Share a weakness with the media and it becomes a caul you can never remove. I lived by this dictum until recently when I received a letter. Short and to the point, it swept me back in time. Back towards memories that I believed I'd buried under the wealth of good fortune gifted to me. I was wrong. The rawness and pain were still there and, so, I met with the sender of that letter. Together, we revisited that stage of my life when it seemed as if my future would be dictated by others. Strangers who were incapable of caring whether or not they broke my heart. How many of you have read The Marianne Diary?'

The snake in the grass, the cobra, asp, whatever, all loose and wriggling. Davina heard the audience's collective gasp as hands shot up and a buzz of conversation broke out.

'How many of you believe it was genuine?' Babs silenced them with the question and hands were raised again. Not as many this time, but far more than the show of hands when she asked the non-believers to declare themselves.

"I have to admit that I was not familiar with the diary,' she said. 'I'd no idea it had been found and was being blogged online. But I did not have to read it to be familiar with every word Marianne wrote during those bitter nights. She laid bare the horrifying conditions that existed in a mother and baby home called the House of Atonement. I was her friend. She helped me to escape and because of her courage I was able to keep my beloved son,

Aaron. The woman who sent that letter to me is Marianne's daughter. She is also the blogger who released the diary. Please give a round of applause for Adele Foyle, who is here to speak to you about her decision to release a story that began here in this lovely village twenty-five years ago.'

How had she gained admittance without Davina's knowledge? She had been missing from Brooklime for over a fortnight. Probably off visiting her fiancé, Larry said when Davina called to his house with her canvassers. She had left with an older man, whom she had introduced to him as Rory. More than that Larry could not say, except that she would be returning to Reedstown. And there she was, all swagger and defiance as she emerged from the wing of the stage and walked towards Babs Shannon, who moved aside to allow her the microphone.

The audience broke into cheers and rose to their feet in a standing ovation as Adele raised a clenched fist. That first time, when she was loitering with intent outside The Lodge, Davina had known she was trouble and here it was, being played out in front of her helpless gaze. Keith stood to attention, unable to move. The video camera swept over the audience for its reaction. Julie, her glasses fogging with tears, took them off and clapped as loudly as anyone else. Davina brought her hands together and forced a smile. She must make it as radiant as possible, despite the fact that her mouth felt crushed with stones.

'Thank you, Barbara,' Adele said when the noise died down. 'And thanks to all of you who responded so kindly to my mother's story.'

The audience was seated again, and silent. Davina longed to press her hands to her ears to drown out that hated voice. She did not want to hear how Adele's search had brought her to Reedstown to find out the truth about her birth. Break-ins and a stolen online identity, guns and masks – she made Reedstown sound like one of those awful drug-ridden inner-city communities. She was convinced her make-up was running in rivulets down her face. Her palms had the same clammy feel. She tried to catch Keith's eye. One glance from her should be enough to snap him to attention; he needed to end this farcical rout – but his fear was captured on the video screen, his furtive half-smile as he tried to decide what to do. It was only a matter of time before the audience noticed that he was shaking and using the podium as a support to hold him upright, but, for now, their attention was focused on Adele.

'How many of you knew about the House of Atonement?' she asked. 'How many of you knew that babies were being sold to the highest bidder? Would this story have ever come to life if it had not been documented by a fifteen-year-old girl from Reedstown—' Her voice broke and she seemed incapable of continuing. Babs took over the microphone and began to speak again.

'You've heard Adele's story but not its ending. She has lived all her life in the knowledge that her mother was dead. Reading her diary brought her to life in a way she had never anticipated and opened up a pathway to an amazing discovery. She has allowed me the privilege of introducing my second guest. My dearest friend, who shared those days with me and who, contrary to what we believed, is alive and here with us today to tell you her story. Please give a very warm welcome to Marianne Mooney.'

Her arms outstretched in welcome, Babs turned again towards the wing of the stage. The woman who emerged to thunderous applause, walked hesitantly into the glare of the lights. A long dress floated around her ankles, cinched at the waist with a wide belt. Coppery-brown hair fell to her shoulders and the haunting familiarity of her hesitant smile caused Julie to utter a low moan. Keith's expression suggested that he was standing in front of a speeding train with failed brakes and he was powerless to move from its path.

Marianne Mooney faced the audience and gave a timid wave. The silence that followed the applause was tense with anticipation. That she was not used to speaking in public was obvious from her diffidence, but the words she used struck a chord with the audience. Her nervousness only added to her appeal as she told her story in simple, stark terms, leaving nothing out except the names of those who had assaulted her. She had left Ireland after her baby was born and moved to New Zealand where she lived in a house with many shadows. She was holding something back, a deeper story. Davina, as sensitive as a wind vane, sensed it but she could not dwell on speculation, only on the unfolding horror drama being played out on the platform that she, herself, had created.

Marianne Mooney was coming to the end of her speech. 'This past fortnight has been one of tremendous emotions,' she said. 'I've lived a quiet life since my baby was taken from me. All I ask is that the Gardai open my case and establish the identity of the men who came that night to Blake's Hollow. The only evidence I can produce is my daughter's DNA, which she is willing to provide.'

The audience was on its feet again, applauding them as they walked from the stage, their arms entwined. They had sabotaged Davina's conference and exposed the ugliness that Jack Bale had tried so hard to contain. How was she supposed to follow them and deliver her keynote address? Would her legs hold her steady as her husband welcomed her onto the stage? He had recovered his nerve and was rousingly eloquence as he introduced her? Political nous, it was inbred in him. His hand was hot, sticky with guilt as he escorted her to the podium. The hours she had worked on her speech, honing it to perfection, but the audience refused to settle, their excited, giddy conversations forcing Keith to demand silence for the keynote speaker.

Did anyone hear a word she uttered? Probably not, until she declared that once she was elected, she would lobby for a full inquiry into Marianne Mooney's case. Keith sounded just as confident when he offered to do the same. The audience applauded at the end of her speech but did not spring spontaneously to its feet. Conversations were breaking out among them even before they stopped clapping, and there was only one topic being discussed.

CHAPTER SIXTY

Rachel

The gates to Holywell were open. Sunlight filtered through the leaves as Rachel drove up the wide, tree-lined avenue towards the entrance. She mounted the steps and rang the doorbell. After ringing it for the third ring and receiving no response, she wondered if Liam Thornton had lied to her yesterday when she phoned to arrange this meeting.

She stood back from the door. Vaulted and studded with metal, it reminded her of a fortified church. The windows had the same arched design. She was about to try the doorbell one last time when he opened the door. He was always impeccably dressed but, today, he looked as though he had slept in his jogging pants and the T-shirt he wore was just as crumpled. His ruffled hair and stubble added to his dishevelled appearance.

'What do you want?' He appeared to have difficulty recognising her.

'We spoke on the phone yesterday. You agreed to meet me this morning.'

'Yes… yes… you must excuse me. My head is all over the place. I presume as you're out of uniform this is not an official call?'

'Correct. I'm back on duty but not this morning. I'd like to speak to you about a private matter. Are we likely to be interrupted?'

'Highly unlikely. My daughter is in France and my wife has moved out.'

'I'm sorry—'

'Indeed.' He opened the door wider and made a sweeping gesture towards the spacious interior. 'Come on in.'

The ceiling soared above her as she followed him through a hall filled with religious artefacts. The room she entered was so darkly panelled that even the sun shining directly through the long windows was unable to penetrate the gloom. How had Julie endured this oppressive house? He gestured at her to sit down but he himself remained standing, his arms crossed, his back to the mantlepiece.

'It's good to see you, Rachel.' He was emerging from whatever haze he had been in when she arrived. 'How are you?'

'Good days, bad days.'

'It'll take time.'

'Ah, yes, time the great healer.'

He looked keenly at her. 'I'm sure you didn't come here to trade platitudes with me. What can I do for you?'

'Were you at the conference?' No need to name it. The publicity had been rolling ever since.

'No, I didn't attend,' he said. 'Seems I missed out on the resurrection from the dead.'

'It was quite an outrageous performance,' Rachel agreed. 'But also extraordinary, don't you agree? A child, that's all she was, driven out of Reedstown and put into your mother's care, goes into hiding for twenty-four years and is then reunited with her daughter.'

'If you like melodrama, it is indeed extraordinary.' He shifted position and unfolded his arms, put them behind his back. 'I presume this conversation is leading somewhere?'

'It's leading to Bob and a question I've often wanted to ask you. What happened to the friendship you had with him when you were teenagers?'

'Friendship...?' He frowned. 'That's not how I remember it. I'm sure you're aware that Bob was a loner with a drug problem. I'd very little contact with him in those days.'

'I've been looking through some archival material in the *Review*—'

'Congratulations by the way.' He abruptly cut across her. 'How does it feel to acquire a newspaper?'

'The price I had to pay was too high.'

'Poor Bob.' He lifted himself on his toes, then settled his feet back on the floor. 'May he rest in peace.'

'I don't believe he's at peace, Liam. Can the dead rest easy when they go to the grave with their crimes unpunished?'

'Is that a theological question or rhetorical?' Once again, he swayed on his feet, his impatience obvious.

'The photographs I found in the archives suggest that there was a close friendship between you, Keith and Bob. Yet my husband couldn't bear to be in the same room as the two of you. Why was that?'

'I was never privy to his thoughts. So, I'm afraid I can't answer you.'

'Was it because you and Keith set him up on a drugs charge?'

'Set him up? He was caught in possession—'

'Which either you or Keith supplied.'

'I'm not sure why you're here, Rachel, or what exactly you're trying to imply. If you'd like to continue this conversation, then we will do so in the presence of my solicitor.'

'Why not do so in the presence of Jack Bale?'

'I'm going to ask you to leave—'

'Did you know that he was in the House of Atonement on the night your mother died?'

'He *what*?'

'He was there, Liam, and he was threatening Gloria. He was good at doing that, still is, as a matter of fact. But I'm sure you're well aware of his tactics.' She held an envelope out towards him. 'It's all in here. You don't have to read it. You can shred it before you even open it. But then you'll never know the truth about her death. That choice is entirely yours. I've left you a recording, also. I'm sure you'll agree with me that it makes interesting listening.'

When he made no effort to take the envelope from her, she laid it on top of a nest of tables and left.

CHAPTER SIXTY-ONE

Davina

When does the dust settle after it has been disturbed by a whirlwind? Three days since the conference and Marianne Mooney's name was still on everyone's lips. The fact that she shunned the limelight and had returned to her sick husband as soon as the conference was over meant nothing to an eager media. The entrails of Davina's conference were being picked over by a flock of carrion crows. The story had gone beyond online prattle and was front-page news. *A Miscarriage of Justice*, the headline in the *Reedstown Review* screamed at Davina. A photograph of a cigarette packet appeared on the front page. Twenty-five years old and found at the scene of the crime, the news item beside it claimed. Shane Reagan was quoted. He called it 'his talisman'. Since when was it established that a crime had been committed, Davina raged. How had the fake diary achieved biblical status when it had been so thoroughly discredited?

On page three of the *Reedstown Review* she saw another headline. *Keith Lewis China Trade Mission a Success.* The feature was a puff piece about how one of the delegates had received a substantial contract from a major Chinese retailer. The delegate praised Keith for introducing her to a whole new market. Only a few days ago, Davina would have welcomed such publicity.

Now, she was filled with the urge to set fire to the glass edifice that Rachel Darcy had inherited. She crumpled the paper and threw it into the litter bin.

Jack Bale rang her again. She cancelled the call. He was apoplectic since the conference. His blood pressure must be through the roof but there was nothing Davina could do to bring it down. He must wait until the by-election was over before making contact with her. The promise she had made at the conference had no substance, she assured him. He refused to be mollified. For the first time since she'd known him, he was afraid. This did nothing to ease her own panic. Was it normal, she wondered, to hide fear behind a mask? Would that mask transform her fear into confidence and, if so, which was real? Which one could she trust? Jack rang again. He was like a bear at her shoulders. He was unsheathing his claws and the longer she kept him waiting, the sharper they would be. Whether she liked it or not, she had to risk meeting him tonight before she went canvassing.

CHAPTER SIXTY-TWO

Julie

Julie's face had healed, as she had known it would. The swelling around her eyes had finally gone down and she no longer gasped each time she drew a deep breath. Overall, she was lucky. Her husband could have killed her. She had sensed it in him. The repressed desire he had kept under control for so long finally finding release. Stephanie had been the pacifying influence that had kept him stable, allowed him to work off his demons on the tennis and squash courts and in the business bearpit. This evening, keeping to his regular routine, Liam would do violence with a squash ball and racquet at the Reedstown Recreational and Leisure Centre. Julie, who had been staying in the Loyvale Hotel, had an hour left to remove the most essential of her possessions before he returned, sated and victorious.

She had attended the Unstoppable March conference. Dark glasses had hidden most of the damage to her eyes but once Babs Shannon started talking, she had taken them off, and wept openly. Davina, who had been sitting beside her had slumped forward, as if her spine had buckled. She had recovered quickly and joined in the applause but the glance she directed at Keith had a laser-like intensity.

How many men would undertake the DNA challenge and rule themselves out of an investigation, if one was ever organised? It wouldn't matter if the entire male population of Reedstown came forward to the police with blood and spittle. No one would test positive because Adele's father was resting in Reedstown Cemetery. This realisation had dawned on Julie when she saw her at Bob's funeral. Standing in the background, an inconspicuous mourner, her face awash with tears.

Had Davina made the same connection? Julie suspected she had but she was afraid to ask. Their time for sharing secrets was long past. That she managed to speak afterwards and give her keynote address was a credit to her steely determination. Like Julie, she must have been confident that nothing would ever be proved against either of their husbands.

Julie thought back to the time she had met Adele outside her husband's office. She should have guessed then. Marianne's daughter… that explained the rage on her face, her lips drawn back from her teeth, a metallic glitter in her brown eyes. She had reminded Julie of the Furies; goddesses of vengeance, seeking the destruction of men.

This would be the last time she would stand in his house. Since she had left, Liam had phoned her every day. He wanted forgiveness. In return, he would sell Holywell and seek counselling to manage the unresolved issues he had about his mother and the strange path she had chosen. Julie had listened to him with a chilled detachment and gave him the same answer each time.

She stopped at the door of the living room, swamped by the memory of their last encounter. Now, like then, papers were strewn across the table. They would not be from the safe; everything incriminating had probably been burned or shredded – but he would discover that there was no such thing as a clean trail.

On the night she left Holywell, she had left a message for her husband. It contained photographed details of an off-shore account she had discovered at the back of the safe. One of many, she said, and all with Gloria's signature. She had warned him that if he approached her again, she would deliver the information she had acquired personally to the Garda National Economic Crime Bureau. Such a weapon was mightier than any fist.

She picked up a letter he had tossed onto an armchair. Her eyes watered as soon as she looked at the cramped words written across three sheets of paper. This was a warning sign that she must not strain her eyes. The ophthalmologist she had consulted had said she'd narrowly missed losing the sight in one of them. She put on the patch she had been advised to wear over the most seriously damaged eye and checked the pages. It was a photocopy of a letter, she realised, and it had been sent to Adele Foyle.

Her incredulity grew as she read it. The man who wrote it was a hoarder of secrets but, then, who wasn't? She stared at two photographs. A scene from hell, she thought, as she tried to unscramble the images. It took her a moment to recognise Jack Bale in the midst of the conflagration. Liam's computer was still on. She could tell by the screen that he had been listening to a recording, which, she realised on closer examination, was on a USB key that he had inserted into the computer.

He would be back soon. She still felt the impact of his foot and his fist branding her. Whatever was going on between her husband and this man, Malachi Norris, it had nothing to do with her.

She drove back to the Loyvale Hotel, passing Hillcrest on the way. Davina must be relieved that there were no longer any bouquets of flowers or message of condolences heaped outside it. As always, Hillcrest stood out from the other houses, the evening sun gleaming on its mellow thatch, the garden in full bloom. The by-election would take place in two days. A tight race, according to the polls. The conference and its heady revelations had increased Davina's popularity, but she must be clinging to sanity by her fingertips, Julie thought.

Inside the hotel, she unpacked her case. She had transferred her clients to other counsellors in the practice and spoken to Valerie, her partner, about taking a leave of absence from the clinic. She had booked her flight to Provence and would travel there after the tests on her eyes were concluded. Chasing butterflies was preferable any day to living in a golden cage.

She ordered food and coffee up to her room and tried to forget about the letter. Liam would be home by now. Would he be aware that she had been to Holywell in his absence? Her tenure there had left hardly a dent on Gloria's dominant presence. She took her coffee outside to the balcony. Hard to tell at this distance who was fishing today, but she recognised the bulky figure of Jack Bale walking away from the river. Clouds were gathering. Dark grey and ominous, they covered the sun and dulled the ripples into a sullen roll.

CHAPTER SIXTY-THREE

Davina

Leaves fluttered before her face as Davina left her car. No need to lock it. Only two cars were parked by this humpbacked bridge with its crumbling walls and overhanging trees. It had started to rain shortly after she left Hillcrest. A difficult night for her canvassers and she should be out there with them instead of trying to appease Jack Bale, whose demands had become impossible to ignore.

'I want you to hear me loud and clear,' he said when she slid into the passenger seat beside him. 'If you as much as mention this farce of an investigation ever again, I've enough information to wipe the Lewis name off the political map forever. As for your husband and his shallow promises, if I go down, he's coming with me, every inch of the way.' No greeting, no preamble, just the threat, and, as he intended, it sent a tremor through her.

'Jack, you have to understand, we were put in an impossible position by that Shannon bitch. It was the last thing either of us wanted to promise. You have to trust us. All this will fade after the by-election. We'll make certain it does.'

'You bet your sweet life you will. The file I have on your husband and his dearly departed father is impressive. Weighty, if you get my meaning. I've always believed the past can come back and bite you in the arse if you're not prepared to bite it first. So, it's all there in hard copy. You can keep your laptops and USB keys. Fat lot of good it did Adele Foyle, as you well know.'

'I'd nothing to do with that attack on her.'

'Oh, aye, there's none so blind as those who will not see.'

'Don't start, Jack. You've closed your eyes to enough over the years.'

'Three blind mice, eh. You're right, I closed my eyes to Keith and that Thornton creep and the other little—'

He tensed as headlights swept over the car. The blur of rain on the windscreen added to the glare. A couple seeking privacy under the rain-drenched trees, perhaps, Davina thought. Why else would anyone come to this forgotten wilderness… unless there were shady dealings afoot. She thought of Marianne Mooney's daughter. To think she had been lying since she arrived at Hillcrest with her innocent smiles and loaded questions that must never be answered. She thought of Grad Wheeler and Bob Molloy, both dead, and was filled with a sudden, overwhelming trepidation. Her antennae, supercharged. Davina held her hands to her eyes, dazzled until the lights were switched off. The driver had reversed and parked directly in front of Jack's car.

He lowered the window. Rain swept into the car and the wind tossed her hair before her eyes.

An interior light in the other car switched on as the door was opened.

'What the hell do you think you're doing?' Jack roared.

A figure emerged, or so Davina thought, but the blurred shape she glimpsed was lost in darkness when the car door was slammed closed. A hand appeared at the open window. Davina cringed against the passenger door as the hand was raised, as if in benediction, before Jack's outraged face. He was muttering expletives as he struggled with his seat belt when the trigger was pulled. A split second, that was all it took, an instant that could have been imagined except that Davina's ears were humming, her eyes rivetted to Jack as he slumped forward over the steering wheel.

The horn blared, like a banshee wailing a warning at death, and the figure at the window bent to look beyond Jack's slumped body towards Davina. His face was a pale moon shining and the plea that came to her lips was barely uttered before he was gone. She watched the light come on as he entered his car. Jogging pants and a loose sweater, a baseball cap low over his forehead, that was all she could register. His headlights flared again but this time he was moving away from her, driving too fast along the rutted road.

She had blood on her face and clothes. Splatters that she would never be able to wash away, ingrained forever on her psyche. Jack was dead. A bullet through his forehead. She was unable to see his expression. No need to guess. She knew that when he was examined by someone else it would be one of surprise. Instant death: she could understand its lure. Leaning forward, she removed the ring of keys that were attached to a loop on his belt and shoved them into her jacket pocket. In the glove compartment, she found a packet of wet wipes. Working fast, she cleaned every surface she could have touched, then opened the car door.

'Goodbye, Jack,' she said and closed it quietly behind her. The horn was still blaring as she drove away. Even when she was out of earshot, she believed she could hear its plaintive wailing inside her head.

She parked outside Loyvale Crescent and ran to his house. No time to lose. Her nerves could not fail her at this point. Once inside, she closed the blinds and found a torch in his utility room. Keeping the beam low, she moved through each room until she found a filing cabinet in his bedroom. The cabinet was locked but one of the small keys on the ring opened it. Each file had a name. Keith's file was next to his father's. Jack was right. They both had weight. Her own was lighter but he had left space for it to be filled. Some people sucked up all the air around them but that never became apparent until they were dead. Only then, did breathing become a freer experience.

She left his bungalow as silently as she had entered it. Back in her car, she drove through the village and out past Rachel Darcy's town house. The lights were on. She caught a glimpse of Rachel as she pulled the curtains closed. Her compassionate leave was over. Life moves on. Soon, she would receive a call to duty. Another shooting. Would she have flashbacks to the night her husband was shot? Was that what Davina could expect? Adele Foyle had spoken about flashbacks. Three blind mice... footsteps on the stairs... a gun pressed against— Davina shuddered away from the image. Such violence, but Adele had brought it with her, stirring ghosts and bringing the past back to life. Her head ached as she parked her car beside a security bollard and ran to the river's edge. Jack Bale's keys fell silently into the water. The ripples spread outwards, a circle within a widening circle that would eventually spend itself and be still.

CHAPTER SIXTY-FOUR

Julie

When darkness fell, Julie was no longer able to ignore the uneasiness she had been feeling since she read Malachi Norris's letter. She had expected Liam to ring after he returned from the leisure centre and when darkness fell without word from him, she broke the promise she had made to herself, and rang him. When he did not answer she left a message on his voicemail. 'Liam, ring me as soon as you get this message. It's important.'

After an hour had passed and she hadn't heard from him, she tried him again. 'Ring me, Liam. It's about Stephanie.'

Silence, except for the slash of rain against the window. How much time had passed since he read that letter? Julie was unable to settle, unsure what action she should take but increasingly conscious that something was wrong. He was never more than a few minutes away from his voicemail and, on hearing Stephanie's name, he should have been in touch with her immediately.

The traffic was light as she drove back through the village. Outside the Flowing Loy, a group of bedraggled canvassers stood under umbrellas and handed out leaflets to the customers entering and leaving the pub. Recognising Davina among them, Julie pulled in at the side of the road and beeped the horn.

'I'm looking for Liam,' she said when Davina approached the car. 'Have you seen him anywhere?'

'No, I haven't.' Davina stretched out her hand and touched Julie's cheek. 'Don't forget, Julie. I need your Number One.' Her eyes, illuminated by street lights, glowed. Julie sensed an excitement about her. A radiance, that was what it seemed like, but Julie was unable to name the emotion that flickered over Davina's face as she shoved an election leaflet at her and returned to her supporters.

Loyvale Crescent was a quiet road of bungalows behind high privet hedges. Julie rang the doorbell and knocked on the windows. Jack Bale was not at home. She walked around to the back of the house and turned the door handle. All locked and secured against intruders.

The local radio station was playing late-night easy-listening music. Suddenly, a voice interrupted the programme to announce a news flash. A body had been located in a car close to the Little Loy bridge. A shooting. Foul play was suspected. No name would be released until family members had been notified. The body was that of an elderly man, well known in his local community. The newsreader's tone suggested he was straining to say more but was confined to just those few, impersonal details.

Julie's hands were slippery with sweat as she drove towards Holywell. Once, she almost lost control of the steering wheel. When she entered the living room, everything was exactly the same as it had been earlier. She placed the letter and photographs under her arm and removed the USB key from Liam's computer. She hurried back to her car. This mausoleum held bones and she would hear them rattle if she stayed any longer.

In her hotel room she watched the late-night news. Cameras poked through the branches of weeping trees and focused on an isolated car where, pending further investigations, the body of Jack Bale still lay.

An hour later Rachel arrived at the hotel. She was in uniform and accompanied by a younger guard, who introduced herself as Garda Roberts. Her expression was grave and sympathetic when she greeted Julie. She was young, still inexperienced, and her mouth had yet to turn steely when she was the bearer of tragic news.

Had her husband been taken from the river, Julie wondered? Or cut down from a tree? The river, Rachel told her, gently. He had been discovered by a homeless man who hung out on the riverbank. She must come with them to identify his body.

Who would officially identify Jack Bale, Julie wondered? No wife or family to mourn him or give him an identity as he lay stretched out on a slab next to her husband. But first, she must ring Stephanie. She needed to protect her daughter. Stephanie would grieve for a father who had lost his footing on the riverbank and was swept to his death on the racing currents.

CHAPTER SIXTY-FIVE

Davina

Rolling news. The gods of Chaos had been set loose and Reedstown had experienced two tragedies on one night. In the mortuary Julie, supported by Keith, officially identified her husband's body. Davina stayed in the waiting room, awaiting their return. She had gone there directly from the Flowing Loy, where her canvassers had gathered for a drink before calling it a night. Keith's frantic phone call had not surprised her. As soon as Julie had stopped her car and asked Davina if she had seen her husband, she had been waiting to another tragedy to break above her head. Far, far above her head. She was untouchable. Faces swam by her, voices too. No one noticed that when she spoke, she was on automatic. No one noticed the blood on her hands, on her face, her clothes. Clean as a new pin, her mother used to say when Davina was going to school, and she was just as clean now. She had to learn to ignore the blood. It was a figment of her imagination and, like all such figments, it could be controlled by rational thought.

That glance she had exchanged with Liam over Jack Bale's slumped corpse. Would she ever be able to forget it? Such a pause... a time-standing-still instant that stretched way beyond the grasp of endurance as he decided whether she should live or die. He had made his decision and sought his own oblivion.

Now, having survived that instant of indecision, Davina's will to live was charged and powerful.

She rehearsed what she would say to the media about the sad and shocking events that had befallen Reedstown. An honoured former member of the police force struck down in the prime of his retirement. Shot by gangsters seeking revenge for his unstinting fight against the scourge of drugs. A successful businessman losing his life in a tragic accident. If she was elected, the first thing she would do was organise security barriers along the riverbank.

Julie was a ghastly shade of pale when she returned to the waiting room but her composure surprised Davina. Keith appeared to be on the verge of collapsing. So much information in those files. She had left him shredding them in Hillcrest while she joined the canvas. Not by a beat would she change her plans. No breath of suspicion must ever touch her. Those files could have destroyed them, crushed Keith's rising ambitions, and her own political career just as it was taking off. She had always known Jack Bale was a weasel but she had believed he was their weasel… until now.

Julie's face had been a disaster after the beating. A map of violence. She was free from Liam now. Free from the shadow cast by Marianne Mooney, as Rachel was. The sergeant had been present at the mortuary, so straight and rigid in her uniform. Two down, one to go. The words came unbidden to Davina and were quickly banished. She checked her self-control, as she would her pulse. Nothing else mattered except putting one foot in front of the other, one word after another, one day to follow the one just gone.

She drove Julie to the Loyvale Hotel.

'Have you told Stephanie?' Keith asked as she was leaving the car.

'Not yet,' Julie replied. 'It will break her heart when I tell her she has lost her father.'

Keith leaned back against the headrest and closed his eyes. What was he thinking? Did he realise how close he came to losing his wife? Did he realise Davina was the only person in the world he could trust?

Squad cars reached Hillcrest as darkness gave way to dawn. Doors opened and figures emerged, moving quietly but with purposeful steps towards the front door. For once, Keith's winning smile failed to disarm the group of Gardai who entered the house. After a brief conversation, she and Keith were allowed to dress. Only then were handcuffs produced, two pairs, efficiently locked. It could have been a dream; all the elements were there: those dark intrusive shapes trampling through her immaculate rooms, disturbing her order, the shape of things to come. A dreadful mistake had been made. Heads would roll, she would make sure of that, but the guard with the stretched face, officialdom stamping her with authority, refused to blink. Keith's smile had a stiff awfulness when he was warned about saying things that could later be used in evidence. What was it Jack used to say? Something about the past coming back to bite one's arse. Crude but apt.

The dawn had given way to a full-blooded day when they left Hillcrest. Such a sun, raging through the sky with its lacerating rays. Seagulls swung past them, wings sharp as sabres, as they scavenged for food.

In the interrogation room, Davina held her head high as she faced those who had dared to make such an outrageous arrest. This belief remained steadfast until Sergeant Rachel Darcy slid a mobile phone towards her. Jack Bale, devious unto death. His voice and hers clearly audible as she listened to the recording of their last conversation. How had she forgotten to take his phone with her? Always one step ahead of everyone else, she had faltered on that occasion. Those meetings in that dense undergrowth, all of it recorded, the ems, ums, ahs, huhs and ' if you get my meaning' verbal tics. Every plan outlined, every fear exposed, every promise secured. Keith – alone – would be charged with the rape of Marianne Mooney and it was her word – alone – that would put him behind bars. She would be charged with what? Obstruction of justice, destroying evidence, refusing to report a murder, being up close and personal to the victim… this list was ominously long. Rachel Darcy's inscrutable expression gave no hint of her internal feelings as she nodded and agreed that it was indeed time for Davina to call her solicitor.

EPILOGUE

Marianne

Crack! The snap of a branch brings her to the window. A deer, she thinks, an elk or a red. The sun is high in the noonday sky, shining like it's just been minted. The ferry has come into view at last. The new arrivals wait on deck for their first glimpse of Cape Maclure. She has set the table and arranged the flowers, snapdragons mixed with sprigs of lavender, and their scent hangs lightly in the air. The ferry is late, fifteen minutes past the time it should have crossed the fiord, but they will be with her soon, breathless with apologies. She will silence them with kisses. Their time together is too precious to waste on unnecessary words.

Fern and cacti sprout between ancient tree roots, sinews that straddle the garden and thrust a canopy of green towards the sky. The house that has sheltered her has open windows. Light fills every room. To move from seclusion and emerge into the glare of anticipation had been torturous. All those expectant faces looking back at her, willing her not to falter when she said, 'I am Marianne.' And when the words came, they winged their way like birds on an updraft towards the audience.

Other voices had reached out to her. Julie Thornton, her eyes reddened by violence, gave her a letter that referred to her as 'the Mooney incident.' Davina made promises that had the substance of quicksand. Keith refused to meet her gaze but language had not been necessary to shackle him to a memory. And she had heard another voice; one she had carried inside her head for twenty-five years. It had deepened since then, a voice that could never again be shocked by sights and sounds, yet Shane had sounded anguished when he phoned her from some war-blasted village and said he hoped to see her soon.

On her return to Cape Maclure, she had been grateful to enter its protective shell and take George into her care again. Amaia had been a good companion to him while Marianne was away but she could tell by the weight he had lost that he had missed her.

She is nervous, apprehensive as she waits for their arrival. Dreams do not always come true and she has been a long time dreaming. She hears music from the veranda and George's voice calling out to her. She has left him alone for too long. He orders her to have courage. As yet, her future has no shape. Impossible to separate it from the days she spends caring for him but she had hope now where, before, there was a broken bridge.

She watches with George from the veranda as the new arrivals leave the harbour. They enter the taxi that will bring them to her. At first, they are too far away to be distinguishable but, as the taxi draws nearer, she can make out their individual shapes. She kisses George on his cheek and leaves the veranda. The front door is already open when the taxi stops. Cases and backpacks are removed and they move towards her with one unified step.

Their voices fill the hall. They remove caps and sun hats, dark glasses are shoved into pockets and hair. Her daughter wears jeans and a tan bomber jacker, a black backpack still slung over her shoulders. She refuses to part with it. Finders keepers, she joked when she showed it to Marianne.

Mam must have taken the backpack from Atonement to her own shelter in the mountains. So many years lost. Marianne aches to think of it, but this is a time to reunite and not relive the past. Rory, as always, is dressed in black; the garb of a man whose soul is still wedded to his ministry. Daniel stands back from the clamorous welcomes. His eyes move between her and her daughter, seeking similarities. How does he feel about this woman who became Adele's obsession, a thorn in the flesh that broke them apart? He meets her gaze and smiles, nods slightly as if acknowledging that she was worth the pain.

Shane approaches her. How familiar he looks yet how different to the youth she loved. His smooth skin has tautened and his black hair is shot through with grey. His blue eyes, once so open and trusting, have narrowed into a commanding gaze that softens when he shakes her hand. This formality is understandable. He is a guest in her husband's house and George is a man to be respected.

They settle around him on the veranda. Amaia brings glasses and drinks to the table, adds crackers and cheese, cashews and olives. A leg of lamb seasoned with rosemary roasts slowly in the oven.

George will have sized up Shane by now. As always, he has her future in mind. He knows that his time is near. He does not fear death. His tranquillity is the source of his strength as he prepares to leave her. Adele will stay on in Cape Maclure and, together, they will ease him through his final months. Afterwards, what then?

They have made tentative plans to visit Siobhan Miley, whose Facebook page has become a hive of information, support and discussion. They will fly to London and spend time with Barbara, meet her family, her husband, Charlie, who hid with her in a bale of hay and delivered their first child in an inner-city squat. Then on to Reedstown to see Rachel and her son, Adele's half-brother.

Adele uses his photograph as the screen saver on her phone. Then they will part. Adele will join Daniel at last. Marianne could move with them to Colorado but she can no longer live under the sheltering wing of others. The future may be blurred but she is the one who must mould it into shape.

Shane is showing his camera to George, explaining its functions, and how he uses it to contextualise violence. How he contains it within a frame. He looks across the table towards Marianne, his gaze as rapt as it was during those stolen hours in Blake's Hollow. Since then, he has seen so much and she has seen so little, yet they both know that violence will only be contained by the courage of the few who dare to call it out.

They came to her through a trail of lupins. Their colours create a speckled palette as far as the eye can see. Birds dart from branches, their iridescent plumage drawing Shane to his feet, his camera ready. The beauty of her surroundings often steals her breath away. Her daughter takes her hand and brings it to her lips. Adele has blessed her with love. She is a mother's prayer that had finally been answered. The struggle is over and Marianne Mooney is at one with the unfolding of the day.

A LETTER FROM LAURA

Dear Reader,

Thank you so much for choosing to read *The Thorn Girl*. If you did enjoy it, and want to keep up to date with all my latest releases, just sign up at the following link. Your email address will never be shared and you can unsubscribe at any time.

www.bookouture.com/laura-elliot

The story had been nudging at me for a number of years before I decided to explore its contentious themes. It is a work of fiction and was not inspired by any one particular event or location. However, there are elements within the narrative that reverberate with memories of every story I've ever heard about women made powerless by circumstances beyond their control, whether it be carried out by one individual, or the combined force of state and Church, aided by a judgemental society.

The only silver lining in this dark cloud of intolerance is that these stories have been heard. They are out there in the open and I, like so many others, have absorbed them into my psyche. It was inevitable that sooner or later they would rise up from the well of my own imagination. I set my story in a more recent era; the last Magdalene laundry would close its door two years later, but exploitation does not need a time frame to flourish.

Nor does brutality, corruption and the struggle to unearth the sins of the past.

I hope you like what I've done with it. *The Thorn Girl* is now at the stage when it no longer belongs to me. It has slipped from my fingers into another realm and is open to the interpretations, insights and opinions of you, my reader. The wrench I feel as this transition takes place is tough but temporary. Soon I will be engaged in another book and the characters and plot of *The Thorn Girl* will assume a dreamlike quality – but your responses and reviews will keep them alive in my mind.

If you enjoyed my book and would like to contact me through Facebook or my website, I'd be delighted to hear from you. Also, if you'd like to leave a review, it would be greatly appreciated.

 lauraelliotauthor

 @Elliot_Laura

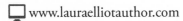 www.lauraelliotauthor.com

ACKNOWLEDGMENTS

Thank you to my husband Sean Considine for... well... everything. You've been constantly loving and supportive, an excellent barista, and my best pal.

To my family, Tony, Ciara and Michelle, and spouses, Louise, Roddy and Harry, and my adored grandchildren, Romy, Ava and Nina. Individually, the gifts you have brought into my life are unique and invaluable.

To my extended family, too many to name, thank you for the songs and the music, the laughter and the long conversations over dinner tables, the shared holidays, the many celebrations, and the sharing of the difficult times.

Thank you to my friends for remaining constant when I've been living in my 'burrow' for months on end and for being there when I finally emerge into the sunlight after writing those wonderful words, The End.

Special thanks to Peter Brunton who, as always, helped me with detailed information whenever I needed it.

My Bookouture editor, Claire Bord, has been a tremendous support to me. Thank you, Claire, for your insightful and sensitive analysis of my work. Thank you to publicity gurus, Kim Nash and Noelle Holten, to publishing executive, Leodora Darlington, managing editor, Alexandra Holmes, the marketing team, Alex Crow and Jules Macadam, to Natalie Butlin, commercial manager, and all who have contributed to bringing my book to completion.

Over my years of working with Bookouture, I've established a wonderful network of readers and reviewers. You are the most important element in the whole process and I'm grateful to you for choosing to read *The Thorn Girl*. To all who have taken the trouble to contact me personally, or to review my books, my very special thanks. It's always a delight to hear from you.